Lion's Creed

From Darkness

Roxanne Ward

Go Go Self Publishing VW

First Publication by Go Go Publishing

Idaho, USA

Copyright © 2023 by Roxanne Ward

October 2023

Cover design by RG Graph X Design

ISBN paperback   979-8-9880010-2-7

Genres: Science fiction, speculative fiction, post-apocalyptic fiction, military fiction, romantic fiction, mystery fiction

NOTICE: This novel contains adult sexual content, unethical behavior, offensive language, and military violence.

file 6

Other Books by Roxanne Ward

To Russ, Aaron, Garrett, and Corrin

Courage is not the absence of fear but rather

the assessment that something else is more important.

Franklin D. Roosevelt

Prologue

Outrage and chaos expectantly ran rampant after the assassination of President Jacklyn Sharp, but with the entire world embroiled in pandemonium, her death became irrelevant to the masses. Over half a decade ago, the universe hurled a storm of meteorites of all sizes at Earth's inhabitants. The assault lasted seven days, leaving no continent untouched. None of the space rocks were large enough to deliver a final blow to the planet's inhabitants, but it initiated a global cascade of failures. The toll on all forms of life and their environments was catastrophic.

Like the tide against a sandy shore, it tried relentlessly to erase the human footprint. The age-old struggle between self-determination and singular domination was set back centuries. Like other nations, the United States held onto its governmental routines, but in the eyes of the survivors, their efforts amounted to a pointless waste of time. The wise words and platitudes from ancient documents couldn't provide the food, medicine, or safety they so desperately needed. For the first time in recorded history, the world was united, but its common theme was abject tragedy.

All the political offices, except for a few Senators at the end of their six-year stint, were honorary or volunteer since even statewide voting was a logistical impossibility. The nation's legislators gathered at the Denver Capitol building due to its central location. The discussion related to the value and validity of the transition of Vice President Justine Rhender to President of the United States. Colorado's Honorary Senator, Banner

Vogel, listened to the irrational rhetoric from the panicked group of dwindling political figureheads.

Unlike President Sharp, Rhender had morphed quite easily into a greedy puppet of the darkly evolving Corporate order. She endorsed the radical renouncement of what she termed pre-storm documents, including the United States Constitution. Temporary orders were logical for desperate times, but she planned to replace them with a new doctrine called The Restitution. It would retain the current oligarchy system with no sunset clause. Shouts and rants roared from the floor of the Senate. It reflected the emotions of the nation—raw, divided, and in a state of frenzied anarchy.

As tragic as the murder of an official was, the United States Constitution provided a plan for uninterrupted leadership and the removal of weak or criminal leaders. But the days of that document uniting and governing the nation had ended. Law and order had morphed into oppression, and decisions were made *for* the people, not *by* the people. All the members of Congress, and every elected official at every level of government, faced the choice of subjugation or elimination.

Vogel rose and made his way to the podium. He gave a sweeping run through his wavey salt and pepper hair and straightened his tie. Amid shouts and shushes, he turned toward the silky, tri-colored banner positioned to his right. Placing his hand on his heart, he began to recite the Pledge of Allegiance. The crowd quieted rather quickly, awaiting the violence from Corporate powers, but none came. Some stood and joined him, while others stayed quietly seated, frozen in horror at the impossible choice.

When he was done, the silence in the room was like time itself had ceased to pass. No one coughed, shuffled, or moved the array of implements provided on every desk. Every face was glued on him, expecting his removal and swift death in the dark shadows. The only event to mark time was dust dancing gently in the sunbeams streaming from the dome windows. After a silent pause of reverence, he began.

"Ladies and gentlemen of the United States Senate,

"This is our last meeting before we adjourn for winter break, or perhaps forever. We have much to discuss. Before I present my proposal, I would like to recount our recent history of heartbreaking misfortune. Bear with me because it is easy to forget who we were as a nation and how we regressed into who we are today. Our ominous transformation was prompted by a critically divided country rendering a series of knee-jerk reactions to a litany of catastrophes.

"There has always been division along political lines. It is the nature of democracy to hash out an answer with many ideas being heatedly debated. Infighting between groups is the essence of the human condition, which is why this document, our Constitution, gave a voice to every thought that *any* human brain could devise.

"Around four decades ago, the people began feeling disenfranchised. They were fed a steady diet of carefully crafted media. Whether imagined or real, trust waned year by year, decision by decision. And eventually, what they imagined to be truth came to pass. Like-minded groups attacked those they disagreed with, but not with lively debates.

"Our first President, George Washington, warned us how political parties, as opposed to individual philosophies and proposals, would lead us away from our fundamental values. He said they would battle each other for power and forsake the common man. He feared '... cunning, ambitious, and unprincipled men would be enabled to subvert the power of the people ...' and we are seeing that in full bloom, but it didn't happen all at once or because of one natural disaster.

"Over and over again, the party in power attacked the minority party by abusing laws and extensive media campaigns to shame and punish all who disagreed with their platforms. Their affiliates and supporters exposed the uncooperative with slander, legal attacks, financial ruin, and even physical assault. Both sides were complicit in the game, volleying nefarious proceedings back and forth, forsaking duty and dignity.

"Rational voters rejected the extreme views and sought the truth, but it was elusive. They demanded consequences for illegal deeds, sensible solutions, and to restore the forgotten art of compromise. They felt frustrated that their choices were limited to one radical side or the other, and they blamed both parties for their state of affairs.

"Bills that could make a difference in the lives of the people were riddled with unrelated pet projects reeking of personal gain. The search for the right party caused the control to flip back and forth while confidence in the voting system crumbled completely. The tear in the fabric of our democracy went deeper and deeper as the rights and laws of our United States were manipulated and whittled away.

"And then suddenly, after all the bickering over borders, regimes, cultural rights, and other sovereign preferences, we were faced with a world-altering struggle for the survival of civilization, if not our very species. The meteorite storm disaster grabbed our politically tumultuous world and viciously shook it to pieces.

"It's been just over six years since a cluster of meteors, initiated by a collision in the asteroid belt, rained down on Earth. The seven-day assault of hundreds of sizable meteorites ravaged every continent, and we assume nearly all countries. The fact is, we don't know. Worldwide communication is still inadequate, and no nation, including our own, is willing to admit how vulnerable the storm left them.

"Most of the projectiles were rather small, but the compilation of them caused uncontrollable raging fires, destroyed vast amounts of resources, and annihilated forty-seven heavily populated cities, causing devastating human loss and a cascading collapse of goods worldwide. Though none were large enough to cause an extinction event, the initial death toll was estimated in the hundreds of millions, but the new estimation has quickly risen to three billion. And the number rises still.

"Those that didn't die in the dust and fire were subjected to illnesses due to the smoke, ash, and dust, as well as diminishing supplies. The infectious hazards from the neglected rotting corpses of humans and animals knocked our medical capabilities down to pre-industrial practices. We couldn't burn the plethora of corpses for fear it would increase the death clouds, nor could we bury them with large equipment until winter precipitation could control the ash from being stirred back into the atmosphere.

"The shared tragedy united the world in a massive humanitarian effort to repair the damage most nations suffered. Negotiations to barter surpluses for deficits brought forth inspirational goodwill and contributions of resources to those countries most affected.

"Health issues united medical corporations around the globe, and they founded a program called AMEC, Allied Medical Emergency Care. The health institutions gathered to plan and address whatever care they could provide by making a worldwide medical supply chain from development to dispersal. But travel was still limited due to the noxious particles hovering over most of the Earth, so much of the work was in theory rather than practice.

"It was about six to eight weeks before the air was deemed safe to go outside with AMEC air suits and breathing filters. Many died in their homes from starvation before help could reach them. The benevolent exchange of supplies lasted less than three months. The extent of the devastation was settling in. It would take years, maybe even decades, to recover from the cosmic battering.

"Both the outdoor workers and medical facilities fought over the air suits and filters. With the excessive demand and the meager supplies of protective gear, their conflict became an actual battle to obtain supplies, further compromised by the black marketeers.

"We began to experience a new cascade of failures, creating rampant poverty and raging pandemics. Once easily treated diseases became death sentences without medical supplies. With the complications of the dust-infused air, respiratory illnesses were killing people in unprecedented numbers, especially the scores of citizens living in extremely poor conditions with no access to medical interventions.

"The AMEC tried to keep up with the demand, but the deficit of medicinal supplies and qualified workers proved to be an overwhelming burden. Fear took over and greed kicked in. Hospitals are now thought of as places where the rich go for treatment, and the poor go to die.

"There was one group of scientists that had a promising chemical solution that sped up the decomposition process with the potential for productive fuel byproducts. They were all murdered by power-hungry elitists with imperial aspirations. The formula must have died with them because there has not been any sign of it being utilized or sold. They created it to save lives, but in the end, they destroyed it for the same reason. How many times must we stab at our future before we learn our lesson?

"A few small and many medium-sized businesses survived the supply shortages exacerbated by corporate resource grabs. Soon, by the thousands, small businesses sold out to powerful enterprises, swelling larger by the day. Yes, I admit it. My own business is one of those that benefited. I did not plan to buy out so many companies, but the owners came to me asking for help.

"Within a couple of years, working conditions plummeted back to the early industrial age. The Office of Safety and Health Administration was disbanded due to the unresolvable air issues. The U.S. Department of Labor and Industries gave out safety waivers like candy on Halloween to maintain the supply chain of goods and services, and the Federal Trade Commission, which regulated monopolies, folded.

"The Organ Harvest Act mandated that blood, stem cells, and other useful bodily treasures were to be harvested for the good of the nation. Soon after this Act was passed, many companies began requiring DNA scans of their workers. But when thousands of healthy laborers across the country began to disappear without a trace, the prevailing rumor was that their bodies were matched for well-to-do patients in need of their parts and fluids. Whether it is true or not, the result is that to this day people are afraid to go to work. That began the work attendance mandates, but the police did not enforce them with the fervor expected, so they were disbanded.

"The federal government had become completely ineffective. The decision was finally made to divide the country into several hundred territories. The prominent corporations within those areas were deputized as government agents to provide for the people and maintain civility in the territories. Though they report to a federal body, without the restrictions of federal or local laws, as well as any form of enforcement, corporations quickly asserted their strict policies to subdue the outrage.

"But citizens all over the country resisted the unelected authority figures. Having lost over half of the population, workers and the supplies they produced were at a premium, so borders began to be fiercely patrolled to retain them. Civil regulations failed to rein in the locals, so ever stricter measures were put in place. People weren't going to work, and the police wouldn't force workers to attend, nor would they control their territory's borders. The businesses struggled, and the people starved.

"Corporate sheriffs appeared on the scene and were given more and more leeway to keep the country moving forward. To keep an eye on the citizens within their neighborhoods, corporations began to generously fund an expansion of the Neighborhood Watch programs. The Corporate mercenaries rapidly morphed into professionally trained armies we now call the Neighwah.

"They follow the Corporate orders without regard to laws that once protected our citizens. There is no Bill of Rights, and our citizenry is evolving into an oppressive three-leveled caste system of Corporates, Uppers, and Dailys. What started as a temporary emergency measure is now on the floor to be finalized into law.

"These disastrous times have also decimated our international alliances. Fear breeds all manner of ugliness, and greed and aggression are two of the worst. As the reality of the situation settled in, the contagious nature of panic demolished reason and goodwill.

"Terrorists seized our television and radio transmissions to air, regular public tortures, rapes, and executions. When people tuned out, children were sought after to increase emotional anxiety. Horrific screams from the torture, rape, and death throes of U.S. citizens trapped in other countries were used to extort resources, and it proved to be a profitable method.

"But people became numb to the painful displays, and they stopped tuning in to the death shows as well as the brutality within their communities. They came to accept their fate, and part of grieving lost loved ones was to view it as a blessing and an end to the suffering of being alive.

"The world and the country have become untraversable, and it will happen to the territories within the states too. The correspondence between territories has been strained, preventing families and friends from staying in touch. Already, content is commonly censored, making supportive relationships extremely difficult.

"Dailys, on the lowest rung of society, now cocoon in their small communities and residences to hide from a world that is no longer a home but a place of hostility. And if The Restitution is put into law, the people will be denied correspondence completely, ending any possible threat to the new order." Banner paused, and the weight of his historical rendition was etched in his expression of deep sorrow.

As he continued, he pushed down the grief and let his anger flow. "Yes, the world, our nation, and even our towns are deep in the worst shit-show drama of modern times." His voice boomed louder as he persisted with his petition. "But no matter what our political affiliations or even the validity of our stations, we still have a duty to our citizens. Our purpose is to maintain our democracy by teaching all Americans how it works and to maintain it with our very lives.

"Education, honest, non-agenda-driven education, is the only way we can restore this nation. Jefferson believed, 'An educated citizenry is a vital requisite for our survival as a free people.' I believe we can still turn this around. We just have to start. Too late, you say? Well, I don't believe in the too-late scenario because I don't believe in giving up. We can choose to gather our courage and fight, or we can hide and save our skin for a year, maybe more, but it will be to live as villains or vagabonds.

"This document right here," Banner shook the rolled-up copy in his hand, "this Declaration of Independence, is a blueprint to target our grievances and direct them at our current mobster oppressors. We need to invoke our militia of millions who hid their guns during the collection mandates. I believe people will join, and they will fight for a cause to reclaim their freedom, dignity, and self-determination.

"We stand on the edge of an abyss. And though we have fallen far from what our founding fathers would recognize as the United States, we are still here. I say get up, make a stand. We must stop bowing down before them like sheep in a slaughterhouse. Will it be dangerous? Hell yes! I might not live the day for this very act, but I choose to fight back. *We* must fight back.

"It won't be the first time we have fought to end the enslavement of our people. Together we can assure "that this nation, under God, shall have a new birth of freedom—and that government of the people, by the people, for the people, shall not perish from the Earth.' Thank you for your time."

Such a speech might have rendered spirited applause in a time when people believed themselves free, but shocked silence was the current response for anything hinting at rebellion, let alone revolution.

Banner knew when the doors opened that the Neighwah guards had arrived. They were coming down the aisle to escort him off the podium, and after that, he did not know. They were civil and careful not to make a scene that could be used against them. They did their forbidden work in their evil corners.

The Senator was escorted from the podium and led toward the exit. As he left, he heard whispers, and then a few people began to clap. Soon more joined in, and some began to stand, and before he left the chamber, many were standing and clapping enthusiastically. *Maybe*, he thought, *maybe it was enough*. When they reached the doors, he was simply told to leave the building. He wondered how the retaliation would come and when. The waiting alone would be a form of torment.

The murders were reported as accidents and random acts of violence, but fifty-six instructors and professors from various schools, along with thirty-nine members of their families, were struck down that month. Banner was pained by the idea that he played a part in making them targets, and he wondered why he was spared. It also was not lost on him that the total number of murdered mentors was the same number that signed the Declaration of Independence, and the family members killed represented the number of signatures on the Constitution.

On the last day of that same month, he was asked in an anonymous note to recant his statement and throw his support to the new order under President Rhender. He refused. The next month witnessed the same deadly statistical numbers, but the victims were selected from the resistant legislators and their families. Senator Vogel resigned before the next semester.

Not long after his speech, an old college friend, Tyson Connor, sought Banner out. Tyson was part of the science group that developed the formula to dissipate toxic pollutants and decomposing bodies. He hoped to create fuel as a byproduct, but the application and dispersal method came with grave potential. Banner thought Tyson was dead too, but it was a ruse that would not hold out much longer. He and his two small girls were in grave danger. Banner helped him and his daughters by changing their identities. Banner set up his friend, now known as Leland Delano, in a secret lab to continue his work.

For several years, Banner kept very tight security around the Delanos and his own family. He also instructed and recorded lessons to groom his son, Bannon, and daughter, Dana, to take over his company and manage his philanthropic projects, which were done in secret now. He worked amicably with the top Corporate leaders in the Denver Territory doing all he could as a shipping mogul to appear cooperative.

They didn't trust him, but they needed his resources and contacts, so they just kept a close watch on him. Banner became a member of a group called Americans for Liberty, Ethics, Citizens, and Truth (A.L.E.C.T.), but their underground contacts knew them as the Robinhooders. It was the hope that someday its well-guarded secrets would restore self-government, but it was a long-term plan that spanned into the next generation. The immediate objective was to train the next two generations while they remained unidentified and alive.

Though Banner stepped up his security, he, his wife, and his daughter-in-law were killed in a suspicious train bombing. Because they had some last-minute work, his adult children, Bannon and Dana, and his young granddaughter, were not on the train. Banner's vast shipping and supply business became the property of his children, along with all his skeletons and secrets in the hidden office on the fifteenth floor of his building.

Chapter One

William Alexander sat up abruptly, his heart racing, his breaths rapid and heavy. Beads of sweat soaked through the cheap, oversized t-shirt that twisted and gnarled around him. The recurring nightmare of dandelion seeds swirling in a red mist was tangled in his new dilemma. When he woke up bandaged and hazy, he recalled the events of that day and realized his stellar reputation as a soldier had been reduced to a deserter and a traitor. He had spent the day running from at least twenty heavily armed, well-trained men. How had his life gone so wrong?

As a boy, he understood his purpose: to stay alive, and that had been hard enough. But that all changed in that desperate moment when he was given a gift. It was a beautiful knife, the most beautiful thing he'd ever held, let alone owned. But so far, besides staying forever sharp, the only power it had was to destroy his life. It was a leftover relic that took over one's future, forcing a clandestine destiny upon its owner.

He had heard of a knife that was needed to save the oppressed people, but it was just a myth, a fairytale that gave no hint as to how a simple knife could perform such a feat against huge armies with an imposing inventory of weaponry. Will found everything about it stupid. It was a riddle he couldn't solve.

And now, the one person who could have explained what was expected of him was gone, and he was alone with a purpose that was a complete mystery. He received it as a young boy on the worst day of his life. He worked hard to put the memory and the relic away, and a decade passed without destiny pressing on his mind. To him, it was all just a desperate whim, a childish myth.

Though he didn't believe in magic, he did believe in hope, but it was the kind that got one out of tough spots. No item, or person for that matter, contained enough hope or magic to set this land free. But now the memories flooded back, and hope was all he had left.

This morning he was drugged, kidnapped, and woke up in the presence of a man from his past. It was a man he honored and respected, and he was dying. Again, he was told he must fulfill his destiny. Will told no one about the talisman or the person who gave it to him, so how could he know about it?

The information he shared was muddled with ambiguous tasks and sketchy details. But the moment left no time for questions because his friend handed him a crude map and a backpack with one hand, and with the other, he pointed, saying RUN. Will ran for hours through the roughest terrain he had ever seen. He felt physically depleted, utterly lost and alone, and failing to do... something.

His injuries ached as he reached for a dry shirt from the backpack and added his coat to the blanket over him. It was all he could do to keep from freezing in the temporary earthen shelter. He needed sleep to continue his escape, but old ghosts strangled his thoughts, and his new burdens further tightened his mental noose.

On top of his current predicament, he was reliving the disbelief and panic of that day so long ago. It was always a struggle to put this haunting nightmare away. His mind knew nothing good could come from reliving it, but in that dark place where terror thrives, the cruel visions cut through logic.

He reminded himself, as he often did, that it was a time past, a deed done, and no redemption to be had. He accepted this in his waking hours; why couldn't his dreams do the same? The undisciplined side of his brain kept drudging up phantoms of futile memories that could not be changed.

The dead could not be raised, nor could the answers that died with them. He shook his head and grabbed his canteen from the floor near his bed sack. The cool water soothed his parched throat, and he settled back into a restless, cold sleep.

His early recollections as a young boy held loving memories of his father, Ben, being protective and kind. Like all workers on the lowest rung of the caste system, Dailys, as they were called, life was difficult and hunger was a familiar feeling. They lived a bleak existence under the domination of the Corporates, their nasty Neighwah soldiers, and the efficient mercenaries called Drangers. Even though his world was precarious, it was all he knew, and he trusted his father to keep him safe with naïve innocence.

Will was too young to remember the meteorite strikes that lasted seven days and devastated the entire planet, but the stories prevailed. During those tragic years without proper medical diagnoses or interventions, every affliction was labeled a meteor sickness. It's what Will's mother died of when he was six years old. He struggled to recall her, but he remembered she looked like him. She had dark ebony skin, big brown eyes, and a smile like sunshine.

He remembered his dad, who was also gone from his life. His dad's skin was bronzed on his face and arms from working outside so much, but his protected belly was like buttermilk. It was his haunting green eyes that Will remembered the most. Will's eyes were brown and scattered with green speckles. His father was tall and strong in muscle tone, and in that way, he was definitely like his father. His parents had both been stunning people and though Will had a mixture of their traits, he felt he was awkwardly pieced together.

Their close friends, Tim and Rita, lived nearby and were kind and supportive after his mother died. Rita worked evenings at home as a computer technician, fixing minor, low-security software problems remotely. This allowed her to care for Will and other children under nine during the day in exchange for work, items, or credits. Her children were grown and on their own, but she loved being a mom. It was a temporary solution while her workplace finished construction. Since it was not yet started, Rita hoped she would have at least a year of remote work.

All Dailys over twelve were required to work, or their food rations would be cut off. If they had children under the age of nine, one of the parents would be allowed to change shifts. If one died, there were three choices possible. Find someone to help, get remarried, or give up your parental rights.

If they couldn't find help or be willing to give up their child, they would be put on the marriage list. Single Dailys were also put on that list when they turned twenty, making arranged marriages common. Ben had been on the list for over a year when someone came into his life unexpectedly.

It was a particularly wet day in late spring when Will was almost eight years old. His dad and Tim went out to hunt antelope while Will stayed with Rita. Hunting wild game with anything more than a snare was illegal since it required weapons that Dailys were not permitted to own. Ben fashioned a bow and arrow set and disguised it to look like a walking stick. The flexible bow was made sturdy and straight by wrapping the untipped and un-fletched arrows around it with the bowstring.

It was simply an interesting walking stick until he assembled it. The stick was stored in plain sight, leaning against the wall in his room. When he went hunting, the fletching and arrow tips were concealed in a pouch tied to his leg and under his boot. At his home, he kept them hidden under a floorboard in his room with his cache of other prohibited items.

When they came back from their trip, they had the quartered antelope draped under their jackets and a young woman walking between them. She was extremely thin and showed signs of physical abuse. They found her where she had collapsed from severe dehydration in the badlands. Ben decided to care for her, and in return, she would watch Will until he was old enough to be on his own, according to Corporate rules. To the Corporates, kids represented future workers, and they didn't want to invest time and credits only to have them die of neglect.

Will's father planned to tell the authorities she was an abandoned hostage of Fringers. Fringers were bands on the run who lived on the fringes of the settled areas. The story would be accepted because it was rumored that the rebel bands were marauding criminals, and kidnappings were among their offenses. No one cared about keeping detailed records on Dailys, and young able workers were very valuable to a township. So as long as she could work, she would be registered.

Ben explained to his son that he didn't know where she came from because she had lost her memory. But Will had an uncanny ability to read expressions and body language. He watched her as his father recited the questionable tale of her journey.

He didn't know her, but he had heard enough covert stories from Dailies with secrets to hide that he was certain she remembered more than she was saying. He also suspected she had escaped from some place important and dangerous, and taking her in was a huge risk. But within days, his father and Tianna were married in a small ceremony in their house with Tim and Rita in attendance.

Tianna got a job in the town fields tending to the garden. It was grueling work, but it was outside and Tiana was allowed to bring Will. The supervisor was skeptical about having an underager in his area, but Will was tall enough to pass for twelve, and he was a good worker.

Will remembered little about his mother, but he remembered everything about Tianna. She was a gentle person with soft, light skin, golden hair, and twenty or so freckles dusted across her cheeks and nose. She had pretty, delicate features, light blue eyes, and a warm, shy smile. Will was the very contrast of her with his rich cocoa skin, thin gangly limbs, tall stature and brown eyes streaked with green highlights. He was in that awkward age of growing and not being in proportion. But she always boosted his confidence and called him her handsome warrior.

Though both he and his father treated Tianna with tender kindness, she was quick to startle, had a timid nature, and experienced random panic attacks that were followed by profound sadness. Even young Will knew something horrible must have happened to her. But whenever he probed, she would just fall back on her loss of memory claim, though she had complete recall of her extensive education.

Will knew there was more to this worldly woman, and he was pretty sure she hadn't lost her memory. She probably remembered everything, but it was too painful or inappropriate to share. He just hoped the world wouldn't invade their home and take her away.

As a surprise to brighten her mood, Ben and Will decided to build her a greenhouse. They gathered scraps of wood, windows, and corrugated transparent roof tiles. He found much of it in the deep woods at an abandoned shack with a collapsed greenhouse. Ben secretly gathered the pieces and brought them home. They collected the bent and dropped nails from construction sites and started building Tianna's greenhouse using rocks for hammers.

Gardening was something she loved, and she talked about it often. She talked of edible and medicinal plants she wished to grow and the need to gather seeds from those plants. She knew they were adding on to the house, but she didn't know what they had planned until she saw the six translucent panels attached to the ceiling beams and windows lining the tops of the walls. The realization brought tears to her eyes, and she hugged them both and gave Ben a shy kiss. Their first.

She immediately started filling the raised boxes with dirt and composting scraps. When the smell became noticeable, she stirred the soil like stew in a pot, pulling the bottom level to the top. The seeds she gathered from the farm and the forest behind their home were planted when the soil became dark and had an earthy smell.

She showed Will how to make a spiral in the dirt with her finger about half an inch deep, in a section of the square boxes. She then put a variety of seeds in different places in the spiral and started again in the next space. Her demeanor and the manner as she floated around her garden were the happiest Will had ever seen her.

"The spiral is the key to growing a lot in a small space. With our food allotment, and the potatoes, the hams, and carrots I grow in the field hidden behind our house, we will always have real food to eat," she would say. "I never want us to eat that supplement stuff. I don't trust the Corporates to feed us anything good or healthy. They keep that stuff for themselves."

Will and his father had added the protein powder to their food for years with no noticeable reactions, but she was suspicious of so many things. Will was a child, and he overlooked the things he did not understand, but he was amazed at how much she could produce in those three boxes.

Before the Township garden closed for the winter, Tianna didn't wait for another job assignment. She offered to do mending and sewing for the managers, and she excelled at it. It allowed her to stay indoors with Will during the cold weather and educate him in secret. After his lessons, they spent time in her garden, and she beamed with joy and sang whenever she worked in the tiny room crammed with boxes of seedlings.

Will learned Tianna went to a fancy school and graduated at the top of her class. She taught him to read, write, and memorize his math tables, all forbidden skills for a Daily in Pueblo territory. He was a quick learner, and soon he couldn't get enough material to feed his learning and reading obsession. Books were hard to find because paper was valued more as fuel for heat, and few had the time or inclination to risk getting caught reading.

Will thrived in the love that radiated from his parents. Though they lived under the oppressive rule of the territory authorities, they were the happiest days of his childhood. He turned ten as the spring snows receded, giving up their blanket to the summer rains. Like all children reaching the age of ten without a younger sibling to watch, Will was assigned a job on the Kid Crew.

Most of the Kid Crew jobs centered on a variety of minor maintenance tasks, like shoveling snow, gathering leaves and broken branches for the shredder, and doing chores for the Uppers, the managers. Some Uppers were deviants and sent for kids wanting to use them in twisted acts. It happened more than it should, and the Uppers were rarely punished.

Though a Daily's complaint was seldom heeded or acted upon, even the Uppers were under the threat of the Corporates. If they disrupted the flow of production, the status quo, by enraging workers, the Uppers could be punished. Punishments included being denied their cushy lifestyle, being demoted to a Daily, or worse. But a Daily's punishments included extra work shifts, reduced food rations, hazardous jobs, or life imprisonment in the crematorium.

One year, the Corporate soldiers, called the Neighwah, were ordered to destroy books from a run-down library building. The two soldiers assigned the task were known for their kinder treatment of dailies, and they secretly let the citizens take books for their heating needs. Will and his parents gathered all they could as fast as they could. They got over fifty books, which they carefully hid under a floorboard in their house. On those nights Will could keep his eyes open, he would stay up pouring his mind through the treasured words like a pirate running his hands through gold.

On the days he got off early, he would rush home to work with Tianna on his studies. She taught him mathematics, Language arts, history, science, and even art now and again. He enjoyed learning, and Tianna said he was the smartest boy she had ever met.

He loved the compliments, even though he could feel the heat of embarrassment. It was uncommon. People didn't interact like that. If it had come from someone else, he would have questioned their sincerity. Yet, he wanted her to be proud of him, so he worked even harder, and when they were done with the lessons, they would tend the garden and talk about what he learned.

"How did you like the story we read today, Will? Tiana asked.

"It's written kind of funny, but I liked it after you explained it."

"Yeah, Homer is difficult to read. It's thousands of years old and written in lyrical form, allowing the blind poet to memorize the *whole* saga by singing it."

"Whoa, that's some memory!"

"Songs are one of the most efficient ways to memorize text," she justified. "What do you think of the story so far?"

Will pause, "This Odysseus seems powerful and confident, and he's fair to his men. But he's ungrateful to the gods. He makes Poseidon so mad, knowing he has the power to destroy him. Why doesn't he just obey so he can go home?"

"It's true. He's quite arrogant to argue with a god, but he does so because he sees himself as an equal and doesn't want to bow down to their decrees of abject authority. He wants to live his own story and decide his own destiny. I think the Odyssey is my favorite story because it's the ultimate adventure; the quintessential hero's quest. Tomorrow, Odysseus fights a giant with one eye!" She spoke with an enthusiasm that tugged at his curiosity and fired his interest.

"Wow, how does that go?" Will asked, hoping she would explain it, so he wouldn't have to struggle through the poetic text. But she just gave him one of her dazzling, warm smiles that caused her eyes to sparkle with mystery while she sang her curious little tune.

Bound by walls that gleam and seep,
Anxiously Liberty waits.
Many quests will seek her keep,
But they drown at Hades' gate.
Yet in the earth so dank and deep
Lies the hope for freedom's day.
Dwelling in the darkest fears,
Where her soldiers bravely lay
The Sanguine blade frees the spears,

To stand against the fray.

She sang it often when they were alone. She said it was a secret song, and he should never share it with anyone, not even his dad. He would watch her as she sang, and he knew it was more than a bygone melody. By the time she went to teach him the words, he had them memorized because he was intrigued by the magic of it.

They sang it together every time they worked in the garden. Will asked what it meant and why was it secret. She gave a mysterious answer about a warrior king sent on a quest to free his true love, Liberty. She was always saying magical things like that, and he liked having a secret. It made him feel special in a world where everyone seemed insignificant.

Will often sat on his bed reading before he turned down his oil lamp at night. One night, he was reading a cheaply published booklet on meteorites and the likelihood of hundreds of them hitting the Earth. It was written six years before the deadly event happened by an astronomer named Harold Seger. Will didn't understand the mathematics that he used to prove his theories, but the booklet included many useful survival skills.

He had been quite curious about the meteorite storm and meteor sickness. He knew his mother died from it, but he was too young to remember much more than flashes of memory. He struggled with the medical jargon, which included a litany of secondary infections and issues the survivors would incur. He was left with more questions than he started.

"Dad, what happened during the meteorite storms?" asked eleven-year-old Will.

"Well, you were about four years old, and we were living near Ogden, Utah. The strikes were forecast to hit in a week, and the impact map had just been released. A large one was expected to hit just west of us, and the prevailing winds tended to travel in an easterly direction, meaning they were headed toward us."

"What is a 'prevailing' wind?"

"It is the overall direction of the wind due to the Earth's rotation. The atmosphere is not attached to the Earth, so when it spins, the atmosphere lags. The pull of the earth, the heat of the sun, and the cooled air from the poles and night sky cause the air to move in certain ways. As the earth spins, heats, and cools, the air is in a constant state of instability, trying to even out the temperature so, voila—we have wind."

"Huh, but sometimes the wind goes in different ways."

"True, the air flows in spirals like the smoke from a candle when you blow it out. There are patterns due to the rotations and the land formations they encounter, and it allows us to predict what is happening and what may happen. That's because along with the variation in temperatures and pressure, gravity also pulls on the atmosphere, and it causes swirls. You see that glass with water and an upside-down bottle in it?"

"The one with all the numbers on it?"

"That is my barometer. It's a primitive model, but I check it every day to see if it's moved. If the water in the bottle is high, it means the weather will stay the same; if it's lower, it means a storm is coming."

"Wow, how did you learn so much about the weather?"

"Your grandmother was a well-known meteorologist. She was brilliant, and she taught me."

Will looked at him with confusion evident in his expression. "If she studied meteors, how does she know about weather?"

"A meteorologist studies the atmosphere. Meteor in Latin means 'anything in the heavens', including our atmosphere. Again, Will science is forbidden, so be careful."

"I know that. So, did we come here because of what you know about meteorology?"

"Partly. We came here to Pueblo because your Aunt Milly lived here, the air was still clean here, and it was on the other side of the Rocky Mountains. It was a newly incorporated city, and they needed workers. The whole world was expecting fires, deadly heated dust storms, and devastated infrastructure, and we thought the mountains would be a good barrier."

"Dr. Seger predicted there would be suicide groups and mass murdering gangs. Did that happen?" Being young and fascinated by intense situations, he found the topic thrilling.

"Unfortunately, those things did occur, and it's why the corporations hired personal armies from the local programs. Neighborhoods formed volunteer groups to watch their communities. They were very popular, but they quickly took on a vigilante approach to enforcement. In other words, people weren't arrested and given a trial to decide if they were guilty. They were often shot on sight if suspected of doing something wrong.

"It didn't take too long before the Corporates figured out they could use these new armies to do whatever they wanted. Those who made the grade joined the Neighwah Army. Those who didn't, became Drangers hired to do the grunt work for the army."

"They knew they could buy their loyalty with credits because independent businesses, like mine, were shut down and the only available jobs were from Corporates. They called for all the weapons listed on the registers, so they could create and enforce any rule to meet their agendas, and no one could stop them. Many hid their guns, but no one was willing to share that information or rally against them, so there was no resistance to the new order.

"How did Mom get sick?" Will noted the heartbreak that pooled on his father's face, revealing the ever-present pain deep inside him. Will felt sad too, but he grieved mostly because he had no clear memories of her.

"On the way, we got in the middle of a pretty bad dust cloud from a small rogue meteorite. We covered our faces, but the dust was thick. You and I recovered, but it got to your mom. We arrived here at Pueblo, hoping she would get better. But when we got here, we found Milly had been injured in a food fight."

Ben drifted off, thinking about the food fights he remembered as a kid. It used to mean throwing food in a mischievous and messy act of childish mayhem. But after the disaster, it referred to the violent attacks on stores, shoppers, and people to steal food.

"Dad?" Will could see his father had drifted away with some memory in his head, leaving him behind.

"Oh, sorry. After the strikes, people carried bats, pipes, hammers, or whatever they could find to fight with, but Milly never learned to fight like that."

"Why didn't the Neighwah keep people controlled like they do now?"

"The Neighwah weren't formed yet, and no one feared the police, so they were overwhelmed. Many people refused to use credits preferring money to buy things."

"Money?" Will asked

"Money was something people carried with them to buy what they wanted without their purchases being tracked. They could get the notes from banks and stores from their accounts, and spend without showing ID."

"But weren't they afraid of being attacked?"

"Yes, and money was soon outlawed, and all the rebellious people who only had money lost their status overnight. And now everything we do is tracked. When a person or business does something, the Corporates don't like, no one is allowed to give or pay them credits. Guns were also outlawed for everyone but the Neighwah and licensed Drangers. Now, without the freedom to speak, vote, or fight, we are powerless.

"But back to your mom. She tried to take care of her sister, but her injuries were already seriously infected before we got there. Your aunt knew she was going to die, and she gave this house to us. When she died, it broke your mom's heart, and she got worse. Her dust cough turned into pneumonia. I took her to the hospital, but they don't treat Dailys who are as sick as she was. They just helped her to die quickly and be out of pain. Those were hard times for you and me. I still miss her." His dad got a melancholy look as if he was back there in that hospital watching his wife fade away and consenting to her death.

"So, meteor sickness is pneumonia?" asked Will. They were back at their house then and stacked the firewood by the fireplace. Will fell hastily onto the old couch, sending a plume of dust into the air.

"The fires, dust, and rampant illnesses made people unwell, and many died. Meteor sickness is just a non-medical term we used to refer to every breathing, burn, or injury issue people got sick from. We didn't have enough medicine or doctors to help everyone."

Will considered this for a while. "Where do people's bodies go?"

"All dead bodies are collected, frozen, and then driven to the Colorado Springs Territory where they're incinerated at their huge crematorium. It is done to prevent another pandemic of disease from untended corpses. There was a time when people were buried in the ground in cemeteries where a stone marked their site, so people could visit it.

"These times don't allow for the niceties of a grave, but we keep your momma's picture from our wedding on the mantle. That's our memorial." His father looked over at the color photo in its delicate bone-China frame where tiny vines bloomed with dark pink flowers.

Will walked over to the fireplace mantle. The faded picture was in a frame that at one time was probably valuable, but the cracks showed signs of a poorly done repair. He often looked at it, but after that day, the image gained new meaning. Will would often stare at it, trying to summon his memories of her, but only blurry shadows bubbled up.

Chapter Two

Will was approaching his twelfth birthday in August. It didn't signify a celebration as much as it meant he was entering his coming-of-age year. During this year, he was required to seek a mentor to train him for his adult work. Training would start part-time and didn't usually involve full-time until one was closer to fourteen. But if he did not have a secure position by the end of his twelfth year, he would be drafted into a service selected by the community supervisor.

That often resulted in dangerous, labor-intensive, and undesirable jobs, including becoming a Dranger soldier. That was a repugnant option Will would resist at every opportunity. The Drangers endured a ruthless training schedule and were required to do the evilest of deeds.

They were moved away from their families, and their only friends were among themselves because they were hated and feared by Dailys. He didn't want that life, but he wasn't sure what he wanted to do. He knew his father would mentor him if there was an opening at the machine shop, which currently there was not. He had time, but the impending date weighed on his mind.

In late May, the Neighwah soldiers started regularly visiting them and harassing his father. He was used to going into the house whenever authorities came to call, but he often watched through the crumpled blinds. Tianna would hide, but she hid from lots of things, so Will didn't pay attention to her behavior. He just let her be Tianna.

He could not hear their conversations, and he was worried it was about a job they wanted to assign him, like a go-for. The Neighwah never drafted children for the core, but if they hadn't secured a job yet, they could grab them for their low work. He spent many sleepless nights devising his escape from such a fate.

"Dad, where's Tianna?" Will asked one morning as they sat down to breakfast without her. He expected an everyday response having to do with taking water to the outside vegetables, picking up seamstress work at the drop box, gathering seeds, or some other subsistence task. But his father's hard expression alerted him to a problem which he had been left out of.

"She went to visit a friend in another section of town," his dad answered.

Will tried to give his father the benefit of the doubt, but he could not come up with one friend Tianna knew well enough to visit in their small neighborhood, let alone outside of it. He couldn't even remember her going anywhere out of sight of their home by herself. He wasn't told why, but her fear of being on her own was palpable.

"What friend, and why did she go alone? She's terrified of being alone. Are you lying to me?"

His father leaned close to whisper his response. "I don't know where she is. We aren't allowed to know. So don't ask questions. Just say she is visiting a friend. Do you understand?" His dad's stern demeanor let him know this was serious, but his ambiguous answers offered nothing but the fear of impending tragedy.

Tianna was missing. He thought back on the evening when she sweetly told him goodnight. He knew something was bothering her, but she was constantly in and out of that state. And now she was gone. His youthful imagination instantly reframed the dilemma. Maybe Tianna, his dad, or both were involved in some conspiracy against the Corporate tyranny of their Pueblo region. In his pretend world, they were fighting for the people, and that better world they dreamed of. He envisioned them as brave rebels championing a good cause. Their efforts in this honorable endeavor were why they were in trouble, and a part of him felt proud and excited.

He recalled the strange little tune that Tianna had taught him, reciting it in his head word for word. She said it was important to remember, and he couldn't tell anyone else about it, not even his dad. It was just between them. He smiled at the memory of them singing it in the garden room over and over. He felt secure again, holding that memory close. That is until something catastrophic happened to suddenly change their fates. He was too young to know what was going on, but everything in his world was about to turn on him.

One night in early summer, his dad woke him, covering his mouth, pulling him out of bed, and signaling him to be quiet. He handed Will warm clothing to put on and they set out with only a couple of prepared backpacks. They crept by the passed-out sentries, and Will wondered if his dad had given them some kind of a sleeping draft. He suddenly felt like he did not know his father.

They bolted into the night, dodging from bush to bush behind their home. When they were far enough away from the city streetlights, they ran without stopping. On and on they went while Will's lungs burned and his energy waned. He had no idea why they ran, but the terror and determination in his father's eyes compelled him onward without question.

A lingering storm had muddied the trail, causing them to slip and stumble. His father slipped into a hole and twisted his ankle, and still, they ran, his dad limping from the throbbing injury. Both were on the verge of passing out from the exertion when the pace slowed, and his father led him into a deep cave flanked by a thick stand of brush.

He expected to rest there for a while, but his father walked to the back of the cavern and rolled out an old but hefty hybrid ATV packed with supplies. Helping his father push it through the bushes, Will caught the glint of a long black barrel, and he wondered where his dad had gotten a hold of a rifle. His father grabbed an ammo box, fully loaded the rifle, and expertly chambered a round with a one-handed move.

It was painfully obvious they were part of an organized rebel faction. Just possessing ammo violated one of the most serious laws of the Pueblo Corporate Territory, but a working firearm was unthinkable. They were in the torture-for-information before-being executed or shoot-on-sight kind of trouble.

The stop at the cave was so short, and the supplies were so strategically placed, that it reeked of a carefully organized and executed plan. How long had they been planning this behind his back? Will's hackles began to rise, and he felt more like a kidnap victim than a rescued child. Through the darkness of night, they rode under the cover of the emerging forest, even when other routes would have been more direct. The quarter moon, dulled by scattered, light clouds, did little to illuminate the shadowed trail, but his father navigated the vehicle with great skill and an apparent familiarity with the route. *When did his parents become so secretive? Did he practice riding and following this trail? If so, when? And most importantly, what were they up to?* Will's questions started stacking up while anger was swelling in his chest and tensing his muscles.

Will was grateful to not be running anymore, but the rough ride gener- ated different aches and misery, adding to the ones he had just racked up from their sprint from home. His body was pounded with every bump and quick turn, and though he was in serious need of sleep, he didn't dare close his eyes for fear of falling off. Finally, as the tree-dappled sun crawled up the horizon, they came to a small, run-down shack tucked against a heavily wooded hill.

It appeared uninhabitable, but Will was so tired he didn't care if he had to share a bed with all manner of critters. He just wanted to collapse, yet as sleepy as he was, the situation had him wary and the need for answers was plaguing his thoughts. *Where is Tianna? Why are we under guard and having to escape? Where are we going? Will we ever be able to go home? What is going to happen to us?*

As he climbed off the four-wheeler, his arms cramped, his back ached, and his legs felt tingly, like they weren't his own. Dizzy with fatigue and his muscles crying out in protest, he grabbed one of the packs and shuffled toward the shanty. He was so urgently in need of a reprieve from his exertion that he decided his questions could wait until he rested.

But then he would insist his father reveal the point of such a journey. He may only be a boy, but this was happening to him too. His life was on the line, and he had a right to know what he was risking it for. As he staggered into the ramshackle hovel, his eyes lit up at the sight of Tianna's smiling face and her arms waiting to embrace them.

"Tianna!" he shouted while his sobs and tears flowed freely. All his pains and questions were temporarily forgotten, and relief flooded through him. He had anticipated and played their reunion in his head since she had disappeared. He refused to think she had met her end alone, so he would fantasize that when he saw her, all the craziness of the past weeks would be over. Then his childhood realm would go back to the way it was. Everything would be familiar again, and they would feel content and sheltered from this frightening new reality. But like most idealized futures, it was tragically flawed.

Holding on to her, he swiftly felt all the terror of the last week returning to suck the joy out of the moment. He was fully aware that they were in dire circumstances. He felt a rush of anxiety at the thought of losing one or both of his parents and dying himself. The last of his childish dreams and wishes faded under the cruelty of his new existence.

Though only eleven, he already had a bead on the ugliness and unfairness of the world they lived in. He had witnessed plenty of brutal violence under the last Corporate regime, but it had gotten much worse under the new one. Despite the reality of hostile and crooked authorities with their ever-changing, murky rules, his father and Tianna grounded his education in a foundation of ethics.

They filled him with the hope that someday leadership embracing justice and compassion would prevail, and Dailys would work for their benefit, not for tyrannical overlords.

His heart knew it was ethical, but his experiences left him doubtful that ethics could prevail. He was skeptical that any amount of valor or magic could change their world. And now the evil and powerful rulers would aim their armies at them. How could it ever be okay again? Tired as he was, his sleep was full of churning nightmares that woke him up and tossed him into the real one.

They slept without detection through the daylight, and all three got back on the recharged ATV at nightfall. His father's ankle was quite swollen when they arrived at the shack, but Tianna treated it with an anti-inflammatory poultice made from herbs she had gathered, and it was already going down. Their goal, as it was shared with Will, was to make it to an area near the boundaries of Pueblo.

Ben had received reliable information regarding an area near the Colorado Springs border, with a small number of sentries. The group had been assured they would be let in, but Will didn't understand why they would. Settling beneath a thick canopy of trees as daybreak's beams began to creep across the wilderness, they set up their simple camouflaged tent.

Tianna and Will took a walk to gather edible plants and herbs to add to their dinner. While they walked, they sang her little song, and she taught him the lessons her life had revealed.

"Never forget who you are and where you come from, Will. Remember the lessons of your journeys and the paths that brought you through them. They shape you and show the way to your destiny." She bent down and made a spiral. "Life is like this spiral. Although it seems to cover the same ground, it expands with each new experience. Even the bad ones can make us better people if we keep to our circle and come back to what we know is right."

Although Will didn't understand the reason, she used strange riddles to get her point across; his intuition sensed there was a warning somewhere in her lessons, but being a young child, his imagination only found the magic in it.

The next evening's travels brought them to a small encampment edged in a ravine dense with tall pines. Will counted dozens of people joining them for the final leg of their journey. The band of rebels greeted the dusty trio with total familiarity. The rest of the travelers were strangers, but everyone interacted as though they understood the shared plan. *It just gets more and more obvious that I was left out of this... whatever it is, and I still am*, he thought.

His father finally told him they were escaping to the Colorado Springs Corporate Territory for a better life. Will wasn't sure why he had been left in the dark for so long about that, and he had a feeling there was more to the plan, but he wanted to believe they were safe now. So he did, and he slept more soundly than he had in weeks. He liked being among this crowd of armed comrades because he was a child, and he gave his trust freely and hastily.

In the morning, they interacted with the group of thirty-three refugees while they waited for the return of the two scouts sent to the border to assess its security. Some shared their tales, but the details were notably censored, and some were the practiced cover stories they maintained. Ben doubted any truths were told at all, but young Will sat riveted, believing every word of the embellished and exciting narratives.

His father and Tianna gave a cover story of them bringing Will along because he was recently orphaned. Will didn't know why being their son was dangerous information, but he played along. Not because he understood, but because he didn't.

That evening, one of the scouts came back and delivered the awaited good news. He reported the border was manned by only two Pueblo sentries. Most territories had arrangements to share the management of the entry and exit points to cut down on needed manpower and confrontations. He explained the other scout was staying to continue the surveillance just in case the situation changed. The band gathered and packed their supplies with an efficient routine that had become second nature and headed toward the electronically armed border.

In the distance, a wounded man stumbled toward the group. They rushed to him, realizing it was the other scout. He accused his teammate of deceiving the group and betraying himself to the sentries. He only escaped because they thought he was dead. Although he was seriously injured, he made his way to this juncture to warn them not to proceed. The women tended to the wounded scout while the men surrounded and secured the traitor, Cole, as he pleaded his case.

"They only want that woman, his woman," and he pointed at Ben. "They will let all of us go through if she is handed over. General Kenner sent them himself."

"And being the idiot you are, you believed him?" Taylor, the leader of the group, asked scornfully.

"I was captured and beaten. Look!" he said and showed them his back where five or six lash marks bit into his flesh. "Then the promise was made. The Pueblo Corporates discovered their arrangement and made a deal with Colorado Springs's more powerful army. They said we could all go through as long as the woman stayed.

"We are to leave her in the open field over the next rise," and he pointed to the hill before them. "They will retrieve her. The Pueblo army has us surrounded on three sides, and the Colorado Springs sentries are on the other. There is no escape, and if this is a lie, it is still our only chance." The traitor turned to Ben and quietly said so others didn't hear, "They said you could watch the others go through. I didn't tell him about the boy with you, I swear. It is very important to them that she is taken alive, so they don't mean to kill her."

Ben knew there were worse fates than death at the hands of these merciless fiends. He gathered his family and turned to retreat from the group. He'd be damned if he was going to give them his wife after all the effort and planning to save her. The leader caught him by the arm and pulled him aside. Will watched from afar as they discussed the situation. The way the traitor said, "That boy with you," confirmed no one knew who he was. *Was this why? Did they expect this to happen?*

Will had heard of this general. He was inventively cruel. No wonder she was scared all the time. He looked over at Tianna, who sat with her head in her hands, shaking and sobbing softly. Will went to her.

"What is happening?" but she did not respond. He felt like he was in a nightmare, and like such dreams, nothing made any sense. He was alone and at the mercy of a faceless monster. Two men came and took her to a tent while Will stood frozen with shock and uncertainty.

"Will," Tianna called her stepson, motioning him to follow them.

He crawled into the small dwelling, and when the two men left them alone, he hugged her tightly as tears pushed at the back of his eyes. "What's going on? Do you know who they're talking about? We need to plan an escape..."

"Will, hush. I need to talk to you. There's not much time. Please, just listen." She had a steely look in her eyes, and Will knew this conversation was critical. "You remember the song?"

"Yeah, but Tianna, this is serious."

"Yes," she stressed and took a breath, "it is, so listen. I'm giving you my coat. It belonged to my dad. Tucked —"

"No, why? You need it."

"Listen, Will! I don't have much time. Tucked into the left sleeve is the Sanguine Blade."

He froze and stared for an extended moment. "It's real?" His eyes were wide with shock, and it hadn't escaped him that she laid the burden of rebellion on his shoulders.

"You must not let it be discovered. It's a well-made blade of superior quality, but it's much more than that. You must keep it safe, and someday, you will discover its true value." She tilted his down-turned face toward her. "William Alexander, your future holds a heroic destiny. There are many others with clues that can end the Corporate rule, but the Sanguine Blade is unique. Learn, grow, survive, and someday you will understand."

He stared at the worn, drab green jacket she held out, and he took it with a sense of reverence for the moment. The jacket was well padded with arm guards built in for defense. He pushed on the sleeve, feeling for the blade, but he discovered it could only be felt from the inside of the left sleeve. "How do I get it out?"

"There is a hidden zipper." He felt around and found the masked zipper in a seam on the inside of the lower arm. The zipper tab was a piece of material disguised as a tear. Opening the zipper, he reached in and pulled out the knife. It was about eight to nine inches from base to tip. The handle was made of deep mahogany wood with a stunning grain pattern and a finger grip shape. Numerous expertly carved markings that he did not recognize provided a solid grip along the handle.

The metal sheath displayed a rugged cliff edge masterfully etched and highlighted in black on its surface. He pulled out the double-sided blade, amazed at its burnt reddish hue, sharp edge, and the mean jagged ridge running along the top. A lightning bolt shot down the blade, etched through the dark, bloody pigment, allowing its silver insides to shine through. He returned the knife to its sheath and then to its place in the man-sized jacket.

"How can a single knife conquer the Corporates? I'm too old to believe that." He pushed the jacket toward her, and she pushed it back. "The jacket is way too big for me, and besides, they'll just take it," Will argued.

"They won't take it because they don't know it's mine. I haven't worn it in front of anyone here. And for now, they don't know you're mine either. You will be safe in the Colorado Springs Territory before they figure it out. Don't worry about the size. You're young now, but you will grow. You will be a powerful and brave warrior like Alexander, like a lion," she smiled. He looked deeply at this kind woman and hugged her, tears welling in his eyes. He didn't know what her gift meant, or what being its owner entailed, and he was afraid to ask. But he knew it was important, and he would carry out her wishes, regardless.

"What's going to happen? How will we get away?"

"There is only one escape for your father and me." Tianna saw the dread in Will's young eyes. "But I want you to know, it's going to be okay. Your father and I love you so much. My time with you has made my life worthwhile. Our hearts are aching now, but you must trust me. Go with the group. Promise me, promise me you will do this one last thing for me, Will."

"I promise," he said, but in his mind, he was stuck on the way she said the last thing. *What did that mean? Were they splitting up?* He decided then and there, he would sneak away to observe this escape plan, and then he would go with the group.

Ben listened to Taylor's plan, which was woefully weak and had little chance of success. It seemed that no one in the group knew the extensive power of the one who chased her. Ben came to the tent and asked Will to give him a moment alone with his wife. Will hugged her and said he would see her soon.

Everyone was grouping up to head toward the boundary. Ben, per the agreement, would be the last to cross the border. He hated their plan, and he had no intention of turning her over. Tianna shook her head. She left the tent and walked a dozen yards away. Ben followed. Will watched them arguing and madly gesturing with wild arm movements.

"NO! I refuse! No, Tianna! I won't; I can't!" Ben roared at her in an uncharacteristically aggressive voice, but at the end of his statement, his voice was cracking. Will had never seen his father raise his voice to her. Tianna was crying and pleading now, though he could not make out her words, her resolve was determined. It was obvious the plan was changing. Then suddenly, she coolly and quietly whispered something to her husband, and his resolve and his body crumpled to the ground like a child. Will saw the rifle she had hidden under her long cloak.

He desperately tried to decipher what just happened to cause such a divide between a couple so in love, or at least he thought they were. He was petrified with shock and pondered with a significant amount of concern what Tianna intended to do with the weapon she held. He stood watching, unable to decide what he should do, or whether he should make a move. He remained where he stood, counting on his father to make it all right.

The rest of the group was also frozen, waiting for an impossible answer to the dire predicament. No one moved to leave, and no one volunteered to help. They just stood there as if time itself would remain stalled in this moment, waiting for someone to take the lead. Their hesitant replies and actions started slowly with a couple of soft-spoken suggestions from the small crowd. It quickly whipped into a furor that ended in Tianna and Ben being restrained, and the weapon taken from her. Questions and demands were shouted at them, and Tianna looked at her husband with pleading eyes.

Taylor Noland, the group leader, waved the white rag above his head several times, and a shot rang out to the left of him, followed by one in the direction they were heading. The first was the signal from the Pueblo leader that the group was okay to leave, and the second was from the Colorado Springs sentries just over half a mile away calling them to head toward the gate.

The next shot would mean the group had safely crossed into Colorado Springs. It's not that Taylor trusted either territory's military, but he knew

Colorado Springs needed laborers desperately after a massive landslide destroyed the worker dormitory, killing and injuring dozens of laborers. His people had a place to go where they needed to arrive alive and well. That was his duty. It was tragic that the woman was doomed, but her sacrifice would buy the safe passage of the twenty-eight able workers and their children.

Ben saw through his binoculars the movement in the next grove of trees, and he knew they faced impossible odds. She was trapped; he was trapped. He dreaded the options before him. He talked with Taylor privately, and the two seemed to agree. They brought Cole, the traitor, into a tent put up for the children and dressed him in Ben's clothing. They were of similar size and build, so the sentries wouldn't recognize him for a while without camo paint on his face. Then, they dressed Ben in Cole's camouflaged clothing and put camo paint on his face. Cole was knocked out and propped in front of the bunker where Ben hid.

Will wanted desperately to believe they had a plan. Despite the recent betrayals, he had the innocent trust of a child unable to imagine vulnerability in the people who had raised him and loved him completely. They had gotten through so many things together, and he couldn't foresee them abandoning him, but he didn't know how they would get out of this. If he had had more years of experience, he would have seen the grave reservations in everyone's expressions.

Tianna dutifully sat in the grass while the rest of the group passed by. Will stopped and hugged her, assuring her they would protect her. She smiled at him, and then Ben kissed his wife tenderly. Will was forcefully separated from her. Ben shook with rage as he retreated, leaving Tianna sitting in the field. Will couldn't comprehend what was occurring. Surely, they weren't going to leave her out in the open. Will's father ducked into a hidden bunker with a perfect view of Tianna. Taylor covertly gave Ben back his rifle in case he had to defend himself.

Will was hopeful this was where he would make his stand and save Tianna. Will was sent with the people walking and driving ATVs ahead. The children and supplies were piled into the carts, making counting the young difficult for the accompanying sentries. This made it possible for Will to separate from the group. As the group moved onward through a thick grove of scrub oaks heading a quarter mile from CS, Will fell behind and hid by a tree.

He had taken the binoculars from his father's pack because with his scope he wouldn't need them. Will planned to lie on the crest of a rise, giving him a clear view of Tianna. He wanted to see the plan in action, as if watching her could keep her safe. He looked behind him and saw the group disappearing over the next ridge, and he remembered his promise.

"Just a few minutes longer," he said under his breath.

He adjusted the powerful binoculars until he had a view of Tianna's profile. She was sitting in the open field in such a casual manner that it completely contrasted with the current situation. It was as though she was safely relaxing in the sun and enjoying the wildflowers waving in the breeze.

She smiled as she picked up a dandelion, tipped her head, and blew the fuzzy ball, propelling the whimsical seeds to dance in the wind. It was plain to see she enjoyed the act immensely, and she quickly gathered up another. Her casual composure gave Will hope that whatever the plan was, it was on track, but it made no sense. *Was the dandelion a signal? How could it possibly work?*

Chapter Three

Nothing about the last week had made sense to Will, but now he was questioning Tianna's sanity. She was easily confused when she was frightened, but she was extraordinarily knowledgeable and efficient in every task she attempted. Will never thought of her as compromised in any way until this moment. *Maybe they had both lost their minds.* All this time he had felt they left him in the dark about their predicament, but maybe it wasn't him in the dark, but them in denial. And yet he watched, still trusting in their abilities to win over evil.

He added up the possibilities over and over, but he could not see a desirable outcome, and his nerve was slipping. She would be directly in the line of fire if his father had to engage the enemy. He had been left in the dark about everything, but surely the side talks he was excluded from contained the rest of a more viable plan. As Tianna blew on the next dandelion, a shot rang out and a spray of red mist joined the gentle, airy dandelion seeds scattering to the wind. Tianna was thrown sideways, ending in a still slump.

Will's screams were stifled by Pierce, Taylor's son, putting his hand over Will's mouth. He noticed him missing and crept up behind him on the hill. It was the last time Will assumed with a childish faith that anyone could protect him or those he loved. *Who shot her? They said they wanted her alive. It couldn't be his dad. He couldn't, he wouldn't.* His mind burned with searing disbelief. *No, no!* His world began spinning, and he became frozen beyond fear. He felt his body being lifted, but he was helpless to understand how.

Pierce lifted Will in his arms and ran, carrying him to catch up with the group before their window of entry closed. They had betrayed the Pueblo deal, and Pierce knew the soldiers would soon charge them, firing at everyone. They were moments from the border when a round of explosions rumbled through the tense air. While being muffled and carried to the rest of the group, Will wondered where his father was and whether those explosions were the soldiers or his father's bunker. His head was in a manic dance, fighting against reality when a strange-smelling cloth was held to his face. His eyes blurred, his consciousness waned, and the darkness took him.

In his first lucid moment, he found himself in a large tent with rows of bunk-style cots. He was utterly confused about what had happened in the field. He was lying on a bottom bunk and could feel a scant awareness of heat warming one side of his aching body. It was coming from the small wood stove in the center of the canvas bunkhouse. He craved more heat than the stove provided but settled for rolling over to soothe his other side.

Facing the tent flap, he concluded he must be in a camp of some sort. He knew they must be close to their destination. Sitting up, waves of nausea hit him, and he thought he must be sick. He tried to recall his unsettling dream he couldn't piece together.

Maybe the nightmare was fever-induced. He tried to recall what happened, but the details were lost in a mist, a red mist. *How did they get here? Were they on their way to another town? It was a huge tent to erect for just one night.* Will's young mind was drowning in questions. Pierce was sitting on a stool and leaning on the bunk pole, fast asleep. His dark, wavy hair was haloed by a low-lying sun, shining through the partially open door flap.

Will tried to sit up, but his head swam. He fell back down on the cot, and Pierce woke up. The bright light from the door outlined his strong, angled chin and the deep hue of his olive skin. He had been watching over Will in big brotherly fashion.

"Hey, come on, wake up. Open your eyes. There you go, welcome back. I thought you were losing it, mumbling that weird tune over and over. What the hell is a "sayway bade" anyway?" Pierce shrugged his shoulders, smiled at him, and handed him a bowl of watered-down oatmeal sprinkled with supplement powder. When Will fully opened his eyes, he remembered Tianna saying... something, giving him something.

"Where am I? Where is my gear?"

"Calm down. All your stuff is secured in our family locker right there." Peirce walked over to the bank of metal lockers and put his wristband on the shiny dark pad. With a tinny click, it popped open. Will noticed at that moment, he also had a band secured around his wrist. He saw his gear bag at the bottom and Tianna's coat hanging on a hook.

"Can I have my coat? It's a little chilly in here." Pierce grabbed it out of the locker and closed it. Will hugged the coat to him. It still smelled like her. He ran his hands nonchalantly down the sleeves and felt for a knife. It was there. A mournful release swept over him, and tears rolled down his face. Not panicky crazy tears, it was the tears of a terrible new reality slowly taking form.

"I saw that woman give it to you and figured it was special to you."

"Thank you. Where are Tianna and my dad?" Will was still hoping for a simple answer, but in his heart, he knew it would not come.

Pierce ignored the question and addressed different answers instead. He explained they were in Colorado Springs Territory on the outskirts of the western side. They were in temporary lodging while they built a new and larger apartment building to replace the one a landslide took out. He talked about the camp and how the work was harder due to the timeline to beat the winter, but the supervisors were not as cruel as the ones in Pueblo.

"That's why we got through because workers are urgently needed here. This bunk tent will be our home until the building is finished. Then we'll get to live in one of the new apartments, and we'll have a place of our own. That's part of what we were promised if we risked our lives to make it here. Just think about it—a new apartment with new stuff in it."

"Again, where are Tianna and my dad?" Will knew they weren't there, but why wouldn't he answer him?

"I guess your memory is still pretty fuzzy. My dad is right outside and he can explain that. I'll get him." Pierce pushed the tent flap aside, ducking so his tall frame could pass through. Will got a quick peek at the bustling camp in the fading daylight.

"Good to see you awake. How are you feeling?" Taylor asked while pulling up a stool.

"Groggy. Why does my head hurt so bad and my arm too? Why is it in a sling?" His head was flooded with images. "All I remember is..." Will suddenly flashed on a fuzzy nightmare of Tianna in a field and a burst of red mist. Shock showed on his face as he dealt with the memories rocking through him. Taylor moved his stool closer to console him and be ready to restrain him, so he couldn't run as he had before.

"Where's my dad? Where's Tianna?" Will screeched. He felt the dread of a horrible reality but clung to the hope that it had all been faked. But he could not unsee what he saw in that field, and it coldly stated the awful truth.

"Shhh, take it easy, Will. Settle down enough to listen. Okay?"

Will nodded. Taylor told him the first time he woke up, he fought them and tried to run back to Pueblo. The Colorado Springs sentries captured him, injuring his arm and knocking him out. Taylor said told them that he had been recently orphaned, and because he was so young, they let him go. They had been giving him a sleeping draft to keep him calm so he could heal.

He told Will that Tianna was an escaped slave, and her owner, Commodore Winston Kenner, was obsessed with getting her back. His ruthlessness and cruelty were legendary, and even Will heard tales of him. Taylor left out the part he knew about his infamous treatment of his female slaves, but he revealed the part Will feared the most. His dad was the one who shot Tianna. Will had seen it with his own eyes, but he rejected the idea that his father would murder the woman he loved so completely.

"Will, I know this is a lot to take in," sympathized Taylor, "but that argument scene you witnessed, that was Tianna begging him to kill her if her capture was imminent. She threatened to do it herself, but it would have to be done after we were across the border. The only way to do that was to deprive your dad of his weapon. There was just no other way to save her and us from Kenner's headhunters. Every one of us would have died that day."

Taylor had his hand on his sturdy chest and looked at him compassionately. Will could see his sad brown eyes framed by the silvery highlights of his curly dark hair. "Though we can't talk about the events back there, we will remember them. We honor and appreciate their courage and sacrifice, as well as yours."

"Where is my dad? Did he die too? What do I do now?" Will helplessly sobbed through his questions without restraint.

"We gave him some explosives hoping he could escape, but we haven't heard anything. They went to a lot of trouble to find her and collect her alive. If they had wanted her dead, they could have easily used a sniper. I don't imagine they were happy about him killing her. They would have tortured the heck out of him to punish him, but what he was forced to do was as ugly as it gets.

"But as for you, you will stay with Pierce and me in this temporary housing and then in our apartment when it's ready. I registered you as my adopted son, and I will care for you as I would my own. No one knows you are Ben's son as far as I know. I believe he will come for you if he can. But regardless, you are safe here, Will."

Taylor took Will in his strong, powerful arms and held him until the boy's tears succumbed to exhaustion, and then laid him gently down.

Taylor looked sympathetically at the boy. He knew Will's path of recovery would be difficult, but he wouldn't walk it alone. He had them.

But Will's thoughts were not as benevolent. He began to blame his father for everything, even his real mom's death. Though he heard his father tenderly cared for her as her cough took a deadly turn, he had lied to him before, so he blamed him and hated him. Bitterness wove its tendrils through his heart, and vows churned in his head, demonstrating a malicious and self-destructive attitude.

He swore it was the last time he would believe in the ethical ways his parents had so carefully taught him. *They could not abide by them; why should he?* Honesty, *my ass*, he thought. They*'ve lied about everything*.

His trust was frayed. If they could betray him, who would not? Will curled into a ball and returned to his dark pit, wallowing in his despair. His memory of the next few days was a blur of feeling drugged and held against his will, more proof that he could count on no one but himself.

They lived on the west side of town, tucked up near the mountain forest, near the lumber camps. They occupied the tent cabin for almost two months. Everyone on the construction crew was double-timing the work to beat the already chilly temperatures.

Will was a go-for and a lumber stacker. He had a brutal schedule, and everyone seemed to be his boss. They yelled for his services, trying to get him to stop his current task to take up theirs. When he got back to the tent, he had cleaning duties while Taylor cooked on the shared wood stove, and Pierce chopped their share of firewood from leftover building materials.

The workload was steady for the Dailys, and though the Uppers and Corporates lived more lavishly than the Dailys could dream of, they were regularly fed. Will was sure the rations contained the supplement Tianna hated so much, but he had eaten it before she came with no ill effect.

They got one day off every other week, but Will, Pierce, and Taylor were off on different days. So instead of doing something together on their days off, they did the laundry, the mending, and stood in the long line to gather their weekly allotments.

It was rumored that when the building was done, and the neglected work was caught up, they would get one day off every week. He often nostalgically reflected on how wonderful his life was before their tragic attempt at an escape. He reminisced about sitting with Tianna for secret lessons, reading, and talking with his father in the evenings. He lost all his books from Pueblo, but he was too tired to read when he finished his work and chores, anyway.

The first snow was blanketing the ground, and tent living was proving unbearable, but finally, moving day arrived. The two-bedroom apartment was quite small. Smaller, they heard from the locals, than the previous apartment building, but it was new, clean, dry, and much warmer than their tent. Sparse furnishings, linens, and minimal kitchen supplies were issued to each apartment. Will and Pierce shared the second bedroom that had a bunkbed and a closet with a built-in dresser at one end. The furniture and bedding were all new, and though it wasn't extravagant by any means, it was nicer than any bed Will had slept on in his life.

Will knew he should be grateful for his life with Taylor and Pierce. They treated him fairly, and he knew they cared about him. Yet he still grappled unsuccessfully with his father's homicidal solution to Tianna's dilemma and the adults who stood by while it happened. All he could feel was an ever-shifting concoction of rage, betrayal, and shame. Though he had moments where he empathized with his father's predicament, he couldn't foresee forgiving him. By keeping him clueless all those weeks, everything that happened on that day happened to him.

Everyone else made choices for him, and if he was honest with himself, Tianna was included in that guilty group, but he could not bring that idea to fruition. His father killed a part of him on that traumatic day. He could not push through the betrayal or release his stubborn anger to begin the healing process. His life, though satisfactory for a Daily, held nothing of the contentment he felt as a child.

He routinely relived his past and embellished it with exaggerated magical times of playfulness and laughter with his stepmother. The angrier and more distant his father's memory became, the more beautiful the memories of Tianna grew.

Will's teen years demonstrated the restless angst that accompanies the transition to adulthood, but it was compounded by a past that he couldn't process. Taylor worried that Will was vulnerable to a host of dangerous choices. Mostly he feared Will would lose the job his friend's dad had secured him in construction. He might be jacked into a Dranger pack or worse, get drafted into a hazardous job assignment.

Will had to admit, he often entertained the notion of wreaking havoc and purging his rage with the soldier rebels, but the Drangers he knew were devoid of purpose and lived in a state of constant instability. They were required to do horrible things to innocent people. And the eventual death, maiming injuries, or recruitment into the Neighwah, held a very dreary future. Although he never seriously considered those options, he threatened Taylor with the notion just to hurt him.

Will's best friends, Calen and Nash, were in Taylor's opinion "one minute away from becoming Dranger scum." Calen and his mom and dad were assigned the same bunkhouse tent, but they came to town two weeks after Will's group. Nash was someone Will met on the Kid Krew. His dad was often in trouble for drinking moonshine, which made him mean. Of the three boys, Will was the oldest, but the younger two were only months behind him.

Will often spent the night at Calen's, escaping the memories his home held until he could cool his temper enough to go back to the apartment. Taylor felt there was something off about Calen, but all he could put his finger on was that he was too outspoken. It didn't go over well when he warned Will he was insolent and dangerous.

The boys connected right away, especially after Pierce moved into the construction section of the men's dorm. He had been the buffer between Will and Taylor, and the tension got uglier when he moved out. Will projected onto Taylor all the anger he couldn't visit on his real father. They both knew it wasn't fair or productive.

Will found himself making constant but warranted apologies, but he couldn't control his anger from the betrayal boiling in his gut. The roller coaster of fighting and resolving was exhausting and painful. But Will, Calen, and Nash developed a tight friendship that gave him the camaraderie his family could not.

The three boys shared many adventures, drowning out the cruel background noise of their painful home lives and their grinding schedules. One summer evening while chasing a rabbit, they pulled the brush aside and saw a large rocky cavern. The cave was probably an old animal den tucked in the hillside. Will estimated it was about eight feet wide, five feet deep, and at least five feet high.

They were all at various stages of their fifteenth year when the idea was hatched to make it into a fort. Their community in Manitou Springs, just west of Colorado Springs, fed the lumber needs of the territory, and there was usually a pile of leftover boards that were not guarded well. The boys took on the task of gathering supplies and constructing their hideaway with great enthusiasm.

Without any formal schooling, Nash and Calen looked to Will to execute the plan and work out the mathematics. He used the lessons he learned while helping his dad build the garden house for Tianna and from watching the crews he worked for. Nails and tools were much harder to come by, but part of Calen and Will's job was to collect the bent and dropped nails on the ground, and some found their way into their pockets. Their measuring tape was a length of used banding material they made hash marks on, and a rock served as a hammer.

Their big score was a small shovel that had been left behind and hidden by a bush. It was called a shit-shovel that workers commonly carried while lumberjacking, hunting, or road repair, but it was more versatile than its name implied. Its compact design made it easy to carry and handy in countless situations, and its sturdy construction made it a hard-working tool.

They were careful to build their hideaway without disturbing the camouflage bushes, so it would not be discovered. Using the boards they had gathered, they built a roof to shed the water toward the back, where a crack served as a natural drain. They made it watertight by pilfering a couple of small tarps from the tent city days. They used a pitch mixture to seal it to the sides, ceiling, and floor planks. They hoped it was sound enough not to collapse or flood under the snow, considering the piece-mill lumber they had to work with.

They became excellent scroungers for items to improve their get-away. An old mat left over from the temporary tent city served as floor covering, and sitting in the center of the space was a wooden crate they rebuilt topped with a homemade candle. It served as a small table and storage area, complete with a cabinet door on rope hinges.

Standing in front of the getaway, one could only see the bramble of bushes growing against a hill. A trapdoor entrance on the side had living branches attached to it, so they could swing out without breaking. Every day at the first sound of the shift horn, they checked in at home and secretly made their way to their place where they made their own rules. In their liberated palace, they shared their dreams of living on their own in the wilderness, free from the Corporate cities. Sometimes they revealed their private nightmares of surviving in this world.

"He shot her?" Nash asked with exasperated confusion after Will shared his last and worst moments with his dad. "All you've ever told us before was those awesome things you did together." Will reflected on the stories he told them. They were true but didn't reflect the way he felt now. Telling them only fueled his sense of betrayal, but he hadn't wanted to open that wound or have them think he was as damaged as he felt.

"Man, that's some severe shit! Did he go crazy or somethin'?" added Calen.

Will had a faraway, lost look in his eyes. It was the first time he had told anyone the story. He shouldn't have revealed they were his parents, but he believed they wouldn't betray him.

"All I was told is that she asked him to do it because she didn't want to get recaptured. I know something bad happened to her, and I know he loved her, so I can't believe he could pull the trigger even if she asked him to. She was the kindest person I ever knew. She made everything magical, and I was so happy. But I don't know exactly what happened because he never came back to explain it."

"Do ya think he's still out there?" Nash asked. "Maybe he's still kickin'."

"Then why hasn't he come for me? It makes me sad to think of him dead. I miss him, but I also hate him. He has a lot to straighten out, maybe too much. But if he is out there, he has abandoned me here without knowing or caring if I'm even alive." Will turned his head to sob, and his friends huddled around him.

"I think ya oughta remember the good times. We got this place built because he taught ya how to," offered Calen. "My parents don't even like me. They only talk to me when they grill me about what I've been doing with you guys."

"Yeah, you have some great stories with him. Remember how you and he made a scarecrow in the field one evening, so the crows would leave your garden alone? The Neighwah on patrol hit the deck when they saw it standing in the field the next morning." Nash started laughing just thinking about the tale and how Will told it.

"Yeah," Will laughed, "they shot the shit out of that thing." They all started laughing now. It was a loud, cathartic laugh that often follows an emotional storm, and it reached deep to ease the awkward intenseness of the moment.

"Man, we should do that here! It would be hilarious." Calen said while laughing. Will was smiling now.

"My favorite story was how he snuck out and got that antelope with a handmade bow and arrow disguised as a walking stick. He even took you with him once. That would have been amazing. Your dad had balls hunting on Corporate land and getting away with it. He sounds totally rebel." Nash said. "You're lucky, Will. Look at my dad; he's a toxer now, and he's getting worse. I'm thinking I should get outa here with my mom and brother before he does something crazy."

Nash's dad had been assigned one of the most hazardous jobs in the territory at the tox factory. He was forced to take it or give up their accidental third child that was on the way. Most workers got sick from the poisonous waste and were sent to the hospital when it finally got too bad to work. But some workers would feel fantastic, and Nash's dad was one of the latter.

At first, toxers would volunteer to do the worst jobs, but the pain of needing a bigger high soon came. Booze and euphoria drugs were hard to come by, but getting tox was easy. They destroyed one's brain thoroughly, but Will could hardly blame Nash's dad. He was forced into it. He tried not to think of the irony of forgiving Nash's dad and not his own.

"Hey, you know what we should do?" Nash was excited by his idea. "We oughta name this place."

"What do we call it?" Calen asked.

"It has to be a word that no one knows," Nash added.

Will finally chimed in. "Gidan Zati."

"What?" said Calen.

"Gidan Zati. It means "the lion's den" in Hausa, a language from Africa my great-grandfather knew. He was my mom's dad. My dad would tell me about him and how he had a dream of living where he could rule himself and be king of his own, be free. He called it Gidan Zati."

"Gidan Zati!" they all said together.

Will thought back to his father's laugh and his gentle eyes, contrasted by his steely nerve. He taught him so many meaningful things, like the blood pact that made brothers out of friends. He locked onto those happy moments and let them roll across his memory, bathing him in the love he felt back then. Calen was right. He should remember the good times.

His dad was the best man he ever knew before he did the unspeakable. There must be more to that moment, for it didn't fairly represent who his father was. For the first time since Will was told what happened by Taylor, he found himself hoping his father was alive somewhere, and he made a new oath. He swore he would find him to get the truth.

"We should seal our promise to keep this secret and each other safe with a blood pact," Will suggested. He explained to his friends it would make them brothers for life, and they agreed to enter into the sacred pledge. Since the blood pact required fire, they hiked up, cleared a spot, and lit their small fire under the tall pines to diffuse the smoke, so by the time it was noticed they'd be long gone. Will took out his Sanguine Blade and bathed the knife in the flame.

He tried to be nonchalant about it, but there was nothing nonchalant about a Daily owning a knife, especially one so fancy. They marveled at its beautiful details and swore to never tell anyone about it. Each boy balled up their fingers, and Will slashed across the business end of their fists with the searing sharp edge. They held their cries as required and joined their bloody fists to seal their oath to each other.

When he got home that night, he apologized to Taylor again, but this time it was with sincere reverence. The two sat up into the night talking in the darkness about everything, including that fateful day. When he finally went to bed, he prayed to the forbidden God that he would see his father again. He slept soundly for the first time since his world died.

The winter snow made it easy to see their tracks, so they agreed to postpone going to Gidan Zati. Several times a week, they would walk within sight of it to check on its condition. In early February, a tree fell and rolled near their precious den. They were relieved to find the Gidan Zati, or GZ, untouched. After they removed some of the branches in their way, they found they could walk behind the log and access their side door. They decided to resume their visits to GZ before adulthood threatened to split them apart.

Will had just turned sixteen, and Nash and Calen would soon follow. At sixteen, they were eligible to move into the dorms. Will planned to live with Taylor as long as possible because he didn't want him to lose his apartment and be moved to the dorms.

Calen wanted to move as soon as possible because he was tired of the uneasy tension with his parents. Nash wanted to move out, but he couldn't leave his pregnant mom and brother alone with his dad. Nash's dad had taken a turn to full-on crazy. Nash secretly worried he would draft him into a tox job or sell him off. He was fifteen and a half, but when he turned sixteen, he was his own man. Well, as true as that could be for a Daily.

Chapter Four

It was late summer, but the evening air was already frigid with icy winds. Calen and Will sat in the fort, waiting for Nash. Old Man River had died, and he had left each of the three friends a gift. Old Man River was the only person the boys knew who made it to an age where his hair was white, and his face was fully etched with the lines and marks of time.

No one knew his real name, so they called him Omar for short. He had gained favor with one of the head Corporates because he could write well and drafted many a document and letter for him. He earned his nickname, Old Man River, from his many fishing adventures in faraway places.

He was a gifted storyteller and spun many a tale of a bygone world with his dramatic renditions of his travels. Most believed he was a dreamer and translated in the current era, meant liar. He was ordered to stop his tale-weaving and warned by his high-positioned friend that he would not defer his deserved punishment again.

He kept to himself, but Taylor knew what few others knew. Omar was once the famous author, Harrison Brand. Taylor quietly revealed his knowledge of Omar's identity, and it forged a friendship between them. Taylor got his fill of stories, and Omar got to be himself. Omar thoroughly loved the outdoors, where he was free to roam and explore. The two men shared many a night discussing a time when people were free, and the world was wonderfully happy and breathlessly wild.

One night, the two acquired some homegrown moonshine, and their storytelling became loud enough to wake Will. He sat near the door, listening to the yarns the old man spun, and he was reminded of his time with Tianna. She also spoke as he did, and he recognized at least one story as a classic she had told him.

Will knew the world he spoke of was unrealistic, but it churned up an expectation of fairness in him that seemed possible and completely reasonable. He made a concerted effort to seek out this storyteller and gain his confidence, and soon he too was invited to enjoy the bard's renditions. Be they true or not, they locked into Will's thoughts a sense of how the world should be.

Many in the town were grief-stricken when Omar died and was unceremoniously shipped off to the giant crematorium in Colorado Springs. Will was especially upset. The thought of him and his world being shipped off and turned to ashes was unacceptable. He needed it. He used it to tether himself to a better place where people envisioned their futures and were free to make them happen.

That kind of humanity was woven into his purpose now. It seemed connected to the ambiguous destiny Tianna planned for him. He was determined not to let his stories or his world die. Before he was sent to the hospital, he gave Taylor three gifts, one for each boy he had befriended. They had not yet opened their gifts because they waited for Nash to join them at GZ.

Time slowed as it does in waiting, but when an hour passed and Nash still didn't come, the two decided to go find him. The boys stowed the gifts wrapped in burlap bags in the crate table, carefully crawled through the hidden door, and walked across the log near the entrance to GZ.

Splitting up to hide any tracks they might leave, they made their way back to town and met at Nash's door. Although they knew where he lived, they had never been there before. A woman swollen with child answered the door with a red and purple shiner swelling on her cheek. The boys were not sure what they should do, so they simply asked if Nash was there. His mother stepped outside the apartment door and closed it softly.

"He sold him," she sobbed as quietly as she could manage. "That bastard sold him to a Dranger pack for the credits he owed them for toxins." She fell against the wall and put her face in her hands.

Calen and Will froze in their tracks. "They jacked him! When?" they said loudly in unison. His mother frantically signaled them to be quiet.

Drangers were known for drafting Dailys into their service. They often inflict debt situations on the vulnerable to grab valuables, including male children as recruits. Although the parents were intentionally tricked into their situation, the Drangers had a legal right to take them. Since Nash was over fifteen and a half and under sixteen, his father could legally conscript him into Dranger service to address his debts. That meant the parent's debt was paid in full, but the recruit was obligated to serve until he turned eighteen. Being experts at creating indebted scenarios, the obligation was indefinite, which meant their lives were often short.

"Last night, they came wanting payment. We had nothing of value to trade, so they took Nash. They said they needed new jacks, so they took him." A loud bang sounded from the street, which might wake her husband, so she told them to go, as she snuck back through the door.

Will's mind froze. He needed to clear his head to fully consider the situation. He was suddenly and painfully aware of his naïve nature. No matter how many awful things he encountered, disbelief was still his immediate reaction. Both Calen and Will had heard stories like this before, and he had seen Dailys treated with depraved indifference. But this was Nash, this was their brother, and his own father sold him. They shared the powerful storm rolling through them as they rushed down the stairs and made their way back to GZ.

"He knew his dad was going to do something bad to him. Why didn't we listen?" Calen wiped the tears from his reddened eyes.

"What could we have done?" Will was revisiting the helpless feeling of watching people he cared about being viciously torn from him.

"He could have hidden in here."

"There would have been a dog team sent out. This place would have been outed, and we'd be in serious trouble too. I mean, we stole material, constructed a dwelling without permission, and who knows how many other rules of the obedience mandate we've broken." Just saying it made Will's nerves edgy. *What if he told them about this place? What if he told them about his knife?* But he dismissed the idea. They wanted a new jack. They didn't have a clue about this place or Will's treasure, so they wouldn't know to ask.

"What are we gonna do, Will? I mean, we're gonna do something... aren't we?"

"I don't know, Cal," Will said, using Calen's nickname. "I'm not sure what we can do. Just let me think about it." He knew that thinking about it was all he would be doing. It seemed hopeless, but he had to do something. He wouldn't live with another tragedy he did nothing to stop.

Word got around that young Nash was sold to the Drangers, and it was the topic of conversation whenever the authority types weren't in earshot. Will and Calen found out Nash was sold to the Colorado Springs Raiders. He would be taken to their training camp at Fountain, where all jacks and recruits were sent.

After that, they would be assigned to a crew. Each crew was run by a pack leader. Rescuing him would be an impossible task for seasoned fighters. They would be completely out-skilled and outgunned. All they had to bring to the fight was their recklessness and youthful rage.

Calen and Will decided they simply needed to get to the training camp, so they could locate him and keep track of him. If they didn't, they might never see him again. New jacks were not allowed to work in their home-towns, and their routes were anything but routine. The two met after work at GZ to discuss a plan.

"How do we leave without getting our families in trouble? I'm not sixteen yet, so I can't go off and look for work in other areas without my parents' permission. They would get in trouble, and though you just turned sixteen, Taylor would flip." Calen's voice rose as reality set in.

"I'm... I'm not sure yet. I need to think." Will was tossing a thousand worries and memories in his head. He needed to be alone to think clearly, but he was resolved it was up to him to intervene. "Meet here in two days after work. Tomorrow, I have an extra shift, and I won't be able to come. I need to work this out. It's complicated."

Will walked back to the apartment just before dinner time radiating his deep, heavy mood. Taylor let him simmer in silence until the shift horn sounded at 9:00 p.m.

"Will, I am so sorry about Nash. It's despicable what his father did. I had no idea what his life was like. I guess everyone does now; he's been the talk of the town. Being jacked into Drangers is no picnic for sure, but it's not a death sentence either. There is a chance he can get out when he turns eighteen." Taylor didn't believe this was likely, but he hoped it would give Will the hope he needed to move forward.

"You know as well as I do that's a lie. They set up debt traps to keep people in until they are dead or so injured they go to the sit-work house. And that is a death sentence."

"Will, there isn't any move you can make. If you run away without permission, you're AWOL from our section. The few scuffles you have been in don't come close to the fighting experience needed to go against their weapons and combat training. I hope you aren't thinking about rescuing him. If you get caught and are lucky enough to survive, the minimum punishment you will receive is being jacked as cannon fodder!" Taylor's voice dripped with fear, his tone rising to an emotional pitch and getting louder with each word.

Will knew he was right. Everything he said was true. Will could see plainly how much he was loved. He would do almost anything not to hurt him anymore, but sacrificing Nash was outside of the almost. They were brothers now. *That's right,* he thought, *we are brothers.* And a very risky strategy began to take form.

Will's mind schemed all night. He went through every move, contingency, and response his young mind could conceive. The next morning, he marched up to the foreman's office fifteen minutes before the shift work horn was scheduled to wail. He knocked on the door with resolved determination.

"Enter," said an annoyed voice from inside.

Will grabbed the handle and pulled with the force required to free the door from its crooked frame. He turned and closed it with the same strength. His every move was empowered by his teetering anger and sense of urgency. "I need to talk with you, sir, please." Will had no idea how this was going to go, but it was Nash's only chance.

"Well, make it quick," the foreman responded without looking up.

"I want to leave to find work in another section. I'm sixteen, so I'm allowed."

"Barely," looking up from his work orders, he took in Will's serious posture. "You turned sixteen like two weeks ago. This is about Nash, isn't it? Why don't you just take a breath here, kid? Do you know how hard it is to break into a new town? You'll get toxer work for sure."

"Sir, I am willing to forfeit all my credits to you, and I understand you won't permit me to come back."

The foreman thought for a minute. Will was a hard worker, and he didn't want to lose him. But as determined as he appeared, he was sure he would just go to the supervisor, and then she would get his credits. The foreman knew how to win this gambit. "Well, you look like your mind is set. Put your hand here and repeat what you just said into the Mic."

Will stood proudly, "I want a witness, my mentor." Will had heard of cases where the recording "failed" and a runner warning was sent out in its place. He could end up losing his credits, being labeled a runner, and getting dragged back to a double-duty schedule. He wasn't going to let anything stop him from getting to Nash.

"You little shit. Who do you think you are?" the foreman's jaw was clenched, but Will stood his ground.

"If it's too much trouble, I could get the super. Of course, you'd lose my credits," Will spoke with a confident, calm demeanor, contrasting his jellied insides. But Will was a meticulous planner, and he had prepared for every contingency he could conceive of.

The foreman knew that if he altered the recording now, someone else would get the credits. He called Will's mentor with the speaker, and soon Calen's dad, Jonah, came through the door. When he heard the reason he was called, he pulled Will outside for a talk.

"Are you sure about this, Will? I can't see how this goes well. There's no way Taylor knows. What am I going to say to him? It's going to crush him. What will I say to Calen? Does he know he's about to lose his other best friend?"

It had been Jonah who made a special request to bring him onto his team because Taylor had no openings. Jonah had always taken a special interest in Will more than he had his own son, and he had spent many nights on his floor when he was fighting with Taylor. He was going to miss and hurt so many good people, and for a second, he questioned his decision. But only for a second.

"I see you are set on your course. If I can't change your mind, let me be the first to wish you the best." For the first time, Will understood why Calen felt the way he did. The Jonah before him didn't look concerned. He looked relieved.

"Please don't say anything, not yet. I appreciate how you have been there for me, but now it's my turn to be there for Nash. I have to do this. If I don't try," Will pushed down the thought of the red mist in the field. "I couldn't live with that again."

"That woman was surrounded by trouble. You should keep that story to yourself," Jonah advised.

Though many knew about the shooting in the field, only Taylor and Pierce knew why it upset him so. Will had told Jonah he had met her at the camp, but he seemed to see through his story. Will thought of his friends and Taylor and Pierce. He was fortunate to be so loved. Nash had no one. No one but him.

"I will, thank you for all you have done. Please take care of Calen and be kind to him. He's going to be upset that I left him too. Don't let him do anything stupid."

"Like you?" Jonah's eyebrows were raised, and his mouth was set in a thin line.

Will smiled, "Yeah, like me."

After that, they went inside and concluded the unpleasant business. As Will walked away, he saw Jonah heading in the opposite direction, slapping his hands together in an odd, finished business manner.

Will thought about the letter he left Taylor on a blank page torn from the book OMAR gave him. He put it between the tin plates in the cupboard. Taylor, Pierce, and Will all were aware of each other's ability to read and write, but it was forbidden. They communicated with symbols, like putting his cup on the table meant he got home from work but went to hang with friends, or a plate meant he was spending the night with Calen, but he had never left a note before. He could only hope that when he didn't show up, Taylor would search through the cupboard for a clue.

He wanted to let Taylor know how he felt. They had just come to an understanding, and their relationship was strengthening. He had to leave, but Taylor deserved an explanation. He owed him that. If he tried to explain it to him in person, he would have never been able to leave. He didn't write a letter to Calen because he couldn't read well. Will had started teaching Calen and Nash in Gidan Zati, but they hadn't had enough lessons to read on their own yet. He hoped Taylor would relay his message to him.

Will set out with the same pack he used on that fateful journey so many years ago. There was no turning back now. His path was set before him, and he only had one option left. Go forward.

Taylor got home and, knowing Will had a long shift, he didn't expect him right away. Calen was knocking at his door soon after he walked in. He must have been waiting to be there that quickly.

"Calen, Will isn't home yet," Taylor said with a yawn, from a hard day and a sleepless night.

"I know. He's gone! That's what my dad told me." Calen looked distraught and discarded.

"What?" Taylor ran to the cupboard, and his heart sank when he felt the paper tucked between the metal plates. Calen followed him in and watched as Taylor read the letter.

Dear Taylor,

You gave me good advice last night, and I did listen. But you have to understand, Nash is my brother. I can't watch another person I care about die in the field without trying something. I have a plan, and it isn't anything that will get me or you in trouble.

I will always be grateful. You and Pierce took me in and cared for me. You included me in your family so completely. You made me feel loved and safe, even though I rebelled against you. It took me a little while to realize how much you did for me. I love you both so much. I will miss you terribly. Thank you for all you have done. Please don't worry about me. I will see you again. I promise.

Love Will

P.S. Please tell Calen I will be back someday. I will find Nash, but he cannot come looking for us, or we'll have to go find him too. Tell him we will come back and be brothers again. Tell him to take care of himself.

The rain fell softly from the flat gray sky, pecking out a gentle beat on the leaves of the vegetation reclaiming the area humans once commanded. The battered pavement was littered with puddled potholes and darkly dribbled cracks. Twisted guardrails revealed a history of fleeing vehicles going too fast and years of neglect by a shattered society. The road before him told a tale of desolation, and he grinned at the irony of following it.

He was reveling in the freedom of walking on his own to a destination of his choosing. He knew he was still within the city of Colorado Springs, but he was in the desolate section of town. He heard the tale of an enormous avalanche destroying the neighborhood here, and from what was left, it validated the story. His freedom was limited because if he didn't check in before morning, he would be considered a runner, but at this moment he was as free as he had ever been.

The rhythmic silence of the rustling trees and the chirping of spring critters allowed his mind to wander. It settled on his regret of having to leave his belongings. He only had a few books, but he would miss them. Remembering stories his stepmom shared threw him back into that fatal day. It was a dangerous memory fraught with fear, anger, and a raging demand for resolution, where revenge was the sole answer.

Now his stormy thoughts battled the familiar waves of aggressive and fallacious emotions. He had been thrown on this course many times, and he steadied his reflections back to happier flashes to manage his way back to stability. He volleyed the persistent memory each time with pure discipline, tugging him back to the present. He set his mind to his plan, which demanded memorization as well as his practiced petition to gain entrance to the well-defended camp.

He had taken only what he needed to make it to camp and carry out his plan. Included in his belongings were the coat that belonged to his step-grandfather, a couple of extra clothes, and three of the barely palatable protein squares. Each family had a day's worth of these bars for times when food couldn't be issued. He justified it by only taking his share of the pack. He over-hydrated himself and then filled his canteen from the community well.

The Sanguine Blade sat in its pocket sewn into the coat, but he would stash it before he was totally out of the wooded area near Cheyanne Mountain. There was no way he would allow it to be stolen when they searched him. He also carried an extra handmade shiv. Hopefully, he wouldn't need to use it because his skills were sorely lacking.

He gathered and reviewed all the information Raymar and Barny, both sit-workers, told him about the camp and the procedures they remembered. Both had been injured while enlisted as Drangers, and both were crippled now from the sit work. They had trained at the Raiders' camp in Fountain. They were all too happy to share countless stories and pieces of advice.

Will knew he had to hide his blade soon before he reached the badlands that stretched between Colorado Springs and the southern border of the territory where the forest cover turned to high desert. The blade fit nicely in a tall, thin canning jar they never used because it didn't fit in their pan. It would keep it perfectly preserved and buried in the ground. As soon as he could, he would retrieve it, but carrying it into a Dranger camp was a sure way to lose it.

Eventually, he came upon a large boulder with a perfect trapezoid shape, resting neatly along the hillside and facing the road. It had been a while since he had studied geometry with Tianna, yet his memory of the lessons was sharp and clear.

Removing the sticky red substance from his pack, he drew a spiral on the side facing away from the road and wrote RIP above it. He hoped it would look like a grave, and no one would be foolish enough to expose themselves to decomposed bodies.

He hiked off the rubble-strewn road and up the shallow bank. A partially burnt tree from a lightning strike stood sentinel one hundred paces behind the boulder. Fourteen strides from the lightning tree, a large log lay on its side, so he climbed over it and took five more long steps.

The sixth was under a bush. Perfect. He lifted the edge of the brush, and with his travel pick and trowel, he dug a two-foot hole. Securing the blade in the tall jar, he tightened the lid and lowered it into the hole. Carefully, he packed the dirt and secured the top layer, so that even if one looked under the random bush, it would be difficult to notice that the ground had been disturbed. As he left the spot, he memorized every step. He looked up and the geometrical rock stood out so much, he wondered if it was too obvious. He settled on the idea that it was only because he was focused on it.

Across the high desert, he followed a road slowly being reclaimed by nature's intended vegetation. The trees thinned out and gave way to dwarfed pines and sagebrush and the occasional remnants of a forgotten society. Over his jacket, he draped a poncho made from a paint tarp. The browns, golds, and tan colors were splattered across it reminding him of the colors in Pueblo. He attached some sprigs of brush to it creating a desert ghillie suit so he could hide from strangers along the way.

Will traveled quite a distance while being lost in his head. He chided himself for not being more alert as he evaluated the unfamiliar surroundings. He had never been this far out of the Colorado Springs city limits. The landscape was dotted with struggling patches of forest among the dominant high desert, allowing him to see the horizon. Down the road, a billowing dust cloud was heading his way. He had no doubt it was a vehicle.

He set his sights on a close copse of vegetation big enough to shelter him and settled next to it to maximize his view. It seemed to take forever for the vehicle to get down the road, and then about fifty yards away, it stopped. *Did they see him?*

His hand was over the shiv he had tucked in his sock. He had been practicing the fighting moves Barney showed him, but he was far from ready to take on a fully trained Dranger, let alone a truck full of them. Through the brush, he saw two Drangers get out, and he remained perfectly still.

Neither of the Drangers looked his way, and he wondered why they stopped. One stood next to the truck and was going pee, but the other one lit a match for a cigarette. Will assumed it was stolen because they were so hard to come by, but Drangers stole things. It's what they did.

Then the other took a puff of the cigarette. He looked straight at Will, and he was sure he was made, but he turned back to his comrade and said something. They finished their smoke, got back in the rickety truck, and drove right by him with their eyes completely focused forward.

He watched them turn and disappear behind the distant brush. The ghillie suit worked like a charm. They both looked right at him and never alerted to his presence. He replaced his makeshift knife and thought of the Sanguine Blade buried in the hillside. He worried about it being found, but it was safer there than with him. He wondered how important it was to the destiny Tianna expected him to fulfill. And exactly what the hell that was.

Will headed toward the road with the utmost care to be on the alert for Dranger crews. The closer he got to the base, the encounters would become more and more frequent. Looking both ways, he jumped back onto the road, feeling a little smug at his cleverness. So far his plan was working perfectly.

Suddenly, three Drangers leaped from under a small bridge onto the road. They surrounded him. He expected this and even counted on it, but this was where his plan got dicey.

"Look what we have here," said the one with the grey coat.

"I think it's a runner," the smallest one said while grey coat shoved Will in the back with his rifle.

"Where ya headed, kid? You got papers?" The third one stood apart with his rifle at the ready. He must be the one in charge, thought Will.

Slowly, Will removed the papers he had received from his supervisor and held them out to the crew leader. The soldier unraveled the crumpled form and checked for the approval symbols. Will assumed he couldn't read because he handed his papers back and asked his name.

"Will Noland," he answered, using his adopted name. He had not used his real last name since arriving in Colorado Springs. He was registered as Taylor's son, and no one had ever questioned it.

"Jeeter, secure the captive. We'll take him to Prefect Ender." Grey coat locked the zip ties around Will's hands behind his body.

"He's a scrawny guy, ain't he?" said the small one, taunting Will for a second time. He was jabbing at Will because he thought it was safe with Will tied up. Will outsized the little shit by almost a foot, and wondered if he had the balls to go one-on-one. But Will kept his cool. The plan was going his way so far. The next step was to get an audience with the prefect. After that, he would be at the mercy of the prefect's decision.

The small guy, they called Fry, continued to bait Will, and his anger started to plot a single strike against this menace. Jeeter seemed to be enjoying Fry's game and encouraged him to torment Will. Jeeter was behind Fry, and Fry was behind the prisoner. Will needed to trick him into getting ahead of him. Will slowed his pace a bit and pretended to stumble, falling on his side. Jeeter jumped around him, staying clear of his reach, but Fry laughed at him and kicked him as he passed by.

Perfect Will thought and swiftly swept Fry's legs out from under him, causing him to hit the ground with a thud. Will quickly bounded up and began kicking him as hard as he could. Jeeter stopped, but did not break up the scuffle. The leader came back and hit Will across the face with the stock of his rifle.

He was bleeding from his lip, and his jaw was throbbing, but it was worth it. Jeeter was laughing while Bandit, the leader, warned Will. "Try something like that again and you'll get this end," he said sternly, pointing his rifle barrel at him. "This is your fault too, Jeeter. Save your teasing for the next run." Then he turned to Fry and slapped him across the face. "Quit being an idiot. I'm getting sick of it. We've got three miles to go. No more shit. Got it!"

Chapter Five

The rest of the trip was quiet. Soon Will got sight of a new collection of buildings in the distance. He saw they were in very poor condition the closer they got. It was unlikely they were utilized for anything but scavenging and rough trouble. Weeds, brush, and pines had wound their limbs around and through the ravaged dwellings, thoroughly reclaiming the area joined by scampering critters and scurvy insects.

Will tried to imagine a time when people tended gardens and children rode bikes down the little roads. Neighbors talked over hedges while a lawn mower's hum rumbled in the background. He caught glimpses of this world in the neighborhoods where the Uppers lived, but he was rarely allowed near that part of town.

He snapped out of his daydream when, down the road before him, he could make out a tall log wall with an opening in the middle. The sign said *Fountain* Camp, *Home of the Raiders*. As he got closer, he could see the wooden wall angled down to a shorter wire fence that continued beyond his sight to border the perimeter. Will wondered how easy it might be to escape through that fence. But the Drangers had eyes everywhere in the territory. It would be hard to hide for long.

Bandit nodded at the guards and walked through the open gate, leading his prisoner and crew with little fanfare. They looked Will over, but they didn't seem concerned. Through the gate, Will got his first glimpse of the camp. It was a run-down little town with buildings that ranged from sagging ruins to patch worked houses.

They brought him to a prominent building in the center of town. It was somewhat better maintained, but at one time must have been beautiful. He reviewed his plan and steadied his courage to pull it off. The doors opened, revealing a large hall with a high ceiling. Will was pushed across the cracked tile mosaic design on the floor, stretching for some distance before him.

At the end was a room with an open door where a man sat behind a massive, ornate desk littered with papers and whiskey bottles. It was an elaborate scheme to fully intimidate frightened prisoners making the long walk to their fate. Will refused to let fear show in his expression. Leaning on his shoulders, they forced him to kneel while Bandit spoke to the man.

"Prefect Ender, we found this Daily on the road. His papers have the appropriate stamps for travel." Bandit laid the papers on the desk in front of him and stepped back.

"It says his whereabouts are to be reported when he arrives, but it does not say where he is expected to report. Where are you headed, boy?" The man behind the desk said aggressively. He had a slashing scar across his forehead and a glove covering his right hand and wrist.

"I was headed here. I have a proposition for you, Prefect Ender." Will stated with all the resolve he could gather.

Laughter rang out from those in the room. Will remained on his knees, silent and still, but he held his head high and his eyes focused on the man behind the desk.

He must have understood the challenging posture because his mood quickly changed. The prefect stood and leaned over his desk. "What could you possibly offer me?" His serious look caused the laughter to die instantly. Will could see he was shorter than the average man, but he had a commanding presence and the power to demand respect.

"Prefect Ender, I wish to invoke the blood pact."

"The blood pact, huh? What is your brother's name?"

"Nash, Nash Genty. We share the blood oath."

"I see," Ender sat back down and sent his chair rocking backward. "Haven't heard that in a couple of years. Show me the mark."

Will was yanked up and marched closer to the desk. His ties were cut, and he held out his hands. Will balled his right fist displaying the slashing scar across his fingers. Barney told him that the blood oath could not be denied, but challenging the Prefect would come with a price.

"Bring this Nash before me."

"All jacks are still out on training drills, sir," said Bandit.

"Fine, lock this buckshit up, and bring him and this Nash to the ring tomorrow morning."

Will was tied back up and dragged out of the office and through the hall. Jeeter loaded him into a cage at the back of a dilapidated jeep and drove him down the road. It was a quick ride to a building with a tall stone fence. Jeeter parked in front of the old iron gate and got out. He grabbed a rope connected to a bell hanging between the blocks of stone and yanked it. It rang louder than such a small bell should, and the tone hung in the air as he got back into the driver's seat.

An old Dranger made a slow walk to the gate. Seeing Jeeter with a prisoner in the cage, he clanked through the huge keys on the iron ring and opened the metal gate. They drove through and stopped when they cleared the gate. There was something antiquated and ominous about this building, but Will didn't know why he felt that way.

Will began shouting from his cage. "Where am I going? Am I a prisoner?"

"An' whadda we 'av here? Some kind o' genius I see," laughed the gatekeeper. He spoke with an accent Will was unfamiliar with.

"He needs watching until tomorrow. He's gonna challenge Denter for a blood pact," said Jeeter with an excited tone.

"No shit? I 'ope I get ta watch it this time. Always stuck 'ere, I am," the guard complained while swinging the gates shut and locking them in.

As they drove into the enclosed area, Will looked around the yard. The side fence ended at either side of the building. It was once a wrought iron rail with an intricate pattern, but it was rusted and leaning now. It must have been a church of some kind. Two concrete benches formed a circle around a shallow, empty pool, and rising in the center was a statue of a serene woman. She was looking downward with her welcoming arms held slightly outward while stepping forward.

Her long dress flowed and draped the full length of her, while her bare toes peeked out of the dress on the forward stepping foot. She had an expression he remembered Tianna having as she nurtured her beloved garden. It wasn't quite a smile, but it radiated peaceful contentment. It was a beautiful, gentle work of art that gave him hope, and he wondered why it was left to stand in front of a jail.

Following the dirt road edging the yard, they stopped at the large double doors. The guard stood at the ready while Jeeter let him out of the cage. He was still bound when Jeeter turned him over to the guard with the odd accent, who led him to the large wooden arched door.

"Come on, then," the guard spoke. "We'll be settlin' ya in the tombs. That be what we call the cells," and he let out a gruff chuckle. "This place were built strong to withstand the tragedy. It was fer a religious group wiff men and women who married the church, not people. We converted their rooms into jail cells. And in case you be wonderin' how fancy they were, they weren't at all."

Will was led down a brick hallway with small concrete cells lined on each side. The guard stopped at one and sorted through the noisy keys hanging on his belt. A wooden bench sat against the side wall, draped with a shabby, thin blanket. Sitting in the corner of the opposite wall was a filthy bucket stained with dried excrement. A single arched window perched on the back wall with a row of bars, and a wooden shutter swung open, letting the cool fall air flow in. The remnants of an old oil radiator rested under the window, but looking at its condition, Will doubted it worked.

They found his shiv and took it away before he was loaded into the cage. He was glad they didn't take his coat, but they had patted it down looking for anything that could suffice as a weapon, and Will thought of the Sanguine Blade safe in its glass tomb. The coat was precious to Will for the sentiment and the warmth it provided, but it was very old, well-worn, and had little appeal to picky thieves.

The guard closed the barred door and had him turn, so he could remove his zip-tie bonds. He felt relief flowing through his wrists the minute he was released. He rubbed them and stretched his arms as the guard locked the door and walked away.

It was several hours later that Will was roused by the scraping noise of a tray being slid under the door. Cold oatmeal mixed with food paste was slopped on a cracked, filthy plastic tray. He wondered how many times it had been used since its last washing. Knowing he needed his strength for the fight the next morning, he ate a few bites to test it. After an hour, he would know if it was drugged or worse. Without any symptoms, he ate the rest.

It was the first day of October, and the nights were getting cold. He was glad he'd be gone before the real winter cold set in. Or would he? Will began to wonder if this prefect had any intention of letting him out. *Why would he? What did Will know of Dranger camps? Maybe they don't honor things like blood pacts. Maybe it was all just rumors and gossip.* Will suddenly didn't feel as confident in his plan as he did this afternoon.

Morning came, and he was allowed to empty his bucket. Breakfast was a repeat of last night's dinner, but since it set okay last time, and he would only be fed twice a day, he forced it down. He sat in his cell as the morning sun moved on to high noon. He yelled for the guard, but he got no response. He had almost given up hope when the guard came down the hall with his heavy ring of iron keys.

"It be your big moment, tough guy. They've sent a ride for ya. I even get to watch. Look, I don't think you got a chance, but I made a tiny wager on ya just the same. I bet you'd last through the second round. Denter is who you be set against. I got a couple tips for ya' just to keep it fun. He's a tough one, but he has a bad right eye, and he gots a mean injury from an arrow in one of his knees. Can't remember which.

"Keep your stance wide when you strikin', and no stupid high kickin'. He'll throw you on your ass, an' you'll be done or dead before you know what hit ya. You're gonna have to eat some punches, that's for sure. If you got a mad deep inside you, an' who don't right?

"Bring it up to the surface and use it. Work it to fuel your rage. You look wiry and fast, so hit, then dodge and dash. Don't make it look like you be knowin' his soft spots. Cuz' when you lose, and ya will, lad. That's fact," he said with a smile. "You'll be coming back 'ere, so don't be stupid. If ya last the first two and make me a little cred, I'll treat ya best I'm allowed."

Will turned to get his zips on. "What's your name?"

"Taggart."

"Thanks, Taggart. I'll see what I can do. I may even surprise you and win."

Taggart gave out a deep and dark laugh. "That's the spirit, lad." He kept laughing as he opened the cell door and walked him out.

Will was loaded in the cage and began planning his fighting moves based on what he had just been told. It was just as likely that the old guard bet against him, but he knew the information was solid. He had been in a few fights in his young life, and the tactics Taggart gave him were effective when executed correctly. He couldn't be sure about Denter's weaknesses until he tested them out. If he had a bad eye, it would make sense he was shot in the same knee as his blind side. Will was so in his thoughts he was surprised when the jeep stopped.

He was led through a gate into a forty to fifty-foot arena encircled by a wooden wall at least six feet tall. Benches sat above the arena wall, and they were already occupied by at least eighty or more shouting Drangers. He was led to a nicer seating area at the back of the arena, where Prefect Ender sat with his favorites.

A Dranger escorted Nash to the arena. He wasn't in very good shape. Will could see his training wasn't going well. He never was very good at scrapping, and he was younger than most trainees. Will wanted to talk to him, but that was not allowed. Nash was led to a holding area and sat down.

Will was led across the arena to stand before the Prefect's box seats.

"Do you know why I am called Ender?"

Will could tell this was a rhetorical question, but he was dying to throw out an answer. He was clearly proud of it, and he would give anything to knock him down a notch. But Will needed this guy's cooperation in his very dangerous and precarious plan.

"Ender was a great warrior, and I learned his legend as a boy. Fast, strong, intelligent, and a natural leader from a young age. He conquered his foe, earned respect, and was greatly honored. I knew I wanted to be this kind of man, and now as your Prefect, I am." The crowd stood cheering with loud enthusiasm.

Will wondered how many times they had suffered through that story. He remembered reading the book *Ender's Game* many times. It was a book series about a gifted boy chosen for special training as a soldier. Will had secretly read the first two in the series from the old library. If that was who he was referring to, he wondered if the prefect had read it. It was a fictional story that took place in space, but this man referred to it as if it were history. Whether he read it or not, he had missed the point completely.

The Prefect continued. "You seek the blood pact with your blood brother, Nash. Here are the rules of the contest. No weapons of any kind may be used. There will be four rounds. The first two rounds are three minutes long, but the next two are five. If both contestants are still standing, a fifth bout will occur until one of you is down. If you win, Nash will be sent home, but you will stay in his place. If Denter wins, you are at his mercy. He can take you into his pack, sell you to another pack, throw you in prison, or end your life. But whatever penalty he gives you will also be given to Nash."

The Prefect bent down toward Will and lowered his voice. "As I hear it, Nash is failing combat training, and you are a scrappy, arrogant little shit. Denter will be happy to be rid of both of you." He stood back up and returned to his booming speech. "If he takes you, you will bear Nash's punishments as well as your own. If death occurs during the contest, it will be considered a win for the survivor."

They led Will to the center of the ring and unbound his hands. The entrance door opened, and in walked a wide, muscular man. His body and the way he strode in told a story of many years of battle-hardened experience.

The crowd was cheering for Denter as he sauntered confidently to the center of the ring. He wore a shirt that barely fit over his bulging biceps. His boots looked heavy and worth avoiding at all costs. A dirty blue band was on his left wrist with numerous decorative metal studs. They were flat, but he was pretty sure they could still leave a mark.

Will was mentally ticking off the advice Taggart gave him one by one. Keep a wide stance. Jab and dodge the punch coming back, then dash away to dart in again. And aim for the right side to test the injury info. Will hoped he was right-handed because a fully functioning dominant side could end this quickly. If he could weaken one side, dominate or not, he had a chance.

They stood before each other with the referee between them, who was more of a glorified bell ringer because the only rule was no weapons. Will wondered how closely that was followed. He imagined Denter had not been frisked for a knife or a set of spiked knuckle rings. Will thought of his Sanguine Blade, and how he wished he had it. Even his handmade shiv would be something.

Then his thoughts flashed on not surviving. The blade and its destiny would remain buried, and Tianna's teachings would be lost forever. His memories brought on the fury of his inner demons, and the paradox of the evil deed pumped adrenalin through his veins. Denter saw the storm brewing in his eyes, and Will thought he saw him flinch. And although Denter quickly put on his deadly stare, it still reeked of overconfidence.

The referee instructed them to stand on the Xs that permeated from the ground. The ref gave the bell one clang and quickly moved away from the two components. The referee saw what the crowd saw: a scrawny upstart against a fully grown, seasoned fighter. His opponent, like everyone else, believed it would be a quick bout.

But Will didn't feel scrawny; he felt powerful and full of determined, dark revenge. He had fought for years to restrain it, but now he let it surge through him, change him, and eclipse any shred of mercy. He was drunk on the wicked pleasure flooding his senses. He visualized the violence and the blood, and he craved it.

Will delivered the first blow. It landed on a rock-solid jaw. He only partially dodged his opponent's right hook, and it glanced off the left side of his chin, But he noticed a slight wince on Denter's face. He danced backward, feeling the heat on his cheek, but it only fueled his mean spirit.

Will was dashing around, and an onlooker might think he was simply avoiding contact, but Will was also assessing his opponent's reflexes. He surmised they were sluggish, lumbering, and favoring his right side. His size was a detriment, not an advantage. Will darted in and kicked his right knee, which spread his legs apart as he turned to follow Will's movements. Will ran at him, and just as the brute's fist was approaching, he slid on the ground through the open legs, bounding up and punching him in the kidneys.

Denter grunted and spun around. He was mad now. There was no way he was going to let this punk kid get the better of him. He watched Will's approach and ambushed him with a gut punch straight on. Will swayed, but his adrenaline-fueled rage popped him up and out of the reach of another assault. Knowing the bell would ring soon, Will used every inch of the modest arena to avoid his opponent's fists.

The ref came out ringing the bell, signaling the end of the first round. Will went back to his area at the edge of the arena. He refused to look at Nash. He didn't want to deal with his friend's emotions right now. He hadn't suffered many blows, but the one to the gut was fierce, and he added its pain to his cauldron of wrath. In this round, he would set his attention to attacking Denter's weaker right side, which was dangerous because it was obvious he had become very adept at protecting it. They were signaled back to the X in the ring, and the ref hit the bell two times.

"Quit your running, you little coward. Get over here and fight like a man!" Denter was taunting him, but Will was hunting him like a coyote, not like a man, and he had no problem using such an effective strategy. He was taking him down one hit at a time and darting back out. Denter got in more than a few rebound jabs, but more often than not he missed. Just before the second bell, Will latched onto Denter from behind and delivered several violent blows to his unprotected backside. The bell rang again, and Will was elated and surprised at how well he had timed the move. Both opponents walked stiffly to their corners.

The bell began clanging again, and Will popped up trying to portray a confidence that was waning with each throb from his injuries. Denter came out with a renewed, steely resolve, and Will wondered what had changed. Before the bell rang out its third clang, Denter grabbed his young opponent and spun him into a headlock. Will was certain that broke the rules, but the ref's whistle was silent.

He felt the sharp stab of a knife point slowly piercing through his ragged shirt and slightly into his lower back. Will winced. He wondered if the rules were enforced, and now he knew. He froze, hoping his plan wouldn't end with his guts all over the yard and his friend receiving the same, or worse. He thought about the scene Nash would be witnessing. The curse would come full circle with his friend haunted by murderous nightmares.

"Listen, kid," Denter was speaking quietly right next to his ear. "I like the way you fight. You're angry, and you use it. You give up now, and you'll live."

"What about Nash?" Will was in no position to bargain, but Denter was asking for his cooperation—odd.

"Him too. You will join my students, and you can shadow him. And when his time is up, you can go too."

Will knew he could leave before Nash because he was older, but that wasn't the point at this moment. "What's the catch?"

"Well, first I'm gonna knock you out, and then the two of you are going to spend some time in the cells doing some special training." The disdain as he said the word 'special' was disturbing, to say the least. "If you get that worthless tadpole caught up, you'll both rejoin the class. If he graduates, and you turn out to be the Dranger I believe you can be, I'll let you both live. So, you in?"

Will wondered what Denter's word was worth, but he also thought of Taggart's information, which turned out to be true and valuable. He remembered the bet that if he lasted through the second round, he'd treat him well. "I agree," he said, as if he had a choice.

Denter swung him out and dropped him with a single shot to the jaw, and Will's world went blank.

Chapter Six

Will woke up in the same cell he started in. He felt disoriented and in severe agony—everywhere. His eyes were almost swollen shut and his nose was packed with something. His anger was overshadowed by a blurry world of pounding pain. He went to grab whatever was stuffed in his nose, and someone grabbed his hand.

"Don't, Will. Keep it in there until we're sure the bleeding has stopped." It was Nash.

"Hey, Bwash. How are t'ings wit 'ou?" Will mumbled through his dazed demeanor and extremely swollen lips.

"It's not funny! What the hell are you doing here?" Nash was holding back his emotions as well as he could. He looked at the only person in the world who had ever stepped up for him, who had ever given a damn about him. "He knocked you out, but he kept punching you. I thought you were going to die!"

"So is dat 'or way ob taying t'ank 'ou?" Will's words were slurred in his effort to not move his split lips and aching jaw. He was also clearly disoriented, but Nash was relieved he was finally awake.

"You should stop talking. You sound like an idiot." Nash smiled. "But yes, thank you, my good friend. I will have your back forever."

Taggart came walking down from where he had been in the hall, sitting vigil, waiting to see if the young upstart would make it through. He had taken a liking to this kid, and he wanted to help him get well.

"Hey," he whispered through the bars. "There ya' be. Thank ya for going the two. I made me some serious creds. But, laddie, do yourself a favor, then, and stay quiet. Here's some bread and willow brew to dull the pain. Denter be wantin' ya' to start training as soon as ya' be waked. You'll do better with a bit more rest. If they don't know ya be awake, I can give ya a couple more days." He handed Nash the bread and the cup with the warm liquid. "Eat the bread first. Willow brew is wicked on the gut." He said no more and quickly walked by the cell door to another detainee yelling several cells down the hall.

Will was familiar with willow brew. It was a powerful painkiller and fever reducer created from the bark of willow trees. He ate the bread, enduring the pain and ignoring the metallic taste of his blood. Then he swallowed the bitter tea. When footsteps approached, he assumed his coma state.

"What's his status, Trash?" Nash bristled at the cruel nickname he was given by the Dranger standing in front of the cell. He was Denter's number one, and he was an evil prick.

"He hasn't moved yet. I've tried to give him water, but he's still out cold. He might die." Nash was eyeing the baton Dread always carried with increasing trepidation. He remembered all the times it was used on him, and he hoped Dread didn't have the keys to the cell.

"If that was you layin' there, I'd say yeah, you were dead. You're a worthless little piece of shit," and he started banging against the bars. "I wish Denter would let me do some more training with you. Remember how much fun we used to have? But now you get to be lazy and lounge away in this cell. We're going to have to start your bruise collection all over." Dread began rattling the bars with his baton. "Wake up, dickhead." He yelled and then stood there watching Nash with his psycho stare.

Will could feel the thick tension of Nash's fear. He was sure Dread could feel it too, and he was drinking it in. The villain returned to rattling their cage, and Will thought of the irony of being behind bars and being extremely grateful for it.

Dread turned his gaze from Nash to look at Will. "Yeah, he'll wake up, and then I get a turn at him." He laughed as he spun around and left.

All was silent for several minutes, and Nash looked through the bars down the hall. "It's all clear."

"Who was dat and why did he call you Twash?"

"That's Dread. He's Denter's pet. Nasty son of a bitch. He swings a mean baton too." Nash was hoping Will would forget his question. He knew what his dear friend was in for, only now it could get worse for both of them because Will would never back down from a bully.

"An, why did he call 'ou dat?" Will repeated the question more sternly this time.

"I'm not a very good Dranger. I'm the smallest and the youngest, and I suck at drills." Nash looked down with his face tilted away from Will. "Everyone gets an insulting nickname to start. But if you pass all the drills, when you graduate you get to pick your name. Dread is a graduate.

"Wad id his name used to be?"

"I don't know. I don't think they are going to let me pass. They cheated me out of passing every drill." Nash paused for a moment, "I don't want you to be responsible for me. It may get us both killed."

"Don't worry, widdle brudda. We're gonna kick ath, and I'm going ta take dat widdle shit down and gib 'im a new name." Will's words drifted off as the willow brew kicked in allowing him to sink into the rest his broken body needed.

Every six hours, Taggart snuck the brew and food down to their cell, and Will was allowed to heal for three full days. On the afternoon of the fourth day, Denter himself came to find Will sitting up on the hard slab. His head was in his hands, and when he looked up, his face still bore the overlapping bruises of various colors and the healing splits on his eyes and mouth. Denter had taken a few beatings in his day, and he had little sympathy for this arrogant little upstart, who needed a lesson on who was not in charge if he had any hope of training him.

"Thought you were brain dead there or faking it." Will did his best to look disoriented, but he was fully back and thinking with absolute clarity. Denter looked carefully at the scrawny teen and wondered how this punk ever got the best of him. "Tomorrow, at five AM, your training," he said, pointing at Will," and his retraining," he pointed at Nash," will begin. If he fails, you fail. And then your second chances are up." With that, he left.

"He only won because he cheated," Will growled between his teeth.

"I know. I found a small knife wound in your back, but that's how things roll here. There aren't any rules, just a nasty pecking order."

"Well, I guess we're going to have to scrap our way up to that eagle's nest then."

Nash admired Will with naïve idolatry. Will faced his problems directly. He didn't start trouble, and though he never ran, he knew when to hang back and plan. He was wicked clever and feral brave. It made anyone who knew him think twice about confronting him. Nash vowed his absolute loyalty to this friend, who had already demonstrated his.

Training day came, and they expected Dread to lead their drills, but another graduate showed up. This trainer didn't look much older than them, but he wore a green band with one brad hammered into the mesh. Nash explained that the bands they wore showed their rank. Nash and Will had yellow ones, which signified trainee; graduates wore green, and different brads were added for awards and promotions. Will thought back to Denter's faded blue band with numerous brads covering the circle completely.

Taggart led the three boys into the yard. The trainer was setting up drill equipment while Taggart walked over to talk to Will and Nash. "That be my nephew Drake, but he goes by Drakon since graduation. I asked if he could come train ya since he be leavin' soon for the southland."

"Hey, Taggart," Will began softly but was interrupted.

"Call me Tag. You made me a bit of coin, you did. I thank ya'."

"Good, I'm glad. I would have lasted..." and he was interrupted again.

"Don't bother whinin', we all know Denter pulled his shanker on ya'. But you'da lost anyways. He were just tired of playin'."

Will gave a crooked grin. "Maybe."

Taggart laughed out loud. "You'll be somethin' if you live long enough, laddie."

"Thanks Tag. You are a good man, not a thug."

Tag looked at him with a woeful nod. "Maybe now. Not always."

Drakon lined them up and began the combat drills. He told them they were a week behind the rest of the class. When they caught up, they could join the rest of the class and graduate. If they didn't catch up, their fate would be decided by Denter. On the first day, the drill lasted for five hours with no break, until the grey sky became so dark and angry the wind started rattling roof tiles and throwing tumbleweeds up in the air.

He instructed them to practice in their cell. He would test them tomorrow. Will and Nash went through the moves until Nash was ready. Will discovered Nash wasn't the fastest learner, but when he mastered the moves, he was precise in his execution of the techniques. Their dinner was wholly inadequate for the energy they spent that day, but they slept despite their growling bellies.

On the second day of training, they began their grueling schedule by cleaning up the yard and repairing the roof tiles that had been dislodged or broken. The rest of their training went on like that for four more days. Tag would wake them up a half hour early and introduce them to the day's moves to get caught up sooner. After five days, they were brought before Denter during his lunch break. They demonstrated their combat drills and waited for his response.

"Trash your improvement is noticeable, but don't think you're out of the woods yet. You must continue to keep up. Blood brother, you will be called Dog until you graduate, if you graduate. You must complete your training and keep Trash on track. Your final score will be an average of his and yours. Do you accept?"

Will swallowed the anger at the insulting names but looked Denter in the eyes and said, "Yes, sir."

"Very well, go complete the obstacle course and report back for the rest of the day. You won't have time for lunch today, but if you work hard, you might make it to dinner." He laughed, and the troop joined in.

Will didn't even know where the obstacle course was, but he assumed Nash did. He looked over at him as they walked toward the first task. "Nash quit looking defeated. If you think I'm going to let you fail or give up, you're in for one hell of a beating, and this time it will come from me. Now, let's do this shit and get to dinner. I'm fucking hungry."

Nash smiled, "I'm ready. I'll show you how some of the bigger kids do it, and you can show me how I can, even though I'm short."

"Done, let's go."

They completed the whole course, assuming they were being watched for any sign of cheating. They made it back minutes after the dinner line began to form. Will looked over his new leader. His arms were folded across his massive chest, and his proud posture and wide stance were foreboding and stern, but his expression appeared observant and evaluative. Will ran through the thoughts buzzing in his head. Maybe he wasn't a mindless brute. Maybe he was a good soldier with a cunning mind. Obedience to such a man could keep them alive, or he could order them to their death.

It was nice to be out of the small cell where they had been locked up for a week, but the trainee tent certainly didn't offer deluxe accommodations. The canvas home teemed with rows of smelly cots and rowdy idiots while the cold wind easily found its way through the canvas gaps. They slept well because they were deeply exhausted, but they turned over and over, trading their warm side to comfort their cold one.

They were on week four of the six-week course, and Nash still wasn't winning awards, but he was keeping up. It was a huge difference from his first week and a stark difference from Will, whose skills were easily the best in the class.

However, since he was responsible for Nash, he was doing extra work retraining Nash at the end of each day. Dread tried to mess with Will about his score since it was tied with Nash's, but he could not deter the talent Will demonstrated during the drills. Although Will was annoyed by his taunts, he was laser-focused on helping Nash graduate.

At the end of the fifth week, all the trainees were lined up according to their evaluation. Out of the twelve recruits remaining, Will ranked third and Nash was tied for fifth. Three trainees had already been ejected. Two sustained serious injuries, and another was sent to detention for disobedience. All three would start the course over in a couple of weeks. Though everyone knew those injuries were due to Dread's harassment, he was not disciplined. There was a place for a cold-hearted bastard in the ranks of the Drangers.

The twelve pre-grads filed over to the trainee tent and waited their turn for branding. All Drangers completing the fifth week were branded with a D on their Upper left forearm. They were required to endure the searing pain without any sounds of the agony it caused. It was intended to make the young men realize they would always be recognized and never escape this life in deed or identity. The reality burned more than the wound, but together they invoked a considerable amount of introspection.

Nash had a serious, wincing look as he wandered over to Will that evening. "I'm sorry, I'm sorry you got messed up in this. All because of my dad. How could he? I'm his flesh and blood!" He was about to lose it.

Will grabbed Nash by the jaw. "Look at me. This mark means one thing to me and everyone else. We are trained to kill. It may turn out to be a pretty handy little warning. But right now, I'm thinking of my new name." He was consumed with the intensely painful brand, firing off a constant sensation of that red-hot iron.

Willow brew would help, but he wouldn't take it, nor would he share his misery with Nash. He didn't need him breaking down in tears. This brand for life was a test, and he refused to fail.

"What is it?" Nash looked over at Will's puzzled expression. "What you're fixated on."

"I'm thinking about my name," he lied. "Haven't decided yet, but I suggest you decide on yours. Don't let them give you the next one."

Each demanding day of the next three weeks seemed to drag on, but when graduation day finally arrived, the past six weeks seemed to have raced by. Most of the eagerly anticipated day was spent receiving a hammer and nail tattoo on their left forearm, directly under the branded D. The hammer had a large, elongated claw that curled down while holding a nail at a sixty-degree angle. The artistic image resembled an R for the Raider clan. The final adornment would be their green graduation band held together by their pack brad, which they would get after being chosen.

Most of the grads would be lined up for the in-camp choosing, but now and then they were sold to the smaller Dranger camps, or on rare occasions sold to the Neighwah. Dread was one of those purchased by the Neighwah, giving Nash a sigh of relief, but Will owed Dread some payback. He hoped he would still have a chance at it.

There were twelve packs in total for the territory, each with seven to ten members. While a leader was instructing trainees, he could keep four of his original members to help train, but the other men had to be taken on by active crews.

There were four off-site packs beyond the cities that patrolled the borders. They had the biggest areas to control and the highest mortality rates, so they were allowed up to a fifteen-man crew, but they chose last. Each pack leader at Fountain Camp took turns at the six-week training duty when more Drangers were needed, so it wouldn't be Denter's turn for some time. Will knew firsthand how deadly the borders were, and he hoped they wouldn't be sent there anytime soon.

They assembled in the Great Hall, which was an old conference room of the hotel the Prefect and his cronies lived in. All the packs gathered at their tables. The packs out on runs, who were low on members, had their second in charge attending alone to choose from the eleven remaining graduates. Will knew the reality of him and Nash staying together was slim, but at least he had prepared him well. It was finally time, and the new graduates were lined up in their graduating score order before the Dranger leaders. The seasoned Drangers from the next trainer's team stood apart to be assigned after the graduates.

"Leaders," Denter began, "I have a fine group before you. One of my best."

Jeers came from the crowd, and someone yelled, "You always say that!"

"It is true; I improve my training skills with every duty." More heckles and roars of laughter rose from the moderate crowd before them. "I will now introduce our new Drangers by their chosen names."

There were many names, but they all had deadly connotations. When he got to Will, he answered confidently, "Dirk". He looked it up in the book of weapons. It was an assassin's knife, usually around nine inches in length with a double sharp edge. It reminded him of his blade in the jar he had buried in the woods, and he wondered when it would be safe to retrieve it. When it was Nash's turn, he yelled out his new name, "Brash." Will was pleasantly surprised. It was a good call name, bold and rebellious.

When Denter finished going down the line, he turned to his audience. Because Denter had trained them, and he was short three crew members, he got to choose his three first. "Dirk, Lynch, and," he paused, but Will thought it was unlikely he would choose his friend. "Brash." Will was both shocked and ecstatic at the same instant. He had come to respect Denter. He had what Taylor called ass-holiness—an asshole with an honor code.

The rest of the pack leaders had chosen their new crew members, but one experienced Dranger remained. His pack leader had traded him for a recruit, so he was traded like a newbie grad. It was Jeeter, one of the pain-in-the-ass guys who hassled him on his way here. He was offered to the pack leader with the fewest members, which was Denter's crew, and Denter accepted.

When the choosing ended, their pack symbol was clamped on, securing their new bands. They had seen the eight banners at the chow hall displaying the eight Packs: Falcons, Spiders, Claws, Snakes, Sickles, Comets, Fangs, and Arrows. He and Brash were Arrows now.

They had earned their spot on the team. They had been well-trained in many combat strategies, from hand to hand, and weapons including a sling and a bow. Bows were taught to all trainees, but it was a prominent part of Denter's classes. It was a smart, quiet, long-distance, deadly weapon. Will was an exceptional bowman.

"Okay, newbies, listen up. This is the Denter Arrow Pack. The rules are simple. Rule one: I'm in charge! Rule two: Don't be getting all friendly with the other packs unless we're on a run together. We're in competition for points, and points get us time off, good grub, and other perks like that, and I like perks.

"Now, line up in order of your rank and give your name to your pack members. Look at your bands. The order of rank, lowest to highest, is stars, laurel wreaths, and skulls.

As he was talking, he handed the three new members a plain grey beanie. It was the only item they got in the way of a uniform. "Whenever you line up, including for meals, we do it by rank."

A skull meant one killed a target, and no new grads had those. Up to two star brads could be earned each year for hard work and following orders on runs, but they could also be taken for punishment. New grads didn't have those either. Laurel wreaths were earned by winning a contest at their annual visit back to Fountain to re-qualify.

Denter had thirteen brads on his worn blue band. Where a grad's star meant six months, a leader's meant two years, a laurel meant two awards, and a leader's skull meant five kills. Denter had four stars, two laurels, and seven skulls.

Donner was Denter's first, replacing Dread, with three skulls and four stars. Then came Rad with two skulls, two laurels, and four stars. Next was

Rumble with three stars and one laurel, Slice with two stars, and Jeeter with one star. Brash, Lynch, and Dirk were at the end with one brad each—their pack brad.

Nash carried his tray past the ugly yellow picnic table he would never have to sit at again. It was the trainee table made of rough-cut pine, and though it was painted an obnoxious yellow, it didn't reduce the irritating splinters. The pack tables were made with thick slabs of smooth, polished wood.

Each one had its pack symbol burned into it. Also branded on the table were the names of its former honored members. An unsettling number had a border around them, which meant they had died in the service of the Dranger brotherhood. Four names were surrounded by eight stars, meaning they had died with honors in battle. One name was blackened out, and asking about it was forbidden.

"Hey Will," Nash called to his friend.

"Don't call me that, *Brash*. It's Dirk now."

"Dirk, then. What do you think our first mission will be? I don't want to kill grandmas and babies."

"I've never seen them do that, but I have seen them attack innocent civilians. I've seen that a lot. We're going to have to get our asshole on. Do as I told you; pull out your angry stuff. I should think your dad gave you plenty of material to get your edge on. If we don't, we'll be dead or worse."

"I saw your hackles fire up when Jeeter joined our pack. Isn't that one of the guys who captured you and brought you here?"

"Yeah, he doesn't worry me. He just did what Drangers do, but he's not much of a team player. He likes to stir the shit, and he avoids doing his own dirty work like a pansy. A guy like that could get someone killed."

"That's what they used to call me, a pansy."

Will tilted his head and turned toward him. "Well, you better not let anyone say that now," he said with exasperation. "If you do, I'll bust you one myself."

"No way. I'm good now. I'm just wondering what his story is." Nash suddenly realized his friend wasn't going to make life any easier, just longer. Well, hopefully.

Later, Will huddled on his meager cot under his thin issue blanket and his precious coat. They were leaving early the next morning, so he was still in the trainee tent for the night. As he lay there trying to get warm, he imagined how much warmer four walls and a better blanket would feel. It didn't strain his imagination to understand such luxuries were the product of theft, bribes, and confiscations. He was beginning to see the Drangers in a different light. They were surviving just like everyone else.

He wondered if he would take a coveted blanket from some scared, poverty-stricken Daily, or freeze to death himself this winter. The answer was easy. He'd find a way to secure a blanket, hopefully without being cruel. And he'd make sure Nash scored one too, by himself. And he would make it happen on the first run because winter was well on its way.

Assignments, or runs, involved traveling to the cities they were hired to address by the Corporates. Since the beginning of armies, a soldier's job has been to defeat the enemy or intimidate them into submission. It gets complicated when the intimidator has friends or family within their realm of control. Tormenting and intimidating the residents was justified by the ultimate Corporate goal of maintaining the status quo. Drangers aren't compensated much for performing their hostile assignments, so allowing them time to form bonds could compromise the mission.

Will was quite familiar with Drangers' activities—from the other side. A Dranger's duties involving disputes were often undeserved and cruelly executed. He realized that a Dranger was who he was now. Someday he'd find a way out, but today wasn't about right or wrong. Today was about protecting his own status quo. And that included protecting his blood brother. He adjusted the rationalizations in his mind to allow him to carry on and compete in this hostile environment by convincing himself there is no such thing as being completely right or completely wrong. There are reasons someone does the wrong thing, and whether it was excusable or not, it was all perspective, and his was simple—win.

Will woke up the next morning and immediately felt for the shoes Taylor gave him when he outgrew his old pair. They were becoming quite shabby, but they didn't have holes. Will was surprised he still had his coat and shoes in this den of thieves. Drangers didn't just steal from Dailys. They stole from each other too, and even though the coat was in poor condition, it did have shields built into the arms, front, and back. They weren't bulletproof, but they could thwart many injuries.

Will had a reputation as a fierce and violent opponent, and so far, no one in his pack wanted to be his target. Will's six weeks of training had churned up and freed his dark attitude, and when he tapped into it, he brimmed with cruel intensity. Somewhere deep inside, he knew this feeling of power was at the subjugation of others, but it was a high he thoroughly enjoyed given the right circumstances.

He worried about Nash's soft underbelly showing, and he decided his charge required additional training. He needed to think more objectively with his head rather than compassionately with his heart. The Dranger world had no room for charity. Nash had a dark past too. They had that in common. Their dads hadn't always been bastards. They were considerate and caring parents at one time, but they turned into monsters, and their boys' lives became nightmares.

Will tried to focus on the current issue. Nash had to let go of the hopeless feeling that he had no power. He needed to tap into the temper that simmered below one's compassionate side. But even Will slipped into the occasional examination of the events leading up to his father's transformation from a good parent to a ruthless murderer.

Would he have made a similar decision on that hill? Will quickly pushed that thought back down into the depths of his psyche. He needed his temper and his selfish viewpoint. It was detrimental to staying alive, which only proved it deserved more development. He pounded the cold earth beneath his cot enough to feel the pain of it. He concluded that being charitable and sympathetic would be a death sentence.

The next morning, they were given their first orders, which were in Security, and they walked the five miles to the town. Drangers earned credits, but they went directly into the Dranger Alliance credit account. Drangers weren't on salary like the Neighwah. Drangers were paid per job, and all those credits went into one big fund to use for the wages and expenses of the whole clan.

Like Dailys, Drangers' needs were marginally met, and they were paid for a job after it was completed. Recruits on their first job had a zero credit balance. It forced them to use unscrupulous means to secure their needs beyond what was issued—like blankets.

The jobs they were hired to do fell into two categories: labor and justice. Labor work meant various physical projects for the Corporates and Uppers. These were the jobs that child labor couldn't handle, such as demolishing dangerous buildings, downing large trees, small construction projects, repairing roads, and other miscellaneous chores. Justice jobs were the uglier side of their duties. They were often about revenge for those who could afford it, meaning Uppers, and it was always carried out on Dailys.

Justice rounds were usually painful warnings given to Dailys for work issues, suspected misdeeds, or retribution for disrespect. The last category was mostly about power and revenge. It targeted those who caused Uppers to feel jealous, rejected, or exposed, but it also included mean-spirited people who liked the power of cruelty.

Since Dailys weren't allowed an official or fair trial, the Uppers could exact revenge on them at will. But it cost a lot of credits, and if one engaged in it too often, or Drangers took the punishment too far, those involved could be punished by the Corporates. The Corporates believed their survival relied on maintaining the status quo, so the Dailys were given just enough support and supplies to prevent them from rallying together.

On Will's first day, he was sent on his own to remove a tree that had fallen on the corner of an Upper's house and repair the damage. He enjoyed the work. He had helped his dad do some work on their own house, so he had some working knowledge of construction and the skills involved.

The job took him three days, and he worked so hard and did such a nice job that the owner wanted to reward him. He said he'd love a blanket, so she gave him one. It wasn't new or pretty, but it was a lot warmer than the one he had. The next few jobs were more of the same, and he was glad he hadn't been asked to make any justice rounds yet, but that would change.

Labor could have one or more Drangers assigned as needed. But justice rounds were always done in twos or threes. Will and Rad were paired together to respond to a reported peeping tom. A young Daily was accused of peeking into an Upper's house to watch his wife. It was true she was a beautiful woman, but she had hired him to trim the hedges around her house while she left her curtains wide open. The teen swore up and down, he never looked up through the windows. It sounded like a setup, but such is the life of a Daily. Will and Rad punched him over a bit and sent him on his way.

Another woman accused a Daily maid of stealing her bracelet, so they trashed the Daily's house, but they never found it. It seemed unlikely this Daily would steal anything because she would be the obvious one to blame. And blamed she was. The next day she was assigned to go-for work at a tox job. If the assignment became permanent, it could ruin her health and future, and she had no power to alter its course.

After spending a month in Security, they headed to Cimarron Hills to do more of the same. The brutal cold of late winter had settled in by then, and Will was thankful both he and Nash had secured heavy sweaters from a house that was strangely abandoned one night.

Occasionally, Dailys disappeared. The most likely scenarios included runners and body dumps, and some believed the Fringers kidnapped people. Cimarron was on the outskirts of the inhabited territory, where the

Fringers nomadically resided. Missing Dailys were recorded as runners, and if caught, they could be executed. Whatever happened to this family, they gathered only what they could use and carry, leaving everything else behind.

As awesome as that find was, they were even more excited that they were getting a ride to the next town. There were extra seats in the four snowplow trucks sent to clear a large accumulation of new and drifting snow. They were deterred onto many side roads before finally making it to the ten or so miles to Stratton Meadows. Will was in the first truck, and it amazed him how much snow was pushed aside by the hefty shovel. The trucks behind continued the process of removing huge amounts of snow from the narrowed and closed roads. Now and again, they would get out and move an obstacle or other such tasks. It wasn't the quickest trip or a very comfortable one, but at least they were inside for most of it.

Stratton was new, but the jobs were the same. Will hated the justice kind of work. He wished it all his assignments were construction and repairs, but the justice work was part of the package. The reality was that he and Nash had to survive in this pack until, hopefully someday, they could leave. He saw his fate as being no more or less trapped than the Dailys. He justified it with the cynical belief that no one was completely innocent or completely guilty. But every justice round made him feel less human, and he wondered if he would be able to return to a more ethical existence, or would he become a Dranger inside.

During their last two weeks at Stratton, Will and Nash worked together. They were told to punish a Daily who had been rallying workers to stand against the supervisor, or so he was accused. When Will and Rad walked up the driveway to knock on his door, they heard mumbling voices in the garage. They abruptly threw open the large door and saw six men standing there, frozen in absolute shock until all dashed out but one. Will assumed it was the owner of the house because where could he go? Their guilt was palpable.

"It's not what you think," the man yelled. "We're, we're..." he was panicking and could barely talk. "He is going to sell our daughters to some general in Pueblo.

Will froze where he stood. *Was this what happened to Tianna? Was the buyer General Kenner?*

"Kenner?" Will said the name with such pure purpose in his tone that its power hung in the air.

"I, I think so." The terrified man answered, not sure what Will's wrath was about and hoping he hadn't fueled it further.

Will was paralyzed with pain and rage, and he radiated wicked energy. This was too much to ask of him. Nash knew this was Will's nightmare coming back to haunt him, so he fiddled with his cell and made it beep.

"Hey Dirk," he said, calling Will by his D name. "We have an urgent call. Gotta go. Come on."

Will forced his body to move. He needed to get away as much as he needed vengeance, but getting away won out, for now. "We'll be back," Will said loudly, not knowing what else to say. When they were out of the man's hearing, Will asked. "Who the fuck called?"

"Your nightmare," Nash said a bit timidly. At that moment, Will was so charged with an edgy rage that Nash wasn't sure Will wouldn't exact his wrath on him. "I knew I had to get you out of there before you went full-on psycho."

Will took a breath and let out an uneasy laugh. "You know me too well. I had total flashes of General Kenner ordering his next victims."

"I know. And you probably started devising a plan to free those girls and kill that bastard. But Dirk, Will, it can't be done. Look, we'll report back and say there was no meeting there, and we'll try again tomorrow. Say we saw the guy and his wife sitting at the table with their daughter and son, so we left before they discovered us there."

"Yeah, we'll say we want to surprise them tomorrow, so they don't change their plans."

Will and Nash went and gave their report to the Neighwah commander. They expected some pushback for not being successful, but to their surprise, he agreed with the plan.

Denter approached Will during dinner, giving him tips on how to catch the rebels in the act. Will did his best to sound interested and engaged, but his anger was still seething under his façade. Denter was excellent at reading people, and when he saw Will walk outside, he followed him.

"Nice sky. Clear and cold as shit." Denter said as he pulled out a flask, took a hit, and offered it to Will. Will considered the rare gift and took a swig. It burned like his mood, and he liked it.

"Ever heard of a guy named General Kenner?" Will wasn't in the mood for small talk. He had a target in mind, and he threw it out there to see what jumped.

Denter let out a long exhale. "Sounds like you had a two-hit day. Ya better take another one." And he held the flask out again. Will took another hit. "Let's take a walk." They moved away from the building and stopped near a collapsed shed down the street. "Kenner is a special kind of bastard. What did you hear today?"

"Nothing just heard his name." Will was in dangerous territory now. He could be punished, and Nash too, if he wasn't careful.

"Don't fuck with me, Dirk! If you have info on that muck-shit, you better spill it. This isn't about you. This is about, about... the shit the fucker does. We dink with people to keep the status quo, but he's a whole different kind of evil."

Denter looked like he had his own bad history with this monster, and Will decided to tell him what happened but leave Nash out of it. When he was done with the day's short story, he stopped. He wasn't stupid enough to tell the full tale.

"Go back inside."

"What? I want to know..."

"Now!" Denter said quietly, but through clenched teeth.

Will stared for a minute and then turned to head back to the warehouse. "And Will," he called him by his true name. Will didn't know he even knew it. Why would he? "We never had this conversation. Tomorrow, when you go back as planned, better look like you're gunning for those rebels."

Will nodded, but he had no idea what Denter was going to do, or what side he was on.

Chapter Seven

The next day, Will had a new partner. It was Slice, not the nicest guy in the pack. Will worried he would be required to tag this rebel hard. But when they got there, the Neighwah were already in the house. Will and Slice weren't let in on the action. There was no sign of rebellious paraphernalia anywhere in the home, but the girl had been taken in the middle of the night.

A significant amount of blood was found in the alley along with her ripped and bloody clothes. The dogs were sent out to find the body. The final report said Fringers raided the town last night and took several girls. It was evident, that the girl fought back, and they killed her. End of story—they were just Dailys. No inquiry was ordered.

Will wondered exactly what part Denter played in this little drama. *Did this girl die, or was it staged? What happened to the other girls?* Did *he help them escape, or did he sell them himself and pocket the payoff? Or did he hand them over to* the Fringers? That might be just as bad.

No one knew much about the Fringers. They were named that because they lived in the wilderness fringes of the territory, but they were always on the run and almost certainly in a constant state of desperation. There were rumors they were human traffickers, so the story made sense. He believed Denter was secretly a good man in a Dranger world, but he'd probably never know the truth.

The pack spent two months doing scrap work in Stratton Meadows, while spring fought against the grip of winter. By the time they left, all that was left of the cold season was the occasional drift of dirty snow. Their next assignment was to be their first combat mission in a town called Stratmoor Hills.

It was only two miles away, but it would take at least a week to get there because they were tasked with doing road maintenance as they went. Denter drove a dump truck with gravel and pulled a trailer behind it, securing their equipment, weapons, and ammo. Those who didn't fit in the cab hung on to the welded platforms on each side of the truck.

Will had hoped the next town would allow him to check on his stash, but they weren't traveling the 25. They made their way down various unmaintained roads in desperate need of brush clearing. It was so overgrown in some places that the pavement disappeared, hiding treacherously deep potholes. Even trees had ignored its boundaries by growing through its middle and getting big enough to fully claim their ground.

Denter, who always toed the company line, grumbled that it was in much worse shape than he had been told. Every member knew exactly what their job was and how to execute it because Denter was a master delegator.

"Donner, you're in front with the chainsaw taking out the nanny trees."

They were called nursery trees, which grow so fast that they give protection to the slow-growing old forest, but Denter liked to spin the names of many things.

"Slice," Denter bellowed, "use the scissor saws to de-limb the downed trees for removal, and take out the pecker-poles. Rad, Lynch, use the trimmers and take down the brush. Brash and Jeeter, you're on debris removal and stacking logs in the trailer. Rummie, Dirk, you're bringing up the rear on pothole duty. I want a road, people. Move it!"

The eight of them created a steady swath as they progressed down the road. Denter did his share of labor while he supervised. After a long morning, the pack leader walked around distributing meal bars for lunch. They stopped where they stood, and at the sign of lunch, they collapsed on the logs strewn across the path. A light rain began to tap a gentle rhythm on the wide leaves and speckle the tired asphalt. Will was hot and sweaty from the pothole task, and he welcomed its refreshing coolness.

Stopping for lunch was a welcome reprieve, but it was hard to get back to their morning pace. They were dog-tired at the end of the first day, but they had cleared half a mile of road. They still had one and a half to go.

Some set up the simple camp while others prepared dinner. Will was curious how Brash got on with Jeeter. It was the first time either of them had been paired with him. After dinner, Brash and Will took their four-hour turn on patrol.

"So, what did you think of your partner today?" Will asked, expecting to laugh at Jeeter's expense.

"Well," Brash began, "I knew he had a story. Did you know he was jacked in like I was? But he got caught stealing. The Drangers have been messing with him and his family since his dad died. He stole a box of food because the Drangers had stolen their rations while he was bringing them home.

"He was late to the group walk because his little sister was sick and the neighbor who watches her wouldn't take her sick. So, he brought her and missed walking with the group. On the way home, they grabbed his box. He didn't fight because he wanted to protect her.

"To pay for his crime, he got jacked. They tried everything to keep him from graduating, so he'd have to do training over, but he's a good Dranger." Brash thought about that. "Well, what I mean is, he's not an idiot. He chose the name Jet when he graduated, but they changed it."

Will was dumbfounded for two reasons. One, he *might* have misjudged Jeeter, and two, Brash had picked up a stray. How many times had Will warned him that everyone has a tale of woe? Everyone! Even if it's true, the fact that he shared it was suspect because it showed weakness. The more vulnerable one is, the more outer strength one should show. Whether the story was a lie or not, Brash now had a pet to take care of.

"Smart people don't spill their guts like that. Do you believe him? There are an awful lot of lies floating around here. I heard I'm a witcher, and I cast a spell on Denter during our fight. That's why Denter had to *do what he did.*" Will used a sarcastic tone. "No one is brave enough to say he cheated. But people, especially Drangers, don't throw their shit out there like Jeeter did. It's suspicious. He might be testing you, setting you up."

"You make a good point. It may have been stupid to share, and it may have been stupid to listen," Brash said with a crooked smile. "And, yeah, he may be lyin', and I told him that. But I also said, as long as he acts like Jet instead of Jeeter, I'll call him that and have his back."

"I guess that's fair. Well done. But Brash,"

"Yeah, Dirk," Brash said with a hint of attitude. He knew his friend still regarded him like a little brother, and he would double down on his big brother advice.

"Don't turn your back on him. Even if he's telling the truth, he has somethin' to prove. Of that, I'm sure."

"Maybe so," Brash knew it was good advice, but he bristled at it just the same.

Though dead tired, they separated to do a perimeter walk around the camp. It was cold that night, and the soft steady rain was pulling that cold through his overly used sieve of a poncho. Will thought of his nice blanket secured to his cot back in the tent. His mark was on it, and no one dared to release his demon by taking it. Eventually, they woke up the next shift and settled into an exhausted but chilly sleep.

Later the next day, Will and Lynch were assigned brush removal with Brash and Jet since they were behind. Although Denter humiliated them in front of the pack, even he knew two guys couldn't clean up debris as fast as six guys could pump it out. Brash was calling Jet by his chosen name, and Lynch asked about it in front of Denter. Before Jeeter went into his dramatic sob story, Brash interrupted.

"They made a mistake with his name on graduation day, and he's been marked with it ever since." Then Brash added, "It doesn't matter why, but it's in the pack's best interest not to have a Dranger that no one takes seriously."

Even Denter agreed, and before long, Jeeter was Jet. Will was observing the whole name drama and decided he would go along. He'd call him Jet until his Jeeter side revealed itself. Then he'd nail him.

After another day and a half of road work, they made it to Highway 16, where they turned west and continued the strenuous task. It was only a quarter of a mile to the highway where their work assignment ended, and this part of the road was in better shape. For the rest of the trip, they would walk unhindered by roadwork the eight-plus miles into Stratmoor Hills. It was late morning when they began the last section of their journey. The weather was miserable, but at least they weren't slogging through road tasks.

While on the road, Will was on full alert to find where he had buried his treasure. He worried he wouldn't recognize the trapezoid rock because it had been moved, altered, or he had forgotten. But it stood out on the side of the forest road like a beacon. He was surprised it didn't catch anyone's eye but his own.

"I've gotta go take a walk in the woods," Will said, signaling he had to do more than pee. As his crew moved on, he climbed up the shallow bank to the backside of the rock and located the red spiral with the grave inscription of R.I.P. above it.

He passed the lightning-charred sentinel and took the fourteen steps to the fallen tree. Climbing over it, he crossed five more paces to stand in front of the bush. It was completely undisturbed, but just to be sure, he took a stick and pushed it into the ground several times until he heard the slight tap on the canning lid. Relief flooded through him. He hopped back onto the road with a lively bounce and jogged to catch up with the crew.

Upon arriving at Stratmoor, they allotted a section of a warehouse that was used to billet visiting workers. They walked into the cold, sheet metal pole building and saw the mess hall with picnic-bench seating and a wall of lockers that separated the mess hall from the dorm room. Numerous cots were parked in rows behind the lockers, and the numbers on the cots corresponded to the locker it was assigned. It was built to hold many more people than they had, and he wondered if they were to be joined by another crew.

A large wood stove sat on the side wall of the dorm room, but they were on the bottom floor with an open loft above them where the pack leaders slept. Though a couple of large fans spun continuously above, Will doubted it pushed down the heat enough to do more than keep the Drangers downstairs from shivering. The bathroom was filthy, with ten stalls and a long wall sink. Next to the bathroom was another enclosed room with clean-up sinks and a huge area where a washbasin and a couple of clotheslines hung.

Denter told them they had the rest of the day to settle in and get cleaned up before dinner at 1700. It would be nice to get cleaned up, but first, he went to claim a bed as close to the stove as he could get. He didn't know how, but he needed to get his hands on another warm blanket. After washing his clothes and hanging them on the line, he lay on his bed.

He wished he had a book and permission to read one. After a dinner of lukewarm porridge and beans, some of the crew played cards in the mess hall. The wood stove was cranking up, and it felt almost pleasant. Will lay down on his cot with his blanket and drifted off to sleep.

Denter had been driving them pretty hard. The road was in worse shape than the reports said, but they were expected that morning and showed up that late afternoon. That made Denter look bad, and the excuses didn't go over well regardless of their validity.

It had been a grueling couple of days, and Will was annoyed with Denter. He thought he was a smart leader. His crew, most of whom were new, had just finished an impossible task in record time, but he treated them like failures in front of the Neighwah soldiers. Will didn't expect a reward, but it was inefficient to belittle one's soldiers just to impress his superiors. It was going to take all his resolve to maintain the work ethic he had begun with.

Stratmoor was like every other town—rundown but hanging on. The rugged Cheyenne Mountain rose in the distance, and Will longed to just take off and get lost in the wilderness like that. Others couldn't understand that dream, which he admitted was rife with danger and tough living. But it called to Will, and after the last couple of months, the call was getting louder. He longed to be his own man, and he vowed it would happen someday.

Their mission was to capture a couple of rogue toxers. The two men had gone AWOL from their jobs after stealing chemicals from their job site. Now, they were robbing Dailys and uppers for food and valuables to trade for stronger tox. They were hiding in the foothills at night and creeping into town after the day shift horn blew. They'd scope out neighborhoods in search of empty houses. They easily broke through the brittle door-frames to seize anything they thought would buy their next fix.

The small territory only had six Neighwah soldiers, including their commander. They just couldn't cover enough ground to catch them, but that's what Drangers were for, backup. Denter would be working under the Neighwah commander, and the pack would be working under him and everyone else. Will had no idea what that would be like, but he was fairly sure the soldiers would be unfriendly, and more than likely, they'd be downright cruel. They consider Drangers a step above criminals.

"Okay, Arrows, listen up," Denter said with his usual authoritarian voice. "I'm getting wind that there's been grumbling about how hard you worked on the road. I strongly suggest you get over it, and quick. That's the life of a Dranger. It can get much worse. Don't make me prove it. Enough said.

"Our assignment on this mission is to split into four teams of two each. Two teams will patrol the neighborhoods during the day, and two will join the Neighwah teams to locate the rebel camp. You'll be armed with a pistol and a rifle, but don't get stupid and shoot a Daily on assigned duty or, worse, each other. If I have to do that kind of paperwork, I might as well shoot you myself.

"This afternoon, we'll be practicing at the shooting range. Tomorrow, Jet and Dirk will take the day duty, and the rest of you are on the night shift. Get your gear and be back down here in five. Dismissed."

Will hated that he and Nash were separated, but if he were Denter, he'd do the same thing. Nash was a grad now. If he couldn't function like one he was useless. Jet was consistently demonstrating that he could be a hard worker and a team player. Though Will hadn't wholly joined the Jet club yet, he was edging that way.

Target practice was the crew's favorite task. They were extremely competitive. The best marksmen with a pistol were Donner, Rummie, and Slice, but Will was improving his way up to their scores. Everyone was pretty skilled with a rifle, but they hadn't shot one beyond fifty yards. Will loved his guns, and he took the time to maintain them. But his compound bow was his favorite. It was an elegant weapon and deadly quiet, and he was more than proficient with it, but he was told to use his rifle for intown duty.

They had an early dinner of pheasant stew since Denter had shot three while scouting the nearby woods. Everyone but Will and Jet was resting before their night shift started. Will and Jet were tasked with cleaning up dinner and setting the camp gear to dry on the empty side of the building. They got to sleep that night after dinner in a quiet house while the rest of the pack went hunting for the toxers.

Will and Jet woke up at dawn and headed down the street to the Neighwah headquarters. They needed to be on duty and set up before the dayshift horn blew. They followed the other five soldiers to the briefing room. Dread was there. He knew he was drafted by the Neighwah, but he didn't know which town he went to until now. Will began stoking his rage and looked Dread right in the eyes, but Jet looked away. They sat down with plenty of distance between them.

"Okay," started Commander Brindle to the small group before him. "The teams last night came across a campsite. We believe it belonged to the pair we're looking for, but they change locations often, and this is an old one." He pulled down a map of the area spotted with three different colors of dots.

"The red ones," he explained, "are the houses that they hit so far. The green ones are houses that are empty during the day, so they are the most likely targets. The black dots are the campsites we've located. As you can see, they camp close to their next set of target houses. We're still unsure how they offload the stolen goods, and we haven't run across a stash.

"We believe they have an accomplice, and they dump before they go back to the woods. The blue dots are where we are going to position ourselves." He then assigned an area to each group of two. Jet and Will were split up to accompany Neighwah soldiers familiar with the town because a third group was joining the day shift. Will found out Brash was doing a double shift, and he was to be paired with Dread in town.

Before leaving, Will told his partner he was going to stop at the bathroom. Jet darted out of the briefing room while Dread was speaking with the leader. He got into the stall next to Will. From under the panel that separated them, Jet gave Will the Arrow's signal for Neighwah, followed by the one for a traitor.

He left before Will could ask him whom his signals were about, but he had his suspicions. Will still wasn't sure if Jet was Jeeter, but if he had a hunch someone was helping the thieves, he'd better fess up the info fast. A Neighwah soldier would have a lot of information to keep them from getting caught. Will tucked that info away.

Will didn't get a chance to speak with Nash, but he knew enough to stay out of Dread's way, and he had the skills to defend himself now. Surely Dread wouldn't be stupid enough to attack the hired help, not on the first day anyway. Will walked up to his Neighwah partner, Brock, and made the small talk necessary for a cooperative working affiliation. Will started the conversation with questions about what being in the Neighwah was like.

"Well," Brock said, "it's better than the Dranger life." Brock then pulled up his right sleeve to show his D brand and A tattoo for the Assailants from Denver. "The food and accommodations are a lot better, and we don't travel as much as you do. Mostly, we patrol the town we're assigned to. Now and then we have to do hard labor, but typically we hire you for that. The best part is we get credits every week. It's not a lot, but we get enough to buy the supplies we need. Drangers get food, a cot, and maybe a few credits when they finish a run, but that's it. When I was a Dranger, I had to steal stuff like clothes and blankets, but now I can afford them. We also can give up our pack name. Are you thinking of applying?"

Will shrugged his shoulders. "How about your boss and the guys you work with? Are they assholes?"

"Well, I said it was better, not paradise." They both laughed.

"You got a Dranger recently, Dread. I recognize him from Fountain. He was a piece of work when I knew him." Will hoped he hadn't crossed a line, but he had to test out this organization, especially Dread.

"Oh, you mean Devon. Yeah, the commander has toned him down a bit. He thought he was going to come in here and take charge. He's quieter now."

That sounded like the Dread Will knew, a self-serving blustery dick. But he didn't believe the Dread, or Devon, he knew, would back down easily. He seemed like the kind of guy who wormed his way next to the top, so he could grab some power and throw his status around. But regardless, this was all he was going to get from Brock. He didn't want him to get suspicious.

The more Will thought about it, the more things started fitting togeth- er. Two toxers couldn't outsmart a whole department of soldiers. Their muddled minds would need help and direction. An accomplice in the department made sense. But how exactly would it work? Whoever it was, he just couldn't dump unearned credits into his account, which was run by the Neighwah in each territory.

He could grab some trading power, but that would be easy to trace. Maybe he could grab some extra trading items, but it would be risky to store them unless he had a buyer. Will enjoyed thinking through a problem, and this kind of warfare was his kind of highway. He would try to get more out of the other guys and piece this puzzle together. Dread was not a likable guy. If he could get them to complain, they might give him useful info. He also couldn't wait to see how Nash's day went.

Brock and Will had checked their assigned territory several times, and they both extended their patrol beyond the assigned area. Sure enough, they came upon a house with the front door lilting on its hinges. Will went to the back, and Brock kicked open the front door. Will saw tracks in the muddy backyard leading away from the house through the hole in the fence. Brock came to the backdoor and slid the glass door open.

"They've been here all right. The place is a mess."

"We might get in trouble for breaking from our assignment. I have an idea." Will's mind was in full investigative mode, and he was loving it.

Later that evening, everyone met in the briefing room. Will was watching for Brash, but he didn't show up.

Will and Brock went to the front to present the report from their team. They had decided to add a reason for going outside of their assigned area to avoid trouble. "We were doing our checks when we saw two guys on Wender Street," Will observed. Dread stiffened at the mention of the unassigned street—*interesting*. "When they saw us, they ran. We chased them but lost them when they dodged between two houses. We were trying to catch up to them. That's when we saw this house with the door hanging loose on its hinges."

Brock took over giving the rest of the report. "We knew it was outside our list, but we had to check it out. Sure enough, it had been broken into, so we called it into Command. I wish I could describe the two suspects, but I barely got a glimpse, and Dirk was even farther away than me." He then took his seat and returned the podium to the commander.

"We checked it out, and it contained stolen goods inside. It was a small enough amount that one man could pack it out. We talked to the residents, but they didn't see anything," the commander responded. "Your number one order is to catch these guys, so you did right. Devon has the next incident."

Dread came up to the stand and paused. "Brash and me were checking doors and windows in our area according to our list. I did one side of the street, and Brash did the other. Next thing I know, Brash was gone, runoff. He always was a coward. He saw his chance, and he took it."

"So," the commander growled, "we now have another goal. Capture the deserter." Will went to stand up, and Denter pulled him back down. The commander issued the next day's assignments and ended the meeting with, "Anything else?" No response was spoken. "Okay, next meeting 0600 hours. Dismissed."

Will turned to Denter, but he gave Will a stern not-now look. He got up with the rest of the crew and filed out of the room. He expected Denter to call him aside for a talk, but it didn't happen. Finally, Denter called Will upstairs to his room. He went in and was told to sit. Denter closed the door behind him.

"Shut up and listen," he said in a rare whisper. "I don't believe it either. That Dread, there's something up with him. We're short a town walker now, so I'm pairing you with Dread. You are gonna look for Brash. I have no idea where he might be, but I'm gonna give you a chance to find him first.

"Tell Dread you want to split up, and then track him. If he's alive, he's been stashed, or he got away. So, Dread will either be checking on him, looking for him, or getting rid of his body. If he's already buried, I doubt you'll find him." Denter didn't say another word until he opened the door. "Like I said, I'm gonna find that little yellowbelly, and I'm taking Brock with me. We're checking the hills. You are going to stay out of it. Understand?" His voice was anything but soft this time because he wanted everyone to hear him.

Will answered with the expected, obedient response, "Yes sir."

Chapter Eight

Will waited outside the Neighwah HQ for his new partner. Dread was visibly disappointed he wasn't working alone today, but no one but Will and Denter seemed to notice. The cruel Neighwah soldier had an arrogant confidence about him that said he hadn't picked up on Will's dangerous demeanor. They hadn't walked far when Dread turned to Will.

"Hey, let's split up. I work better on my own, and I don't need no newbie D following me around like a kid who lost his puppy." Dread stood with his hands on his hips. Will couldn't believe his good fortune. He wasn't sure how he was going to bring up separating without looking suspicious, but more importantly, it was a sign Dread had unfinished business. Maybe Nash was still alive.

"Works for me," Will spoke with a shade of contempt. Though he didn't know exactly what Dread was up to, he intended to find out.

Tracking Dread would take all the stealth skill Will could muster. Dread had a lot more experience, and Will was pretty sure he was the inside man involved in the robberies and abductions carried out during the last couple of months. Nash probably discovered this, and he was silenced, or about to be. Will focused on the outcome he wanted and pushed the unthinkable to the dark recesses of his mind.

He headed in the opposite direction, but he used a mirror to watch Dread's feet. It was a trick his father taught him. "If you point the mirror at their feet, you won't alert them with a reflective flash." Will's pace slowed as he faded back into his better memories when he saw Dread turn suddenly up the next street. Will turned up a parallel road and ran to the next that would cross the one Dread turned on. He couldn't lose track of him. The street sign said Wender Street. It was the one yesterday's robbery was on.

Hugging the side of the house on the corner, he peered around with his mirror looking for Dread. He caught a split glance of him entering a house a couple of doors down from the one he and Brock had investigated yesterday. When the door closed, Will darted down the street. As he reached the house Dread entered, he quickly deduced it was uninhabited.

It was among the many unlivable dwellings that patiently waited between the occupied ones. They hung on like old clothes in a closet for those just-in-case times. Many of the windows were boarded up, and the roof wasn't likely to take too many more years of snow without repairs. He put his cup up to several windows, but there were no voices or rumblings. Just then, Will heard footsteps heading toward the back door. He hid behind an overgrown bush tucked up against the house.

Dread came out dragging a large bag. *Shit!* Will reached for his weapon and aimed his sight at Dread.

"You murdering piece of shit!"

Within seconds, Dread had the knife he held pointed at the bag. "I wouldn't if I were you. He's still alive, see," he said kicking the bag invoking a soft moan from inside. "I'm hoping to remedy that soon, but you don't have to join him. There are plenty of ways I can sneak credits to you. Do you want to have this gimped-up ball and chain 'round your neck forever? He's not worth it."

Will thought for a minute. *He thinks I'd turn on Nash.* He scrambled to decide how to use this information. All he came up with was to keep him talking.

"He has been more trouble than I anticipated, but I don't believe you can *sneak* credits under the Corporates' noses. You're lying. Pocketmen always get caught." Will had witnessed several thieves and extortionists, called pocketmen, hauled away. "The Uppers may get away with it once, maybe twice, but a newbie Neighwah and a Dranger—not likely."

"Well, look at the high and mighty moral wonder boy. Maybe you *are* smart enough to dump your trash. Let me tell you, it's very possible to get away with it. I have access to a computer, and they don't know how good I am at getting into their files. I created a new identity. I'm paid with credits or goods. I sell the goods to someone in another town. Then the credits go right into my alter account, so they're legit. I use a disguise, and I spend my credits easily. I've gotten away with it for months. No one is even close. The Dailys are more than happy to donate their stuff, like food, meds, and homemade goods, to keep their brats alive."

"Why make it look like a robbery then? Why not do it undercover without involving the soldiers?" Will was hoping to get a shot with the rifle he still had trained on Dread. But he had to be sure it was clean enough that it wouldn't allow Dread to slash what was undoubtedly Nash's throat under the body bag.

"Well, those stupid Robinhooders caught wind of it. One of the Dailys told someone who reported it to the RH band." *Denter*, Will thought to himself. He must have connections with RH and got them involved.

Dread continued, "That's why I had to teach them a lesson with that girl. I had a sweet deal with General Kenner's men. It was going to set me up as an Upper in Pueblo. I could have made a killing on that deal, and the general was going to help me, as long as I supplied him with girls and smuggled his high-end drugs. It's all okay now. Those idiots learned their lesson, and they still have one kid left. I shouldn't have to teach it again, but I could," Dread smirked.

Will held back the abject hatred he was feeling. He needed to get the shot. He was about to engage in making a deal when a dog ran from between the houses and started barking up a storm. It caused Dread to turn his head just enough, and Will took his shot. *BANG!*

Down Dread went like a stone, blood pouring from the hole in his forehead. The dog stopped barking and ran to the Neighwah soldiers coming out from behind different houses with guns up and ready for any other criminals. The Neighwah commander followed.

Will ran to the bag, ripped open the top zipper, and sliced the side to assess his friend. Nash's face was badly beaten, and he had two gunshot wounds, one grazed his shoulder and another on his left knee. He let out a weak groan and lost consciousness. "I got ya buddy. That bastard's dead. Everything is going to be okay now." He had no idea exactly how bad Nash was, but a cart pulled up, and two Neighwah loaded Nash. The commander looked Nash over and sent the cart off. Will wanted to go with him, but the commander stopped him.

"Don't worry, I already cleared him to go to the infirmary. I heard the whole dialog. It's a good thing he's dead. I would have hurt that son-of-a-bitch hardcore and then hung his rotting body before he could die. But you did take this into your own hands without letting me know, and now we don't know who he was working with. You have a radio, and you should have used it. In case you didn't know, I'm in charge here, not you." The commander was stern and noticeably pissed, but at that moment, Will didn't care about anything but Nash.

Will knew he had gone rogue, killing the one man with information who also happened to be one of the commander's soldiers, and he waited for his punishment. But the commander went in a different direction and called Will off to the side.

"Kid, you cut me out of the loop. I hate that. And you owe me. I'm going to help your friend here. And then you are going to owe me more. And someday soon, we'll be settling this. Deal?" and he held out his hand.

Will expected him to penalize him here and now for disobedience. It reminded him of how Taylor would make him wait for his punishments to build up more trepidation. He found, more often than not, it made the punishment seem easy. But he had to admit, it would increase his guilt. But unlike Taylor, this guy didn't have Will's trust or best interests in mind. Will wasn't sure what he meant, or if there were any limits on the ask.

"What exactly does this deal look like?"

"Well, I want you to join my team voluntarily. In return, I'll get Brash the best care I can provide, which is a thousand percent better than what Denter can do. This move will have to wait until Brash is done with his treatment because I can't take you from the Drangers before the end of your first year. Then they're gonna make me pay for you. If you say yes, I'll take you at your word." And he held out his hand.

"Why are you so interested in me?" Will was afraid he knew the answer, but it might confirm the man's suspicions if he didn't feign ignorance and ask.

"I think you'll be a good soldier. You're smart and loyal. That makes you better than most of my men who grew up soft as Uppers."

It was a plausible answer. "What would keep me from backing out after Brash is better?"

"Gun accidents are an awful tragedy. I'd hate to see the poor kid end up with his other leg messed up. That would be just sad."

"I see." Will looked the man straight in the eye. "I guess that settles it." And he held out his hand, wondering where this would take him in life. *What if Nash couldn't work? Would he be sent home to rot in a sit-house? At least he would be alive to go home. One shit-show at a* time, Will thought.

The Arrows were scheduled to stay in town another couple of weeks to assist in tracking down the smugglers and hopefully their contact from Pueblo. Nash was being treated at the infirmary, which was the same one the Uppers used. His knee was in bad shape, and as a Dranger, he could have died from infection or been left crippled and poverty-stricken. But with good doctors and medicine, he was expected to walk again, but how well was unknown. The other Drangers and Nash thought it was because he helped solve a big crime ring, so the treatment at the Neighwah facility was donated. Will knew different.

That evening, the Arrows and the Neighwah got into four teams of three. One team was scheduled to search all the empty houses to see if there was more hidden contraband. The other three would canvas the surrounding area to track down the toxers, and if they were lucky, they may trap the Pueblo contact too.

Jet, Will, and Brock were assigned the NW2 section. The quarter moon was filtered on and off by the scattered clouds, making a red halo around it, and a cold wind billowed and bit at their inadequate jackets. The shrouded moon softly illuminated the snow with a clean white glow in open spaces, but the wooded areas complicated their progress, and images of wicked creatures dwelling in the inky black world played with Will's head. Benign noises one ignored in daylight were brought to life by the vicious shadows in his mind. Brock broke the silence, but his words brought no comfort.

"The witches call this a blood moon. It's a death warning."

Jet jabbed back. "Thanks for that happy thought, Brock,"

"Is this witch reference referring to my luck in the ring when I declared the blood pact rite?" Will chimed in.

"Yeah, but it's only half out of the clouds, so it means we'll only get half dead," Jet tried to keep a straight face, but they all broke out laughing.

"We best keep our noise down, though," Brock added, and the quiet hike continued.

In the dark forest, they used Neighwah night goggles to make their way. It eliminated the candle-in-the-dark effect that might warn their enemies they were approaching. The toxers would probably use firelight to ward off the evening's chill, which would further blind them to approaching foes.

Though spring was waning, she was known for sudden stormy tantrums, and they were expecting a mean one. They received a weather report of sorts, which simply told of a sudden drop in air pressure, calling for a storm. They prepared for that with the meager gear they had access to.

As they made their way through the trees and brush, the clouds thickened and blotted out the modest moonlight they depended on. The temperature dropped significantly; the wind picked up, and one by one, snowflakes began to make their sideways trek to the ground. A few turned into more, and then there were so many it blinded them, making their progress impossible.

The three teens found their way to a large spruce tree with old snow-laden boughs creating a generous area underneath. Settling on the lee side of the wind, they assembled their connectable waterproof ponchos to construct a tiny shelter. They were issued two chemical heat cans that could provide about forty minutes of heat each. Vigorously, they shook the first one, and soon their ungloved hands were gathered around the small can. It would not be comfortable, but it would be survivable if their supply held out longer than the storm.

Their last can had given out about fifteen minutes ago, but the storm was dying. As quickly as its fury descended upon them, its howling stopped, and not even a whispering swoosh through the trees could be heard. A dizzy melancholy filled the young men, who soon realized they were buried and their air supply was dwindling. They disconnected the makeshift dwelling enough to reach out. Using their combined strength, they pushed on a bough, bringing the icy drift down on them, but it achieved their goal, and they made their way out. Shaking off the frozen flakes, they saw little bits of the sky peeking through the tired clouds.

A wispy wind suspended the snow in the air as if the storm still lived, but the heavens above were quiet, and a gibbous moon peeked out between ebbing clouds, illuminating the brilliant white blanket. The moon's light allowed them to continue the mission without the goggles. Trees were shedding snow in terrific whomps, and each step required more effort and caution.

Walking through the drifts of fallen and discarded snow was arduous work. To keep his mind off the labor, Will quietly contemplated how the toxers dealt with the storm. Without reports of its approach, it was reasonable to assume they had been caught off guard. One more advantage for them.

They had traversed a mile, but it seemed like five. They were panting and sweating, which could mean real trouble in the cold. In the distance, a sudden ruckus of movement and the murmur of aggravated voices disturbed the silence. As they approached, the words rang clear enough to hear.

"What the fuck is going on here? I waited on the 115 forever. I'm lucky I wasn't had, and hiking all the way here pissed me off. That road is unused for sure, but they still drone it. I crept by the stash house, and a soldier guarding the door. All the curtains were open, and there were lights on inside."

The panicked toxers had just been dug out of their temporary shelter where a tree shedding had effectively trapped them. It was sufficiently covered, but Will estimated it was about seven or eight feet square. He noted the chimney and the hooked fresh air tube that protruded above the snow. *How is it that something like this evaded their week and a half of searching?*

Although it could probably be broken down and moved, it would take something to haul it and cover the tracks. And surely someone would see the smoke. Then he remembered Dread was their computer guy. He must have been in charge of setting up the search patterns. No doubt, he carefully calculated the past and current placement of the shack.

The toxers were shaking, but whether it was from the cold, the drugs, or the assault rifle trained on them was a mystery, but all the above was probable. *Where did he get that gun?* Will noted the weapon's huge ammo clip and thought of his rifle, which required constant reloading.

"It's not our fault …" Their answers were overlapped and anxious.

"Yeah, that Neighwah never came."

"We figured he'd be here after, after…" his broken mind seemed to lose his thought.

"After the storm. Yeah, after the storm." The other man picked up the answer as his friend swatted at imaginary issues. "The storm, bad storm. Couldn't get out." The drug-crazed men nodded at each other, their faces tweaking with contorted expressions.

"Last week, no girls!" the man yelled. "Now, no supplies. No weapons, no ammo, nothing. The general is going to have my head, but not before I take yours."

The general's goon shot the two toxers with a cold round of bullets while they huddled together. They screamed and writhed on the ground, but only for a moment. Brock took off to position himself for a better shot. A sudden thump of snow shedding reverberated through the forest. It was right behind Jet and Will. The goon changed his barrel toward the brush where the two Drangers hid. He pulled the barrel high, and Will knew he would miss them. Then he moved his aim lower, directly where they crouched.

As Will laid himself on his belly and took aim, Jet popped up. It startled Will, and before he resettled to pull the trigger, a round of four or five shots rang out one right after the other, followed by a single shot from Brock's position. The goon toppled, and Will turned to scold Jet, but he was crumpled on the ground. Will never even got off a shot, and Jet lay oozing blood from multiple hits.

"Shit! Jet's hit!" Will's shout brought Brock leaping out of the brush to Will's left. Will grabbed Jet and held him in his arms. The blood seeped out of the back of his jacket, running through Will's fingers. They opened his layers of clothing to put pressure on the deep red cavities swelling with red, pulsating puddles. His chest was riddled with them, and air bubbles fizzed out of the wounds. He took multiple shots in his left lung and one near his liver. He had seconds left.

"Why did you do it?"

"Saw you." Blood spurted from his mouth, and speaking and breathing were a visible struggle. "Brash," he coughed, and another round of blood poured out of his mouth, "he," more coughing and gurgling, "needs…" His ability to speak ceased, and his pupils rolled out of sight. The convulsions didn't last but a few seconds, but they were traumatic, and helplessness burned through Will. Then he was still, leaving the expression of death frozen on his young face.

"Why did you do that? You made yourself a target." Will was sobbing. How could he have ever doubted this man's loyalty?

Brock arrived and saw the man lying motionless in the cold snow. He put his hand on Will's shoulder.

"He was a good soldier. He will be missed."

"He saved me. The bastard was aiming right at me. Jet sacrificed his life and left me unscathed. How do I live with that?" Will curled Jet's still body to his chest and wept uncontrollably.

"We lose good men sometimes. Jet died a hero because it was *his* choice, not yours. If you try to own it, you'll diminish his sacrifice. Thank him, honor him, remember him."

Will looked up at Brock as tears streamed down his cheeks. He closed his eyes and nodded. Then he looked at Jet's face. It was still, and his jaw hung open. He closed it and spoke softly.

"Thank you, and I will honor your sacrifice by taking care of Brash. Your name will be on the table and on the honor wall at our dorm. I will always remember what you did. Sleep easy Jet. You will not be forgotten." He spoke in an honest, heartfelt whisper. Then he kissed his head and laid him down. He looked at Brock. "I don't care if crows and predators rip the shit out of those losers, but Jet's coming home with us."

"Not even a question."

They fashioned a litter from branches and a blanket found in the toxer hut. Brock grabbed the AR and the bullet belt strapped across the goon's chest.

"I wish I could keep this mother-fucker," Brock said as he secured the strap of the impressive weapon and its ammo around him.

"I definitely was having some gun envy back there," Will added.

"Yeah, his was definitely bigger than yours, and now it's mine, so yeah." Brock laughed.

"Well, enjoy it while it lasts. That big gun-dick will be seized before we even begin our report."

"I'd love to keep it. It sure does pack a punch." As soon as Brock said it, he looked back at their fallen comrade. They stayed mostly silent as they made their demanding trek back to town to give their report.

Two teams were sent to retrieve the bodies and gather evidence to send up to Corporate. It was certain there would be words about Pueblo's General stealing from Colorado Springs. More than likely, a favor and supplies would be given to the Colorado Springs Corporates to appease them for breaking the territory alliance. They would probably give bonus credits to the Neighwah soldiers, and the Drangers would get something, but the Dailys would see nothing for their loss.

Exhausted, Will went to his bed and finally settled into a restless sleep of mingled nightmares. When he rose, he walked to the infirmary to visit Nash. He was awake and propped up with his hands cradling his head on several pillows. A gray blanket lay across him diagonally, allowing his heavily bandaged leg to rest in a sling hooked to a rail above him. He looked quite comfortable.

"Wow, nice slack work. Does Denter know they're softening you up?"

"Well, they did a pretty good job fixing my leg, but they're awful stingy with the pain meds. The Uppers and Neighwah patients get more."

"Yep, soft as butter and complaining to boot. Denter's not going to be happy, and he's probably gonna work up a rough ride for you." Will was laughing for now, but he knew he had bad news to break.

"Heard you guys found the Toxer camp. Exchanged a bit of lead too." Nash changed to a more serious mood.

"Yeah, we did. We lost Jet. He popped up and made that Pueblo shithead change his aim from me to him. It's killing me, but I'm trying to respect his choice. You gave him back his dignity, and he all but said so before he died. He's getting his name carved on the table and on the Arrow plaque too. If I have to take Denter on by myself, it's happening."

"Well, you did that before and lost, but I bet you won't have to fight for it. He came in here himself and told me about it. He said he was proud to have him in his pack. He's holding a service this afternoon sometime. I wish I could go. Tell me about it."

"I will." The two sat talking until Will had to leave.

The Arrow pack gathered around the body bound in plastic material. Denter bowed his head for a moment of silence before he gave the eulogy. "I can't say I was happy when I was given Jet as a pack member. They called him Jeeter as an insult, and I wondered what problems he might bring. But it was Brash who turned everything around. He convinced us all to give him a chance, and we did. He was a good man, a team player. He gave his life for his pack and completed the mission. We thank him, honor him, and will always remember him."

Everyone removed their caps and answered, "Here, here."

Jet's body was loaded into the refrigerated truck bound for the crematorium near the Neighwah Territory Headquarters outside of Colorado Springs.

Later that week, the Arrows left for a new assignment at Big Johnson Reservoir. It was hard to leave Nash behind, but he was improving every day. Will took comfort that they were giving him the time he needed.

Spring had been fully replaced by summer, and they were hired to repair the roads on the way, inspect the dam, and do minor maintenance on both as needed. Any major discrepancies found at the dam would be reported to Corporate for a specialized maintenance crew. The reservoir was a major water source for much of the Colorado Springs Territory.

The road was in bad shape, but within two weeks they were close to being done. They just had to check the dam. They started on the spillway side of the structure, checking for cracks and bulges. They found it to be in sound condition.

Will and Rummie were excited about taking a couple of boats out to check the lakeside of the dam. Though he had never been on a boat before, he remembered Old Man River's fishing stories. He showed him the rowing motions and how to position the oars in the water. He quickly mastered the motion between the launch site and the rim wall of the dam.

Will found the roll of the gentle waves calming, and he wondered what bigger waves would feel like. He almost regretted the experience, knowing he would miss it. There was little chance he would have a job on the water or be allowed to enjoy it. The dam was in excellent shape, so they had a couple of hours to kill before they went back to their campsite.

The heat of the day was taking its toll on the crew, and Denter decided everyone in his pack needed to learn how to swim. He gave a brief lesson on arm and leg moves as well as breathing information. Then, one by one, he tied ropes around them and threw them off the dock. There was a lot of panicked splashing after being tossed into the chilly water. Not one knew how to swim. Some had to be hoisted up, but after a few minutes, most were staying above the water on their own.

Will took to the water immediately. As tall and slim as he was, he sank a few times before he got his fish skills working. As soon as he did, he untied his rope to enjoy the refreshing cool-down and the weightless feeling of the water's support. Lynch was also devoid of buoyant body fat, but he was faithful to the pack and worked at the task until he too was holding himself above the water.

Rummie was rounder than his pack mates. He wasn't graceful by any means, but his main goal was to make the pack proud of him, not to excel or enjoy the experience. Yet, truth be told, he admitted it was fun. Donner, Slice, and Rad were familiar with Denter's unconventional antics, and they had come to relish the way he provided a constant stream of new experiences.

They had been a team for almost a year, and Denter had driven them pretty hard, but it was time to make a trip back to Fountain. They would spend two weeks at camp getting new orders, restocking, re-qualifying, and a bit of recuperating time too. They would also be replacing their fallen member and maybe two more if Nash didn't qualify and Will was taken by Colonel Brindle.

Every summer the obstacle course was altered, and twice a year training classes were held. As each class finished, four of the eight packs would meet to get requalified and choose recruits. The assessments were set up as contests, and reward ceremonies honored the best competitors at the end of each one. It promised to be an easy week of playing hard, sleeping in the pack's dorm house, and breezing through the light workload.

Will had heard many stories about the contests, and he looked forward to the event. He was also looking forward to getting his new brads and seeing Nash after being informed he would be there. Though there had been no word on his condition, Will was excited to see him and assess him for himself.

What Will dreaded was the deal he had made with the Neighwah commander. His mind was tangled with dangerous scenarios. *Was Nash well enough to join the pack again? What if he couldn't qualify? What would happen to him? And what about this deal? With the Drangers, he had the hope of getting* out, *slim as it was. How would he ever get out of being a Neighwah?*

Chapter Nine

The Arrow pack strolled through the big log gate to the familiar camp. Will reminisced about the first time he crossed this threshold a year ago. Back then the camp seemed foreboding and full of danger, but now he welcomed the sight. The team needed a break, and though they would have a work assignment, it wouldn't be strenuous, hazardous, or guilt-ridden.

Though the time he had spent, there was mostly unpleasant at best, it felt like coming home because Nash would be there. One thing that would be new was staying in the Arrow house, not the trainee tent or the jail. The last night he spent here, they departed early the next morning, which made moving to the barracks pointless.

Along the road, he was told about the contests and the reward ceremonies. They would get their brads for the deeds they accomplished that year. Everyone would get at least one star for completing a year, and some would get two if they did well. It was the skulls that made real rank. It was a gruesome brand that he had conflicting feelings about, but this was his job. This was his life for now. He wondered if any of it would transfer to the Neighwah he was soon to join. As far as he knew, it was a secret, and he had not spoken to anyone about it. Putting aside all the worries and concerns swirling in his head, he focused on seeing Nash.

The Arrow bunkhouse was in a brick building that used to be a large condominium. The front area was a great room with a table on the back wall, and in front of it was a mix-match of a dozen chairs facing a podium. The kitchen was rather small, but it was only used for morning meals since all others were served at the dining hall. The walls hadn't been painted any time recently, and the floors throughout were a shabby linoleum, but everything was clean even in the corners.

The bathroom consisted of three stalls, a long urinal trough, and an extended sink with four faucets. Will was surprised it didn't smell, but that only meant Dailys were hired to clean it before they arrived. Denter had a room to himself, but the Drangers' sleeping area was one large bunk room with five bunk areas.

Each one was tucked behind half-walled nooks and partially blocked off with large lockers, so a door-sized opening led into a space with just enough room to get dressed. In the middle of the sleeping area, were two tables with six chairs each. A deck of well-used cards and a couple of dice sat on one, and a couple of checkerboards were painted on the other, sporting rough-cut wooden wafers for pieces.

"Do we get time to play?" Will asked.

"Sometimes, if we get our work done early enough," Donner answered.

Donner was Denter's highest-ranked member, and he got the bunk nook with a single bed. They had started with eight Drangers and one leader, so there were still two empty beds with Jet gone and Nash not there yet.

Will yelled, "I'm going to take this nook and save the bottom bunk for Brash." It was a statement, not a question, and no one rejected it.

"Have at it. We'll be getting some newbies, and if Brash doesn't qualify, you'll be bunking with one of them. Just sayin' is all," Rad added with a grin.

"Whatever," Will knew there was no reason to get comfortable here. He wasn't going to be allowed to stay.

They settled in and got a chance to play a game or two. The next morning, they had wheat porridge for breakfast and headed to the Great Hall for the group meeting. Will noticed Jet's name was newly carved into the tabletop with four stars above and below. It was the highest honor to lay down your life for the pack. Denter had called it ahead, and before they headed back out, they would add his name to the plaque at the dorm house.

They got the schedule for the qualification course and the rest of the events. Will continually looked around, but no Nash yet. The crowd was filled with high spirits, and it reminded Will of the false hope he felt about leaving Pueblo and joining the Colorado Springs Territory. It was an ominous thought, and he pushed aside the superstitious foreshadowing running through his mind.

There were three other packs at the camp for annuals. Another pack was also there, as they were permanently stationed at Fountain. They were an older crew that worked at the mess hall, equipment maintenance, miscellaneous, and if needed, runs close by. The packs here for re-qualifying included the Arrows, the Snakes, the Claws, and the Comets. There were also some Drangers needing make-up qualifications and those trying out for number one and pack leader positions. All in all, there were twenty-nine Drangers up for course qualification.

The qualifying contest involved the obstacle course, but the equipment had been altered and the order of the challenges changed. Three teams of four and two teams of three would get two chances: one practice and one final. The four competitors with the best final scores would then compete for the win. The leaders and applicants for promotion slots were not required to run the course to qualify. They only had to pass the officer battle tests. Drangers also competed in the battle tests, which included target shooting, arena fighting, and a team paintball game between packs.

Will was eager to participate in the contests. As each team left the starting point, he grew more excited for his turn. Physical competition made him feel alive and free, pushing his body through each grueling task. The sport of it was its own kind of battle, and battle time was when he allowed his demons to come out and play. They made him a tenacious and fearsome opponent. Will was in the fourth group, and the four contestants lined up waiting for the starting shot. He could see a couple of them eyeing him in his periphery, but he stayed focused on the path before him.

Bang! He sprinted the half-mile run at the beginning, charged up the climbing wall, and tackled the hand bars. So far, the course was the same as it was the first time he and Nash ran it. The rest of the challenges were new. He had to climb up a rope and traverse one of four rough suspension bridges over a mud bog. Immediately after that, he had to run and jump to grab one of the lines dangling across the other end of the same mud bog and swing back across. If he fell on either, the mud would prove he failed that skill. He took just enough time to familiarize himself with its requirements. He had no intention of walking past the spectators looking like that. That being said, he knew he had to improve his time on the final run.

He tried not to worry about the one contestant slightly ahead of him and concentrate on memorizing the course. He had an incredible memory, and on the next run, he'd attack it with everything he had. Another half-mile run led him to the open area where a net of wires was positioned about one and a half feet off the ground. A rough drawing above the entrances showed a person crawling under the wires and a lightning bolt where his butt hit the wire. It was all the instruction needed to explain the task, but it was harder than it looked.

Will had passed his opponent during the run, but he was in a hurry, and he hit the wire when he started. It burned like a brand. He heard the zaps behind him informing him every time his challenger hit it, which was several times, and he swore on the last bite it gave him. If Will wasn't so engrossed in the task, he would have laughed, but he stayed focused. By the time Will got to the other side, he had figured out a crawl that kept him free of the stinging wires.

His time was third overall for both runs, but being third wasn't his goal. The notion of not winning ramped up his fighting spirit. He was now in the final run with the top four contestants. He looked them over, searching for advantages, his and theirs. They did the same.

One was burly with biceps like an ox, but that made him slower. His name was Hulk. He was in fourth place. The guy in second was jumpy and nervous and probably fast, but he was likely to make a mistake. Will didn't catch his name, but for reference's sake, he nicknamed him Twitch. The guy with the top score was built like Will, but not as tall. He had a mean side and a determined attitude, like himself. This was the guy to beat. His name, fittingly, was Rival.

The next morning came, and Will was excited about the competition. He ate a modest bowl of oatmeal and headed to the gym to stretch out. From his practice run, he learned the course and went over his strategy in his head. In the first round, each man had his own path. Every challenge had four of everything, so there was no fighting for it. This time, fighting was part of the game. The crowd cheered when a large screen was rolled into the arena, and it was announced a drone would record and broadcast the front-runners.

When the pistol rang out, Will and his opponents took off. He and Rival were both built for speed, but the twitchy guy was fast too. Will got to the climbing wall first, but Rival was right behind him and pulled him down. He started up the wall with Will scrambling on the ground, but Twitch showed up and Will tossed him up the wall and onto Rival.

Twitch grabbed Rival's ankle and pulled him off the wall, causing them both to tumble down, allowing Will to scale the wall in time to avoid Hulk on his heels. Will quickly traversed the bars before Rival could catch up. He ran full speed and leaped onto the rope climb. Rival was on his heels, so he pulled his feet up to position them high on the rope and pushed himself up beyond Rival's grasp.

Just then, a massive tremor shook both him and Rival to the ground. Hulk started up the rope before they could get back on their feet, while Twitch sat on the ground nursing a flowing bloody nose and watering eyes. He wasn't going to challenge them much anymore. The two enemies looked at each other, and in a short second, they became a team. Throwing Hulk off the rope was not possible, any more than knocking him off the bridge, but the jump may not be his forte.

They could outrun him if they had enough distance, but the rope swing was only fifty yards away. Will signaled to Rival on the way, and they both leaped in the air, grabbing a branch from a dead tree hanging over the path. It broke easily under their assault, and they carried it over their heads down the trail. Even with the limb, they caught up to Hulk. The path led up to his side, and he was just starting his long run to leap for the rope, and with his size, he needed the distance. Will took the back position, and they both heaved it in front of Hulk as he made his run toward the rope. He successfully hopped over it but missed the rope and landed in the mud.

The partnership ended in that second, and they were enemies once more. They sparred along the edge of the pit when a loud grunt came from behind Rival. Will had seen Hulk pulling himself up the ridge, but Rival turned, and Will ran and jumped. He wasn't sure he would make it because he didn't get a long enough run to launch, but he grabbed the rope. He caught low, so he had to swing his feet way up to catch the other edge, but he did. Hulk had thrown Rival down in the ravine mud, and it was down to Will and Hulk now.

Will quickly built distance between himself and Hulk during the half-mile trek, but not by a lot. Hulk was determined. When he hit the dirt to begin the crawl, several strategies popped up in his head. If he went too fast, he might lose points for tripping the wires. He quickly decided on a new idea. While he had a head start, he began kicking the sticks that held up the wires as he went. Finally, one gave way, and he darted his leg out of the way of its sharp zing.

Hulk began his crawl and approached the fallen pole where the wires drooped in his path. He swiftly reseated the pole and crawled forward. He was pulling himself with his colossal arms and digging his feet for the additional push. Will was almost through when he felt Hulk clawing at his feet. Will used his other foot to catch the already dangling lace of his loose shoe, and it came untied. When Hulk grabbed it, the shoe was all he got.

Will sprang out of the wired tunnel and darted toward the flag, fiercely grabbing it off the pole. The crowd was around the bend, but he could hear the shouting. He was catching his breath when he saw Hulk charging him. He was still in the game, and the flag was not his to keep yet.

Hulk threw a heavy punch, and though Will ducked, it skimmed his head enough to send him to the ground. He jumped up fast and, using the technique he used on Denter; he slid past him on the ground and, leaping up, he delivered his best punch to his kidneys. It surprised him more than wounded him, but it gave Will a chance to start running.

As he sprinted one-shoed into the arena, the crowd was already on their feet and going wild. Will was drunk on the adulation. He held the flag aloft and spun around to show it off. It wasn't long before Hulk and the other contestants showed up. They quietly climbed up into the bleachers to join their packs without challenging the obvious winner.

Prefect Ender stood, and the crowd died down. He motioned to Will to approach the imperial box where he sat. He went to one knee and looked up at his leader.

"This was a most enjoyable game. The top four contestants fought well, but as in battle, only one may be victorious. Dirk, you have earned the laurel brad, a symbol of victory. I remember you, Dirk. You've come a long way from the scrawny teen who challenged the blood pact. Rise and collect your award."

A Dranger came next to him and crimped the winner's brad onto his band. Will was anxious to see it all new and not scratched like Rummie's. The small metal disk was made of bronze and had a raised relief of two fern-like branches crossing at the bottom and curled into a circle. It was highly detailed and skillfully crafted, much better quality than the roughly made stars and skulls. Will turned to the crowd, holding his armband up.

The assembly rose and cheered with claps and whistles. It was then he saw Nash vigorously joining the exaltation, and sitting by Brock, the Neighwah soldier from Stratmoor.

Will walked up the bleacher entrance, but he was met by a Neighwah sergeant who rose from his seat and blocked his path. "You need to come with me." Will knew all the soldiers from Stratmoor, but he didn't know this one.

"May I know where we're going?" Will was firm, but not disrespectful. He knew there would be a meeting to conclude his admission into the Neighwah forces, but having a stranger abduct him at the games seemed unnecessarily aggressive.

"To see your new commander."

Will quietly followed the soldier to the Great Hall. He saw the Stratmoor commander sitting with another Neighwah superior. He was silently motioned to approach the table.

"Well, congrats on the contest, Dirk." The new man held out his hand to Will.

"Thanks," Will said warily as he shook his hand.

"Sit, sit," he answered. "I'm Lieutenant Garriset, representing General Dermit from Colorado Springs, Neighwah Headquarters, and you've already met Colonel Brindle from Stratmoor."

Will shook Brindle's hand with trepidation. Something was happening here. These guys were way up the food chain, and it felt like he was on the menu. "Can I ask what's going on?" Will inquired cautiously.

"I came down to watch the contest, and I must admit, you impressed me so much that I wanted to recruit you. But then I heard you were already spoken for." Will looked at Brindle. He felt his deal was falling apart. He didn't even know if Nash was done with his treatment or well enough to be a Dranger.

"He knows all about our deal, Dirk, and he's willing to honor it." Brindle didn't sound like this was the plan he wanted either.

"What about Brash? How's his knee? Is he able to be a Dranger still?"

"Hold on there," Garriset said. "Look, I could just take you, but like Brindle, I want your full cooperation. Brash is doing okay, but he still limps a bit, and he isn't going to qualify to remain as a Dranger. I'm willing to take him home, where he will get his old job back. Maybe with the training he's had, he can even get something better. That's up to him."

"Okay, what's the catch?"

"No catch, except if you screw up or run, I'll go after him."

"Can I ride home with him?"

"That could probably be arranged, but I ain't promising that one."

"But he goes back and doesn't get put in the sit houses?"

"That I can promise, unless he does something to get himself in one."

Brindle had stayed suspiciously quiet. Will had to ask. "What about the medical treatment? Is that still paid for? I want Commander Brindle to tell me if that's allowed."

"General Dermit has paid for all of that, and he paid our precinct for the rights to you too. I'm just sorry to lose a good soldier. Now I have to find another one."

Will thought of Rival, but he would have no idea what he was getting into. He wasn't about to get him mixed up in this... whatever it was.

The three men shook hands, and Will left to find Nash. He made it to the Arrow dorm door and found Denter standing there.

"Been waitin' for you. I know you want to see Brash, but this can't wait."

Wow, Will thought, *I just keep getting waylaid. Is this all because I won?*

"I'm listening."

"Let's take a walk." He walked him toward the empty barracks, where the streets were unoccupied. "I knew about the deal with Brindle. That seemed legit, but this Dermit guy is really high up the chain. This is more than winning the race. Do you have secrets?"

"Like what?" Will barked back.

"Remember the girls General Kenner wanted? Well, the Robinhood pact moved them quietly in the night to other families in the territory. Even the one everyone thought was murdered, that was just rabbit and pheasant blood." Will thought of Dread's boasting and was glad it wasn't true.

"That general is after some guy who shot his prisoner. He was trying to get info out of her, but now he's looking to get it out of the guy who offed her. Witnesses say it was her husband. Whatever he thinks he might know, it's big. Rumor has it they had a kid, a tall, dark-skinned kid named Will. Most thought he was too young to be of interest, but it seems that has changed. Dermit wants to get the information first, and I'm betting he thinks you're that kid."

"What is the Robinhood pact? Do you belong to that?" Ideas and memories were racing through his head. The song and the blade came screaming back to his mind. Pure fear was gripping his resolve, and he tried to dial it back.

"Hell no, I don't, but I know where to leave information for them to act on. But stop avoiding the question. Do you have a secret?"

"If I did, I'd be stupid to reveal it. What do you want from me?" Will snapped back, trying to look more pissed than scared, but he couldn't keep his eyes from turning away.

"Too late. I know your tell. True, you should trust no one. But this may be even more than the mighty Dirk can manage. Just give me this sign," and Denter rolled his band around his wrist with two fingers. "If you are that kid, Dermit might know that. If you give me that sign, I'll do what I can for you. Now go that way, so we're not seen together."

Will took off not even knowing where he was heading. Just twenty minutes ago, he was a hero taking his accolades from a screaming crowd. The next thing he knew, he was being traded like property, and now he was back to the scared kid in that killing field. How quickly he could be toppled from the powerful warrior he had fought to become.

NO! he yelled in his head. *I won't be undone.* He got back on track to see his friend, the one he had risked everything to save.

Chapter Ten

Will took a slow walk back to the Arrow barracks. He went from his highest high to his worst paranoia in under twenty minutes. Denter was warning him he was in danger, and two Neighwah precincts were fighting over him. Sure, he had won some contests, and he was proud of his contributions while on their runs. He was loyal to the well-respected pack, and Denter often told him he had extraordinary potential, but this was something more.

He was only seventeen. Neighwah recruits of that age were usually gofers. These guys were paying a hefty price for him. Denter was right. They must know or think they know something about him, and he feared it centered around Tianna and General Kenner.

He was standing at the door thinking when it opened, and there stood Nash. His mood brightened instantly, and he quickly grabbed his friend in a rough embrace and gave him a harassing greeting. "Man, it's good to see you out of that bed, slacker. How are you doing? Is that knee working again?" Will had already heard the prognosis, but he didn't want to let Nash know that.

"It's just about back to normal. The doctor said it will be a slow process, but my progress has 'demonstrated a steady upward trend'." Nash spoke the last part with the pomp of his Upper doctor, and they both laughed.

Denter was striding up the walkway behind them. "Are ya' gonna stand in the doorway all night so no one else can get through?"

Nash ushered Denter and Will in and walked behind them. Will was greeted by his celebrating team with cheers and slaps on the back. He had brought honor to his pack by winning first place on the obstacle course, but it was only the first of four contests. They had the chairs positioned in a circle in the main room adjacent to the entry. Will noticed Nash had quickly found a seat before he could evaluate his injury.

"I saved you a spot in my bunk nook," Will said, sitting in a chair next to Nash. "Of course, I get the top bunk, just in case you were wondering." He punched his shoulder, and Nash shoved him back.

"Yeah, I already put my gear in there."

"Hey, let's go to the game table. I need to beat the shit out of someone in poker." Will's ulterior motive was to see Nash walk, but a couple of rounds of poker to delegate his chores to the losers sounded like a good idea.

"You're on, braggart," yelled Rummie. "I'll be happy to give you some of my menial tasks. Doing my laundry comes to mind. I don't wash my stuff so often, so it's a bit of a chore when I finally get to it."

"Come on, Brash," Will said, grabbing his friend's shirt to yank him up. "I need a witness."

Nash reluctantly stood and gave his best interpretation of a perfect gait, but Will could tell he was still dealing with pain and stiffness. No way he should run the course. No way he'd qualify. He was scheduled to make up the obstacle course run two days from now. That and the shooting range were mandatory for qualifying.

The arena fights and the paintball games were done by representatives from the packs, and no one would nominate him for those. It would damage the pack's reputation. Nash would do fine on the target range, but the obstacle course would most certainly reinjure his knee. He was doing quite well for only a month and a half of healing a gunshot wound to the knee. If he could go home, he'd heal up the rest of the way, and get a job instead of a death sentence. Well, that's if the Daily community didn't see him as a Dranger.

Will lost the poker game, getting stuck with Rummie's stinky laundry, but maybe it would give him a chance to talk to Nash alone. Tomorrow was the arena fights, and Will opted out against many loud objections.

"Hey, don't you losers want to win something? Do I have to do it all? Besides, we agreed we would all have a chance to be in a rep contest. If I do this, I'm out of the paintball. And I want paintball bad."

It was considered bad form to send one person to win everything. It meant that the rest of your team was worthless. The teams started with two members, and Slice and Lynch were elected. Both were good in a scrap, and they had a decent shot unless Hulk or Rival were fighting. He had a feeling Hulk would be on the docket because being a brute was his talent, but he hoped to see Rival on the paintball field.

Eight contestants entered the arena fights. Four fights would wind down to two and then one for the final being held tomorrow. The other contestants were unfamiliar, but Will recognized Hulk from the Snakes pack. Rummie lost his first fight, but it was with Hulk. Lynch won his fight with the Claw member, and the final fight would be tomorrow between him and Hulk. Will had mixed feelings about what it would be like to fight him hand-to-hand. Though these fights were not as ruthless as a pack challenge, being in even one would be brutal for sure. If he won, he would be seen as a total badass, but the pain would linger for days. Will met with Lynch and gave him his best tips.

After the initial fights, Nash and Will saw Taggart at the Great Hall, so they stopped and sat with him. Both shared their tales of the year and listened to some of his. Taggart asked Nash to speak with Will alone, and Nash walked over to the Arrow table. Taggart spoke of a prisoner who was pretty beaten up.

"Well, 'e were unconscious most o' the time, beat real bad by someone. 'E told me ever'one was lookin' for a man who 'ad the secret to a place of great power. 'E said the man they wanted was a man 'ou kilt his own wife. Her departed dad knew 'bout the place, and they was thinkin' 'e mighta known and told 'er about it. One night jus' before the poor guy took 'is last one, he says to me 'The knife's the key. Then 'e jus died. I never told the Prefect. I figured it would jus' lead to me own torture for stuff I don't know. 'E were probably crazy as a loon after they worked 'em over. 'Is head weren't right. Weird, it was. I jus' had to tell someone, an I trust you."

Will sat frozen on the bench. "Probably screwed up his head with their beatings. Stupid way to get info anyway because a guy will say anything. Better to gain his trust. I feel sorry for anyone involved if it's true. 'Place of power' whoo-oo," Will said and twisted his hands back and forth with sarcasm, "sounds like the superstitious stuff the mean Dailys make up." Will took a breath and brought his story home. "Yeah, when we were in Cimarron Hills, some superstitious Dailys killed a baby because it had a birthmark they said looked like a comet."

Taggert shook his head at the wretched act. "Ah well, shame upon them to kill a wee babe. Shame be upon them for sure."

"Don't worry, Tag, I won't tell a soul. It could go badly for both of us if they think we know more." Will was getting more and more nervous about his Neighwah choice, if it ever was a choice. *What could they know? Why were people choosing to confide in him?* He was totally in the dark about the point of it all. They could torture the life out of him, but he had no answers. All he had was that stupid song and the Sanguine Blade. He hoped it was still safe. He had no way of knowing, and checking now seemed reckless.

Winning contests earned packs more food, more credits, and a better shot at choosing the best graduates or transfers. Every pack was allowed a leader and seven to eight members, depending on the number of Drangers on the block. Packs were allotted a token for each member they needed to fill the missing slots. They put their tokens in the buckets for the newbies they wanted most. Whenever the team won a contest, they got an extra token for each new required member to improve their odds. The most popular buckets would get the fullest, and they would be pulled first. The

Arrows needed three newbies. In one annual, Denter lost Jet, Dirk, and Nash.

The next day, Lynch met Hulk in the arena. As expected, Hulk won, but Lynch gave him a good run. Denter commented on the dash-around technique that reminded him of someone.

"Well, it might not win the game, but it won me something. I'm not dead at the front lines, and I think it got Lynch some serious respect. I doubt anyone will want to fight him."

"Yeah, well, that might feel better after his bruises heal."

Will wanted to add that at least Hulk wasn't allowed to pummel him while he was unconscious, but it seemed too far over the line, so he just smiled.

The target range was also very competitive, but not being a contact sport, it was much calmer. Silence by spectators wasn't enforced so much as interest in the results of each round created a quieter audience. Each member had to qualify on two weapons. The choices included the pistol, the rifle, the bow, and the slingshot. Will didn't like the slingshot, since on runs they used poisoned spike-balls. It was used only on people they wanted to take alive to torture, so he never had the desire to master it. But he was a genius with the bow and quite excellent with a rifle too.

Nash chose the slingshot and the bow. Only six contestants chose the slingshot, and he felt good about his chances. When the contest concluded, Nash got fifth on the bow out of eight and second on the slingshot. His scores were not bad since he had not been able to practice much during his rehab. Will made first on the bow and fourth out of thirteen on the rifle. With Rad getting first on the pistol, that gave the Arrows two more sets of tokens.

The team paintball game was set for the morning after next. A day was given for the work assignments and other management issues. The Arrows were tasked with cleaning the Great Hall from top to bottom, including the kitchen. Denter assigned everyone to start with the kitchen, and when

Lynch warned the cooking crew not to get too messy with lunch, they complied, remembering his tenacity and fighting abilities in the ring. They finished up quickly after lunch. The paintball team went to the range to practice with the slingshots they would be using tomorrow in the contest. After dinner, they had several hours to themselves.

Will took his time to walk in the uninhabited areas of the compound. He had to think on his own. He wanted desperately to believe that it was all just hearsay, but too many details were lining up. The plan taking shape in his head involved making it look like they had his complete cooperation. But he drew the line at the blade and the song. He also knew he needed to take Denter's offer and give him the two-finger sign to seal it.

The paintball rules were discussed in the Great Hall to all, but especially for the twenty contestants. The first officer under Prefect Ender put up a series of diagrams to explain the rules to the mostly illiterate group.

We play with slingshots. We don't have paintball guns like the Neigh-wah.

Your equipment includes a helmet and a vest in your team's color, one slingshot, and twenty paintballs in a pouch with a belt.

Rules:

Kill shots include the torso and the head. They're worth five points.

If you are shot in these areas, you will show your surrender by walking to your starting point with hands raised

Anyone caught shooting a surrendering opponent or confiscating ammo will be eliminated

Receiving shots to limbs doesn't count, but can get you eliminated at break if you have a lot.

There will be four, five-minute rounds with three breaks to separate them. When the break horn sounds, you must freeze.

Points will be tallied each break by drones that can detect where you've been hit and by who.

Kill shots are worth five points for the shooter and his team.

Friendly fire hits and hits on surrendered players are minus three points for the shooter and team.

At least four members will be eliminated each round. If less than four have surrendered, eliminations will be decided by the number of hits received, the amount of ammo left in the pouch, drone footage evaluation, or a combination of the above.

The remaining opponents will receive five more balls after the second break.

The first horn signals to get ready, and the second starts the game.

The member winner is the last one unless they have less than three kill shots, then the player with the most kill shots wins.

The winning team is the one with the most team points.

A token will be awarded for each of these wins.

"Each team has a starting area at opposing sides of the course. Your team will be led there, and the games will begin and stop at the sound of the horn. Here is your map, which designates your starting area. You will now be given a map of the course and twenty minutes to choose a leader and plan your strategy."

The maps were handed out, along with their blue gear. The Arrows were led to their area to plan. They looked over the map and the battle area where the four teams of five would battle for the title. It was a black and white drawing of a fourteen-acre square area with rounded corners. The letters from the familiar compass they all had been taught were marked on the border of each side. The Arrows would start on the W, the Snakes on the N, the Claws E, and the Comets on the S.

Two hills dominated the center, one larger than the other, and both were strewn with large rocks and tall grasses. On either side of the mounds were small ponds, and running between them and across the course was a creek. There were several large boulders, six small treed areas, and two small ponds. Cover could also be found behind dilapidated man-made objects including a brick building, a truck, and a collapsed wooden stable. These all provided excellent cover if one could get to them. But they were obvious hiding spots, and hiding was not the point of the game.

The first order of business was to choose a leader. Donner was their second in command, and they unanimously agreed he should lead. Looking at the team, Will was optimistic about their chances. Nash may not move quickly, but he was a hell of a shot with a sling, so he would make a stand that didn't require much movement. They put on their gear and their blue helmets as they discussed their plan.

"Splitting up would cover the most ground, but hanging in pairs allows us to have more eyes and communication to ambush our opponents. So, the pairs are Dirk and Rad, and me and Rummie. Dirk and Rad, you move up the big hill on the east side. Move from rock to rock and military crawl through the grasses."

"Yes, sir," both responded while studying the topographic map.

"Nash, you will cover this area here, and you will travel with Rad and Dirk through this wooded area, then split off toward your assignment," he said, pointing to the truck between their start and the northern entrance where the Snakes started.

"Yes sir," Nash answered.

"Rummie, you and I will go through the ravine toward the building ruins."

"Got it," he said.

"Take your time to get a good shot. The goal is to move around enough to get hits and stay in the game, especially for the first round. For the rest of the rounds, you're on your own. I don't know if we get any regroup time during any of the breaks, but I'm not counting on it. Don't use whistles or other sounds we use with non-combatants. These are all savvy soldiers. It will only alert your opponents to your position, but by all means, use rocks to rustle them out and hone your slingshot abilities. Use hand signals to communicate with your partner only."

Will studied the map and the plan. "Looks like we're focusing on the northern and western teams first. How or when do we engage the south team?"

"There's a lot of open ground between them and us. That should slow them down a little. I expect they'll make a run for this bolder on their northeast and this small hill on their northwest. By all means, watch your six, but if possible, get in position before you engage."

The team nodded.

"How will we know who's left?" asked Nash.

"Well, like real combat situations, we won't." Donner's answer conveyed a grim revelation of the game's true purpose. "Besides, if we were to get word about our team, they might too. Sometimes, if there are too many left at mid-break, they'll pull all the survivors and restart them in a different location to keep the game exciting for the audience. If they do that, we'll have a few minutes to re-strategize."

A signal horn called for the teams to be ready to start. The Snakes were in red helmets, and the Claws were in orange. Will could see Rival wearing the green Comet colors. Rad whispered to Nash, and through their tinted visors they glanced sideways to see Rival looking straight at Will. Both Will and Rival were smiling. Rematch time.

They followed the path and were led inside their gate and shut inside. There were three courses in total, and they use a different one each year. The whole course was behind a chain-link fence, and going out of bounds was not an option, whether as a strategy or an error. They each whispered their assignment and got positioned to run.

"Woooo" went the ready horn, followed by the go horn. They shot in different directions. Will, Rad, and Nash swiftly made it to the wooded area, and right next to it was the truck. Nash crawled under the truck, where he had a good view and a fallen door to cover his back. Will and Rad headed up the hill double-timing, panting for breath, and ducking between rocks and below the grass for cover.

They were near the top when Will saw the red splat hit the bare dirt beside Rad. Quickly, they tucked behind a large speckled rock with grey and black crystals. More splats hit the rock they hid behind. Their position was not a secret. Will motioned that he was going to move up the hill. Rad nodded and put two balls in his sling knowing he wouldn't hit a target, but it would cause the enemy to believe they were both shooting from the same place. Will leaped to the next area of cover and made his way to the other side of the hill. He was about to crawl above them when the first horn blew signaling the first game break nu.

He froze flat on the grass. It seemed like a long time, but it was under a minute before a drone flew by, and then the horn blew again. *Game on,* he thought with glee. He slowly and silently made his way over to the opposing players. He could only see one, but he took his shot. Blue paint exploded on his foe's helmet.

He heard a cuss word, and the player stood with his hands up. Will rolled down the hill and quickly found cover behind a shrubby bush. He heard the player coming over the hill, and he shot a rock hoping he would follow the noise. As he came into view, *SNAP*! Will nailed him in the back. He too raised his hands and walked northward to his gate.

Will headed down to where he had left Rad in time to see him halfway down the hill with his hands up. Will started back up the hill to see who else he could find, but before he got to the top, the second horn blew, followed by an announcement for all players to go back to their starting gates.

Waiting for them were Rad and Rummie, both eliminated. Rummie took a headshot from the Comets near the pond before he got to the ravine, so only Nash, Donner, and Will were left. The teams were switching sections to keep the game interesting. The Arrows were now northeast; the Snakes were in the southeast; the Claws in the southwest, and Rival's team went northwest. They had no idea how many players were left on the other teams.

"Okay," Donner said, "we got five minutes. Listen up. Brash and Dirk, head to the closest group of trees and then to this one. Dirk, break off and head up the east side of the hill. Brash find a good spot that will give you a shot at the brick building here," and he pointed to the map. "Someone will hide there, no doubt."

"Will do, boss."

"I'm charging the grass to the trees here. I'm betting they'll use the same cover we did on the west side. Then I'll make my way up the hill for a good vantage point. He paused. "This whole area is new to us, so be vigilant."

The horn blew, and the team got into a ready position to wait for the second one. "Whooo" And they were off. The first section was through open grass, but every team had that landscape to begin with. Will took off and looked behind him where Nash was limping significantly, and Will grabbed him under the arm.

"I'm fine. Keep going." Will ignored his retort, ripped off one of his long sleeves, and wrapped Nash's knee to give it more support. He accompanied him to the next group of trees instead of heading up the hill. The two treed areas were close, and they easily made it.

"Can you get up that tree? There's a nice sitting limb with lots of foliage to hide behind."

"No prob. Now go."

Will ran through the trees that edged up the hill. It was a well-covered path to his goal. When he reached the last tree, he edged his way to the bolder on his originally assigned path. Peeking over the large mountain of a rock, he saw Donner was pinned by Rival. He tried to maneuver around to flank Rival, but suddenly a shot winged his bare arm.

It stung like crazy. His eyes watered, and he stifled the screech building as the pain increased. He looked down to see green paint dripping down his arm, mingling with red blood. He fell back behind the hill and regained his resolve. He pressed the pain down easily and moved to find better cover.

"Whooo." The horn blew, and he froze. Again, the drone flew over him and flew on. He was organizing his thoughts and making his plan. When the horn blew again, he noticed his trail of small red and green drips. Grabbing his neck bandana, he wrapped it around his arm, tying it with his other hand and teeth. He fell back onto the bolder and found his nook. He could hear Rival trailing him, so the rematch was imminent.

He saw quick movement dash behind a large rock. Will shot but missed his target, and he shouted to his opponent.

"So here we are. We know each other's positions. Come out and I'll shoot your helmet, not your soft spots."

"You're funny. I like that. Saw the blood trail. Bet that hurt. How about *you* come out, and I won't make you bleed more?" Rival could hear Will's chuckle.

"It's just a dribble, but it makes me meaner."

"I took out your partner," Rival boasted.

"Yeah, but I'm still here."

"That makes two of us."

"Are we going to throw words or paint?"

Both adversaries took a couple of shots without reward. Will rolled to another side of his bolder to get a better view. As he did, Rival moved too. Will tried to taunt him to get a bead on his position, but no response. Just as he moved to get better a view, he felt the bump on his helmet and saw Rival standing on top of a rock outcropping at the top of the hill. *Shit!* he thought, but he also smiled. Rival was a worthy opponent.

An announcement came over the intercom. "The game is over. We have a winner. All players, please proceed to the nearest gate." Will was heading for the east gate when Rival caught up with him.

"That was fun, Dirk," Rival said.

"That last move was brilliant. You earned the win," Will conceded.

"True that, but it could have gone differently. So, what the hell happened to your sleeve, anyway?"

"Long story," answered Will.

"Aren't they all?"

They both laughed as they approached the gate and split off to meet up with their teams.

Chapter Eleven

The final ceremony awarded champion brads to Rival for winning the combat game and the five competing Arrows for their team getting the most kill shots. Star brads were presented to all pack members for completing their annual tours, and some, including Will, received skulls. Will looked down at his band. He had two champion brads, one skull, and two stars. It was impressive for a first-year Dranger. He wasn't proud of killing and beating people, but a Dranger's job wasn't all about cruelty. Drangers did their part to keep order, and order saved lives too. He chuckled to himself at the irony of his new perspective.

In this realm of brothers, the brads signified rank, strength, and accomplishments. A man got them without political interference because his brothers witnessed his kills, contest wins, and years in service. The Neighwah were recognized by their appointed rank only. There were no awards or achievements displayed on their uniforms to tell the story of their advancements.

Will looked at his band woefully. He didn't want to leave this world, not really. It was familiar, and he was respected and successful here. He had re-identified himself as Dirk, not Will, not Noland, and not Alexander. His secrets didn't live here. He was a warrior who was well-received and celebrated. Everything he worked so hard to earn wouldn't matter in two days when he left for the Neighwah command. Will thought of his new supervisor. He doubted he was someone like Denter, whom he respected and trusted. Racing back to the forefront of his mind was the critical question. *What do they* know or *think they know?*

"Dirk!" Nash said as he came up behind him. It reminded him of another discussion Will had to have and soon.

"What's up?"

"We're going home! That's what they told me. I can't qualify, and your term was to end when mine did. That was the deal. I got good medical because we solved that big smuggling ring, and I'm old enough that I don't have to live with my dad. My luck is finally turning around, and it's totally rack that it helps you too. Who knew getting shot would be so lucky for us?" Nash was almost bouncing.

Will had time to give his friend the news of his leaving since he was told he could accompany Nash home and see his family. He could tell him the news away from this camp and the people in it.

Will worked up a convincing happy face for Nash, and they headed toward the barracks to break the news to the pack. Tomorrow was choosing day, and the next day, they would head home. Will assumed Nash was worried about his knee holding up for the long walk home, but Will knew they would get a ride. The Neighwah general wasn't going to let his new prize out of his sight. Will thought back to his anxiety when he entered this camp. How odd that he was right back in the same predicament. He pondered his future, and it looked bleaker than ever.

When they made their announcement, mixed replies and gibes filled the room. Denter looked at Nash's pure joy and figured out that Will hadn't explained the deal to him. They exchanged glances across the room, and both left it at that. All those with a winning brad were awarded bigger helpings at dinner and got to be the first group, after the leaders, in line. Those who had two, like Will, would get the same privilege tomorrow. Will intended to thoroughly enjoy this most treasured reward. He wasn't starving, but he was always hungry.

Will went to dinner, and he saw Rival in line with two people between them. He liked this guy. Nash was his dearest and oldest friend, but Rival challenged him, and Will liked that. He wished there were a way to hang out with him, but it was impossible. Denter would tan his hide for befriending someone from a competing pack. Even his name said off limits. They were going in different directions on very different teams.

The two weeks they had spent here were some of the best of his life. The workload was light, and the games were better than fun. It was all so unfair. He felt alive and settled, and for the first time in his young adult life, he belonged. He traced the new carvings by his name, feeling the marks of his achievements. Unfortunately, it was all coming to an end like it always did. He suddenly felt very alone even though he was surrounded by his pack brothers at their table. He'd miss working for a man he held in high regard, but he pushed his melancholy aside. He didn't want to feel that, not yet anyway.

The next morning at the barracks, Will began to feel twinges of danger all through the disturbing web of lies and secrets he had constructed over the years. Lies to Nash, lies to Taylor, lies to Denter, the secrets he kept from everyone, and even more perilous were the secrets kept from him. He couldn't share what he knew, and couldn't get to the secrets he needed to be the holder of the *key*. Which he hoped was still buried out in a jar in the woods. A single lie was hard enough to keep, but he had so many that he was caught in his own web.

He was alone and vulnerable, not knowing whom he could trust. He desperately needed an ally despite the risks. He had no idea how Denter and his Robin Hood band might be of help, but he respected him and he believed he was honorable. He made eye contact with Denter as Lynch and Brash yelled breakfast was ready. On their way to the kitchen, Will gave Denter the signal they had agreed upon, and he gave a subtle nod in return. Surreal was his only word for it. His life was just changed by a twist of his band. Whatever it meant, it was done.

They got a ride home in a Neighwah troop van accompanied by three Neighwah soldiers. The explanation for the ride was to deliver protein powder to this section, and they did have several boxes to drop off. But it wasn't the reason the soldiers were there.

Nash was so relieved to be going home, he was oblivious of the company. They both had all of their belongings stuffed in the empty seats in front of them. Nash had stayed up most of the night and fell asleep quickly as the sun beat through the window. The drive should have been a short one, but the van moved slowly on the broken road, extending the time. Will was mesmerized as he watched the world go by his window. He stared without really seeing the scenery, but his cluttered mind was set in motion by the easy task of riding.

He wondered if this ride provided the right time to let Nash know he was leaving for Neighwah headquarters. There was no good way to say goodbye to him or to everyone else. He knew he was loved, and he knew it would hurt them. They would never understand, and some would hate him since he planned to say he wanted to go. He didn't want Nash to ever find out he had made that deal to save him from a short life as a cripple at the sit-houses. He didn't want Nash to feel responsible for the decision he made willingly. But he would be lying to himself as well if he didn't acknowledge the dreadful possibilities he faced.

He settled on the idea that he would tell Nash and Calen together when they visited GZ. GZ, that was another thing he was curious about. *Was their secret place still there? Had it been discovered? Did Calen still go there? Should he even go with the Neighwah tailing him?* Everything was so complicated now, and there was no relief in sight.

He was momentarily rocked from his introspection when he spotted the rock marking the stashed knife. He quickly returned to his contemplative state as the last words of the beaten prisoner rang in his head. *"The blade's the key."* He felt his chest tighten at the thought of Calen accidentally letting it out. He told them not to tell anyone, but he had no idea how important it was then. Frankly, he still didn't.

He set his focus on being happy to return home, and he was. The closer they got to seeing Taylor, Peirce, Calen, Jonah, and so many more people, his spirits rose, but not enough. He would have to put on a good show of happiness. Happiness at seeing them would be easy; explaining his decision, not so much.

Taylor was the first to greet them, and he grabbed Will into his arms. Nash's mom, Francine, was holding a baby girl, and she looked happier and healthier than the last time he saw her. Davy, Nash's little brother, was taller than he remembered, but his dad was missing from the crowd. Hugs and excited greetings rang through the group.

"Whose place is this?" Will asked.

"It's ours," Taylor said, tucking Francine into a side hug. "Some things have changed since you left."

"Ya think!" Nash said with a bit of bewilderment.

"Let's go in, and I'll explain," his mom said.

Due to the new housing arrangement, no one noticed that Will didn't grab his gear. They all walked into the house, which looked like every Daily house, tired and worn down. But in the nooks and crannies, Will could see loving attempts to make it a home. Cans of living wildflowers were nestled on several windowsills accompanied by hand-carved figurines. Patchwork rag rugs decorated the entrance and the kitchen, making the house look well-loved despite the decay.

Will was busy talking to Pierce, so Francine handed the baby to Taylor and pulled her son down the hall. "Your dad is dead, honey. He was just sick about trading you away, and he overdosed on some work chems. Before he died, he wanted me to tell you how sorry he was. It was only because of the baby that he turned into that monster. I hope you can forgive him."

"I know, Mom. I'll try, but you have no idea what it was like. The training was brutal, and some of the jobs were ruthless. You have no idea the beating Will went through to join my pack and help me. He saved me, Mom." Nash looked away to compose himself. "But I remember how Dad was before. I know he took the bad job for Clare, and that was a noble thing. But then he sold me for tox, and he left you in a bad way." Nash swallowed hard, took a breath, and let it out through pursed lips. His facial expression demonstrated his conflicted feelings without any attempt to hide them.

Francine recalled the hurt of that decision too. "I know, I know. But you're home now, and I can't be happier."

"So how did you end up here?" Nash asked.

"Well, after he died, I was on my own with your little brother and a month away from your sister being born. I had to leave your seven-year-old brother alone every night, then I was put on the marriage list, and they said because of my kids, I needed to fast-track my decision. I had one month to hook up, or they'd take my baby. Taylor found out and started watching Davy at night. When he was told he was going to lose his apartment and be sent to the worker dorms. We decided to enter into an arranged marriage. And with a family of four, we got a house.

"I'm sorry, Mom. I should have been here."

"Not your fault. We both know that. I didn't expect much from Taylor. I didn't even know him, but he has been so kind and so good to us. He helped bring little Clare into the world. I don't know what I would have done without his help. It happened slowly, but we fell in love. And now, Nash, I'm so happy."

"I see that, Mom, and I'm glad."

"I hope you can accept Taylor, Pierce, and Will into our family."

"Mom, Will, and I are brothers already. I don't know Pierce except through Will, but he seems like a good man, and so does Taylor. I can see he makes you happy, and I'm glad he was here for you. I will, however, have to get used to him kissing my mom. And now we need to rejoin the group, and I need to meet my little sister."

"Yeah, and I need to get some sleep before work. I work nights now. You and Will can bunk in Davy's room. We'll put him with Clare. Taylor can help you guys secure jobs and get you in the dorms."

They hugged again and went down the hall. Francine said her goodbyes and headed back down to her room to sleep.

Taylor walked with her. "How did that go?" he said when they went through their bedroom door.

"He understands. He's not angry. He said he was glad you were here to help. But what we have slowly grown into over a year, he's had ten minutes to adjust to. Give him time. He'll be fine." She smiled and added, "He said he and Will were already brothers. How about Will?"

"I don't think it's the same as finding out his dad died and his mom fell in love and got married. He's a great kid, and I love him to death, but we're not related. He was just about raised when I took him in." Taylor smiled and kissed her forehead and stepped toward the door. Turning, he said, "Get some sleep, babe. If you can. We'll try to keep it down."

Calen, Nash, and Will were in the backyard, sitting on log stumps covered with old carpet pieces. To Will's relief, Calen gave the sign for GZ and smiled, meaning it was still good. He hoped nothing had been said about the knife. He didn't know if he was bugged or the place was. It wouldn't be hard to do if they were close enough to pick it up. He had told Nash long ago that he had lost the knife to thieves on the way to Fountain. He said it was a relief to be rid of it because it would cause him nothing but trouble.

They went inside to get with the friends and family that had taken the time to welcome them home. Will threw out a couple of smiles, backslaps, and hugs before he made his way to the front door. He sat down on the stoop when Nash and Calen came through the door and sat with him. They would have asked Will what was going on, but Taylor came through the door right after them.

"So, what do the two of you think about everything that's happened here? It's a lot to absorb."

Nash was the first to speak. "Well, Taylor, can I call you that?"

"Yeah, that works for me."

"I want to thank you for taking care of my mom. She looks healthy and happy. I spent many a sleepless night wondering how she and my brother were doing. I think I'll grow into the rest, but it's weird. It's just really weird."

"I like that answer. It's honest. You've grown into a man, Nash. I look forward to getting to know you all over again. But hey, can you guys let me talk with Will alone for a bit?"

"Yeah, we've hogged him. It's your turn. Come on, Calen."

Will looked right through the house across the street where his eyes were fixated. He had a hard time looking Taylor in the face. He had a whole new lie to tell him, and he wasn't sure he had the stomach to hurt him again. He had done so much for him, and all he got in return was pain and trouble. He didn't even know if he was doing the right thing anymore. Everything was so messed up. Every time he tried to fix it, things got worse, and he was caught in a hell-bound current of good intentions. He felt the swell in his throat, and if he tried the speak, the dam might burst.

Taylor pulled Will into a side embrace, and he broke down like a child. "My dear son, you are a man with the world on your shoulders. I can only hope you have come to trust me enough to let me help you."

"I want to, but you have no idea," Will sobbed out.

"Does it have anything to do with the fact that you didn't grab your gear out of the van, or that the Neighwah soldiers who brought you here are still parked down the street?"

"Shit! Shit!" Will instinctively froze and carefully glanced down the street. "I'm usually more aware. I didn't even notice." His sobbing was momentarily replaced by panic.

"It's normal to let your guard down when you come home. It's a place of being protected, not protecting. It's why you could be so rebellious."

Will held his head, shaking it from side to side. Taylor was right. He had let his guard down because he trusted Taylor to have his back, but it was Will's turn to have his. He should have known what he was up against. "I need to protect the people I care about. I joined the Neighwah force to," he was sniffling and gulping back sobs, "to save Nash. He got hurt, badly hurt, and they said if I joined of my own free will, they'd give him Upper hospital care."

"I wouldn't exactly call that willingly. They blackmailed you. It's what they always do. They need you for something."

"That's the crazy part. I know nothing. I have nothing. What could I possibly give them?" Will knew they were listening, and they probably knew he knew. But most of what he said was true.

"You have been with me too long for me to believe you will give them a secret they would benefit from. Kids slip up, and you never did, not even a little." Will noticed he was talking in a normal voice, so the men in the van could hear clearly. "These guys are like vicious dogs. They get excited when they think they have tasty prey in their jaws, even when it's an old shoe. They lock on and don't let go until they're bored, or they set sight of the next shiny thing. Make sure you still have value when they get bored with you. When do you leave?"

"Tonight, around 6:00," he was still sniffling and teary-eyed, but the intensity was easing. "I think this whole thing is going to go badly no matter what I do. Apparently, they know who I am, which is funny as hell because I don't," Will hissed out a cynical snicker. "I wanted to talk with Calen and Nash about leaving in private. I have to lie and say I wanted to, so promise you won't tell them. I don't want Nash to do something stupid—like I did."

"Yeah, no kidding. Don't worry, the last thing I would do is tell them and risk that again." Taylor let out a weary sigh. "Maybe these people have access to info that may help you find one of your family members. When you feel up to it, come back in. People will be leaving in about twenty minutes , so don't take too long. We'll let Calen spend the night here, and I won't tell them about your deal. But I will find a way for you guys to talk in private." Then he leaned over and whispered, "Not at GZ."

Will turned with a look of exasperation while new fears bloomed in his already crowded brain.

"Chill," he said while sneaking a peek at the van. He stood, and so did Will. The men hugged, and Taylor whispered, "I knew. You were young, and I may have followed you. I mean, what did you think, Will, that I'd let you wander out of my sight when killers and thieves are everywhere? And besides, you guys threw out clues like I wasn't listening or too stupid to figure it out."

"How can I ever repay you? You've been so good to me, and I've given you nothing but grief."

"That's what teenagers do, and that's without having a past like yours. And there is something you can do, but let's save that for later. We have more to say, but we need to get off this porch." Taylor stood up, and Will did too. "If you need a moment ..."

"I'm good, Taylor, thanks." Will felt a sense of relief. He knew it was temporary, but being honest with Taylor gave him the release he needed. It didn't matter whether he could do anything or not. It was nice to tell someone and trust someone after so many had let him down. Now, no matter what happened, someone knew, and he wasn't alone.

He felt a glimmer of hope grow inside him because Taylor understood. He had no idea what the Neighwah or Denter had planned or what their motives were, but he knew Taylor would think of him, remember him, and honor him because he cared about him. He only hoped he hadn't snared him into his conundrum.

Will, Calen, and Nash sat in the small shed behind the house. When Will told them he had joined the Neighwah, they were stunned.

"Why the hell did ya' do that?" Calen demanded.

"Were you forced?" Nash asked with a suspicious look.

"It's the only way I can find my dad." He thanked Taylor for his suggestion of a sound explanation for such an outlandish choice.

"Well, I guess I can see that. I haven't heard one peep about finding your dad this whole year. I didn't know it still was a thing." Nash looked like the lie had worked, and to be truthful, the goal was settling into Will's sights too. These people have their agendas, so why shouldn't he have one too? Like the analyzing planner he was, his chaos began to coalesce into a strategy.

Chapter Twelve

The goodbyes were tense, killing the earlier mood of the joyful reunion. Will gave a round of hugs to his family and friends. Taylor grabbed this son he loved, this young man with a burden beyond his knowledge, and hugged him tight. When the embrace ended, he held him at arm's length, looking into his eyes that were drained of the fire and fight he needed.

"Will," Taylor spoke firmly and quietly so no one could hear. "You are a warrior entering the next battle. This is not the time to feel sad, worried, or tired. Find your power and use your head. Fight well, my son, and come home. Don't you dare lose yourself in their world out there or the one you keep in your head. Focus, stay the course, and come back to us."

Will returned his gaze, trying to tap into the inferno that blazed inside him, the one that would show Taylor he hadn't given up. They each gave a nod of unspoken understanding that said more than their words could. It felt like the moment he signaled Denter. It gave him hope that he wasn't lost at sea by himself. No matter where he was, people were watching out for him and over him. They crossed thumbs in a soulful handshake before reluctantly letting go.

Will sat in the front seat next to the driver as he rode away from the only place he wanted to be. It was some time down the road before he tuned back into his surroundings. The two Neighwah soldiers in the back were talking about their girlfriends while the driver drove the rutted road. His thinking was that he could befriend this soldier to adjust to his new life, but there was so much on his mind. He wasn't sure how to clear his head enough to be good company, but he had a ton of questions, and maybe the answers would ease his emotional suffering.

"So how big is this unit I'm joining?" he finally asked.

"There are about thirty of us soldiers there permanently, but we're not all in the barracks. Some have families, and they live in houses. But lots of soldiers from all over the Colorado Springs territory come there for training, and they stay at the barracks. I've seen as many as two hundred billeted there."

"Really? Wow. So this Headquarters covers the training for all the Neighwah in CS?"

"Mostly. Some survival drills are done in the wilder places, but only special forces take those courses. You're gonna like being a Neighwah a lot better than being a Dranger. Things are different when you don't move around all year," and he showed Will his Dranger tattoo. "Decided what name you're going to use? Noland or Will? Or maybe you want to use Dirk. Most people use first names for friends and last names for everyone else. You should decide before we get there."

"Either one works for me. What's yours."

"Garler," the soldier answered. Will assumed it was his last name. It was a message of how this man rolled and where he stood.

The silence took over for a while until it felt too awkward.

"Look, Noland," he used Will's adopted last name," I know how hard it is to leave home. If you need quiet time, I'm okay with it, but you should know that you can get passes to visit home sometimes."

"Wow, you're right. I think being a Neighwah is going to be a lot better." *If they don't have an evil agenda for me, and what they think I know,* he added in his head. "Thanks for the option, but I think I need to get out of my head for a bit." Will decided to get to the question that he most needed to know. "What jobs do HQ Neighwahs do if they don't manage a town?"

"We have run-about jobs and stuff that needs clearances for newbies, but we also coordinate a lot of investigations. We work at exposing the bigger crimes and rebel militias." And there it was; his fears confirmed. They needed him close to find out what he knew about Tianna's secret and the whereabouts of his father. But he knew nothing about anything but the blade, and the extent of that knowledge was its location.

"I love that kind of work. I'm feeling better and better about this whole thing." Nothing could be further from the truth, but lying was going to be his new normal. He better become extremely proficient at looking credible and totally on board with their goals. Maybe if he was lucky, they were going after his dad, and he would have a chance to find him first.

Garler continued their small talk about training and the gear he would be issued. Before he knew it they had pulled up to the gate of a fenced compound. A freshly painted sign hung above the entrance saying Falcon Field. Everything about this place looked much more professional than the Fountain camp. The small building parked between the ingoing and outgoing roads had two guards standing inside. One of them came out to meet the van, and he called Garler, Gary. They exchanged the paperwork through the window and had a relaxed conversation, as friends would.

The guard went inside, and the gate in front rolled out of the way. The buildings and roads inside were in good repair, and lights lit up the grounds. Will had never seen so much electricity being utilized at once. He had heard that HQ Neighwah soldiers lived like Uppers, but he thought it was just a sales pitch. Looking around, he couldn't help but be impressed. He hoped he had a chance to live like an Upper before he became a prisoner.

"Nice neighborhood, hah?" Garler was smiling and proud of his home.

"Yeah, I'd say. What do the barracks look like?"

"Well, you're a new cadet, so you'll share a room. The beds and the furniture are clean and in good condition. The rooms are big with closets and desks, *and* they're kept warm in the winter and cool in the summer."

Garler emphasized the 'and' because he knew the plight of sleepless nights caused by miserable temperatures.

They pulled up to a lengthy, six-story building with a copious number of windows. Bright electric light poured through the open curtains, where silhouettes moved about. The bottom floor was a parking garage. Very few vehicles were parked there, and all of them had Neighwah emblems. They parked near the door in a reserved spot, and Will got out and grabbed his gear. Everything he owned still fit in that infamous pack from so many years ago.

Inside the door was a modest office area, and they walked up to the check-in counter. Garler handed papers to the woman in a Neighwah uniform sitting behind the desk. Will tried not to look shocked that a woman could join the Neighwah. She handed Garler a keycard attached to a cord, saying the room was on the fourth floor.

As they walked past the counter to a door on the right, he whispered to Will. "Don't react to anything you see in here. I'll explain it to you once you're settled in your room." Will gave him a curious look, but truth be told, he already had a question about the presence of a woman.

Will was led to a door that slid into the wall, leading to an empty and ridiculously small space. Will stepped inside, but he put his gear on the floor just in case he had to defend himself. Suddenly, he felt the floor move under his feet, and he grabbed for the rail. He heard Garler chuckle, and within seconds, the door opened again to a different room.

It was a large space where men and women were playing games. Will's attention was drawn to a massive table lined with green material, edged with pockets, and scattered with colorful balls. Players wandered around it, trying to hit the balls into the pockets with long sticks. There were several tables where casually dressed men and women sat, played games, or just talked. A large screen was parked against the wall, and two men held units that manipulated the video. Four other people were hitting a small white ball across a long green table divided by a short net.

Several rows of chairs faced a screen in a room with windows, but the curtains were open enough for him to see the people inside watching a puzzling video. It looked real, but people were fighting a creature that didn't exist, at least he hoped it didn't. Will was startled and stopped when a large explosion rocked through the video room and a fireball billowed across the screen. *Yep,* he thought, *the questions were piling up.*

A counter was on one side of the room with beverages and snacks laid out. He wondered about the food he would be provided. If this was any indication, he might go to bed without a growling gut. It excited and bothered him. He had never participated in this level of decadence, but there was no denying Dailys and Drangers slaved and died for this opulence.

Dailys and Drangers were prisoners in their territories, and all they had was what they were issued. Every Daily over twelve worked long hours for meager rations. They had no given medical care beyond what they concocted themselves and had short lifespans. They owned nothing because it all could be confiscated for no reason. They were issued a ridiculously small amount of credits, which did little to improve their condition.

The Uppers had supervisory jobs, and only one person per household was required to work. They also were issued a standard food allotment, but it was fresh and plentiful. They earned a generous amount of credits, especially if more than one person wanted to work. They could afford lavish things and excellent medical care. But they also didn't own their homes or the land they sat on.

If the Uppers and Neighwah lived beyond Will's imagination, he wondered how the Corporates lived. He heard Omar, Old Man River, talking to Taylor one night, and he called our government an oligarchy with two-tiered socialism below the rulers.

"They keep the lowest group illiterate, ignorant, and tired. They are fed enough and afraid enough that they don't rise up against their oppressors. They keep the middle group fed plenty and in adequate comfort. They won't rebel either because it would mean moving downward. And the

Corporates live like kings," he had said. Will bristled to himself at his new collaborative position.

They went back into the small room to go to the fourth floor, which opened onto a hall full of doors. A soldier dressed in casual attire walked past them wearing his card around his neck, and Will noticed it had the man's picture on it. His did not. Garler stopped and put the card up to the shiny black surface, and Will heard a click. Garler swung open the door, and there stood his new roommate—Rival.

"What the..."

"I found out you were coming yesterday," he said. "Lieutenant Garriset asked me to join when I won the combat contest. Welcome to HQ."

Will stood there, still holding onto his gear. He was tired of feeling shocked and surprised. "I don't know what to say except I have a ton of questions." One of the questions Will had was whether Rival had been sent to spy on him, but that one could not be asked out loud.

Rival laughed aloud and slapped Will's back. "I imagine you do at that."

Rival and Garler gave Will a tag team of answers while he secured his gear. They explained the things he saw in the game room, and that the video wasn't real; it was just a recorded story. Women were allowed to hold Neighwah jobs, but they tended to be desk jobs. The key card is for this building only. He was instructed to pick it up when he checked in and drop it off when he left. It opened all the places in this building he was allowed to go into.

Rival continued, "The dining hall is on the other side of the game room. Most jobs have three shifts: day, swing, and night. They are all nine hours long and overlap thirty minutes at each end to allow for debriefings."

Garler pointed to the closet. "Tomorrow, you will meet with Lieutenant Garriset in his office at 0800 hours. There is an alarm on the wall," and he pointed to a digital clock. "It will wake you up at 0700. You'll need to report in uniform, which you'll find in your closet. There is also a change of casual clothes fitting your new status. When you check in tomorrow, you will get issued a permanent card with your picture. You'll get the rest of your gear issue and an advance on your credits to buy some things at the commissary." Garler told Will he would pick him up at 0745 in the morning for his new cadet briefing and said goodbye.

Rival continued with the information he thought Will should know. "Our supervisor is Lieutenant Garriset. He reports to Colonel Burke, who reports to General Dermit. Unless you're good friends with someone, we tend to go by last names. My last name is Rival. My first name is Dean. How about you?"

"I'm Will Noland. What should I call you?"

"Dean is good; Rival is familiar. You choose."

"I'll try Dean, and see if it fits you. You can call me Will," he said, remembering the advice of keeping friends close and enemies closer. He had no idea who this Dean Rival was or why he was there and chosen as his roommate.

"So, Will, we have enough time to hang in the game room. You up for that?"

"Absolutely, but can I get a quick shower first?"

Dean showed him the clean bathroom with double sinks, a walk-in shower, and a separate room with a flushing toilet. He explained that the door on the opposite side led to another dorm room. They shared this bathroom with them, but they were on the night shift, so it shouldn't be an issue. Will took a quick shower in the bathroom, thinking how nice it would be to only have four people sharing it.

The water was perfectly warm, and he wondered if it would fluctuate or run out like the Dranger showers, but it stayed warm. Regardless, it beats heating just enough water on the stove to get clean with as little soap as possible, like his days as a Daily. Even the shampoo and soap were provided in wall-mounted dispensers. He could definitely get used to this and find it hard to give up.

He wanted to dress quickly, so he didn't keep Dean waiting, but the stiff feeling of his new clothes did not escape him. He had never had new clothes before. Most were made from softened, worn-out things the Uppers discarded. The new jeans were snug and didn't hang loose like the clothes he was used to. These fit him well. The t-shirt was pale tan with a navy Neighwah insignia on the top left side. It was a brand of sorts, but a removable one. He walked out and looked in the full-length mirror on the other side of the bathroom door and liked the look.

Dean showed him how to work the elevator on their way down to the recreation room. Will grabbed some food from the snack table, having missed dinner. Then he tried his hand at the pool table, finding it much more difficult than it appeared. Ping-pong wasn't any easier, but he looked forward to mastering these games. The good news was that Dean had only just arrived yesterday, so they were well-matched.

They tried to watch a video on the screen, but it didn't hold their attention with so much going on. Dean took him to the back of the room to a set of five slanted tables called pinball machines. He had missed it during his walk-through, but in his defense, this recreation room had a lot to take in. He loved the single-player challenge of it, and the noises and bumper lights were exciting.

Everything was so new to him, and his lack of skill made him feel awkward, but he knew that feeling would soon be replaced with a competitive determination. Will and Dean made their way back to their room, racing up the stairs rather than taking the elevator. He found out in a short time that they had a lot in common. Both were tall and lanky, enjoyed a challenge, and learned quickly and effectively.

Dean was eighteen and a half, just over a year older than Will, who was seventeen. But both were quite young to be assigned to HQ, where most people were in their twenties and thirties. Will was painfully aware he was chosen for reasons other than his skills as a soldier, but why was Dean bumped? Will didn't want to breach that quagmire. Not today, anyway.

Will discovered Dean grew up in a neighborhood of dangerously superstitious meddlers. He didn't toe their line, and he worried they would accuse him of some witchcraft junk, so he joined the Drangers to get out. He had been a Dranger for two years. Will shared stories about Pierce, Taylor, and some about Calen and Nash, but he made sure nothing of his secrets escaped his lips. He trusted no one and nothing about this place with all its tempting enticements. Despite the worry-filled day, he slept well on the clean, firm mattress with the soft, warm blanket.

Will's slate blue uniform fit him well. The pants were even a bit long, which was a luxury to someone who usually found pant legs lacking in length. The snap-up shirt was full of pockets and straps to hold gear he didn't have yet. The trousers were equally outfitted with pockets on the front, back, and on the sides, just above the knees. Noland was on the right lapel, and the Neighwah insignia was on the left. He walked downstairs because he had time to spare and he was full of nervous energy.

At the counter, he handed a different woman his badge and lanyard. "You normally here on the day shift?" he asked while he waited for his ride. He noticed the name on her lapel was Fuval.

"Yep, three and a half days a week."

"Wow, why only three and a half?"

"I work twelve hours each of those days, and I split this duty with another woman who watches my kids while I'm on, and then I watch hers. It gets my family extra credits, and I like working." He saw her silver ring with a sparkling green stone.

"Oh, that's nice." He thought about the strangeness of a job that allowed that. How different this world looked in contrast to his own. His ride pulled up, and he pushed through the door toward the van.

They drove out of the barracks section onto a street congested with buildings. The van stopped at an intersection in front of a magnificent piece of architecture that towered into the sky. It had to be one of the biggest ones Will had seen. His life in Colorado Springs had been spent on the outskirts, where most structures weren't so massive and high.

"Nice looking place," Will said, pointing at the triangular sculpted building.

"Wait until you see the inside. It used to be a church, but now it's a courthouse and a hall for large gatherings. It's where the biggest cases in the territory are tried."

"What does 'tried' mean?"

"When someone gets into trouble, they have a trial. They have lawyers to tell the different sides, and the judge decides the punishment."

"Sounds a lot more formal than the person in charge saying how it will be." Dailys and Drangers didn't get their troubles sorted out this way. Will had never heard of getting to formally plead one's case as a Daily, but he knew some sort of process was available to the Uppers and Neighwah. He was also pretty sure the Neighwah *were* on the same rung as Uppers, and now, so was he. A lot of Dailys worked toward this goal their whole life and never made it, but Will had mixed emotions about his unsolicited status change.

The sign on the door said Captain Garriset. Evidently, he had been promoted since yesterday. Will couldn't help but think that finding him was the reason. He sat behind a prominent desk marbled with a rich wood grain. Will gave his best salute as Garler and Dean had taught him. He even practiced it in the mirror a dozen times this morning. The powerful man saluted back and beckoned Will to sit in the chair facing him. "At ease, soldier. So how has your stay been so far?"

Will knew this was not an actual question; it was a call for the appropriate response, so he gave it. "It's been awesome, sir. I've never stayed in a place so nice. I had my first meal this morning, and it was excellent."

"Good, we like our cadets to feel welcome. You must have questions about why we chose you. You are rather young to be drafted into HQ. I've never had a draftee. Normally, people build up their resumes and apply to work here."

"Yes, sir, I am curious about that." This *was* the question, the elephant in the room, but he did not expect an honest answer.

"This is a new program. We get mostly Upper kids here. Their parents are granted a favor, blah, blah, blah. We have an increasing number of cadets whose work ethic is seriously lacking. We need fresh blood from a class that knows what hard work looks like. We're hoping you'll challenge them. When they see someone promoted over them, they assume it's a favor, and it has nothing to do with effort. We're hoping if they see a Daily get promoted over them, maybe they'll get it."

Well, this was worse than the secret agenda. Hard work was not an issue, but it would make him a target for his peers. And it struck him that he only had one peer here—Dean. The setup was clear, and the warning was clearer. This was the first of many tests.

He was given a pile of additional uniform items. The one he had on was his dress blues for special occasions, like meeting one's supervisor for the first time. The rest of his uniforms were various pieces in a camo pattern for everyday attire. He also received a training schedule. For two months he would attend classes to learn basic skills like reading, writing, and math. His territory had allowed the teaching of rudimentary skills, but because of Tianna, his abilities were probably better than many Uppers. He would need to feign struggling through the material, so Tianna's influence wasn't noticeable.

He was dismissed, and Garler was waiting outside the door to take him to his other appointments. They stopped at the hospital for a checkup and some vaccinations. Dailys got vaccinations too, but not the newest, safest, or freshest versions. He was brought to the commissary, and it was his first time in an Upper store.

There were so many choices, and they were all clean and new. He purchased a couple of outfits, shoes, and a coat for the cold temperatures that were already being carried on the wind. At Garler's suggestion, he bought two pairs of sweats for working out and playing sports. He looked forward to that. He was amazed he still had credits left, and he would get more in two weeks.

Garler drove past the chapel, whose metal structure artistically rose high in the sky with a series of triangular spires. This base had been well maintained and had many beautiful places to visit. They returned to the barracks for lunch, and Will's first hamburger, fries, and milkshake meal had him holding back moans of joy. He had to admit he was enjoying the luxuries and the environment he lived in, and he wondered how long it would last.

He was given an electronic notebook and told to watch the introduction videos. It was in short segments, but it was an extensive amount of procedural protocol. He took several well-needed breaks to keep from dozing off. The pad was assigned to him, and he could recall any chapter for review as required.

Dean found Will sleeping with the notebook on his chest. "Boring as hell. I fell asleep too."

Will was startled and then lay back down. "Beyond dull, for sure. I'm guessing you know what my day was like because you did the same thing yesterday."

"Always a day ahead of you," Dean snickered. "We have an hour before dinner. Let's go throw this thing." He held up a football.

Will had seen Uppers throwing it before, but he hadn't ever tried it. "Is this another learning curve thing?"

"Yeah, it's not easy to get it to spin, but practice helps. It's fun, and they have a game they play with it. It's hardcore contact, and I want to play when the time comes. They have different sports throughout the year. Football practice is starting now."

"I'm in." It wasn't easy at first, but before long they were bulleting it back and forth. After another amazing meal, they hit the rec room. They turned in and got ready for school the next morning. Neither had any idea what to expect.

They walked to the nearby prep school and into their classroom. They took a series of tests using their notepads and earphones. Both showed disappointment that much of their academic lesson work was on their notebooks. Will thought to himself it would be easier to fake his learning speed because he would go through the lessons on his own time to finish the tedious tasks quickly.

After lunch, they got on the bus to attend what the other cadets called soldier classes. First was a history class. Approved history started with the meteorite storm. Nothing before was ever covered or up for discussion. Will had already understood that there were numerous versions of the story. This was the Upper version.

They called it the Great Purge and said it brought much-needed order to a country in chaos. Will had never heard it called that before, but he had heard the government that had given a voice to all people was purged. After the meteor catastrophe, the corpses of animals and humans created rampant diseases, compounding the problem. The population was once just over six million in the former state of Colorado. It is estimated there are less than two million now.

Most people died from preventable diseases that followed the global event, not from the meteors. That was why the Corporates needed to take control to help the people. A Neighwah soldier's job is to maintain the status quo, so all people are safe and fed. They made it sound like the Corporates were the saviors of humankind. It was not the story he grew up with, but it was his new lie. More warning bells sounded in his head.

After three months of training in academics, combat, protocol, and driving school, he was given his job assignment. He was designated to pick up cadavers from the three main territories: Colorado Springs, Denver/Boulder, and Pueblo. Will had no idea that these territories had connections with each other. He was excited about being able to travel into the Denver/Boulder territory, but he wondered what awaited him in Pueblo.

This, of course, resulted in three more weeks of training. He was instructed in the use of the DNA scan they would use on every body collected. The training was done using the device on animals, each other, and themselves. He was relieved when his scan registered him as William Noland, not Alexander.

He would travel with another soldier, Travis Colter. They were tasked with scanning each body for DNA and dangerous diseases and loading them in a refrigerated truck for transportation. When they got back to the crematorium near Falcon Field, they unloaded the bodies. Each community had a designated morgue with a refrigeration unit, and their route brought them by once a week. They had five routes a week, and each one took a full day with many stops.

It was well into winter now, and tomorrow was his first day, and Pueblo was their first route.

Chapter Thirteen

Highway 25 was a road Will was very familiar with. He wondered how many more times he was going to pass his buried treasure before he could finally hold it again. The large refrigeration truck rocked noisily down the potted road adding to Will's edgy mood. Going back to Pueblo was risky. He doubted anyone would remember the scrawny kid, especially in uniform. People focused on the uniform and didn't tend to look too hard at the person inside.

But what if they knew he was coming? It wouldn't make sense to train him all this time just to hand him over. The thoughts roiled inside him and hopping out of the vehicle occurred to him more than once. They probably did have an endgame, but he did too, and evidently, neither felt it was the right time to make a move.

Will rode shotgun for now, but he was told he would get his chance to drive on the way back. Travis Colter liked using last names, so he was Colter, and Will was Noland. It might help him stay unnoticed since anyone who might remember him in Pueblo would know him as Alexander, not Noland. Plus, Taylor and Peirce Noland weren't even from the city of Pueblo. They were from a tiny town within the territory called Canon City. Even Kenner wouldn't remember him or recognize him because they had never met face to face. At least, not that Will knew of.

An endless stretch of chain-link fence signified they were at the border of Pueblo. They stopped at the gate. Will sat up casually, but he was watching the guards intently. They were calm and greeted Colter with routine familiarity.

"Got a newbie, I see," one of them said.

"Noland, it's his first day."

The guard looked into the truck cab at Will, nodded, and proceeded to swing the gate while the other guard stood in the booth. Colter waved and they drove on through. Across the brushy sea were the bleached and broken frames of rural flotsam. The bones of a lost time were typically scattered in forgotten places. Will's mind called up the ghosts in his thoughts, imagining a time when self-determination thrived, and prosperity and happiness were attainable. It was several minutes before signs of inhabited civilization emerged.

Will was shaken out of his dream state by the truck rocking back as it stopped. A steel building loomed, and a bay door was pushed open by a man in a rubber apron, gloves, and a mask. Colter backed the truck into the building, jumped out, and walked to a large, heavy door. Will followed. Colter handed Will a mask and some gloves while he put his own on.

"Can't be too careful around these bodies," Colter said. "Bad germs can kill ya'. We don't always know what they die from. Grab some body bags."

Will had been fully trained in this, but he pretended to appreciate the advice, knowing many trainees were poor listeners, and people in charge liked to throw out orders. He complied and grabbed a bag. As they walked toward the metal door, the two Dailys in rubber aprons followed behind them.

Inside the cold room, long shelves lined the sides. Four naked bodies lay on them, and the rest sat empty. It was ominous how the cold slabs lay waiting for the next heart to cease beating or for a catastrophe to fill them. He had been taught that dead bodies were quickly retrieved, too quickly in the minds of grieving family members. But the possible devastation from decaying bodies was ingrained in the minds of all. Immediate reporting and pick-up were mandatory, and not complying was a punishable offense.

Will lay the bag open on the table, and the two Dailys lifted one of the frozen rigid bodies onto the cold metal gurney. It was a woman. She wasn't particularly old, but the deep gash on her leg was the obvious cause of her death. Colter handed Will the scanning device. He had scanned dummies and living people, but this was his first dead person. She had a real life, and now it was over. He watched the red light move across her face and Upper torso as her information flashed on the screen: Janet Hill, 38, leg injury.

They zipped up the bag and loaded her into the truck. There were two shelves on slides that rolled out with rails on the sides so the bodies could be piled one on top of the other. They heaped the lifeless black bag onto the bottom shelf and walked back to retrieve the next. The others were men with various injuries and one whose cause of death said simply: illness. They completed the other three in silence. Their next stop in the Pueblo territory was Ordway. After Walsenburg, they stopped for lunch before continuing to Canon City.

"So," Will asked, "what other stuff do we do for the Pueblo and Denver territories? I mean, why are we taking their bodies? There has to be a trade."

"They make different supplies than us, and we trade for them. Like we have a lot of lumber and livestock, Denver has tons of manufacturing companies that make fuel and machinery, and Pueblo does a lot of assembly and textile work making material and clothing. Plus, all the territories mine for various ores, and send them to Denver for refining. There's probably other stuff too."

"Okay, I get that, but how hard is it to build a crematorium in each territory or just burn the bodies in an open pit? Why do we drive all over hell to make pickups?"

"Don't ask that question out loud or you'll get thrown in the brig. We don't get to question the way things work. We just don't."

Will digested that for a while and decided to let it go. Although it seemed like poor planning, it wasn't the first time he'd seen that. It was what it was; it had to be done, and it was their job to do it. When they returned to the base at Falcon Field, they drove to the crematorium building and unloaded the body bags from the frigid truck into the chute, making sure they slid down. They packed more bags into the box and headed back to the barracks.

Rival was there, studying his tablet. His academic lessons were taking longer than Will's because he didn't have a teacher like Will had. No one said anything about how quickly he mastered the reading skills required by all soldiers, and Will didn't explain. He thought he had spent plenty of time faking his abilities, but he still excelled at an amazing speed.

He had a plan; he always had a plan. He would tell anyone who asked that when he learned the primary lessons taught to all Daily children, he became interested in learning more. He began to seek words to sound out. He read signs, directions posted on walls, and any other print he could find. The notebook lessons only helped him improve, and he found he loved reading. He didn't break any laws; he learned naturally by observation.

Will hopped in the shower, anxious to wash away his newfound paranoia. He hadn't touched any of the bodies; they just scanned them, zipped them up in sterilized bags, and tossed them in the truck. Though he wasn't around when the sickness from rotting cadavers devastated the health of millions, he had no desire to test its power.

Throwing on his sweats and hoody, he walked out, rubbing the final drops of water from his hair. He had kept it half-inch short ever since he discovered the barbershop on the bottom floor.

"How was your first day?" Dean said, looking up from his tablet.

"Well, it was a little rough. I mean I've seen dead bodies, hell I killed one, but they were enemies. These were people, Dailys mostly probably, hard to tell without clothing. I couldn't help thinking they were someone's mom, dad, or brother, and one was a baby that died at birth. I guess that happens a lot. That... that got to me."

Will walked over to the laundry basket and tossed his towel in. The bag was almost full, meaning they needed to bring it to the laundry room down the hall and check it in while picking up their clean laundry. Behind that neat process were Dailys working long hours through hunger and fatigue, all to make his fat life easy. After tossing their dead bodies all day, he felt ashamed.

"So let me get this straight, you get to look at titties and snatch all day long?" Will knew it was wrong, but the irony of Dean's unexpected response had him laughing out loud.

"You're sick, man," Will said, still getting his laugh under control. "Hey, you want me to help you with your shit, so we can go see some living women? Colter said a group of female soldiers checked in today for their two-week training. They won't be naked, but..."

"We could fix that," Dean finished his sentence before Will had a chance. Will just shook his head and felt the heat flood his face. "Holy shit, Will! Are you a virgin? Didn't you get any when you were a Dranger?"

"We never had time. We worked long hours and moved from town to town. I never had the chance to meet any girls enough to... you know. And no," Will said with conviction, "I wouldn't be shitty enough to join any rape gang. Still won't."

"Okay, seriously, rape ain't sex. It takes a sick shit to act a woman like that. I'm talking about hot-steamy-grinding-gimme-more sex. For that, you need to meet the wrong kind of girl to have the right kind of time. You got your shit shot, right?"

"My what?"

"When we lined up for vaccines, do you remember them telling you what all the shots were for? Did you get the one they said was for fluid transmission diseases and preventing pregnancy?"

"Yeah, the pink-looking stuff."

"Perfect, then you're ready."

"So what, I go stand in the rec room, and some girl will walk up and say let's do it?"

Dean shook his head. "Okay, let's make a deal. You tutor me out of these boring lessons, and I'll teach you how to pick up women."

"I'm not sure you're as qualified to teach me as I am to teach you," Will replied. "But yeah, it's a deal."

Will shared little tricks for reading and remembering material, and Dean gave him his find, meet, and treat method of cutting women from the herd. "Everything hinges on eliminating the competition. Then you just charm them with questions about themselves and listen. Even if they bore you to tears, smile and listen."

"That's stupid. Why not get her to talk about something we both like?"

"Dude, this is not about the conversation. It's about the endgame."

"Sounds like a trick."

"Yeah, well, I've heard it called that by pros. Look, I'm memorizing 'if two vowels go walking' gibberish because I need the education. You do too. It's going to take a couple of tries at this before you knock it out of the park. Trust me, you're heading toward eighteen. You are definitely behind the curve."

"Most Dailys like us just get married. We aren't out playing around. We keep our women away from older boys and men because they are the ones who are likely to get messed up."

"Yeah, I know. That's Dailys, but that's because they don't get the shit shot. For them, it's a gamble for sure, but even still, lots of Dailys risk it." He had a gleam in his eye as he shared that. "But we do get the shot, and you aren't gonna get pussy if you act like one."

Will thought about that for a moment. He grew up as a Daily, and they weren't given protection from STDs. And they were only given birth control when they were married and had two live children. He was taught to see women as vulnerable and at risk when it came to sex. Dailys didn't attend school, and parents kept their young girls away from the men of their communities. They worked in all women's factories and as nannies for the Uppers. They were often forced into arranged marriages as early as sixteen.

Taylor further explained that it is women who are at the most risk when engaging in sex outside of marriage. It was women who could become pregnant, and if a child's father didn't want to get married, it was the woman who was put on the marriage list. In addition, women's anatomy made catching a sexually transmitted disease more likely than a man's. They internalized the fluids where the skin is thin and susceptible to micro-tears, allowing germs access. The thought of Tianna being raped repeatedly by a brutal bastard also did much to quell his sexual ambition, but not his appetite.

It's not like he was without desires. They overwhelmed him at times. Maybe if these women were protected, they would be open to having sex. The thought made him entertain the notion, which quickly became a determination.

"Hey, are you overthinking this like you do everything?" Dean asked after several moments of silence.

"Probably," Will chuckled. "Okay, we'll study for an hour, then head down to dinner."

While Dean was in the shower, Will changed out of his sweats and into a dark pair of jeans. He evaluated his look in the mirror, with a light blue Henley shirt in hand. He had grown a good two or more inches since he began this whole Dranger-to-Neighwah adventure. At last check, he was six feet and three inches. His face had grown out of his awkward teenage appearance and had been replaced with a strong jawline like his father's and a smile like his mother's.

He had filled out to be more than just toned, his muscle definition exuding power. He and Dean made regular visits to the gym and the covered track on the fourth floor. They played in the weekly scheduled sports events. Both treated all areas of physical exertion as a contest and an outlet for their fiercely competitive nature. They were warriors by training and design.

Will put on the long-sleeve, button-up t-shirt just as Dean came out of the bathroom. Dean put on faded skinny jeans and a tan and black dress shirt. It was a good shade for his tan coloring and brown eyes. He was over six feet, but Will had him by at least an inch. Will had a dressier shirt in his closet, but he didn't feel comfortable wearing it in casual settings. Dean got him to try on skinny jeans at the commissary, but he hated the tightness, and it accentuated his height, making him feel too gangly. But Dean had told him to wear what gave him the most confidence, and laid back felt natural.

The rec room was more crowded than normal. Will guessed the news about the visiting women had gotten out. They strolled over to the beverage bar and grabbed a couple of beers with their credits. They had saved up quite a few since they spent more time at the gym than here. They only stopped in on their off days, Saturday and Sunday. Today was Wednesday.

Sitting at a table with no available seats were six women. Several men tried to break into their circle with no success. Will and Dean walked right by without vying for eye contact and went straight to the bar counter.

"They're locked up," said a guy at the bar. "They made some kind of pact."

Will laughed out loud. "I like it. They're smart."

The rest of the night was spent playing pool and pinball. The women never gave up their fortified circle. Thursday night, they went to the gym and then to the rec room, but when they saw the women's resolve was unshaken, they returned to their room.

"It's like that sometimes. You know how we played baseball last week?" Dean asked.

"Yeah, very strategic game. I liked it."

"Well, it's been said you hit one out of every ten balls, and only some of them are home runs. You're lucky to get a base hit and work your way around the bases. Picking up women is a lot like that game—lots of strategy, lots of work, and tons of patience. Just as well, I haven't told you what to do when you catch one. That's even harder, if you excuse the pun."

"I'm a reader, Dean," Will said, pointing at the shelf near his bed full of books he had purchased and checked out, "an avid reader."

"Well, that might help if I knew what you read. Hey, maybe that kind of literature would encourage me to read more. Maybe we should hit the library."

They expected the girls to still be locked in their fortress on Friday, but it seemed a couple had broken ranks. Will had locked his sights on one still at the table. Her dark brown hair was shiny, wavy, and full. A small lock of her hair was secured in the back by a blue leather bird clip with its wings out. It was held by a formidable stick pushed through it. *Smart*, Will thought. *She found a way around the no weapons in the barracks rule.*

He stepped near the table and turned to make eye contact. She was absolutely beautiful. Her soft bone structure and full lips had his mind reeling, and her dark eyes bore right through him. She looked back and smiled. As Dean would say, that means he's on the batting lineup. But try as he might, he couldn't get her to leave her friends.

Dean had made some progress, and he was still swinging at the mound. The next morning, they went to work off their frustration. Will was pumping weights in a white t-shirt and sweatpants, and there she was. Riding a stationary bike with a book in hand, she just kept checking off boxes. He was losing hope he'd ever get to talk with her, but he wasn't ready to quit. He climbed onto a bike next to her. She smiled slightly, never taking her focus off her book.

"So, what do you think of the base so far?" he asked.

Innocently, she looked up like she hadn't noticed him sit down. "Oh, okay, I guess. The chapel is stunning, and the commissary is nice. The food's good too, but this isn't my first time here. I came for training on some new equipment we're getting. How about you?"

"I'm stationed here. I work as a driver and travel between the territories picking up stuff. Have you had any fun here yet? Lots to do." He wasn't about to confess he was in the dead body business, and he'd lie if she asked. That had to be a deal breaker.

"Kinda bored so far."

"Well, if you're willing to climb over that woman wall, I'd be happy to show you around." Will hoped he hadn't crossed a line, but he tended to be a direct person.

She laughed. "Yeah, we agreed to take our time meeting guys. Not all men are ... trustworthy."

"That's smart. There are some assholes here for sure."

"Of course, I'm sure you are a complete gentleman."

"Well, I am until I'm permitted otherwise," he said, giving her a sly smile.

She laughed again. He could get used to that laugh, that smile, those eyes, and those lips. "Fair enough. Meet me at the rec room in an hour."

"I'll be there. I'm Will. What's your name?"

"Molly," she said as she hopped off the bike and went to the abdominal crunch bench.

He stayed peddling for a moment and headed to the hall stairs to the fourth floor. He was skipping two steps at a time; he was so pumped. He showered and dressed in casual attire so quickly that he was left with a thirty-minute wait. He decided to read the rest of the chapter, but he got too tired to finish the night before. He sat on his bed against the wall and settled into a comfortable position, or so he thought.

His mind could not focus on the words, and he flipped through pages he couldn't recall. Looking at the clock, only five minutes had gone by. Time seemed to slow down just to torture him. *How can time be so distorted from one circumstance to the* next, he thought? Somewhere, someone was begging for time to slow down, while he waited for the passing of every agonizing second. The science of it intrigued him enough for four more minutes to slide by. But time did pass, as it will, without any regard for its prisoners. Five minutes before the hour, he left the room.

Will and Molly walked all over the grounds, talking and sharing the whole time. Untrue to his man-training, they both shared ideas and safe information about themselves. Passed houses and all sorts of buildings that were empty or had unknown purposes, they strolled. When it started to rain, they headed back, but not quickly.

They paused, and he wrapped her in his jacket, carefully securing the hood over her damp hair. He was facing her, looking into her eyes and trailing his gaze to her lips. He closed his eyes and breathed her in. Tenderly, he bent down, touching his lips to hers. It was soft and gentle, and then he parted ever so slightly from her. She had heavy eyes and licked her lips as if to prepare for another. He took her lips again, this time with more passion. He had kissed a neighbor girl once, but not like this.

When they pulled apart, Will spoke first. "I had the feeling I was permitted otherwise."

She beamed that intoxicating smile his way, and he felt his insides melt. "You read right, but it's time I get back. Lunch is looming, and I don't want the squad to run you off or damage you."

He laughed, "Got it." He took her hand in his and set out for the barracks. This wasn't an at-bat. It was at least an inning, and maybe a whole game, and he was all in. He didn't just want her physically. He liked her. That was also against his man-training, but he was beginning to think he couldn't be that guy anyway. He wasn't in love, but he was in paradise.

Chapter Fourteen

olly and Will became a familiar twosome in the dining hall, the rec room, and the gym. Will had discovered Molly was twenty-one. That was three years older than him, but she said he was an old soul. Omar said he had an old soul too. He spent a considerable amount of time trying to analyze what that meant before finally asking her. He had heard the term soul and that it had to do with religion, but it was very hard to get a hold of the material that explained those beliefs. Though it was referred to in some of the books he read, it was an elusive concept, so to have an old one furthered his confusion.

"A soul," she said, "is like your spirit, the essence of your personality, and it's separate from your physical body. An old soul means your soul is wiser than your years. It's like you have the wisdom of experiences without having had them. You're probably older than me."

He laughed, but he of course had to chase the concept around a bit. The very irony of his mental quest struck him, and he grinned. *I guess I do carry a chorus of advisors.*

Dean was more than disappointed that Will wouldn't share any details about his time with her, but he had secured his typical two-week girl from a different group. Before the classes started on that Monday, three more groups from various towns in the territory had shown up for the one-month course—all of them women.

Dean had shared his exploits, and in his thinking, Will owed him some. Truth be told, there wasn't anything to share. He had spent three days with

Molly, and they were still trying to interpret each other's unspoken signals, enticing both of them to sink further into a bond. Dean scored on the first night, but he had chosen the type of girl who oozed sexual tension. He seemed to know what he wanted and how to get it. Will had no idea what he was doing. He only knew he wanted more.

By Wednesday, Will had been on all five routes. The Denver/Boulder territory had three routes because it was so big and populated. According to Colter, a typical load for the smaller territories was between twelve and fifteen bodies, but in Denver/Boulder, twenty-five to thirty was the norm.

It was difficult to spend time between his work and her school days, but they often met at the gym, and again at dinner, ending their day in the rec room. On Thursday, they met at the gym as usual.

"So I'll see you at the dining hall in an hour," Will said, kissing her forehead.

"I want to show you something. Can you come to my room?"

This was new territory. He had never seen her room, nor had she seen his. "Okay, can I grab a shower first?"

"Just bring your clothes. You can shower in my room." Her demeanor was nonchalant, but it didn't stop his body from flooding with a warmth that settled in his groin. He was glad his hoody jacket was tied around his waist with the sleeves hanging where he needed them. If he was reading too much into this, he couldn't help it. His thoughts took on a singular direction, like a locomotive bound to a track. No matter what happened, he'd need to shower because he had been primed for days now, and this was murder.

"I'll be there, " he answered, and they went toward different stairwells. He ran up the stairs and tore into his room. Dean was opening the door.

"Hey, I need the room," Dean said.

"No problem, just let me grab my clothes."

Dean slapped him on the back as they walked in. "You dog. Are you gonna shower at her place? Doesn't she have a roommate?"

"I don't know."

"First time?"

"Dude!" Will was becoming annoyed by Dean's constant need to discuss their 'baseball stats'. He believed his friend was trying to be helpful, but Will liked Molly. Sure, her body was the initial draw, but the person she was had endeared him more with every day that passed.

"Hey, I don't have lesson time, brother. Good luck."

"Whatever, man. I'll be back at ten. It's a work night." With that, Will grabbed his gear, left, and passed Dean's girl in the hall.

He hesitated before he knocked on the door of Molly's room. Maybe she did have a roommate, and he'd have to regain his self-control. He knocked softly, and she answered immediately. She was still in her workout gear, as was he. She pulled him in for a kiss, and he dropped his gear where he stood.

"We need a shower," she said as she grabbed him through the door.

"I know I do. Just to be fair, I'm taking in a ton of go-ahead signals. Please tell me I'm not wrong." He was breathy and half moaning the words.

"No, you're right on the money." She began tugging his shirt over his head. "Wow, you are well built." She ran her hands up his chest, and he grabbed her and kissed her while pulling off her shirt.

Her breasts were full and seductively outlined by a black laced bra. "As are you." He'd never removed one, but ran his hands up her back and found the hooks. Dean had said this was usually a clumsy moment, but the bra fell open easily. Gently and slowly, he lifted the straps off her shoulders, freeing her sexy curves. He spied the only bed in the room and put away the roommate issue. He picked her up as she wrapped her legs around him and set her on the bed.

"These have got to go," he said in a low growl as he slipped her yoga pants down her legs. He kissed his way down her neck, taking in her scent and feeling her blood pulse. She moaned when he held her breast and teased her nipple to a point with his tongue. He returned to her lips and then traveled down the other side to have his time with it. She was arching toward him, and he wanted to slow down, but she sighed and reached to yank his sweats off, so he helped.

"You may have boring skivvies, but what's inside looks very hungry," she teased.

"You, however, have very lovely panties," he said, tracing his hand over her lower abdomen and slightly breaching the appealing attire. "And you have no idea how hungry it is."

"I'm building up an appetite myself. It's been so long," she was breathing heavily as she reached down under her black lace panties and began to stroke herself, moving, moaning, and radiating the heat of pure want. He was intrigued. He thought about taking over, but she looked very engaged in her pursuit, and he was extremely turned on by it. "Now," she begged. "Please."

He didn't need to be asked again. He slid the delicate garment off, and she opened up to him. Slowly, he pushed inside her. She felt so good, and he let go a breathy groan and began moving as if the knowledge of lovemaking was born in him. He tried to hold back, but every caress of her heat had his senses driving him to satisfy an incessant need. He felt her moving with him, guided by her own greedy desires. Her sighs of pleasure pulled him closer to the cliff.

She called his name and began bucking and wildly crying out without hesitation or shame. She was so free and in the grips of her pleasure, and it sent him over. Deeper and faster, he pushed inside her, releasing sounds of ecstasy to blend with hers. He felt like he was soaring in every direction at once. It was all-encompassing and beyond any previous experience he had had on his own. He was enjoying the boundless release that ended too soon. He lay slightly to her side but still on top of her and inside her, enjoying the afterheat of skin-to-skin and sweat-to-sweat.

Pushing up and off of her, he saw her sated expression. Both were beginning to quiet their breathing when she put her hand on his chest. "Your heart is still beating so hard."

"I can feel it." His expression was tender as he traced his finger across her forehead and down her face to tuck a stray lock behind her ear. His hand continued down, settling on her chest. "Your heart also has a powerful beat." He settled in beside her and drew her into the curve of his body.

"I'm glad we met. I have only done this once before, and it was ... well, not like this. You are a wonderfully kind man and an exciting lover. And you're a warm big spoon too. I'm glad we did this."

Will wasn't sure if this was the time to tell her it was his first go, or that she had taken on much of the work he had expected to fumble through. "I am grateful for all our time together, but this time was especially incredible. Lying here tucking you next to me, I am truly happy. Nothing in my life has come close to the bliss I feel right now. You are extraordinary."

Molly slid onto her back to face him. Her smile was genuine, and she gave him a quick but affectionate kiss. "Well, I think we should take our long-awaited shower now."

Will gave her a mischievous grin. "I can't imagine anything else I would rather do."

Will returned to his room just before midnight. He crept in quietly, and Dean never stirred. He was relieved his woman wasn't nesting in their room. Sleepovers were not permitted, but nor were they policed with any diligence. The rule was to be in bed nine hours before one's work shift began.

He should have been exhausted, but he was bathed in pure joy. How sweet to have someone to live for as opposed to someone to fight for? He had never felt so secure and full of hope. He lay awake for some time listening to the happy voices of his chorus. Of course, that one constant voice of paranoia echoed in the background, but he wouldn't listen today.

Friday morning came, but despite his lack of sleep, he felt more alive than on any morning he had slept in. His life had finally become his own. He felt so good that he began to devise philanthropic plans to help the Dailys around him. He floated to work and showed up ten minutes early. He didn't pay attention to the two soldiers waiting at the clock-in office, but they were paying very close attention to him. When he went to go to his truck, they blocked his way.

"Private Noland?"

"Yes." Will immediately thought of the hall cameras and his late-night return.

"Come with us, please."

Will was led to a car and motioned to sit in the back. He knew better than to ask these order followers what was going on, so he sat quietly. His paranoid voice was gaining support as they parked at the officer's building.

They walked upstairs past Colonel Burke's floor and up to the next. He was led into a huge office and motioned to sit in the large soft chair on the other side of a formidable desk. Facing him sat General Dermit himself. Now, that paranoid voice had the whole chorus screaming. He'd have to be an idiot not to know the gist of the coming conversation.

"Relax, Private Noland, I just need some information to complete your file. So, Will, can I call you Will?"

"Yes, sir, of course." Will knew better than to believe this high-ranking officer had been relegated to registry clerk.

"Well, good because I'm not sure I should call you Noland. Because the fact is we have no record of you before you transferred here from Pueblo at eleven years old. Your records from Pueblo were unavailable." The General let that sink in to detect a response, but Will sat cool as a cucumber.

"I was adopted at the border, sir."

"So please enlighten me, in your own words."

Will had practiced this speech in his head a thousand times because he knew it was coming. But this was his first time telling it out loud. And he better tell it well because his life and the lives of others were hanging on it. He blocked from his mind all the people it could also affect. This performance was his one shot.

"Well, sir, I have to admit I don't recall a lot from that time. I vaguely remember traveling to the border with my father and stepmother. They needed workers here, and my father thought it would be a good start for us. But something happened, and I still don't understand it. On the day we were set to cross the border, all the adults started yelling and going crazy.

"They said everyone but my parents could cross the border. They sent me to travel with the group, but I snuck away to look for them. I saw the only mother I ever knew sitting in a field, and the next thing I knew, my father shot her. I'm told I lost my mind for a while, and it must be true because I don't remember much. All I know is that my father murdered my stepmother.

"Taylor Noland took me in, and he did his best to raise me, but I was angry, and I got angrier day by day. He was a good person to me, but I wasn't to him. When one of my best friends got jacked into the Drangers, I went to help him using the blood pact rule. Nash wasn't strong in mind or body, and I knew he would die if I didn't.

"I took the name of Noland because I couldn't stand the name of Alexander." Will pulled up his dark angst, which was not an act. "I was registered as a Noland, and we were told that was all the legal information required under the adoption process. I apologize for not volunteering that information. It's not a memory I like to visit. It brings out the worst in me."

"And your father?"

"My father never made it to Colorado Springs. There was an explosion at the bunker where he hid, and with that and all of the soldiers in that field, there was no way he survived. At least he better hope he didn't because if I ever find out he is alive, I'll find him and kill him myself, slow and mean-like." The pure hatred in Will's eyes was actually for Kenner, but it worked well for the story he told. All but the real target of his murderous dramatics were true. When planning it out, he knew the closer to the truth it was, the less likely he would slip up.

Dermit looked hard at the young warrior sitting before him. His emotion matched his tale, and the tale matched everything Dermit had on him. "So, your stepmother..." he paused, waiting for Will to name her.

"Tianna, sir."

"What do you remember about Tianna?"

"Well, she was pretty and kind, but she was mostly quiet. My dad said he found her wandering the woods while checking his rabbit snares. I was around eight years old, and I was watched by a remote worker because my mom was dead. Tianna needed a place to stay because she didn't remember who she was or where she came from, and my dad needed someone to watch me.

"She had to have a job away from people because of her terrible panic attacks. My dad said it was hard to find her a job because her attacks made people think she had a sickness. But I guess she was good at gardening, so they gave her a job at the farm. She brought me with her, and I worked the farm too. In the winter, she took in some sewing for the Uppers to get food credits, and she was good at that too. Soon she was doing lots of people's sewing work."

"Did she ever talk to you, tell you stories, or secrets?"

"She never said anything because she couldn't remember anything. I remember she sang to keep herself from getting scared. There was one called 'Good Vibrations'." Will sang part of the chorus, "I'm pickin' up good vibrations." He choked through the lyrics. He didn't have to fake the sadness that overcame him, and he leaned on the arm of the chair, pressing his thumb and pointer finger against his eyes. "Sorry, sir."

"Sounds like you two were close."

"Well, as close as someone can get to her. I mean, my dad was married to her, but I never saw them kiss. She would pull away from him and me, but she was always gentle and kind. She could cook and clean, but she was more like a child than a mom. I remember my real mom; she was strong and made me behave. Tianna was the kindest person I ever knew, but she lived alone in her little world. I'm sure she had secrets, but they died with her."

"If your dad killed your stepmom, do you ever think he may have killed your first mom too?"

Will felt his blood boiling over. Not because Dermit had crossed a line but because at one point he had thought that. Will knew he had only thrown it out there to bait him into an emotional response. This guy had an agenda; that much Will knew, but he did too. For the most part, their goals were the same. They were both interested in finding his father to retrieve information. Their plans only differed in how that intel would be used, as well as his father's future. It was time to use his anger to convince Dermit that he could be a loyal ally.

"Sir, permission to speak freely."

"Permission granted." He was staring right into Will's eyes, and his confidence that he controlled the conversation was palpable.

"Am I being investigated for blanks in my background, or is there something else?" Will didn't have to feign his bottled fury. He was seriously fearful, but that emotion always seemed to turn into anger.

"We opened an investigation because your records were incomplete. Everything you told me confirms what we discovered. We may have more to discuss, but I have nothing more today. You are free to go Private."

During the whole conversation, Dermit's demeanor never changed. He was all business and totally in charge. He stoically punched a button on his desk phone and called the soldiers back in.

"My men will take you to meet up with Sargeant Colter en route to the CS city morgue. Dismissed."

Will stood and saluted. Dermit returned the gesture without leaving his chair or looking up from his computer. Will followed the soldiers out the door.

"What was that about?" Colter asked Will when he was in the van.

"I guess my background info was incomplete. It seemed pretty routine, and it got straightened out, but I thought I'd piss myself when they led me off." Will didn't mention he had been questioned by the General himself. He was pretty sure that was not normal procedure.

"Yeah, I think they like to remind us who's in charge. We get this great life with safe work, but not all soldiers live this way. Some are sent to 'gather' supplies and 'acquire' new properties." Colter stressed the words gather and acquire.

Will knew some Drangers, and Neighwah saw combat regularly. If he pursued his goal, he would be one of them. The people he loved might be sacrificed or used as leverage. That part of his plan was in flux, and he constantly strained his brain to develop a solution, but it evaded him. Now, however, the journey had begun, and he better work it out soon.

This was their short route day, and it zoomed by. As he stood in the mandatory rinse box at the end of the shift, he thought about Molly. Being called in to speak with the officers had a habit of getting around. He needed a plan to tell her about his day because she was bound to ask him. He decided to tell her the safe story to keep her out of his threat zone. He'd start by saying he was called in to complete his records.

If she pressed him, he might say the question was about his adoption, but he knew that might open up a whole new can of snakes. He could say they simply wanted his parents' full names. Beyond that, he'd have to shoot her inquiries down, saying he wasn't comfortable sharing private info, which was also true. But his favorite idea was distracting her with more interesting activities.

They took a pass on working out since it was Friday. A military movie called *Top Gun* was playing in the movie room for the last time that night.

It had caused quite a few exciting discussions, so they secured two seats to see it. To Will's surprise, Molly didn't pry further than his first explanation, but Dean was fascinated and, per his normal curiosity with all dramatic events, he wanted more details. Will blew him off, acting like it was the nothing moment he wished it was.

Chapter Fifteen

The second time he was pulled into Captian Garriset's office, it was done discreetly, and Colter accompanied him.

"We have a job that will be considered classified. You may never discuss it, not even between the two of you. Understand?" Colter nodded his head, and Will just sat there waiting for the information.

"Good. We have a situation in Cripple Creek. A Daily couple with one child gave birth to triplets, and amazingly they all lived." Dailys prenatal and birthing care was non-existent, so living triplets would be nothing short of a miracle. But it would bring out the crazy witchers, who purge the possessed from their community. A lot of superstition surrounded multiple births since many produced unhealthy and malformed infants.

"The midwife ran her mouth around town, and that brought out the witch hunters. The soldiers went to the house to find three hunters covered in blood from their evil duty. They'd killed the whole family, all six of them. We have the bodies hidden in a vacant warehouse outside of town along with the bodies of the three witch hunters executed at the family's house.

"Five workers and four children—gone! The witchers left families with young kids, and now their widows are bound for the list. It's a labor nightmare. If people hear too much about their murders or executions, we'd have a political mess on top of it all. It would rip the status quo to pieces. If they just turn up missing, we could say the family ran away to the Fringers, and the witchers went after them. The people would assume the Fringers took them or killed them. No mess. Got it?"

"Yes, sir," they answered.

"Look," the sergeant said, "I heard your family lives in Cripple Creek, Colter, and Noland, you have a girl there. There are no pickups in Fairfield, so you guys could take a long break at the department building. Hell, I'll even set it up that you get a nice lunch."

Will did get it. He got the whole disgusting business, and it brought him back to a reality he could not escape. He had indulged his senses in this place of temporary privilege. It seduced him making him find justifications for his participation, but he kept coming back to the truth. He was part of the wheel that ground people down.

It all started when he tried to do right by his friend. No, that wasn't completely true. His father and Tianna roped him in too. But he was well knotted now. An honorable destiny, yeah right. How would he ever break free to fulfill anything? He liked to think he was so clever, but nine people had been murdered, and now, with his help, they will conveniently and silently disappear.

Perhaps that was his fate too? He was locked in. If he made any move against their machine, he'd lose the ones he loved. Nash would be crippled, and they knew about his family and now Molly. *Fuck,* he thought. *What have I done?*

After collecting CS's bodies, they headed east to Salida. Without having to hit the northern cities, they had time for a two-hour visit to Cripple Creek. They still had to make their covert stop before they headed back to base, but they had more than an hour before they had to take off. Colter dropped Will off at the Neighwah building and headed to see his family at their work. No one would stop a soldier from pulling someone off the job for a few.

Will sat outside the lunchroom waiting for Molly, and wondering if he should. But when she walked up, she glowed with happiness. He drew her into an embrace. Physical displays of affection in uniform were frowned on, but a kiss was out of the question in the open.

"Follow me," she whispered as though she knew he was coming. "That's my dorm building," pointing across the street, she grabbed his hand and led him.

Will smiled. He hadn't expected anything but a sit-down lunch, and that was if he could find her. His normal route didn't allow for much more than a quick lunch most days. Today, however, they had some time to be together. He was surprised and horrified his superiors had arranged his rendezvous, but he followed her like a found puppy.

He knew he had to cut ties with her to keep her safe, but not today. Seeing her smile and the touch of her hand was the definition of happiness. Her room was simply decorated and quite small, but it was all hers. Once they were secure behind the privacy of closed doors, he hugged her off her feet and kissed her deeply.

"I missed you, Will. I did."

"If I caused you to be even half as lonely as I've been, I owe you an apology."

"Well, I can think of a way to settle the debt between us."

They kissed and enthusiastically embraced each other until it wasn't enough. Their clothes peeled off quickly, and being skin-to-skin again took them to the next level of intimacy. He traced her luscious curves and grabbed her firm, round bottom. She hopped into his arms and maneuvered herself until she settled him inside her.

He set her on the bed separating her from him. Will shook his head with a sly smile. "No, no Molly. I plan on savoring my lunch slowly."

"You'd torment me?"

"I will take every minute of this time to torment you, and I'll enjoy doing it." He lay beside her and brushed her hair aside, exposing her neck and caressing her with his mouth. Cupping her face and tracing her mouth with his thumb, her lips red and plump from his kisses. Taking his time kissing her, he was amazed at how overwhelming and tantalizing the effect could be. He was consumed with touching her lips to his lips and tangling tongues until he moved to her ear and down her neck to where it joined her chest.

His hands each seized a breast as his thumb swirled maddening circles around her nipples. She followed his lead and began her own torturous fondling of him, mimicking his every move. When his mouth moved down her belly and past her navel, she spun her body, so they were pointing in opposite directions. Will paused for a second, but not more. He drew in her heady scent and gently tantalized her with his tongue.

He was relishing the task when she began her titillating assault on him. He took a hefty breath when she drew him fully into her mouth. His body took over slowly, rocking in and out involuntarily. She too was indulging herself, yearning to breach the final barrier between her and climax. He held his body back, but when she tipped over the edge, he exploded with pleasure.

Ravenously, they moved in harmony, each movement matched by the other. They lay on the bed, still juxtaposed, feeling the pounding of their hearts and satisfied moans of deep breathing. Propping up, they smiled at each other, only adding to their overwhelming sense of fulfillment and the luxurious warmth leftover from their lovemaking.

After a cuddle filled with the soft voices of contentment, they had enough time for a quick shower. Will felt the familiar hole of emptiness as he told Molly goodbye. He didn't know when they'd meet again, or if they should, but he was drunk on her body and addicted to her company. How could he give her up? Colter was waiting in front of the chow hall when Will showed up, and he snickered at Will's love-sick appearance.

"I picked up a chicken sandwich and an apple for you. I figured you probably didn't eat. I don't suppose you are gonna return the favor and share any details about the lunch you got."

"Thanks, and no."

The truck was already running, and they took off for the clandestine pick-up. Ten miles down the road, they saw the old warehouse off to the side in a neglected state. Will and Colter both gave each other a look.

"If this smells like rotten death, I'm out," said the seasoned Colter.

"Yeah, I'm pretty sure there isn't any refrigerator or power to run one in there." Will backed the truck up to the rolling door, and the two geared up with more consideration than normal.

Bags in hand, cautiously, they opened the lock with the key provided, rolled the bay door up, and moved inside. They detected no foul odors, but a hum came from a sizeable box parked on the edge of the left wall. Realizing it was a refrigeration unit, and the sound was its working compressor, they both relaxed.

The pull-down latch popped the door open, and the cool air drifted out. Will was relieved to see that the bodies were already bagged. They were instructed not to scan these bodies, and he was relieved he'd be spared from the disturbing task of looking at them.

They both counted only six bags. Interesting. They lifted two adult-sized bodies into the truck, but when they grabbed the third, it was in pieces. The realization that all three infants and the young child had been piled into one bag stunned both men. It felt cruel and uncivil. But civility didn't live here; cruelty did. And now these souls were free of it.

The sign on the unit said to turn the temperature to 45 degrees if all the contents were removed. Will adjusted the thermostat and closed the door. *How are they getting power out* here? When they locked the bay door, Will did a walk around. On the backside of the roof were large black tiles. He heard about those once from Tianna. She called them suntiles, and they collected power from sunshine to create electricity.

Will sat in the passenger seat, relinquishing his driving turn. Colter believed it was about missing his girl and wasn't far from the truth. It had not escaped Will's attention that the dead bodies he had just loaded onto the truck were an opportunity to disrupt the status quo. All but three of those lives were entirely innocent. He thought about his desires and his choice to bring Molly into his life, and he found them selfish and cold-hearted.

He had to let Molly go. He had to do it in a way that convinced his superiors that she wasn't important to him, so they wouldn't use her as leverage. But that gave no sanctuary to the rest of his family. For all he knew, he was the last of his bloodline, but there was more to family than blood. He must find a way to protect them too. It was becoming more vital to know if his father was alive. If he was, finding him was crucial, and to do that he needed out of this stop-and-toss job. He required a job that allowed him to hunt the territory for his query, and his query was information.

The road passed by without Will noticing. They arrived at the crematorium and fed the bodies into the chute. Behind the wall were convicted prisoners who removed the bodies from the bags and loaded them into the furnace while sending the unzipped and splayed bags through a sprayer. Will wondered how many inmates were in the facility because it was the only prison for three territories, and no one ever got released once they were incarcerated.

It couldn't take that many people to run the small operation, so sadly they must be executed and cremated when their sentence was done. Will and Colter ran the only morgue route for all three territories, but that didn't include soldiers who died on the borders. They had their own body runners. Will picked up the eighteen bags he needed to replace the ones from that day and threw them in the truck.

The next time they visited Cripple Creek, Will didn't show up at the lunchroom, but he left Molly a note at her dorm's front desk. It said he was getting a new job, and he wouldn't be able to see her again. It was a cheap shot. She deserved more, but he hoped the cold move solidified his claim she was not hostage material.

Will put in a request to meet with Captain Garriset. Later that week, he was called in after his shift. He told him he loved his new life, but he missed the excitement of combat missions. He explained he had been told he would be working as an inquisitor before he was switched to HQ.

"Tired of tossing bodies, Noland?"

"No disrespect, sir, it's important work, but I think I could be more helpful in an inquisitor position or, better yet, a search and capture position. I realize it's more dangerous than my cushy collect job, but I like action, taking risks, and winning."

"Well, you're timing is perfect. We had one soldier wounded and another killed in action. We're down combat men."

"Yes, sir. I had heard that," Will responded.

"Let me float it up top."

"Thank you, sir. Thank you very much."

Will was asked to report to General Dermit the next day. "Have a seat, Noland. I've decided I am going to honor your request. When I hired you, I was looking for a soldier, not a grunt worker. I thought you'd want to keep your job, for a while anyway, since it lets you see your girl every week."

Will shouldn't have been shocked, but it confirmed his suspicions. It made him wonder if Molly had been planted to get close to him and get his secrets. "We called it off, or rather, I called it off. She wanted more than I had to give. She didn't say it out loud, but I could tell. It's too much to ask for a one-hour-a-week fling." Will answered in a cool, unruffled manner.

"I see. Well, you're young. You will report to Sargeant Abbott on Monday morning at 0700." It was a quick-to-the-point response, too quick Will thought. He wasn't sure if his request had interrupted the General's agenda or accelerated it.

"Thank you, sir. I hope Private Colter gets a decent replacement." Will hadn't ever made any real connections with his partner, but he felt bad about abandoning him.

"There's plenty of soldiers we can transfer into that position. That job doesn't require much intellect or labor. Pick up your new orders at your dorm desk along with your pass badge on Monday morning. When you get on the bus, let the driver see your badge. You're all set. Any questions?"

"No sir."

The whole process seemed too easy, and he wondered exactly what he was in for now, but one thing he knew for certain. He'd better find out what they know or think they know. And he desperately needed to find out the whole story behind the secret key shit before they did.

On Monday morning, Will reported in. The first case he was assigned involved finding a lost Corporate kid who had wandered off. The case morphed into a murder case. The evidence pointed squarely to the murdering rapist being the Upper father of the girl's good friend, but a Daily toxer was put to death for it. It didn't escape Will's attention that Drangers had visited that house on a justice round before the evidence was found.

Will had to admit, a toxer was off the streets and the Upper suspect was quietly reduced to Daily status in another town along with his wife and two children. The status quo was intact. It wasn't about justice; it was about order.

Will worked for less than a month as an inquisitor before he realized the potential value of Dean's job as an inventory clerk. Will fished for information under the guise of being interested in his work. Though Dean had access to a computer, it was limited to the supply files. It was his job to manage the shipping and receiving of goods to other towns around the territory. Will was sure there were valuable pieces of information, but true to Dean's nature, he wasn't sufficiently interested in connecting the dots.

Most days, the work was, on the surface, legit investigatory work. A theft at the warehouse, a murder from a domestic dispute, or an accident on a job site were believable tragedies. But often, just under the surface, there was the convenient outcome, and like the justice rounds of the Drangers, some days required his full consent to ensnarl himself in the cruelest of orders.

It had been one of those days, and he was locked up in the dishonor of it. He felt the web he was tangled in, and even a vigorous workout didn't help his mood. He was tasked with hiring Drangers and overseeing a justice run to remove a toddler from his Daily parents. The boy was the planned product of a childless Corporate couple and fathered by the Corporate man and the Daily woman. Will could imagine how unpleasant the conception had been. Now that he had been weaned from his mother, the Corporates were to deliver him to his new home.

The scene at the Daily home was as heartbreaking as the joy at the Corporate house. The couple had made the deal for medical attention for their young daughter and two years of better food rations. The medical attention consisted of one week of ordinary but life-saving antibiotics, and the better rations had everything to do with the new child's health. It was an untenable choice, in an untenable land.

He realized his emotions were hardening to complete tasks where mercy and purpose had no place. He hardly recognized the calloused person he faced in the mirror. He knew better, but knowing wasn't doing, and knowing and not doing was worse.

Will thought Dranger work was sinister, but as a Dranger, he just followed orders from the Neighwah and the occasional Corporate. He didn't know the details, so it was easy to imagine there were reasons. He soon learned that the Neighwah orchestrated the merciless Corporate agenda with wretched complacency.

Dailys and Drangers were simply pawns in a grand scheme. They ruined people, manipulated their lives, and used their very existence to feed their insatiable schemes. People were either working cogs in the machine or bumps on the road. They didn't look back at the trail of broken lives they left in their wake. The machine just kept marching forward, and all were slaves to its needs.

With every justice they ignored, with every truth they twisted, the closer they came to their demise. How exposed and fragile the threads of oppression were. It balanced precariously between malice and subsistence. On one side was the threat that, like a strike of lightning, could turn a life onto a harsher road. On the other side of the scale was just enough. Just enough food, enough protection, and enough shelter to keep the people from risking change. Even the Corporates on top cower under the same threat they impose. The ultimate question was, what would it take to unravel this evil that blankets his world? Will's mind was firing off ideas and forming a new purpose beyond using this job to find his truth.

A month later, Dean was transferred to the same department, but not the same team. Will was disappointed he would lose access to the computer records. Even though Dean had not given up any clues, Will was sure the supply records held critical clues to their weaknesses.

It had been two months since Will had broken off his relationship with Molly, but he still missed her. He missed her smile, her sense of humor, and her luscious body in his bed, causing him many sleepless nights simmering in desire. It was because he cared for her that he stayed away. He had no idea what she thought of his insensitive letter. He wrote that he had enjoyed her company thoroughly, but he was getting a new job and would be unable to see her anymore. It was written like a thank you note, which only added to the sting he intended her to feel. He doubted she pined over him or if she knew how much he pined over her, but he did, terribly.

"Will," Dean spoke, raising his pitch as if to wake his friend from slumber. "It's Friday night, and we're off till Sunday. A new crop of girls is showing up for training tonight. You blew off the last one, but you gotta move on dude, before your dick gives up and dies."

Will laughed. Dean could always make a situation funny. "Yeah, okay, I'll go. I want to get to the commissary. I need some new duds."

"Now, you're talkin'. I know just the look to guarantee a wild night."

"I didn't say I was losing my mind. I said I'd go out and get something to wear. Your style works for you, but I couldn't pull it off. Besides, it might make me give up altogether." Will turned his head and held his heart to feign despair.

"You're not quitting! I know you better. Throw a little competition your way and you see red. You know it's true."

"Good thing we like different women." Will had no interest in trolling for women who could become new targets, but it would look good to anyone watching him.

At the commissary, he picked out a pair of black jeans and a light, wheat colored, waffle-textured t-shirt with a zippered collar. June was heating up, so he bought a pair of shorts and a workout shirt too. And to his surprise, the chestnut tweed loafers Dean suggested appealed to him, so he got those as well. He hadn't been spending many of his credits for months, and he had earned a couple of bonuses, so his account was quite full.

With that in mind, he bought a watch too. He wore his issue watch even when he was off duty because it was accurate and comfortable, but plain. This one had a black face with a gold rim and shiny blue crystals to mark the quarter hours of its old-fashioned analog style. It seemed classier than the common digital kind. It was flashy and strictly an off-duty accessory, and he chuckled at the thought of Dean rubbing off on him.

Will looked in the mirror and felt better than he had in a long time. He knew everything about his look and mood right now was fed by everything wrong in his world, but tonight he needed a break from morality. Tonight, he needed an emotional and a physical release. They walked through the rec room door, and the first thing Will saw was Molly.

Will froze in his tracks. Her back was to him, and she hadn't seen him yet. But it was her. He knew every curve of her, every tip of her head as she spoke in her delicious warm voice. To make matters worse, she was being flirted up by the meanest asshole in the place—Becker. Women who left with this guy had a habit of getting battered.

Dean quickly grabbed Will and held him for just a second to get his attention. When Will was still Dirk, Denter taught him two looks. One:

whatever you are doing right now, stop. And two: they're on to you. He taught those same looks to Dean without explaining their history.

"It's basic bro-code for stuff that shouldn't be said out loud because of the company we're in," he had told him. When Will looked at Dean, his friend gave both of those looks. Will wasn't sure why Dean would care if he showed emotion toward Molly. It made him wonder what he knew and which side he was on.

Will thought he had covered his bases on this issue, but evidently, he had been brooding more outwardly than he intended. Thinking back, not being social, engaging in vigorous workouts, and not spending his credits were classic heartache signs. He should have known and been more careful. He'd have to make it look like he was okay with her stepping out, but did it have to be with this fuckshit? He put on his game face and walked over to her.

"Wow, Molly, how are you doing?" he said it like they were old friends with no past between them.

"Oh hi, umm, Will, right?" She said it with a cold tone in her voice.

"Yeah," he deserved that, but he didn't flinch.

"Can we talk somewhere?" She asked, and her look softened.

It was killing him because all he wanted was to pull her in and never let go. His mind went through the true happiness of their time together and the pure pleasure of their lovemaking. But he had to protect her even if it meant a night of getting a rough go by this dick. At least she wouldn't be tortured or worse.

"Gosh, I'm sorry, Molly. I've started seeing someone else. But I wish you the best, I do." He walked off before he could hear her response. He couldn't hear it. It would kill him if she sounded hurt, and it would kill him if she didn't.

He couldn't go off and sulk either. He had to conclude this performance as an insensitive prick for the watchers. That included staying cool and finding other entertainment. And that didn't take long. Out of the corner of his eye, he saw Molly leave, followed by Becker. They were going to test him fiercely, but he had to stay the course. Becker had never been accused of rape or damaging anyone to the point of needing medical attention, but Will wasn't sure she meant for him to follow her. Will tried to get Dean's attention, but he was kissing some easy meat in the corner.

This was unbearable. Will tried to focus on the woman he had been crushing at a game of pool. His next move was to get close and teach her how to hold a cue, but he needed to take a minute. He asked to excuse himself while he used the restroom and got a couple more beers. In the restroom, Dean met him. Again, he gave him the "whatever you are doing right now, stop" look. Then he patted him on the back and began to discuss who would get to use the room. Will knew he was right, and he played along.

The next morning, Dean came back to the room with the news of Molly's evening, of which he had been conveniently informed. Before he started, he gave the "they're on to you" look. Will knew the correct response was to play along, and he also knew the information may not be true.

"Molly had a couple of visitors last night, I guess. First Becker, then Lewis."

"Who the fuck is Lewis?" Will hoped his response sounded more curious about who Lewis was and not why was Molly with him. But Dean's look told him otherwise. *Why was Dean taunting him with this information?*

"He's some guy who recently got a divorce."

"Wow, a divorce. I knew Uppers could get those, but I never knew anyone who got one. That must be weird."

Dean just shrugged his shoulders and left the conversation at that. Will had so many questions. *Who told you this? Did you see her?* His heart was begging for the news that Molly was okay, but if he didn't keep his cool, she wouldn't be. Will believed she wouldn't purposely put herself in danger, and he clung to that.

"What do you want to do today?" Will asked. "I heard a new movie called Aliens is in the film room. It's about some space monster. There's an early showing and a late one." Will knew he had to show up at the rec room tonight, or it would look like he was avoiding it. He also knew that when he walked in, he would be looking for her, analyzing every inch of her for injuries, and if he found one, all bets were off.

"I got a better idea. There's a party at one of the old houses tonight. Some guy from Operations was awarded a case of whiskey for decoding and fixing a computer virus. Let's go there."

"What's the catch? Is it sanctioned fun or big trouble?"

"It's a 'they'll turn the other way unless we get real stupid' kind of party."

"Well, that's a precarious standard if I ever heard one, but I'm in." He smiled, but inside he wondered how he'd ever find out about Molly. The ache in his belly was causing actual physical pain. He thought of his father participating in his beloved's demise to save her from something worse. He had come full circle, from a self-righteous judge to a compliant culprit. He was getting rather good at hiding his emotions. It seems he's been practicing it his whole life, except for the time he spent with Molly. He was truly himself then, and he wondered if it would be the last time.

Chapter Sixteen

"Come on," Dean said as he jumped up. "Let's rent some bikes and go for a ride. I know a cool place."

"I'm in," Will said as he grabbed his tennis shoes and began tying them. He and Dean had never ridden bikes before joining the Neighwah, but they had become proficient quickly and had been talking about taking a longer excursion.

When they ran, it was usually along the Falcon Trail, but since they were on bikes, Dean took Will a different way. They started on Faculty to Interior and made a turn on Academy Road. When they hit Pine Drive, they headed south. It was free of people and buildings and Will enjoyed the scenery. A cool morning breeze ran its fingers through the aspen leaves flashing and fluttering them while the birds added their melody to the calm June morning.

The speed and the energy spent were liberating, and both men were pushing each other's skills and enjoying the competition. No words were said between them until they turned on a little road that ended at a remote lake. Not a soul was there, but Will could tell by the picnic tables and outhouses it was meant for visiting. There were several minor lakes on the base, but he had never been to this one.

"So," Dean stood straddling his bike and gestured toward the small but crystal-clear lake. "What do you think?"

"I think we should hop in sind cool off." They stripped down to their briefs and bounded into the water. Will was surprised to see Dean was a good swimmer. Few people were taught that anymore. When they made it to the middle of the lake, Dean leaned back and floated.

"Will," he said almost too soft for him to hear, "they can't hear us here if we talk super quiet. The few cameras they have here are the fisheye lens types that don't zoom in well. She's okay. Lewis waited a couple of minutes and headed down to her room. Becket blackened her eye and bruised her arm when she fought him off, but Lewis sucker-punched him and broke his nose. Needless to say, Becker left."

"I wish I could have delivered that myself. Did you set that up?"

"Sort of. I told Lewis that Molly was on the rebound, and if he saved her from Becket, then…"

Will was silent and not sure if thank you was what he deserved, but Dean did step in on her behalf, unlike him. "I guess I should say thank you, but I don't want to hear the rest."

"Fair enough."

"How did you know they were on to me? And what are they on to?"

"They started asking me about you. What did I know about your past, how much you were involved with Molly? They were subtle, but I came from a town of witchers, and they ask stuff like that before they 'purify' the community." Dean's voice was dripping with sarcasm as he said the word purify. "It doesn't take a genius to figure out you have something they want, whether you know what it is or not."

"It's something about my dad and my stepmom, but I was just a kid when they both died. I ended up being raised by a man we traveled with. I don't know anything." He wasn't going to spill his story. Even if he could trust him, it would put him in danger.

"Well, I wouldn't let them know that. These guys don't believe in the I-don't-know scenario."

"You're a good friend Dean. I hope my shit doesn't rub off on you too."

"Hey, they think I'm an informant, or that's what I'm going to go with for now. That being said, I'll be asking you questions. If I were you, I'd let some info out like you don't have anything to hide. You're a guarded person, and that screams secrets. Don't make stuff up you can't manage, sound real sincere, and know it's going to get back to them."

"I kinda figured that the first time you gave me "the look" saying stop, they're watching me that you were involved in my shit." Will paused for a moment and added, "Do you think Becket will bother her anymore?"

"Dude, you said you didn't want to hear the rest. She's good now. Please, leave her be."

They were silent for some time and enjoyed floating on the serene water. The sun danced and twinkled stars across the lake while the sky sculpted its puffy clouds stretching and curling them into amusing images. Will was content. This place was still and peaceful, and he hadn't enjoyed moments like this, where his muscles relaxed and his mind quieted, for as long as he could remember.

The magic of the water soothed him. He hadn't realized how much he needed this respite, and he drank in every second. He had no idea how long they lingered there, but he knew it was enough when the billowing clouds morphed into Molly's voluptuous curves and gentle movements.

"I'm ready to ride back. You done, Dean?"

"Yeah, I was just gonna say that." Dean looked at his friend and wondered if he was going to stay the course or be Mad-dog-Will tonight. No matter what, they had to attend this whiskey party. The stage was set, and the night had to go on.

The ride back was slower, but they talked the whole way. Not like the honest and meaningful conversation they had on the lake. This discussion was superficial and included false plans for the evening's exploits. At least, they were false to Will. The whole night ahead felt obligatory to him, but he knew he had to show up. *Please don't let Molly be* there, he asked the sky as loudly as an unspoken voice could manage.

Will wore his black jeans and one of his new workout t-shirts. It was nice enough to hang out, and he didn't feel up to going on the prowl tonight. He'd let the prowl come to him, and if it didn't, so be it. He'd just exchange a little noise with the guys and grab some laughs before his workweek started. It would be an early night anyway because 0600 hours comes early.

It didn't take Will long to ascertain that Molly was not present, but neither was Lewis. Dean's advice to let her be echoed in his head. Lewis, according to Dean, was a nice guy, but he was on the rebound like Molly. They were primed for a hook-up that Will had all but set up himself. Though her safety mattered greatly to him, it taunted his feral temper thinking about her in this guy's arms.

Will grabbed a shot glass of golden liquid and enjoyed the slow burn of the whiskey. He remembered his introduction to it by Denter. This whiskey was much smoother and he could have easily downed a couple more shots, but he couldn't afford to give his internal guard dog the night off. He poured himself a watered-down version of whiskey and coke and took his time on it.

He was having fun sharing Dranger stories with a group of x-Drangers like himself. He was surprised the line about recruiting them to teach spoiled Uppers wasn't pure fiction. Dean had scoped out his query and was just about to make his final move.

"Will," he said, looking his friend over to assess his sobriety, "I'm heading upstairs for a while. Get home on your own."

Will simply gave him a thumbs-up, smiled, and faked a stumble to make his performance believable. Dean could tell he was lucid and returned to his conquest. Will went back to his group when he caught Becket out of the corner of his eye. He was arguing with a couple of women and propping up another under his arm. The whole group was suddenly focused on the event.

"Let us take her to the dorm!" one woman screamed.

"I said I'd get her back to her room. I promised, and I'm gonna do what I said." Becket stumbled but regained his balance. Will could tell Becket was cornered. He'd be smart to give up, but he was an idiot, and more so now that he was saturated with whiskey. Will could tell he wasn't going to give up his trophy.

"Dude, let her go. You already have a broken nose. Look around you. There are a ton of witnesses here, and two nights in a row of trouble is going to have the Corporates looking to jack you up." Will saw the crowd and deduced he had quite a few willing whiskey fists ready to get a fight rolling.

"This is your fault you, trader!" Becket had let the girl fall to the floor, and her friends were picking her up and heading toward the door. "I don't know what they want from you, but they set that whole thing up to get to you. They think it's my fault you didn't flip your shit. But I can see why you wouldn't fight over that frigid bitch."

Will was shocked. "You're letting your mission secrets spill out all over the place, and I'm the trader? I don't know what they want with me, but I'm going to get a couple of fucking names out of you, asshole. I'm begging you to resist, you fucking prick. I'll fuck your nose and the rest of you up so bad, you won't want to wake up."

Will couldn't hold back anymore, and he didn't have to. His hateful demons were at full throttle now. He had maintained control for so long, but now he had a legitimate fight that wouldn't endanger anyone but himself and this low-life.

Will charged, and Becket saw the rage in his eyes and turned to run. Will yanked him back by his collar and jabbed him in the kidneys. He turned back toward him and held up his hands. Too easy, Will thought, and he gut-punched him anyway. He was rolling on the floor when he motioned for Will to approach. The crowd was whooping and yelling, thoroughly enjoying the fray. Will knew he was ready to confess, or he was so dumbed up on booze, he'd try something. Will grabbed his shirt collar and propped him up, cocking his fist, hoping this moron would do something stupid.

"Dermit," was all Becket said before Will let him fall in a heap on the floor. I

t was then that Dean came running downstairs barefoot, pulling on his shirt, and yelling. "I left you for ten minutes! Ten fucking minutes and you go off the deep end." He was juggling his undone clothing as he spoke.

The whole room was laughing, and another round of shots was sent through the crowd, which was already primed for brawling. Men were slapping each other on the back too hard and delivering playful shoves as they debated the incident. Dean knew at any moment sides would be drawn and more fighting would erupt.

"Come on," Dean said, "we're leaving. Pretty sure that qualified as really stupid. I don't want to be here when this party gets noticed."

As they walked out the door, Dean turned to Will. "You know, *friend,*" he said with sarcastic angst, "you could have given me at least thirty minutes more with that nice lanky blonde."

Will didn't stop to listen. He was cranking down the road. Not even the cool breeze helped to calm him down. He explained the fight to Dean. There was no need to worry about listening devices and no reason to hold back. He was sure Dermit would have twenty versions of the story by morning.

Will wasn't surprised when he was summoned to the upstairs office at 0630 on Sunday morning. He took several deep breaths before he walked through the door. He stopped, saluted, and took the seat when Dermit motioned at him without looking up. Will looked right at the general without any hint of shame or regret. When Dermit looked up, he leaned back in his chair, causing it to squeal and creak.

"Big night?"

"Permission to speak freely, sir."

"Granted."

"You set that prick after me and my friends. Why?"

"You have something I want, and I wanted to find something you would be willing to trade for."

"Let's stop playing footsie here. What the hell are you after?"

"The red key."

Will realized Dermit didn't know what he was looking for, and it assured him his knife was still secure. But Will had practiced this moment for years, and he gave him his best expression of confusion and recollection for his response. "I'd say what red key, but you already believe I know something. But just for fun, what's a red key?"

"Tianna, whose real name was Miranda, had a father who was a very important man. He gave her a key before he died rescuing her from General Kenner. I need that key."

"Tianna, or Miranda, said she lost her memory and didn't know who she was. All I knew was something bad had happened to her because she was scared all the time. If she had a key, she probably gave it to my dad. Why don't you just break open whatever it goes to?"

General Dermit was silent. "Oh shit, you don't know what it goes to." Will shook his head. At least he wasn't the only one in the dark. "Okay, I don't have your key, so where does that leave us? I could be a prisoner or an asset. I make a much better asset."

"What if I told you I know where your dad is?"

"I'd say so do I, burned up in the shed he shot my stepmom from. I know I said I wanted to kill him, and I do. But in all honesty, after all this time, I think fate beat me to it."

"What if I told you he was alive?"

"Are you telling me that?" Will narrowed his eyes and let his ire show through. He even rose out of his chair ever so slightly, letting his voice rise as he did. Though the real demon was Kenner, he needed to make Dermit believe he would betray his father. "I'd kill that murdering bastard. She may have been crazy, but she was kind to me. She was his wife, for God's sake, and he shot her dead. What kind of bastard does that? I'd drill a hole through him for every drop of blood he spilled on that field. But he died in the explosion. There's no way he got out and escaped."

"He was never caught in that field, and we didn't find a body in the blown-up shack. I heard rumors that Pueblo had him in custody, and that could be true. They wouldn't have let me know they had a high-level informant because...," the Dermit paused.

"Because you wouldn't have let them know either," Will filled in the obvious answer. "Are you looking for him?"

"Are you interested in finding him?" the general probed.

"I have unfinished business; you have something you want. Is there a deal here?"

"You need revenge, but I need answers. I can't have a half-cocked gun taking him out before I get those. In the half a year I've had you under surveillance, you have not demonstrated any attempts to contact anyone or search for anything. I think you're a pretty good actor, and I still think you might know exactly where the red key is located. But your story has proven logical and factual, and I have to be open to that."

Will sat silently without offering any expressions that would betray the multitude of ideas and collaborations stored in his head. This wasn't the first time he had run through the possible scenarios of working for Dermit. He didn't think Dermit had been completely honest with him, and Will certainly hadn't been honest with him either. Everything Dermit did, took into account his future moves. Will liked to think he thought several moves ahead too, but Dermit was better at it because he had the power to execute his plans and his enemies. Will did not.

Odds were against any outcome that didn't end with him in the crematorium as a body or a prisoner, but he had to make a move. He had a destiny and a key to unlock something so paramount it had triggered countless covert operations and deaths. Whatever it was, he had to find his father to understand it. He thought of Odysseus alone at sea against the power of the gods. He hoped that when the time came, his destiny included taking down Dermit's greedy power and the depraved Kenner, like Odysseus in his hall of wana-be kings.

Dermit leaned back in his chair, and its squeaks broke the heated silence. Will could tell Dermit saw him as an opponent, and he'd be unwise to see Will in any other way. He sat back up, sending his chair into its natural position.

"Okay, here's the deal. You can work on the team searching for your father. And I'll even let you talk to him because there is no evidence he's given up anything after all this time. I'm counting on him talking to you. That's the only reason you're of value to me. But know this: if you try anything against me, I'll go after everyone you care about."

"So nothing's changed except my assignment, sir," Will surprised himself with his disrespectful retort, but he was weary of the cat-and-mouse game. Will regretted saying it, but something more than Becket's confession had altered the General's timeline. Maybe he did know where his father was. One thing was for sure: Will hadn't talked this formidable man into anything he didn't want to do.

"Watch it, Noland. I've invested resources and called in favors to secure you, and I'm questioning those decisions. If your story about not knowing anything is true, you better hope your dad gives you something, or you're nothing but a waste of time to me."

"Understood, sir."

"You're clever, Will Noland or Alexander, I'll give you that." And he paused as if he were reevaluating the last ten minutes. He folded his hands on the papers strewn across his desk and leaned toward Will. "This meeting is off the record. I know you're close with Rival, and he's going to want to know what we talked about. Rival knows you're an orphan due to a violent past, but he doesn't have to know the guy we're after is that man.

"Tell him it was about the fight last night. As far as Becket spilling his guts, say I told you it was all untrue, and he will be dealt with. Not the most believable lie, but you can also tell him you don't buy it. If he asks if you're being watched, say you don't know. That makes our lie believable, and I have a feeling you're good at pulling off lies and hiding secrets."

Will caught himself before he answered with an affirmative response lest it be taken as an admission. It was the kind of question intended to trick him into untangling a "yes sir" meaning. "You can count on me, sir."

"Yep, very clever," the man grunted under his breath seeing he had avoided his trap, and with a shoddy salute, he dismissed Will from the room.

Will was reassigned to investigations, Dean's team. It made him wonder if Dean had already been investigating the possibility of his father being alive. Maybe he didn't even if he didn't know who he was. Was his commander satisfied with his behavior over those five and a half months, or was it truly because Becket had disclosed his mission and forced the timeline forward?

Will wasn't sure what was going to happen to Becket, but he heard he was transferred to another base. He was only chosen because he was the standout womanizing bully. Dermit knew he'd get Will's attention, and when it didn't work, he probably blamed Becket. The guy had been bought, sold, and shipped out before he even knew what happened.

On their first tour, they were to secure a path for military transports by clearing brush and droning the area for potential attacks. Rival was on the classified team but at the lowest intel level. He didn't know who they might need to transport with so much military support, but Will did.

Soon they would approach the Pueblo border and go a mile inside. They would end up in the very field where Will's life took a severe turn. Will had driven to Pueblo on the main highway near this grave field, but it couldn't be seen from the road. He realized he hadn't faced the power it may hold over him. *Was this part of Dermit's plan to watch me fall apart?* Will buried his fears and drew up his confident power and his anger, hoping it was enough.

Day after day they worked on the road and mapped out the route for military transports. The only difference between this and typical Dranger work was that this was a top-secret operation. That night in camp, the officer in charge gave a briefing that defined the mission goals and parameters.

"We are here to make a prisoner exchange with the Pueblo territory. When the van with prisoner Robin arrives tomorrow, we will proceed into Pueblo, where we will make the trade for prisoner Adam. The prisoner exchange will happen west of Old May Ranch in an open field. Red team, you'll lead the convoy, blue you'll drive the van with the prisoner, and green you'll head up the rear. This is a high-value prisoner, and there is no room for error. Questions?" It was pretty straightforward with very limited specifics, and no one raised a hand. "Dismissed."

"So, Rival, what team are you on?" Will caught up with him on the way to the dinner line.

"Well, as luck would have it," Dean gave him a downward scowl, "we are both on the 'head up the rear' team." They laughed loudly, enjoying a welcome release from the escalating tension.

"Later that evening, Will lay on his cot and tried to sort out some kind of plan. *What if he did get the chance to talk with his dad? And if he did give him some information, Dermit would get it also, then what? How would he save him or himself?*

This was the most dangerous scheme he had ever concocted because he had no outcome that left him or his dad alive. The gist of his fly-by-night strategy was to talk with his dad and hope he had some gestures that would help him figure it out. *Was he thinking his shackled father could save him?* He had trusted him once before, but sometimes there are no solutions. It was more of a fly-by-nightmare than a plan. He was way over his head and unable to sleep.

Breakfast was cold oatmeal and a stale fruit bar. The hot dark coffee hit the spot though. Will had become accustomed to having it since Dean introduced it to him. Everyone stood around waiting for the van when it came down the gravel road billowing a cloud of dust in its wake.

Will got a glimpse through the caged window at the prisoner. She was a young woman, her blonde hair matted with blood. She turned toward Will, and her hollow eyes and tear-stained face told the story of the cruelty she had endured. Her only crime was Kenner wanted her. She was more than likely the daughter of an Upper, and Kenner's price for the prisoner Dermit wanted. But Will couldn't help her.

He had an impossible mountain in front of him, and adding her troubles to it would help no one. He had to talk with his father, though he wasn't sure he could save him. He also wondered if he would fall on this sword of destiny without accomplishing anything.

She looked down, and Will walked toward his vehicle. He would let Dean or Tanner drive. His nerves were igniting the fire of his anxiety. His whole body ached, and his stomach was churning. He knew it was just his past coming to haunt him, and he focused on loading his gun and taking his position.

They came to the cursed field and stopped along the dirt road facing the convoy with the prisoner for trade. Will strained to get a visual, but his head was spinning. Was he freaking out at the scene that marked the end of his childhood? He tried to gain control, but something was happening to him. It didn't feel right. He turned to Dean.

"Something is wrong," he managed to say, trying to focus enough to see his friend. He was struggling against the spell he was under. The world swirled, and its hues grew unnaturally bright and vivid. *Not nerves,* he thought — something, *something else.* He heard Dean call his name, but he was unable to respond. He could not move his body, and he crumpled to the floor in front of the side door.

He was awake enough to hear gunshots reverberating around him, but out of it enough, they sounded like a strange underwater echo. Bulletproof windows splintered and cracked from the multiple impacts coming from every direction. It was an ambush! He tried to call out to Dean. No answer. With all his might, he rolled over enough to see his friend slumped against the steering wheel. Will was powerless. His body refused to move. All he could do was watch a stream of blood seep down Dean's limp arm and drip into a red puddle.

Chapter Seventeen

Fighting to stay awake, Will tried to crawl over to Dean, but his body did not respond to his commands. He pushed his effort with all the strength he could summon, but his determination could not overcome the weakness gripping his body. He tried to fight it until his vision faded and darkness surrounded him.

He woke to intense pressure in the hollow of his shoulder. Several men with distorted faces hovered over him and held him down. He felt the rocking motion as he lay on his back on the floor of a van, not the vehicle he arrived in. He wanted to fight them, but his body was dead, and his hazy state muddled his reasoning. The men loosened their grip when his wild, desperate eyes confirmed he was completely paralyzed. He felt them pulling out pieces of his body, and he heard a tinkling sound when the assault stopped. *Had he been shot?*

One man took the tray containing the piece and handed it to another, who fussed over someone else lying next to him. He was not in any pain, and soon he lost all concern regarding his dilemma, relaxing into the familiar rocking of old roads and drifting into a deep sleep.

He woke up in a dimly lit brick building. It was not much larger than a shack, where a strange pipe structure sat prominently at the center. His mind was clearing, and he surmised it was a pump house, but the motor was still and quiet. His arms and ankles were chained to the pipe, but he could struggle and move his body within the restraints.

At the other end of the small room, he saw the lifeless body of a tall young, dark-skinned man dressed in his Neighwah uniform. He looked disturbingly similar to himself, and he deduced that this man and he would trade identities because he noticed he also was dressed in different clothing. The items were old and frayed, like the clothing Drangers wear. He must be in Pueblo, and Kenner had him. But what the hell was he up to?

He cried out, "Kenner, you gutless bastard. Can't fight a real man. You have to drug him and tie him up." He was about to continue his verbal attack when the door opened.

"Wrong again, Will." Denter walked in rifle in hand and collapsed heavily between Will and the other body.

"Betrayer!" Will sneered at him and strained against his tethered limbs.

Denter gave Will the stop look. He looked pale and weak. "I don't have time to explain, so listen up. When I see the drugs have worn off enough that you don't fuck this whole thing up, I'll untie you. Nod if you understand." Will nodded.

"We set Dermit up to think he would get your dad, but you were right; your dad died long ago in that field. The Pueblo soldiers did find a body, but it was kept secret from the other territories. They felt the search for him would turn up something to lead them to Cali Bantu." Denter could see Will was about to interrupt. "Do not stop me. They are coming, and they'll be here soon. No one knows what Cali Bantu is, but everyone wants it.

"There is a key that they believe you have or know of, and they will stop at nothing to get it. They want it enough that hundreds, maybe more, have died trying to find it. We need to find it first." Denter struggled to get up and free Will from his bonds. "There's a pack over there. It contains the coded book your father left with the Robin Hood pact." Help me tip this pump.

Will stood up, shaking off the last of his dizzies, and the two of them tipped open the machine, revealing a hole where a motor used to be.

Denter was visibly in pain, and blood was leaking through the lower end of his shirt. Will helped him sit back down. "Under this pump is a tunnel. It will take you out and away from here." Denter let out a moan and held his gut.

"You're hurt. Let me help you."

"You can help me by getting away. That kid over there has your blood type and build, and we inserted your ID chip in him. I have this place rigged to go up so hot, the tunnel should remain a secret. With that kid over there, they'll have proof you died here. Are you clearheaded enough to understand what I said?" Will nodded.

"Did you kill him to save me?"

"No," he said, but Will didn't believe him. It was too convenient.

"Where should I go?"

"As soon as you crawl through the tunnel, follow this map and the trail of chalked trees." He handed Will a hand-drawn map. "Spray the marks as you go, so you won't be followed. You have to hurry. It's going to rain something awful in a couple of hours, and all the marks will be gone.

"When you get to X, there's a simple shelter. Walk one hundred paces northwest. Then, with your current position, do a grid search. Don't stay more than one night, and then head west into the wilderness. Find a place to live until you figure out your dad's book. We can't decode it, but he told a Robin Hood brother that you could."

"I don't know any codes."

"Think Will. It's in there somewhere." Denter pointed at Will's head. "Dig for it. You're good at that. When you gave me the sign, this all went into action. You have it. It's up to you now. Go, fulfill your destiny."

"What's going to happen to you, to my family? Do you know where Rival is? Is he okay?" A shot popped in the distance.

"Damn it! Will, get the fuck out of here! Now!"

Will grabbed the gun and ammo box sitting on top of the pack and secured it in the holster on his hip. Throwing the pack over his shoulder, he hopped into the hole. Landing about eight feet down, he jumped up, grabbed the rope attached to the pump, and pulled it back over, sealing himself in the earthy pit. The beanie on Will's head had a headlamp, and he hit the light. The space was cramped, and it stretched endlessly until the darkness consumed it. He never had a fear of tight spaces, but this seemed to push at that boundary.

Ignoring his cramping legs and arms, he crawled military-style through the tunnel, pushing the large pack stuffed to the brim with unknown supplies. On and on it went as the ceiling sent tuffs of dirt down on him, threatening to bury him alive in a sudden collapse. He shimmied through the hole like a worm, wondering if he had taken a wrong turn and if it was even possible to go backward. But he knew better. There had been no option but forward. It finally stopped as abruptly as it had started in that pump house.

A wooden disc stood between him and daylight, and he quickly removed it. Attached to the lid was a wire that led deep into the soil. When he opened the lid enough to climb out, he heard the rumble deep inside, and dust and dirt billowed out of the hole, meaning the tunnel had collapsed. It shocked Will, making him jump. He also was aware of the finality of the journey and its intention for one person to escape.

He took a moment to stretch out his screaming muscles, and the brief pause set his mind to wonder what happened to Denter. He looked up at the heavily forested area and spotted the first chalk mark. Denter's order kicked in. He unhooked the hanging bottle and ran to spray it with water to erase it. Then, he moved onward, continuing the routine until a loud boom in the distance rocked the forest, sending birds scattering from their perches. But to Will, it meant Denter was gone. He steeled his emotions. He couldn't get into that now.

He was glad he and Dean made a habit of running every day. He was only slightly winded after thirty minutes of going at a steady quick pace with a pack of significant weight. But it was the canteen that had been bobbing and sloshing along as he ran that called him to a halt. He enjoyed the first few gulps so thoroughly that he had to stop himself from drinking too much. He didn't know when he would get more, and throwing up would leave an easy mark for the hounds.

A few raindrops hit his face, and he wondered if it had just started or if he hadn't noticed it. A quick observation of the dry forest meant that the white chalk marks ahead were still visible, for now, but speed was crucial. Securing his canteen back onto his pack, he ran on.

Hours had passed, and the rain was getting heavy and steady. The marks were getting dimmer with the increasing rain and the fading of the day. Will hoped they held out long enough for him to find the shelter. The excursion was finally taking its toll. When Will saw the fading X dripping down the tree, he was so excited that he made a misstep, sending him tumbling onto a fallen tree branch. The gash he received hurt like hell, but it wasn't serious.

He started his grid search and within thirty minutes he located an area against a ledge that had a familiar brushy look. He swept the branches aside with his hand, and there was a small cave complete with rustic accommodations. *Looks like GZ* he said quietly to himself. Storing his pack inside, he left to collect a plant he had seen during his exploration. Tianna had taught him many medicinal remedies from native plants, and a poultice made from Oregon grape roots and plantain has an antibiotic property to fight infection if used early.

The mountain shadows were overtaking the daylight, so he settled into his shelter for the night. As he waited for the water to boil on the provided camp stove, Will took in his new surroundings. A bed sack stuffed with straw and covered with a wool blanket was parked at the back of the cavern. A low table, just right for floor sitting, held a battery lantern and the single burner stove with a pan on top, while two full canteens sat under the table.

While the water was heating, he unpacked the pack hoping it contained soap. Inside he found a pistol, three boxes of ammo, dried food packets, binoculars, a compass, a camo/infrared blocker tarp, and many more compact survival items. But his favorite was a bowstring and twenty arrowheads, and under the med kit, he found five bars of soap. No wonder it was heavy. He had the feeling he was expected to live out here for a while.

The last thing Will located was the book Denter said was his father's. It was hidden in a protected compartment under a false bottom section of the pack. He pulled it out gently, and recognition hit him instantly. This wasn't his father's book. This belonged to Tianna.

He recalled her sharing her drawings, and poetic thoughts as he thumbed through the familiar pages. She drew wild vegetables, herbs, and medicinal plants in perfect detail. There were recipes for soups, stews, bread, and household products. At first glance, it didn't hold the secret to world peace, but it would be a great asset living on his own.

He quickly located his favorite page. The swirling design showed the cross-section of a seashell. She even had a seashell once and showed it to him, but it was lost to the past now. She said the shape held math magic, but Will hadn't learned what that meant. It dawned on him it could be the secret to this destiny thing he kept being threatened with. In his mind, it felt more like a cruel joke than a grand heroic plan.

The water was bubbling in the pan, and Will set to cleaning his wound vigorously with soap and warm water, causing it to bleed. Then, he made the poultice and held the mash in place with a piece he ripped from his oversized t-shirt. The size made him believe it was one of Denter's.

He threw the crushed wildflowers into a cup of hot water and let it steep. The med kit had some medicines, which probably included antibiotics, but he didn't need that kind of help, not yet anyway. He could wait until he was far away. Tonight, he desperately needed to rest, but a sound sleep was highly unlikely.

His analytical mind wouldn't settle down. He went through a series of schemes to get him into the lost zone. It was the unplotted line between the Corporate zone and the Fringer zone. He decided he would secure the infrared-blocking side of the tarp over his pack and head while he walked to conceal his heat signature from the drones. Along with keeping him dry, it would make room for the empty bed sack and stove.

He had plotted out a path during his search the evening before, so he could start before dawn. The throbbing in his leg was settling down as the purple coneflower tea kicked in. Willow tea would have been better, but it was harder to find. The next time he was near a creek, he'd look for it. Will felt his body and mind relax and fall toward sleep, but his rest was periodically plagued with worry, pain, and the cold of a wilderness night.

The Neighwah may believe him dead, but that wouldn't stop them from sending the dog teams out. He was too close to the pump house, and if he remained he would be found. The blanket was warm, but the night was colder. Will tried to calm his mind, but his sleep was wrought with the agitation of being hunted and the worry both his friends were dead. In the morning, he sorely missed his strong black coffee. It was the first of many comforts he would miss, but those indulgences had made him weak, and weakness was a luxury he could no longer afford.

The skills he learned in his year with the Drangers and then another year as a Neighwah helped him do the hard labor required to live, eat, and seek shelter. He also knew how to do the ugly work to defend his domain and remain hidden. On the second day of his journey, he came upon the downed fence that bordered the edge of the monitored area.

The way the wire had tuffs of black fur and had been twisted while the posts were ripped from the ground, made Will believe a bear had gotten tangled up in it. The overgrown vegetation told him it had happened several years ago, and it surprised him that the border was so unmaintained and therefore unmonitored. Just to be safe, he crossed the breach at night with his bulging pack and lumbered like a black bear.

He lived the nomad life to be sure there was no one after him. According to the hash marks he made in Tianna's book, he had been on the run for three months. Autumn's warm colors signaled the coming transition toward the monochromatic winter months. He needed a more permanent shelter to survive the cold at this altitude.

The abandoned but sturdy cabin was well disguised to blend into its forested environment and tucked against a rocky bluff. It was a cabin built for the dying times after the meteorite shower. It was in Fringer territory and despite the rumors of their wicked deeds. He felt safe there and thankful he had found it.

It was much sturdier and less covert than Giden Zita, but he called it GZ2 just the same. Although it was in rough shape, Will could make the needed repairs. Inside he found a strong wooden bedframe, a table, a desk, a chair, a sink, and a wood stove. Will scrubbed the rusty spots on the iron stove, worried they hid holes, but he was happy to find it didn't leak smoke when he stoked it up. Although smoke could be seen for a long distance, it would be attributed to one of the many Fringer fires.

The remnants of human engineering could be found easily enough in the ghosted areas that once entertained camping vacationers. Will gathered scraps of metal and made spikes for winter climbing and a smoke box for drying meats and fruits. He was ecstatic to find two of the three plants in Tianna's notes that could make a coffee substitute.

Drying lamb's quarter seeds and roasting mountain ash berries, he made his caffeinated beverage. It wasn't coffee, but he got used to it, and it gave him his morning jolt. He made little improvements to make his cabin feel like home. He built a shelf for his homemade tin dishes and hooks to hang dried herbs and fruits.

The Neighwah and the Drangers wouldn't search this far for a dead man. This was Fringer territory, and it was forbidden to engage them. The Corporates were afraid if the Dailys and Uppers found out the Fringers weren't the cruel, murdering outlaws their rumors made them out to be, they might be influenced to join these free-living troops. The Corporate order needed its slaves docile, but continually hunting down the Fringers in their endless wilderness was unsustainable. The Fringers didn't have the weapons to overtake their soldiers, but they could hide and elude them indefinitely. So, an unspoken truce existed between them.

Will had observed the Fringer tribes in his area, and he learned that they just wanted to live free and be left alone to live their hunter-gatherer existence. This life was hard and dangerous work, and it left little time to get in malicious trouble. Will had overheard them talk about a band that goes around murdering and robbing the tribes, but he had yet to witness it.

He ate wild game and harvested food from the forest with the help of Tianna's drawings and notes. He slept warmly on his bed bag stuffed with dried grasses and pine boughs and covered with a blanket made from bear hides. He sewed himself a coat of tanned deer hides. Will had two bows. One was a simple bow he made when he arrived at the cabin. The other was a compound bow he made with pulleys he salvaged from a ghost town. It took months to file and sand it into a piece of art perfectly balanced and lethal. He spent many nights fashioning arrows using flint and salvaged metal for the heads.

He couldn't believe his luck when he found a sealed spool of strong braided fishing line to use for bowstrings. It had a hundred yards of line, and he couldn't imagine using it all. He loved to hunt, and he was very efficient. The cabin had all the trappings for sustaining him, and he wanted nothing more. Although he started diligently pouring over the book trying to decipher its mysteries and riddles, he did that less and less as time went on. He relished his freedom and enjoyed the life of a solitary predator with no need for destinies or companionship.

Often at night when he sat by his fire, he thought of his other life. He thought of Dean and Molly, of Taylor, Calen, Denter, and Nash. He remembered the nights laughing with his Dranger brothers and the adventures he had with Dean. On this particular night, Will turned nineteen years old. He was safe from the cruel world of Corporate control, but everyone he cared for was not.

More and more, he felt the pangs of guilt for abandoning them to the brutal rule of the oppressors. He thought of the friends and family he had left behind and whether they had been gathered by the Corporates. *Did Dean survive? Who were the other people who helped him escape?* He thought about Denter telling him that his dad gave the book to a Robin Hood brother. *Who was that person? Could it be Taylor?*

The people were waiting for their warrior to save them. He didn't believe it was him, but if not him, then who? *What power did he possess to end Corporate rule? Was he to blame for the innocents still trapped in the Territory cities scampering to the dark hiding* places, *hoping something worse wasn't lying in wait?* He wanted to be done with death and battles, and the same old argument kept him from finding the Robinhooders and joining the fight.

He hadn't solved the book, and he found no reference to a Cali Bantu. He remembered the way Dean challenged him at every physical task, and how hard he fought to move when he was drugged. That was what trying looked like. *Had he tried that hard to solve this mystery, or did he just give in to his lack of understanding? If he felt he had tried his hardest, would he be able to accept that he was given a critical task and failed?*

He still was strong, but only he benefited from his efforts. He would happily follow a strong warrior leader against the Corporate devils, but he didn't believe he was that man. He wished he could relinquish this burden, this destiny, but who would take it? Dermit, Kenner, they would take it.

It wasn't more than a week later, when Will was hunting, that he saw two men chasing a girl through the woods. Through his binoculars, he could see she was bloodied, and her clothing was torn. The pure terror in her eyes made his decision easy. He aimed his bow, *thwack.* The leading man dropped. The second stopped and looked around for his enemy. *Thwack,* the second man dropped, and Will could see no other pursuers. He charged off the hill, leaving his gear. When he reached her, she was barely conscious.

He picked her up and carried her over his shoulder. He knew there was a Fringer camp half a mile away. Most Fringers migrated between a summer and a winter camp, and this was their summer camp. Carefully, he edged near the camp. The people were sitting in a group under the guard of three men. The girl began to stir, and he set her down and covered her mouth before she could scream.

He put his finger to his mouth and pointed to the scene below them. He pulled his bow and took out the guard standing away from the group. He went down behind a tent wall with little fanfare, and his fellow Drangers didn't even notice. He readied two more arrows and waited for his moment. *Thwack, thwack,* the other two men were down in seconds.

"Were there only four?" he asked the terrified girl. She nodded her head. "Tell your elder to leave my arrowheads on the large sun rock a mile from here. Do you know the one I mean?" Again, she nodded, and Will left her alone to climb down to her camp.

Will was battle-charged with edgy exhilaration. Killing people wasn't something to be proud of, but killing the murdering, raping, and pillaging assholes had its appeal. He remembered what it felt like to be a part of something where he belonged and had a purpose in the world. It was then that he decided to decipher the book. And he needed to retrieve his knife.

Chapter Eighteen

That night, Will was plagued with thoughts of his family, friends, and the rest of the Dailys and Drangers picking out an existence while he was free, fed, and warm in his cabin. He had left them to the Corporate carnivores, and it bore into his core where Tianna's tender lessons haunted him. That was where the platitudes of morality and compassion lived, but he rarely unpacked them. They had been dangerous to speak of and impossible to live by. He contemplated the dangerous trek to retrieve his blade, but then what? He had no plan after that because he didn't know anything about the big secret.

He had tried endlessly to decode the shell, but it eluded him. He knew it had to do with the mathematics of a spiral, but he hadn't had many lessons in math beyond the basic algebra he needed for crime scene reports. The closest he had come to the geometry of spirals was its use in search patterns. It was becoming increasingly evident that a Highmind, a genetically enhanced human, set this whole thing up, and it would take another to unravel it. Will thought of himself as clever rather than smart, and he was highly intuitive, but he was no Highmind.

One conundrum at a time he concluded. He set out the old map book of Colorado he had found in the cabin's desk drawer under a still-wrapped ream of lined paper and beside a collection of pencils. He turned to the well-used page of the Colorado Springs area.

The map had a small X marked near the Skagway Reservoir, which marked his cabin's location. Will visited the lake often to fish and swim in its crystal waters. He could see where the old waterline had been before the dam cracked open. The new growth was flanked by the old forest and the leftover lake. The deep gouge in the cement barrier released a steady stream of water into Beaver Creek. Though the remnants of the dam seemed stable for now, Will had no doubt the compromised structure continued to disintegrate slowly, reverting the lake into a flowing river.

He traced his finger northwest and landed on the town of Cripple Creek. His touch lingered there as if he could feel the heartbeat of a certain resident. His reality could have been so different with Molly instead of some enigmatic destiny. Several times when he was choked with loneliness, he thought about glassing the town to catch a glimpse of her. It wasn't far. If he hustled, he could make it in a day.

But it was an outskirt border town whose purpose was to diligently survey the area and protect the territory. He wondered if she had heard about his death and whether she had cried. He wouldn't blame her if she didn't. He wouldn't blame her if she hated him, but that wasn't her style. He hoped she had simply let him go, and that she was as safe in her disappointment in him as he was heartbroken in his love for her.

Until now, he had primarily used the atlas to plot out his hunting and gathering trips. It was invaluable for finding old towns and roads. Though they were reduced to collapsed structures and forsaken asphalt, they held numerous treasures. The countless lines spidered out to every named spot on the diagram. Numerous roads ended in the middle of nowhere, left to the ravages of the encroaching forest. It was a tragic metaphor for the times.

Though overrun with plants and obstacles, the old roads offered less treacherous routes with gentler inclines, which were preferable when packing supplies. The pre-disaster maps in the book revealed how densely populated the region had been. He was surprised how quickly fires, harsh weather, and indigent gatherers had completely erased the efforts of human endeavors. It was nothing like the maps he used as a Dranger or a Neighwah. Those maps only reflected the existing features, considerably smaller towns, and currently used thoroughfares. He wished he had a copy of that version for comparison on his trips.

With his compass and the rough map he drew, he should be able to navigate a safe path to the remote area where he buried the knife. He recalled the spot along Interstate 25 where it intersected the abandoned road. This map showed it was Highway 85, but it had changed since this map was made. He heard that the intersecting roads went over Interstates, but those bridges were left to fall. Using whatever routes they could, Dranger road crews made the shortest path to connect with I-25 at ground level. *What this world must have looked* like, he said to himself while looking at the busy metropolitan map.

Will woke up with the sunrise and pulled on his pack. It was a gorgeous September day, and he followed his route with his compass in hand. Although he had an extremely keen sense of recall, he left small notches on trees, five rocks, or lines drawn in the dirt to mark his return trip. The first two days of the journey, he was safe in the unpatrolled zone.

He found the old roads valuable for location checks, but whenever he could, he used game trails to prevent being found. He was a lone Fringer now, and lone Fringers were seen as vulnerable or dangerous to other Fringers. The ones he had encountered were mostly peaceful, but some were hunters, and they hunted groups and loners to rob them. Will had confidence in his combat prowess against other Fringers, but being ambushed changed his odds.

On the third morning, he continually glassed his surroundings, making his progress slower. Before he crossed the accepted border between the Fringers and the Corporates, he stopped for the night. He had the last meal he would allow himself time for until he was back behind this unwritten boundary. His forest harvest had been fruitful this year, and he brought dried meats, berries, and crabgrass flatbread with lambs quarter seeds. They were wrapped in packets he wove from sweet grass and yucca plants.

He held the handwoven pouches and remembered mastering the art of weaving while being locked in the boredom of his warm cabin last winter. The morning chill made him think of the coming winter as it edged closer despite summer trying to stave off its inevitable slumber. He ticked off the list of tasks waiting to be finished before the snows came and recalled the peaceful nature of that life. He needed that time, that respite, but now the people needed their suffering to end, so his destiny needed to begin.

When he left the Fringer territory and crossed into the Corporate one, the armed drones would make his trek much more dangerous. They traveled far and used heat-seeking cameras, and though he had his infrared tarp converted into a poncho, it was not foolproof. It wasn't meant to be a garment, and the longer it remained close to his body, the warmer the fabric got.

As uneventful as the first leg of this journey had been, he expected serious trouble in this place. If he were found, especially after he retrieved his blade, they would have it, and they would believe he possessed the very information he still sought. His life would be a nightmare of torture until it ended in a welcome death.

The blade was buried just north of Stratmoor. It was in an unpopulated section where I-25 and Highway 85 crossed and then paralleled each other to Fountain. Although the book's map was littered with bustling communities, the current reality was not. The old still-standing structures did offer some cover, but they were precariously unsound. He remembered working on these roads as a Dranger, making them conveniently familiar.

Working in the Neighwah high command gave him access to camera placement, and he hoped they hadn't been changed. He didn't know how often the cameras were moved, but he had been gone for well over a year.

Detecting warm bodies with infrared was less effective during the day, so that's when he made his methodical excursions. That being said, visual sightings were much easier during the day. He made his way through the old zoo because it was a forbidden area and the cement structures made for excellent cover.

Sitting in a densely forested section, he watched two Drangers walk down I-25. Their casual demeanor and loud voices told Will he had not been detected. He was close now, and he was poised to sprint across the road to his buried treasure.

It had been easy so far, and he fought the battle between being impatient and lingering too long. Glassing down both directions of the road, he could see no one coming. He dashed past the rock and into the wooded area. He felt his tarp catch and tear with his careless haste. *Damn it,* he muttered under his breath.

Going through the memorized series of tallied paces, he moved the bush aside and quickly dug up the glass jar. A thick layer of determined dirt covered the glass, and he couldn't see the blade. He shook it and tried to open it, but the lid was rusted shut. With his thumb, he wiped away enough dirt from the side that he could tell it was his blade in the container.

Will stuffed the jar into his pack and crept toward the road. Making his way to the rock, he glassed both ways before he dashed across and into the cover of dense vegetation. He cautiously but quickly made his way back to the zoo and into the old bear tunnel. He relaxed for a minute, thinking through his next move. He believed he was through the worst, but he needed to keep moving. While between two buildings, he heard voices.

"Just a minute, Shank. I gotta pee."

"Hurry up, we're finished with the border walk and I'm hungry," the other Dranger answered.

Will heard the Dranger's clumsy footsteps coming right toward him, and he sprinted for cover of the trees. The Dranger turned his head, but he proceeded to the side of a building and unzipped his pants. As he peed, he looked around, searching for what had made the shuffling noise. When he finished, he walked around the building, assumingly back to his friend, Shank.

The next sound Will heard was the snap of a twig behind him. The Dranger had doubled back. He could not put his covert identity in jeopardy or even have witnesses report Fringers were in the zoo. It might bring out the inquisitors and worse after that. He stayed silent, knowing he had a large tree trunk to block a shot. Will heard the final crunch of pine needles right on the other side of the tree. Will ambushed him and snapped his neck, with the only sound being the separating vertebrae.

"Brute, what's taking you so long? Come on, Shank, let's go find him." That meant there were two coming his way, and the voice that spoke was close. Will readied his bow and two arrows. He pulled his neck scarf over his face and came around the tree. *Thwack*, the slender arrow went right through one of the men's hearts and out his back. One down.

"Shit!" came a voice too covered in the brush for Will to locate him. All Will could hear was the snapping and swishing of branches as the Dranger made a hasty retreat.

Will couldn't risk taking the time to hunt him, especially if their pack was close. This Dranger was on his way to report some Fringer killed two Drangers. And then it would get to the Neighwah. Within an hour, this zoo and the area surrounding it would be crawling with armed drones, and soon after the drones, the soldiers and their dogs would follow. He needed to retrieve his arrow and run.

He proceeded with more attention to speed than caution. Not going fast enough or going so fast that he got injured were both fatal mistakes he couldn't afford. What took him almost a day to traverse, took him under four hours to cross. He stopped when he came to a creek with a steady stream. He splashed the cool water over his face and ran upstream to confound his scent for the tracking dogs.

He felt himself slip, and his left arm slammed into a boulder. He thought he heard a crack, but he couldn't stop here in the open. His legs were still strong, so he kept moving, his arm throbbing with every footfall. He used his compass more than the slashes and other markers. He would climb a tree or even the ridge if he got lost. From there, he could locate a familiar landform. Under the heavy canopy of the forest, he stopped momentarily to wrap his arm. Using his spare shirt, he secured it to his chest. Then, he moved onward.

He had to make it into the abandoned lands. The Neighwah wouldn't enter deep into the Fringer's territory and break the peace that existed between the realms for two dead Drangers. They would probably just check their satellite feed to ensure they weren't dealing with more than a single renegade. That is unless they thought it was Will. Dermit's desire for Will to be alive would drive him to pursue him with a mighty force despite the overwhelming evidence of his death. That scenario could have every Fringer at risk.

Will came to the same place where he had spent his second night. He was somewhat relieved that he never heard any dogs howling or low-flying drones buzzing. It would be hard to track him through the heavy forest without flying low enough to distinguish him from an elk or a bear. He would be more relieved, but his arm was causing him intense pain. He unwrapped his makeshift bandage to triage the injury. If it was broken, it was just a thin fracture. The bone was still properly placed and would heal.

He was feeling reassured that he had escaped successfully. Although he was still watchful and critical of the results, he congratulated himself for recovering his knife. Tucked neatly inside a shallow cave, he took his food pouches and the jar out of the pack. While munching greedily on his flatbread and jerky, he looked at the jar and then at his arm. He tried holding the jar with his feet and turning the lid, but it wouldn't budge. He continued to work at it until finally the rusty canning ring was freed.

Tipping the jar, he let the blade tumble into his hand and pulled it from its sheath. He had worried water might seep inside, but it was completely dry and wonderfully preserved. When he buried it, his skills with a knife were nonexistent, but he was quite an expert at wielding a blade now. He went through the moves he had been taught over the years of soldiering.

He quickly discovered his other arm was needed for balance, and moving around was painful. He sat down, staring at the mysterious key to some place called Cali Bantu.

It was elegantly weighted, and his hand fit securely in the shape of the handle. The red blade was still razor sharp, and it easily sliced through a piece of tough dried meat. It was a magnificent weapon. He knew he wouldn't be able to carry it around as a lone Fringer. It was more than a weapon. It was the key to Cali Bantu, whatever the hell that was. He stared at the beautiful burden, feeling his worries wind through him again.

He laid the enigma down, and with a sigh, he went to the mouth of the cave. Gazing out at the dark sky littered with stars, he focused on the familiar hazy band of the Milky Way that divided the heavens. His world was quite exquisite when he paused to take it in. This incredible expanse was as magnificent as it was malevolent.

A random herd of frozen rocks had somehow found its way to this tiny world and altered its order into abject chaos. *How arbitrary is our existence?* He said to no one. His problems felt small, and he felt smaller. No matter his fate, the stars would shine, and the seasons would change. He turned and checked on the willow bark tea he had started brewing to ease the pain and swelling in his arm. He drank the bitter fluid with a grimace and lay down to get some much-needed sleep. Tomorrow was another day of hard travel.

It was early the next day, and Will's arm was feeling better than he expected. He had slept hard, and believed his injury to be no more than a bad bruise. He made more willow tea brew for the swelling and secured his arm in a loose sling, allowing him to remove it quickly if needed. Though his pace was brisk, he didn't run. By tomorrow, he would be at his cabin, and then he would have to decide what his next move was.

The rest of the trip home was wonderfully ordinary. Will felt confident he had escaped exposure, but he constantly glassed the area for any sign of Corporate intrusion. He unloaded his pack and looked at the tall jar with the blade inside. He had to find a safe place to store it away from the cabin. At least until he figured out how to fit it into his future. There was a cave about a mile from here that was home to thousands of bats. Dailys and Fringers feared bats and the diseases they carried, so they were the perfect guardians of the Sanguine Blade.

After settling the blade, Will felt a huge weight lift off his shoulders. The sun was setting when he hiked to the creek to take a needed bath. The cool water soothed the aches and wounds he could finally let himself feel. He was collecting scars at a rapid pace, but right now he relaxed. On his way back, he gathered some greens for a salad and discovered a rabbit in the snare he had set before walking to the creek. He was safe at home with fresh meat and salad for dinner.

Chapter Nineteen

Will had fully recovered from his escape, and his paranoia had waned into sensible readiness. He had harvested the bounty of his surroundings and began to gather his winter stores. While out on a hunt, he saw the same camp of the girl he rescued before, but they were in a different place. It was only a couple of miles from their last sight. He assumed they had moved to avoid the same marauders but stay close enough to harvest their garden.

He could see six men and two boys, but there were no women, which was unusual. Though Fringer tribes moved several times a year, this camp was still being set up. At least one female should be there helping complete the process of setting up the camp. They couldn't all be in their canopy houses at the same time during daylight.

The light of day was precious time for working, gathering, and meal prep. Where was the girl he freed before he left to get his blade? The Drangers must have come back with more troops and firepower. He was in full cover and hidden on the outskirts as he listened to the Fringers' conversation.

"We have to attack before they take them further south," said the bruised man with the bandages on his hand and head. He was either their leader or he had been randomly selected for a beating.

"With what Wurden? They took most of our weapons, and they have guns. We need a plan to get their weapons," replied the one with the green wool beanie.

We don't have time for that. We have to ambush them before they reach Route 24. No doubt they have a vehicle stashed there," the bandaged man replied.

"We need to find that arrow guy. Maybe he'd help. He did before," the only child piped in.

It dawned on him that he had completely forgotten to check for the arrowheads he told them to leave on the sun rock. He stayed hidden. Surprising them could leave Will with a limited number of homicidal choices in his defense.

"I believe he has moved on from this area. He didn't even retrieve his arrows. We should probably go collect those for our bows," said the short man with dark hair. He sounded like Tianna did when she imitated her favorite teacher.

"But then if he comes back, he'll be mad. He saved Jellybean, and he didn't have to. She said he was strong and very tall. He can fight, and he hides in the shadows, slipping in and out like a, uhh, a what's it called again Relic?" The young child had the same hero dream most kids had. It was one they grew out of too quickly.

"I think you mean a ninja," the teacher type, Relic, replied.

"Yeah, a ninja." The boy began to go through a series of amateur fighting moves while chanting attack calls. Will smiled. He liked this kid.

"Dart and Tommie, go start breakfast. We have to talk." Dart followed the teenage boy, but he kept going through his moves as he walked away. Will was reminded of himself as a child, thinking he could challenge the world.

Two more men came back to the group. "We carried Cutter and Miles to the grove and covered them up with brush until we can bury them. What's the plan, Wurden?"

Will surmised Wurden was the leader. He was the oldest and built like Denter. Will listened as they discussed an attack plan. He learned that all of their women and girls, seven of them, had been kidnapped by the

Drangers, who had shown up an hour ago. Will had a terrible feeling these Drangers were doing Kenner's work.

But that would mean they were Pueblo Drangers in Colorado Springs Territory. Dermit would be furious to find out Kenner was riling up his Fringers and violating the Sovereign Territory Treaty. His trafficking in the CS towns no doubt ended in severe sanctions. It also explains why Will escaped without being pursued more intensely. They probably believed it was a revenge hit, not a rebel on the run.

Why did that bastard need a steady supply of females of all ages? Will realized the answer too quickly. He had heard rumors of a brothel down south from soldiers discussing visits to Pueblo. Will assumed by the soldiers' accounts that the women were willing, but fear creates its own kind of willingness. Will felt the rage in his gut swell, and his fists tightened. *Your day will* come, *Kenner, and before you die, you will beg for mercy, but it will not come.*

Pueblo was the poorest of the three territories, and it was always hungry for credits. The women were kidnapped because they needed fresh working girls to keep the elite customers willing to pay the big bucks. He couldn't take his own residents' women for fear of a revolt. Even if he took them from neighboring towns in his territory, the word could get out where they were. But taking the females from Fringers and Dailys from other territories gave him an endless supply. It also provided him with an ongoing threat, convincing husbands not to fight if they wanted to save another family member, like a child. What Will wouldn't give to set his sights on Kenner.

As he listened to the plan to rescue their people, he shook his head at the likelihood of its success. Drangers were more alert and highly trained these days, and they were funded and supplied with guns. Their plan would fail, of this he was sure. He felt something deep inside calling him to be more than alive and alone, and he wanted to be a part of this hunt.

He needed to talk with them, but getting that opportunity without being killed or killing them, presented a formidable dilemma. He slipped away and decided to take care of problem number one, finding and disabling the transport vehicle.

He remembered the back road called Turkey Creek from his map studies. He had no doubt it would be the route they took to get to Highway 24. It was only five or six miles away as birds fly, but traversing the thickly forested land added quite a bit more distance. According to the Fringers, the Dranger band had a twenty-minute head start, but they had women and children to drag behind them. He was sure he could get ahead of them. What concerned him was the idea that a couple of Drangers would be guarding the truck.

He didn't count on finding the Drangers so soon. Four Drangers were leading four women and three girls tied together at the waist. He saw that the girl he had rescued a week ago was unsteady from new injuries. They probably punished her for escaping. This was not good. She was slowing their progress, and it was highly likely they would kill her if she couldn't keep up. It would slow his progress too because he couldn't allow them to kill her or entertain themselves before they did. They were stopped for a water break, which was not extended to their prisoners.

A small child with big brown eyes and no more than five years old tugged on her mother's tunic. "My daughter has to pee. May I take her?"

"Let that one take her," he motioned to a woman looking angry but pale and weary. "If you take too long, I'm killing this one." The Dranger motioned to the injured girl while holding her by the hair. Will saw that the girl's eyes were dull and lifeless. He detested the thought of the punishment she had received. The woman grabbed the child's hand, nodded at the mother, and walked off the road.

Despite her bedraggled appearance, she was quite beautiful. Her hair was a mass of copper waves held captive by a low-slung ribbon at the back of her head. It was a simple but appealing arrangement. On either side of her forehead, braids drooped backward and were plaited together above the ribbon, which kept her hair out of her way but delightfully loose at the same time. He was glad the striking trait of copper hair didn't die out due to the genetic experiments in the pre-meteorite days. But it made her a prize for her evil company.

She pulled the child off the trail on the opposite side of Will, but he could not risk crossing the path. When she returned, they began their trek down the path cluttered with vegetation and fallen trees. Will slunk behind them, waiting for some unforeseen opportunity allowing him to act.

There were four Drangers here, and he had killed five to save the girl before he left to get his knife. Border Drangers usually traveled in packs of ten to twelve, so with five down, it was likely two were waiting at the vehicle.

It didn't take long before the injured girl stumbled while climbing over a fallen log, taking several more captives with her. Will heard the snap from where he sat, and he hoped it was a branch. *Ouch!* He thought at the same time she screamed in pain. This was not the distraction he had hoped for, but it would have to do.

"Damn it! You're a pain in my ass, you little bitch," the pack leader yelled and slapped the poor girl across the face. "Untie her from the group." Two Drangers leaped over the log and proceeded to untie the injured girl's rope from the main line. None of the other prisoners seemed injured by the fall, but one Dranger's expression betrayed his adverse opinion about this Dranger run. Will wondered if he had a possible ally.

"What do ya want me to do with her, Brute?" the other Dranger with a black front tooth asked. He was no ally, and he had an evil look in his eyes.

"The rest of you keep moving and hurry them along. Now that this ball and chain isn't holding us back, we can make good time and get to the truck. If CS sees that truck in their Ter' it would be bad for Kenner and worse for us. You two keep these bitches moving. Me and Carver will catch up."

The rest of the troop continued down the trail despite the sobs from their hostages. Will was happy the two men decided to step toward his side of the trail. They didn't step too far off before laying the injured girl down, ignoring her cries of pain. They tied her arms to a tree, and one of them began to unfasten her trousers while the leader began undoing his belt.

Thwack! The leader dropped immediately. The other one stood up, and before he could grab his pistol, an arrow protruded through his chest where his heart used to beat. Will leaped down from his perch next to the stunned girl and stifled her screams. When she saw him, she stilled, and he released his hand from her mouth.

"You," she said weakly, "you came back. How did you know where we were?" Will didn't take the time to look at her during his first encounter. He was jogging and carrying her over his shoulder. Her blue-grey eyes were wild with fear as he untied her hands. He could see she was young, and she needed reassurance before he left her here to pursue the others. If he were to guess, he'd say she was sixteen or seventeen. She had an old scar on the side of her forehead that her blood-matted hair no longer covered. Both her cheeks were marred by red slap marks and new bruises that mingled with the previous ones. She was light in his arms, but she winced and moaned when he picked her up and carried her to a place near the trail with high grass.

"You need to let me see your leg," he said.

She nodded. It was clear she trusted him and let him continue. He sliced off her pant leg near the knee. Her ankle was already swelling.

"I need to move it to check it out. It's going to hurt, but you cannot yell out and alert the other Drangers." She nodded again apprehensively.

He gave her the pant leg to put between her teeth. Feeling along the injury to check the bone's position caused muffled cries into the cloth followed by short pants to regain control. She was writhing in pain, and tears flowed freely from her swollen eyes. When it looked like she had regained some control, he continued to the more painful part of the exam.

She winced and muffled a scream into the cloth while he pulled and turned her foot to assess the damage.

"I don't think it's broken, but you will have great difficulty walking. I am going to immobilize your ankle." For the third time she nodded, but she was beginning to shake.

Will knew she was in shock from the pain and the trauma. He had meds to ease her physical suffering, but she would have to deal with her ghosts on her own. He opened his pack and gave her some natural pain-relieving leaves to chew on.

He proceeded to immobilize her ankle with sticks, the pant leg, and his homemade twine. If she had to move, it would hurt like hell, but the ankle should remain stabilized. He wasn't a doctor, but he had extensive first aid training from the Drangers, the Neighwah, and Tianna's book. The rest he gained from experience and experimentation.

"I'll be right back," he said, and he ran up to where the dead men lay. He retrieved their canteens and quickly inventoried their weapons. Grabbing one of the pistols, he checked the clip and headed back down to where the girl sat. He knew he had to catch up with the other group before they got to the truck. If they arrived before he did, he'd have to deal with all four Drangers at once along with the hostages, but he needed information.

"What can you tell me about this pack of Drangers? How many came to your camp? Did they say anything about others waiting at the truck or where it was?" Will asked. He sat back, waiting for her response while closely monitoring her condition.

"They came in before dawn and killed Miles when we were sleeping. They grabbed the children and held guns to them to make us obey. Once the women and girls were tied up on the line, they tied our men together, and the leader told another to run ahead to check the trail and wait with the other guy at the truck. Two others held a gun to two of our men. Before we were out of sight, they shot Cutter as a warning not to fight back or try to escape like me. He was to be my husband when I turned eighteen." Her eyes filled back with tears, but Will needed information quickly, so he got her back on track.

"Well, when I saw them, they were free, and the Dranger was gone. So it sounds like there were six total that you know of. Who do you think freed your men? Was one of them hiding?" Will suddenly worried there was a rogue Fringer out looking for the women, and he would be considered an enemy.

"No everyone was out and being held at gunpoint. The Dranger who shot Cutter and Mills caught up with us, and the other one was told to stay behind and take care of the rest of them. The leader told him to catch up when he was done. We assumed the left-behind guy killed our men and boys because we heard eight gunshots," and she started to sob. "It wasn't long after that he caught up with us."

Will wondered how they had escaped their bonds, and why they had been left alive. He thought of the reluctant Dranger. Not all Drangers had the stomach for slaughtering innocents.

"Was the guy they left behind one of the ones who cut you free? The one with light brown hair and of medium height?"

"Yeah, he was the one who stayed. You say the men were alive and free of the ropes. Did he free them? He seemed to hesitate when the leader told him to be cruel. The other guy with the black coat and missing tooth didn't seem to care about killing our men."

"Okay, so I killed five last week and two more today. Two are traveling with the hostages, and two are at the truck. Does that seem right?"

"Yeah."

"Look, your people are on their way," he said, and he handed her the two canteens and a jacket he had pulled off the dead Drangers. "Wait here. If they don't come by, don't worry. I will be back. Hopefully, I'll have your people with me." He handed her the pistol he took for the dead men. "Use this if any Drangers come this way."

She looked at the gun with hesitation, but she spoke confidently to the heroic stranger. "I can't thank you enough. What's your name? Are you Robin Hood? Mine is JayBee, but everyone calls me Jellybean," she said, a slight smile forming on her face, giving a spark of hope to her sad eyes.

Will smiled at her belief that Robin Hood was a man. She was young and had been protected, but she had probably overheard bits and pieces about the sect. Yet, asking his name caused him to think. Having a name hadn't mattered while on his own, but if he was to interact with people, they had to call him something.

The name Will was a target, as well as Robin Hood, Dirk, Noland, and Alexander. He had been known by so many different names and lived so many alter egos. It was no wonder he struggled with his identity. But inside he knew what he stood for, and one more name wouldn't change that. He thought for a second and smiled to himself.

"Ninja," he said, and he disappeared back into the woods.

Will stopped to pull the still useful arrows from the dead Drangers. He hid their weapons and ammo, made his way back to the trail, and moved on leaving their bodies to the wild things. Will wondered how many brads he would have on his band now, six, no seven. He left civilization to survive and didn't miss being ordered to do things that crossed his moral line. Now that he had reentered this world, he had killed seven men. He wasn't disturbed that he had killed them. It was not being disturbed that killed him.

He sprinted parallel to the trail in his quiet predator fashion and quickly caught up to the slow-moving traffickers. He followed them for a bit, waiting for a clear shot. He was debating whether it was worth his time to cut the soft-hearted guy from his pack. To his happy surprise, another pee break was required.

This time the band moved on, and the soft-hearted Dranger was instructed to wait while the woman and child peed and for the two Drangers to catch up. The woman and girl, about nine or ten, crouched in the tall grass. This guy was a lousy soldier. He was not surveilling his surroundings and seemed unalert when Will seized him from behind, putting a pistol barrel to his temple.

"Use this knife to untie yourselves," Will said as he tossed the woman his handmade knife while his prisoner stood completely still. "Jellybean is down the trail, and your men are on their way."

"What about the men who took her?" she asked as she handed him back the knife.

"Don't worry about them," he said. "Just run, go."

She had so many questions, but she took the child's hand and moved as quickly as they could down the broken trail.

"Okay, Soft-Heart, give me the short version of this run." He reminded Will of Nash. He was too young and reluctant to be a pack member. Both lacked the predator instincts to survive in the Dranger world.

"My name is Hunter. My dad died from the virus, and my mom was really sick. Brute took me from my mom. He's a total dick." Hunter couldn't see Will, but he could feel his muscular arm around his neck and his height towering over him. Escaping this man and his deadly purpose diminished with every second.

"Was a total dick," Will emphasized the word was. "Talk faster, Soft-Heart. How many are left?"

"There is one with the group and two at the truck. I'm assuming your 'was' reference refers to Carver too. Look, I'm not like them. They ..."

"I swear I'll blow your brains out your face if you don't get to the point. Where's the truck?"

"It's a quarter mile south where this trail hits 24. It's tucked in a pull-out we cleared. What are you going to do with me?" Hunter wasn't sure he wanted to know.

"Well, first I'm going to use you to distract your packmate, so I can free those females, and then we'll play the same game at the truck."

"Okay, and if I do all that, then what?"

"You're assuming you will survive that. You have no loyalty to your pack brothers. Why would I trust you?"

Hunter had no answer for the impossible situation he had been in or the choice he had made, so he stayed silent. Will motioned him forward as he hid in a tree, ready to shoot. Hunter ran toward the group, yelling that the prisoners had run off.

"You idiot," yelled the other Dranger. If he had more to say, he wasn't given the chance. Hunter heard the arrow hiss by him as Will sent the Dranger a quick and silent death. Hunter realized how dangerous his captor was. Will's accuracy with this primitive, but stealthy weapon was as impressive as it was terrifying.

Hunter used Will's knife to free the women and girls. He repeated the escape instructions given to the last pair, and he and Hunter moved on to the truck guards. Will heard the lazy dolts laughing out loud and smelled their cigarette smoke long before he saw them.

He decided he didn't need Soft-Heart to take out these pathetic soldiers, so he tied him up to a tree and gagged him. Will wondered if he had ever been as unaware as the men in this pack. He thought of the intensive training he had received from Denter, and the answer and the reason were clear. Their weak leader made them easy prey and done in seconds.

Will fired up the truck and loaded the bodies in the bed while harvesting their weapons and ammo. He drove the truck a short distance and tossed their bodies into a gulch. Then he hid the truck a mile up the road. It could come in handy someday.

Chapter Twenty

Will pocketed the truck keys and returned to his detainee tied up in the woods. "Where did you train, Dranger?" Will asked as he removed the gag from Soft-Heart's mouth.

"At the Pueblo camp. You know a lot about Drangers, and you use our words. Were you in a pack?" asked the Dranger.

"I ask the questions. Were you taking those women and girls to the brothel?"

"I assume that's where they would end up, but first they go to General Kenner. He sends us on a run like this once a month. We've never tried to transport this many before. It's usually two and sometimes three, but when we came upon this camp with so many nice-looking females, my leader thought he'd impress Kenner."

"Kenner is one bastard I'd like to have in my sights."

"That's a run I want to go on too," the captive said, trying to endear his abductor.

"How is it all the men were freed after you left?"

"I was left behind to murder them, but I couldn't. I gave one of them a knife. I was hoping they could free the women, and I said I'd be on their side if they tried, but I expected it to be a bloodbath. I'm just tired of doing these things."

"You had poor training, and your pack offered nothing worth belonging to."

Will wondered what he would have done if asked to make a run like this. Would he desert his pack, or turn on them? He wished he could share his own experience and his deep respect for his pack brothers and Denter, but he couldn't. He wasn't sure yet what he should do with his enemy, but if he let him live, every piece of information could lead back to him and reveal he was still alive. He needed to get his family safe before they figured that out or Denter's sacrifice would have been for nothing.

Will untied the man. "Get up."

"What are you going to do with me?" His voice quivered slightly while he held his head down. He couldn't look this man in the eyes lest it be his last moment.

"Honestly, I don't know, but right now we're going to the camp."

"Let me work with you. Teach me how to shoot a bow, and I'll fight in your army. I would rather die in your service than go to my grave without making amends for the things I've done."

Will laughed. "Do you see an army? I fight alone." Will looked back at his captive. He was looking up now, and Will could see the freckles scattered across his nose, just like Tianna. He was young, and his plight had been forced upon him.

"But you don't have to fight alone. Imagine how many people we could save. You have no reason to trust me, but I want to belong to something worth believing in," and he smiled. It was an apprehensive, timid smile, the kind that hoped and doubted in the same instant. It was the kind Tianna had.

Will was silent and turned his attention to the matter at hand. The man's words had value, but if the territories thought a renegade was organizing the Fringers, they'd storm the place and easily eliminate the problem. "I need silence. Just walk."

Will's first thought was to return him to the Fringer tribe he allegedly assisted to be an indentured servant. But it seemed too risky to leave this soldier among them. He was poorly trained, making him more dangerous, not less. That he saved the Fringer men and betrayed his own may turn out to be true, but that wasn't a trustworthy trait. What he should do is kill him. But if he killed this man, it would feel like murder, not battle, not defense. He also didn't know if he could aim death at this frightened, freckled person with his pleading eyes and not see Tianna, and one more skull brad stamped on his humanity.

Will cursed the destiny thrust upon him. He liked people, but he liked them in small doses. When they gathered in groups and civilizations, it exposed the ugly side of humanity that craved wealth and power. How was he expected to save humanity from something that was inside them?

Still deep in his thoughts, they arrived at the camp. Several of the men quickly greeted Will with thanks and appreciation. A few thanked the prisoner for his assistance, but he looked down and didn't take credit for his good deed. Will was increasingly conflicted about Soft-Heart's fate with each display of decency he witnessed. Even though he didn't trust him, he couldn't kill him, but that left the more daunting task of keeping him.

One of the men and several of the children were off harvesting vegetables from their summer garden while the pretty redhead and Dart tended the venison quarter cooking on the spit. Most Fringers moved between two areas. One was where they grew their garden, and the other was where they sheltered for the winter.

The injured girl was sitting with her leg propped up with cool towels, attending to the swelling. She motioned to Will to come and sit. After a litany of thank you's, she shared her story.

"Last Harfest, Cutter and I met. He was so kind and good-looking. We fell in love," Jellybean blushed. "We were too young to marry, but he was allowed to join our tribe. I'm eighteen now, so we were to be married at this year's Harfest," she added with noticeable sorrow.

"What is Harfest?' asked Will.

"Harfest is an annual gathering of Fringers for trading and fellowship."

"Do you have to wait for Harfest?" Will asked.

"No, couples can get married earlier, but most tribes have a waiting rule. Not everyone meshes with their betrothed or their new tribe. It allows the couple to change their minds or join another tribe. Harfest lasts two nights, and there is a big wedding party on the second night. Everyone we know is there to celebrate with us."

"When is Harfest? Is it in the same place every year?"

"It's usually during the first week of October. Every year the elders decide where and when it will be the next year. Our elder, Wurden, told us the date just a couple of days ago. We don't know where it is until we go. I've never heard of the festival being attacked, but some of the elders remember when gatherings were dangerous places. This year's celebration is a week and a day away. That's why you see all our carts packed to leave for our winter sight."

"Do you bring your supplies with you to Harfest?"

"Yeah, but we camp within walking distance. Three or four people stay behind with the small children to guard it."

Will thought of the vulnerability of those left at the camps and those at such an event. He shook his head and muttered concern under his breath. He was a stranger, though a helpful one so far, and she was spilling out their logistics. They thought they were safe now, just as they did the last time he had to intervene.

He wondered how long it would take Kenner to realize his dogs weren't coming home, and whether it would be worth searching for them this close to winter. It was unlikely Kenner had any idea of this tribe's whereabouts because the pack discovered them after they arrived. None of the Drangers had communication devices on them, but he found a broken one in the truck.

The Pueblo Drangers were much poorer and less organized than the CS Drangers. But this Harfest was a strategic boon for an attacking enemy. Did Kenner or any of the other Corporates know about it? Will had never heard of it, and he worked at HQ and lived out here for well over a year.

He hoped it was a well-kept secret, but it was clear Jellybean hadn't been briefed on its level of confidentiality. He'd have to talk with Wurden about tightening his security.

During the evening fire, Will was introduced to everyone in the tribe by Wurden. Jellybean's family consisted of her parents, Baylee and Jeff, and her twelve-year-old sister Cammy. They were the farming experts, and Will had to admit, their garden was remarkable.

Ventura and her husband Kory were the parents of Dart and Filly. Kory learned construction from his father, who passed it down to him. Ventura, called Tura, was the healer, but she also made pottery and wove baskets and mats to trade at Harfest. The leader, Wurden, was a widower. His wife and son died while they were escaping the Pueblo Neighwah soldiers seven years ago.

Wurden had worked as the head mechanic at the Pueblo auto shop. His daughter turned sixteen last month. Her given name was Tomina, but she was called Tommie. Her parents nicknamed her and dressed her to look like a boy for her protection. When Will saw her with the men, he assumed she was a teenage boy.

Leita was the beautiful redhead who was also pregnant, but she wasn't due for five months. She was the main cook, and her knowledge of wild herbs and forest food surpassed anything Will read in Tianna's book. Miles, one of the men killed, was her husband. Will could see she was weary, but she set her pain aside to perform her duty. She wore a long black scarf banded around her head to memorialize her loss. Tura sewed ribbons with tear-shaped beads to the scarf, which she tied together at the back of her head.

Her busy movements caused them to rattle and sway while the waves of heat wafting from the stove caught the delicate dangling scarf ends in a mesmerizing dance. Will thought such an accessory did more to attract a man than to deter one, but maybe this was their take on a marriage list. Regardless, this was their culture, and he had much to learn.

The family introductions were finally done, and Will hoped he wasn't expected to rattle off everyone's names correctly after only one pass. He had no plans to remain, so knowing them was irrelevant. He had to decide what to do with Soft-Heart. Every minute he remained alive made the obvious choice more difficult.

The dinner yell was made, and everyone lined up to fill their plates. Soft-Heart was sitting on the bench with his feet tied together. Will's decision was getting increasingly complicated. It frustrated him when he saw Tommie bring him a plate like he was a new pet.

Plate in hand, Will walked over to the other side of the fire pit where the three young bachelors were laughing. Remi and Dixie looked like they were in their twenties, but Relic was older, maybe thirty-something. They were exchanging hunting tales and talking about how they looked forward to seeing the new women in the single circle at Harfest. Only girls over eighteen were allowed in the circle, so every year new girls joined the group.

"I hope Brindle is still unhitched. She turned eighteen last year, but she didn't join the circle. If she's still unmade, I'm callin' dibs." Dixie took a bit of the pasta on his plate.

"Ya can't call dibs on a person, Dix. You gotta get a trinket from Tura. I suggest it be something about elk hunting. She stayed single because she didn't want kids keeping her from hunting."

"Tell her you want to take her hunting with you." Everyone looked at Will. It was the first time they had heard him speak.

"Ya know," said Remi, "that's a good idea."

"What if she's no good at it?" said Dixie with a bit of a pout.

Will laughed, "You're not ready for a woman."

"It only took him one talk at the fire to figure you out, Dix," Remi chuckled and took a hefty bite of venison meat. "How about you, stranger? After all that time alone, are you ready to get hitched?"

"Hitched, no, a nice romp, yes," they laughed. "I had a good friend who was always giving me dating advice. Man, I miss that guy."

"What happened to him?" asked Hunter, speaking up for the first time.

"I don't know." It wasn't a lie, but the omissions were vast. Will looked down at his plate as he stuck a piece of meat and scooped up a wild onion with his fork. He was surprised by the savory herb seasoning he didn't recognize. "Why don't you date the women from your tribe?"

"Well, we can, but genetically speaking, it's ill-advised," Relic added.

"Spoils the herd," Dixie pipped in. "Relic uses words like Leita uses seasoning. No one can figure it out but we profit from it. He's wicked smart and usually boring." The rest of the men laughed, and Dixie slapped Relic on the back.

Relic ignored the minor jab and picked up where he left off. "What happened to him?"

"I was captured, and he was unconscious and bleeding when I was taken. What is this seasoning? It's amazing."

"Okay, tell us your story, Ninja. And by the way, how did you get that name?" Remi wondered how long this guy had been spying on them, and though he was glad for today's results, he questioned the agenda of this deadly assassin.

"I was hunting when I saw Jellybean being chased last week. This morning, I admit I was checking on you guys to see if all was well. It wasn't." Will gave Remi a side glance. "I heard Dart call me a Ninja, so I used it."

"What name did you have before?" Relic was still digging down now. Will realized he had said too much.

"I'm going to get more of that pasta. Is it made from wheat flour? Leita's an incredible cook." Will got up to leave when Hunter handed him his plate.

"Can I have a bit more? I mean, if it's to be my last meal and all." Hunter's inflection told Will he was more curious than scared.

"I'm not going to kill you, Soft-Heart. Not yet, anyway." The other men let out a chorus of oohs as Will walked away. Only he and Soft-Heart knew it wasn't a joke.

Will ate his food while standing at the grub table. Leita was leaning heavily over the stove while the washing water heated. Will walked back to the all-guy-gang and grabbed their empty plates. He brought them to where Leita sweated by the stove. "You can be done for the night. I will finish this off."

"You don't know all the things I do to close up. Everyone has their jobs, and I can pull mine."

"Not today, Leita. Go sit."

"It's okay, thank you, but I'll get Dart to help me. Besides, it will keep my mind off ..."

"Your mind needs to be on your loss and your traumatic day. Shoving it away doesn't work. Sadness and fear grow bigger in the shadows. You look ready to collapse. Go sit down."

"My grandmother used to say something like that. She'd say, 'Your monsters grow stronger when you shut them in the shadows,'" Leita sighed. "Thank you, I'll be over there by my tribe sisters."

"Sisters, huh? What are the men called?"

"Trouble," she said with a rare laugh. Will smiled. She looked pale, and he called Tura over to tend to her. Tura helped her into one of the tents.

He worried about this tribe. He worried Kenner would seek revenge, but with winter so close, it was unlikely he would trek into the mountains. Will thought about his interaction here, and once again he had put people in danger by trying to save them. This world needed to change. He even held the key to it, apparently, so why did he resist? He wasn't afraid of dying. He had faced death many times. He was afraid to risk the lives of others, but it may come down to that.

His adversaries were active and determined, while Will tucked his responsibilities neatly away, waiting for the perfect time and the perfect answers. All the while the danger was growing, and the monsters were planning. He wanted to help bring about this change, but if he was honest with himself, he didn't believe in it. He was swatting at flies and ignoring the grand scale. The Corporates, however, were not wasting time with minutia because they believed in the people's power. They were terrified of it, so it must be possible. Perhaps it was time to fully embrace this destiny to which he was fated.

He was in a trance scraping and washing when a hand took a rinsed dish from his hand. "Tell me, Ninja, who are you hiding from? Should we be worried?" It was Relic.

"You ask me to confide in you with one hand and confess your distrust of me with the other," Will replied.

"We should always respect the enemy in our friend."

"Nietzsche," Will responded.

"You have been well educated like an Upper, but you wear the Dranger brand. I suspect you were hired up to the Neighwah, and you did more studying than was required of you."

"I am not your enemy. I am guarded for the benefit of your tribe of innocents."

Relic laughed so loudly that the people looked over at them. "Let me start with a secret, then you can share one in turn. Six years ago, I escaped the Highmind encampment. I know many of their secrets. This information is confidential. The only other person who knows is Wurden."

Will considered his declaration. If it were true, it made him a valuable target indeed, and he wondered how he had escaped. This tribe had a habit of displaying their vulnerabilities like laundry on a line. "You share too much with strangers. But I will share something of myself to honor your trust. The capture I spoke of was during a battle between the Neighwah and the Robin Hoods." This was getting dangerous.

"We need to talk, Ninja, and we need to talk tonight." Relic put the dishes he had dried away in the wooden cabinet and walked toward Wurden.

Dart came over with the last of the dirty dishes and helped Will finish up. They talked about fishing, hunting, and how Dart gave him his name. The kid was pretty proud of that.

Leita was resting quietly. She had lost her husband and now she had miscarried her child. It should have made Will sad, but he felt anger at the continued waste of life. After the meal was complete and the kitchen closed down, the tribe gathered around the freshly dug graves and told their friends goodbye.

Chapter Twenty-One

W ill sat on one of the many stumps at the fire, staring at the flames and thinking about his prisoner. The smart thing to do would have been to kill Hunter and not reveal himself to the kidnapped women. Their people would have found them. But now, Soft-Heart was hanging out with the guy gang at their tent.

First, they agreed to call him Hunter, which is a name of power. Will gave him the weak name to control him. He discovered from the men's discussions at the fire that he had kept his given name, like Rival had. Also against his advice, they unhobbled him and tethered instead. Though they promised to keep an eye on him, he was a trained, captured soldier, not a pet. His training was pathetic, but even he could get out of the leash they fashioned. Basically, if he wanted to, he was free to run.

Will was pretty sure Soft-Heart was trying hard to fit into this tribe because it was undoubtedly a better place than anything he had experienced so far. But his life expectancy was uncertain, and he knew that. The only thing that would make him run and betray them was if he lied about not having any family. Though he left his mother alive, from the sounds of her condition, she probably died soon after he was taken.

It was unlikely he'd return to the Pueblo Drangers. Reporting back to Kenner to say he failed the mission and was the lone survivor of a massacre would earn a torturous death, which would have this weak man pouring out his tale. And that would mean the hunt for him would resume.

So far, Soft-Heart made no moves that suggested he was a danger to this tribe, and he had freed the men against his pack leader's wishes. But maybe he would make his move at Harfest. It would be the perfect target for an angry Corporate General like Kenner if he were stupid enough to risk the wrath of the CS army.

But he could not ignore Soft-Heart's petition for mercy. He even offered to join his cause, whatever that was. The offer was likely more about survival than loyalty, yet a part of Will believed him, but he shouldn't. It was an amateur move and a dangerous viewpoint. Every kill he had made so far was in battle, but killing this prisoner would be murder. And though Will wasn't ready to become a cold-blooded murderer, he was thinking about it.

In all honesty, Will was happy to be rid of him for a while. If he ran, he'd run him down, and then killing him would be easy. He had bigger problems. He was exposed now. Every time he got mixed up with people, he made critical errors.

He was at a standstill with Tianna's book. He desperately needed to discuss his secrets with someone who could fill in the missing pieces, but he knew no one trustworthy enough to breach the subject. He couldn't get close enough to trust anyone, and no one should get close to him. True, Relic had shared that he was a valuable target of the Neighwah, but what if it was a lie? His head was in his hands, and he didn't realize how weary he looked until Wurden sat beside him.

"You look like a man with the world on his shoulders," Will thought back to the day Taylor said that. It was exactly how he felt.

Will let out a puff of air. "The world seems to land there sometimes. What's on your mind, Wurden?"

"Follow me." Wurden led him past Kory, who was noticeably pulling sentry duty with rifle in hand.

Will saw Relic go and talk to Wurden right after their conversation without trying to hide it. Will assumed they were going to tell him he needed to leave because they didn't want to endanger their tribe. He wouldn't blame them, but the other possibility, which was equally likely, was that they were going to pump him for information.

Will was tired of hiding, tired of lying and keeping secrets, tired of not understanding what he was hiding from, and tired of not knowing what he was supposed to do. The thought of letting them in frightened him. That he was entertaining it frightened him more. Relic was a Highmind, or so he said, but he talked like one, making it believable. Perhaps he could help him. He grabbed the coat he had taken off in front of the fire and followed Wurden into the woods.

They came out of the trees onto a rise, allowing them an impressive view of the star-filled night. It was exceptionally clear. Will bathed in its cold serenity, looking deep into its darkness, where the stars and planets reigned. Out there in the endless expanse, he was just another speck. And a speck was not so important, not so powerful, and not so obligated.

Though there was a lonely aspect to its infinite space, it winnowed his burdens down to mere tasks on a tiny rock spinning precariously along. No destiny he wielded could keep Earth from its fate in the universe. It didn't care if he succeeded. It didn't care if he failed.

"What can I do for you, gentlemen?" Will asked. "Have I worn out my welcome so soon?"

"What was your name before it was Ninja?" Wurden asked. Will appreciated a man who got straight to the point.

"My name is of no interest to you."

"Hmmm, humor me while I tell you a story, Ninja. I know a Robinhooder named Deeds. He told me about a young Dranger who challenged him and joined his pack. Deeds was impressed with the kid's moxie, but he thought he was just another hard-fighting Daily. It didn't take long for him to figure out he was more. Some very powerful people were looking for this kid, and the kid seemed oblivious. It was either that, or he was damn good at keeping secrets."

Will stood still watching their moves like a feral cat. He didn't want to give them any kind of tell, but he was slowly reaching for his knife.

"Settle down, Ninja," Wurden said. "We are unarmed." The two men lifted their arms and opened their coats. "Let me finish my tale before you gut us from dick to chin." Will lowered his blade, and Wurden continued. "So, Deeds, his pack knew him as Denter, told me the Neighwah took the kid, but the Robinhooders had a plan to send him here to these very woods. He told us to be on the lookout for a tall, dark, young man who could shoot a fly off a branch with a bow and arrow and goes by the name of Will."

"Lots of people use a bow, and if they aren't good at it, they starve or worse. You're reaching at best." Will was trying to hide his surprise at their knowledge of his story with Denter.

Relic replied. "We aren't this Will's enemies. We are supposed to help him."

"Son, you look like a man arm wrestling the universe, and you reek of destiny," Wurden said, folding his arms in front of his chest.

"And if you find him, how exactly would you help this dark young Will?"

"We are supposed to help him fulfill a mighty purpose. We can provide him the answers he has been looking for," Wurden answered.

"I think it's your turn," Relic chimed in. "You look like you need to trust someone. And if you are that Will, you need us."

Will paused for a long moment, and the three exchanged frozen expressions waiting for someone to blink. Will relaxed his shoulders and looked down, and his arms fell lax beside his torso while his knife fell to the ground.

"Why me? I'm nobody. I was the desperate last choice of a woman sentenced to die in a field. She was my stepmother, his wife, and my father murdered her right in front of me. I was eleven! How can any kind of destiny fall on the shoulders of a distraught, orphaned, Daily kid?" Will fell to his knees and pounded the ground.

"I'm not any better than anyone else," Will confessed. "All I have is cocky overconfidence, and so far it has done nothing but get people hurt and killed. What if I start a war we can't finish? If Dermit finds out I'm alive, he'll kill everyone I care about. How is that helpful? All I want to do is kill Kenner. He is my destiny as far as I'm concerned."

Relic smiled, "Yenoli."

"What?" Will wondered if this was one of those educational Relic moments the guy gang warned him about. It was suddenly clear how Relic got his name.

"Yenoli," Relic stated, "is a myth about a man who was transformed into a demon. He was a good son and husband until a beast murdered his wife and his widowed mother. The creature was so big and fearsome, the man wasn't strong enough to save them. After that, he questioned if he had done all he could. He never asked his people to help him defeat the monster for the good of the community. He just wallowed alone in his torment and filled his heart with hatred and dread.

"Over time, he evolved into a trickster and shapeshifter with a vicious appetite for violence. Now he is bound to chase the darkness across the sky, changing his shape until the hatred eating at his heart is avenged." Relic pointed at the moon in the darkness.

Will pondered the myth, and it brought him back to the stories Tianna would tell him. He looked up at the crescent moon with its wide mouth biting at the sky. He thought of his many identities, and he imagined his bow in the arced shape. "Huh," was the only response Will had, but he concurred with the truthful comparison.

Wurden broke the silence. "Killing Kenner is not your destiny, although it may be part of the plan. Everyone has a destiny, and as an oppressed people, ours is freedom. Your part may be grander than others, but whatever it is, it isn't yours alone. It belongs to every man, woman, and child who wants to be free.

"I don't know how you came to be a warrior, but that's what you are now. You're also a natural leader. This whole camp is abuzz with admiration for you. You may lead this rebellion, but you don't get to own it. We all have talents, and when we work together, we are a force to be reckoned with." Wurden put a hand on Will's shoulder.

"Every fire starts with a spark, and that was what your stepmom gave you. You've been burning blind without a compass for some time. But now you have one. Now, we all do." Relic said while Wurden offered Will a hand and pulled him to his feet.

"We'll keep your name as Ninja, for now," suggested Wurden. "We have a lot of work to do, and we don't need the Corporates to begin combing the woods for you or piling up your kin."

Will imagined his purpose was going to involve a lot of killing and a lot of sorrow. He felt his resolve wavering at the thought.

"Wurden, there's something you should know. Denter died helping me escape. He was gut-shot extracting me. I wanted to stay and help him, but he made me leave. I'm sorry."

"Will, you aren't responsible for the safety of everyone you encounter. Every person chooses to accept the status quo or fight for something better. No option guarantees a long, conflict-free life. You didn't cause Deeds's death, and he didn't die for you. He died for something bigger than one man. Deeds is forever a hero. We will thank, honor, and remember him."

That reminded Will of Brock, who said those same words over Jet's body. It was self-centered to think people's lives revolved around his choices alone, but death did shadow his every move.

Will recalled all the good men he had fought beside. Rival, Nash, Lynch, Brock, Denter, Jet, Rummie, and the list went on. Some results were tragic, but not as tragic as accepting evil and doing nothing. He didn't even know if they were all living, but he wished they were here. He knew what he had to do. He would train those around him to become a serious fighting force.

He wasn't comfortable being in control of the situation, but he felt the power of responsibility regarding his role in it.

"Gentlemen, I guess we have an army to raise."

Both men were smiling. "Welcome back to the fray, Will," Wurden said.

Will told Relic about his stepmother's book and explained his belief that the shell drawing inside was important.

Relic was excited and relieved that a book protected by the Robinhooders was in Will's possession. "Ah yes, it sounds like the Fibonacci series."

"What? Was that English? I have no idea what you just said."

"It is a series of numbers where each entry is the sum of the two preceding entries. The ever-expanding shell spiral follows this pattern. It is the basis of many structures in nature. It's even used in many things like predicting population growth, architectural design, philosophical probabilities, and more. It's math magic."

"Wow, she used to say that, math magic, but I was never taught anything like that. I don't think Tianna would have expected me to figure that out on my own."

"She'd run out of time. Wait, did you say Tianna? Tianna was the one shot at the border about ten years ago? Oh my gosh! Your stepmother was Harrison's daughter, Miranda. Wow!"

Will was stunned. How could he know that unless he was in with Dermit or Kenner? Had he let himself be fooled?

"Put away your guard dogs, Will," Relic said, seeing Will bristle at his confidential knowledge. "I met Harrison when I lived in the Highmind Center in CS. He was a Corporate at the time, and I was eighteen. We were working on the food shortage problem because Dailys were starving and the death rate was interfering with the status quo.

"Months later, we were told he and his daughter died of a virus, but the underground rumor was a general from another territory wanted her and kidnapped her. In Harrison's effort to save her, they were both killed, or so we thought. Years went by, and I found out her father died, but she escaped and took the name of Tianna.

"She was highly educated, and her father told her Corporate secrets. He had been out on a geological dig looking for something called the red key found in an undocumented Highmind's diary. One of his co-workers was tortured and confessed Harrison had found a red key.

"Harrison had already left to rescue his daughter. They knew where he was headed when they found out he was gone. He had a day's head start and had succeeded in freeing her. But he was captured by the Pueblo soldiers. He gave them the key, and they slit his throat in return. It would be a miracle if didn't fall into the wrong hands. Are you saying it's her book? Have you had this with you the whole time?"

"Yeah, it's hers. I saw her write in it, but I didn't have it. It was in the pack Denter gave me when I escaped. I don't know where he got it." Will thought back to the cave with the four-wheeler. Perhaps it was left there. Or hidden in that shack they stopped at. He had no doubt the Robinhooders orchestrated their escape, so maybe she gave it to them. He wondered why Tianna didn't hide or turn over the blade to the Robinhooders instead of giving it to a kid. "How do you know all this high-level intel?"

"Wurden and I are the Robinhooders' contacts for this tribe. Harfest isn't only about trading supplies. What else do you remember, Will? Think."

Will fought the demons that guarded his secrets. This man knew everything. He was a Fringer and a Robinhooder. Though Highminds were kept confined, they lived a privileged life, and he gave it up due to his ethical philosophy to live on the run. If this wasn't the time and the man to reveal what he knew, there might never be one.

"They don't have it— the red key, I mean. Tianna gave it to me. It's not even a key. It's a blade. She called it the Sanguine Blade. She taught me a secret song about it too."

"The red key is the Sanguine Blade? It's real? You have it?" Relic stumbled, lost his balance, and fell over.

Will laughed. It was a needed release from all the tension of late. The look on Relic's face made him laugh harder than he should have. "I have it hidden," he said between laughs.

"This is ... extraordinary!" Relic exclaimed while Wurden and Will stifled the remnants of their uncontainable laughter. "Yeah, haha," Relic dusted himself off. "I wonder what Harrison gave to Pueblo?"

Will shrugged his shoulders. "It's supposed to be ... like, magic or something. It is nicely made, but the only thing I ever used it for was to make me and my friends blood brothers."

"They've seen it?" Wurden asked. Will nodded, his laugh gone now. "Well, that complicates things a little. Did you call it the Sanguine Blade?"

"No, I didn't tell them anything except not to let anyone know I have a knife, and they promised not to tell anyone." Will realize the stupidity of it, but he was a child. Still, if the Corporates found out, they would torture them to get at what they knew.

"It's fine. We'll figure it out. For all we know, Pueblo believes the other territories have it, or it's just a myth," Wurden said, attempting to calm his fears.

"Yeah, but CS doesn't know that. They're still looking. Maybe we could spread the rumor in CS that Pueblo has it. That would be fun." Will was trusting strangers and spilling dangerous secrets. It just kept tumbling despite his chorus screaming at him to stop.

"Clever idea," Relic agreed. "That could protect your people too. I can see why you are so valuable to so many. You were just a boy. I guess that made you above suspicion, but that's a lot for one so young and alone. You are something, you know. I can't believe that as a kid you carried all this, kept it safe, and never lost sight of your duty. You have denied yourself so much because you could never trust anyone. That ends now, Will. You can trust me, and you can trust Wurden. Keep your blade safe for now, but tell me your song."

"Do I have to sing it?"

"I don't know. Do you?" Relic said, shrugging his shoulders.

Will tried to say the words without the melody, but he was unable to get it right. It had been a while since he had sung it, but the words came easily when married with the tune.

Bound by walls that gleam and seep,
Anxiously Liberty waits.
Many quests will seek her keep,
But they drown at Hades' gate.
Yet in the earth so dank and deep
Lies the hope for freedom's day.
Dwelling in our darkest fears,
Where her soldiers bravely lay
The Sanguine Blade *frees the spears,*
To stand against the fray."

"Oh, my God! Do you know what this means?" Relic was pacing, trying to manage the surge of energy exploding in his mind. Holding his cheeks, he blurted, "Oh my God! Will, I know what this means! It's a clue to Cali Bantu. It suggests it is a cache of weapons in a cave. I mean, we suspected, but now there's evidence. I wonder how many people have been taught this song. Oh my God. I'd never heard of a secret song."

Will watched Relic wind himself up into a rambling mess. "Based on my research, I believe there are five pieces to the Cali Bantu puzzle, and in one day we got three! I don't know where or what the other two are, but today we have three! I'm guessing that's three more than those Corporate bastards have."

Will shook his head, but his fear was growing as fast as Relic's excitement. *What the fuck!* He thought. All those years, when he was just a child, he had been carrying around the key to an armory. He wasn't sure if he hoped it held a lot or a little. He thought his life was dangerous before, and he thought knowing why would ease that. Wrong again. It didn't.

Wurden spoke, "We need a three-tiered plan. First, we have to plan for Harfest. Second, it's time to prepare for our move to our winter site. Third, we need a plan to recruit an army."

Relic chimed in with the update. "Kory is in charge of Harfest prep, and last I heard he was on track, but that was before the attack. As far as the RH meeting, I agree we need to shore up our story about losing Miles and Cutter as well as the rumor we want to spread. I'll get to work on those. And Will, could I see the book?"

"Yeah," Will answered. "I have to pack up my cabin. I'm anxious to see what you can tease out of it." He appreciated the efficiency of their get-to-the-point approach, but this was moving fast, very fast.

"Okay, both stories must be ready before we head out. The tribe needs to practice its responses. Lots of gossip gets thrown around at the trading booths and more at the parties. Check with Kory on his work status. I believe Cutter was on his team, so we may need to reassign people. We should talk about our winter site. We've gone to the same one for three years in a row. We should find a new lowland."

"Hunter and I can do that. I have a map of pre-meteorite Colorado," Will said. "I decided to let him live and train him on the bow. He wants to learn, and though his Dranger training was poor, I'm sure I could get him up to speed with a little suffering."

"Okay, I'll get you the area criteria we need to survive with the materials we have. We're keeping that on the down low until we leave Harfest. Lastly, we should probably move over the divide next spring. It would be the best area to grow and train an army over there. It's hard to get to in the snowy months and not monitored as closely."

Like the tortured moon man Yenali, what he had needed was a team, and now he had one. With a simple twist of a band, his path was finally much clearer, and he had Denter to thank. He knew now it wasn't his destiny alone. Wurden was an amazing organizer, and Relic could do research in his head. The people of this tribe each had their parts to play too, and hopefully, more would join. All this time he had been searching for the right answers to reveal what was expected of him. What he should have been looking for was the right people to work with.

Chapter Twenty-Two

Will left the camp to return to his cabin about five miles away, and he took Soft-Heart to keep an eye on him. The information exchanged the night before made him worry more about having an enemy in the camp with untrained men guarding him.

He left all the guns and ammo he collected from the Drangers with Wurden. Will trained Remi and Dixie on the guns and set up the placement and schedule to guard the camp. If a search party came, they'd be as ready as he could make them.

He needed to get himself ready too. The cabin would probably be located next spring when a search party was sent out to the area. He had to erase his footprint, so the story of his demise endured. There were several things he needed to collect and some he just wanted.

Even though his mind was occupied going through his plan and what it would take, his pace was quicker than Soft-Heart's. Will was frustrated by the continual pauses for him to catch up when he carried very little on his back. It wasn't an easy path, but he had hunted these mountains for well over a year now and was intimately connected to the area. He was on his way to believing Soft-Heart's new loyalty to the tribe, but he was still mindful of what he shared with him.

With Soft-Heart's stumbling pace, it took over four hours to get there. The tribe wasn't leaving for six more days, and Will wanted to spend some time teaching Soft-Heart to shoot with a bow. He would train on Will's old bow and teach him to make arrows. He had three days before he planned to return to the camp. He said he would search his map to find a new winter camp. He had much to do and little time to do it.

Will invited Soft-Heart into his sanctuary as he put his pack down on the bed. This was his first and only visitor. He had entertained fantasies where he kidnapped Molly and brought her here, but that would make her a prisoner and him a villain.

"You might want to gather some bedding material. You aren't sleeping on my bed. When you get back, we'll go over what we need to accomplish here." Will handed him the hand saw that leaned against the wall.

Soft-Heart nodded his head and left the cabin with the tool in hand. Will lay down on his bed with the blanket he made from a big horned sheep. He looked around his home. He was going to miss this place, and he didn't think he would ever be able to return. There were many things he would have to leave behind. Sitting in the corner were the racks he planned to carve into handles, buttons, and many other useful items. He would take all he could to trade at Harfest. He'd roll up his bed and pillow sacks, but the carefully gathered down from hunted fowl was too bulky to bring.

He made a pull cart to haul firewood and hunted game during his first few months. He'd have Soft-Heart pull it while he wore the pack leaving his hands free for defensive moves as required. He was feeling optimistic about how much he would be able to take. Just then, Soft-Heart walked in with an armful of pine boughs and moss and dropped them on the cabin floor.

"Here help me move these antler racks outside. You can bunk here," Will said pointing to the side wall. Use my extra blanket to cover you and these hide pieces to lay over the bedding you found." Will threw his thin wool blanket from his escape over to Soft-Heart. "We have a lot to do before we leave here in three days. But first things first. You must swear your loyalty."

Soft-Heart tensed up when Will brought out a knife and began heating it in the fire of the wood stove. "Is this a brand thing?" he asked nervously.

"Make a fist Soft-Heart, and don't cry out, or I may decide it would be easier to gut you than train you." Will slashed his fist and then Soft-Heart's. He held strong much to Will's surprise, and then they bumped fists. "We are blood brothers now. 'With this oath, I pledge to fight at your side for the glory and allegiance that brings a better fate to all.' Now you repeat it after me." Soft-Heart said the words and Will could sense his reverence while saying them. He believed he was capable of it, and it made him feel better about coaching him. He hoped he was ready to train with the diligence the oath demanded.

"If you betray me or the oath you swore, it will be easy to kill you. I've decided to train you to shoot a bow. The one with pulleys is mine, but the other one will be yours to train with. There are some exercises you can do to strengthen your arms. From now on, you will volunteer every time there is a need to chop down trees and split wood. Did you ever work out to strengthen your muscles as a Dranger?"

"Just the walking and work we were assigned."

"You're weak. You've depended on your guns, but guns get taken. We'll fix you. It will be painful, very painful," Will smiled, "but pushing through it will build your confidence as well as your body." Will demonstrated pull-ups with the bar he had installed by the door as well as other exercises that Soft-Heart could do on his own.

The three days zoomed by, but they got the cabin cleaned out. Will thought about burning it down, but that would cause more suspicions than just leaving it as he found it. It was unlikely they would find it or investigate it in-depth unless he gave them a reason, like burning it down.

After the winter snows receded, it would be hard to find his DNA outside the cabin. Though he swept out the cabin thoroughly, he had lived there for over a year, and if they worked at it, they could find it. The day would come when they knew he was alive. He looked forward to it, but not yet.

The journey back to camp was arduous, and Soft-Heart struggled under the demands of the labor required. In several places, it took both of them to get the pull cart over logs and up steep inclines. Soft-Heart would be tired and sore after this trek. His strength was a fraction of Will's, but hard work was the only solution to that issue. Will wasn't without sympathy, but these supplies were for both of them now, and Will couldn't carry all of them. It was part of his training and nothing Will hadn't done by himself many times.

Soft-Heart collapsed on a stump near the fire when they arrived at the camp. There was a lot of business going on, and Will told Soft-Heart to help out. He mumbled out an expletive and begrudgingly stood up to help Remi roll up a bundle. Will went to Relic's tent. He'd probably be too busy to look at the items Will brought, but they needed to discuss how to secure them. He also wanted to talk about the choices he had for a new winter site.

"Come in Will. Do you have them?" He was excited, and Will set down his pack to retrieve the source of his enthusiasm.

"I'm assuming I'll crash here like last time." Will was holding his sheep-skin blanket, waiting for permission to lay it down or repack it.

"Of course. And Remi and Dixie mentioned to me that Hunter could bunk with them again."

Will set his bedding down and removed the items stored in the false bottom of his pack. Relic's work area was well lit by an open roof flap on his canvas home. On each side of the tent, half of the roof could be flipped to the other side to let in a square of light above his desk or bed.

When returned, it was watertight and double-insulated. Will lay the jar with the blade and book on the sunny square of his desk. It was quite sturdy, which meant it was probably too heavy to pack. He assumed he would have to leave it, and it made him think of all the handmade amenities he had to burn in his fire pit or throw into the woods.

Relic quickly unwrapped the blade and marveled at its perfect balance and decorative embellishments. He slid it out of the sheath, and the shiny metal flashed its eerie red hue on the tent wall. "Look at the workmanship. I don't know whether to be amazed at the one who crafted it or disappointed it was made so desirable. A key, huh," Relic said under his breath as he turned it every which way.

"I didn't think you'd have time to deal with these now. How is packing camp going?"

"Actually, we are right on schedule, which is surprising with fewer hands. We spoke with the tribe, and they know to keep the talk down and report anyone who gets too nosey to Wurden."

Will felt anxious about the upcoming journey with vulnerable women and children. "I feel like I should be helping get the camp ready. Isn't Harfest in two days? How far is it? How much of your stuff are you moving?"

He looked up concerned for a moment. "I imagine a party would be intriguing after so much time alone. But Will, you do know you can't show up at Harfest."

Will smiled. "Yes, I did know that. Soft-Heart and I will stay with the kids and Leita if she's still feeling poorly. If I were you, I wouldn't mention the deaths of Miles and Cutter. Say they stayed behind."

"Well, I guess great minds do think alike. That is exactly what we decided. As far as Leita, Tura says her body is healing fine. She's keeping the rest of her pain to herself. Now let me see this other gem," he said as he returned the knife to its sleeve.

"Relic," Will's voice showed his unease about Relic's lackadaisical approach to their excursion. "Harfest is only the first leg of a much longer journey. We haven't even discussed the new location or our defensive strategies while traveling."

"Will," Relic stood up and put his hand on Will's shoulder. "We do this twice a year. We know so many trails around here, we can pretty much go where we want. That being said, at Harfest we'll get the update on what's going on in the world of the Corporate territories, and that'll be a big part of the decision too.

"If you want to go around the camp to take an inventory of the progress, I would appreciate that, but I'm going to spend a little time with this book. If something were to happen to it on the way, I have excellent recall, and I want to put as much as I can in my memory. That is if you trust me to hold these."

Will let out a huff and a smile as he opened the door flap and waved goodbye. The first thing he saw was Soft-Heart getting a shoulder rub from Leita, who had put a bandage on his fist. "What are you doing, Soft-Heart?"

"Quit your military crabbing. He tweaked a muscle." Leita chided.

"Oh, I see. Well, the best treatment for that is cold. Come with me, Soft-Heart. We'll fix you right up." Will was smiling wickedly as he pulled the wrap off Soft-Heart's fist and led him toward the river trail.

"Why do I think your treatment isn't going to be as comforting as hers?"

"He's right," Leita agreed. "Dipping in the creek is good medicine."

"You're going to throw me in the fucking creek?"

Will had a cocky grin. "Well, I have to admit, that would be fun, but no. You are going to lay your shoulder in the creek to reduce the swelling."

"It will feel good after the initial chill, so put that pout away and go," Leita said as she turned and left Soft-Heart at Will's mercy.

After Soft-Heart was set with his cold soak, Will left to scope out the camp's packing progress. The Drangers had burned most of the camp's bows during their last visit, so building more was a job Will began working on.

"We can trade for them," Jeff, Jellybean's dad, stated when he saw what Will was up to.

"Well, we won't have to trade for as many. I figure I can make two before we leave, and two to three more while I wait with the supplies. Then we can trade for arrowheads."

"Yeah, but the season to gather and braid the grasses is past for the bow-strings. But we may be able to trade for ready-made bowstrings without the bow."

"I have some braided line that's perfect for bowstrings. If you have a skilled arrow maker, that would be helpful."

"Well, the Drangers burned all our bows, but the good news is, they only got half of our arrows. It would still be prudent to make arrows. Levi is the best at it, but he's been busy fixing the wagons. Tommie dug the arrowheads out of the fire, and she's been looking them over, seeing how many could be saved. She could help you make the bows and the arrows from good heads, but you would have to teach her."

"I can do that."

Tommie came over with her bucket of burnt arrowheads. Will looked through the arrowheads, which were all made from scrap metal. He discovered the heat had warped and weakened them. All but a couple were worthless. He picked out five that were still in decent shape and set them aside.

"We need to gather up shaft wood. What do you use?" Will asked. He was testing her.

"We look for strong wood that grows straight branches."

"Not all wood makes a good shaft just because it's straight. Its strength, springiness, weight, and stability are important. Dogwood is best. Do you know where dogwood grows close to here?" Will asked, but Tommie shrugged her shoulders. "Come with me. We'll find some."

"Did you learn this from your father?" she asked.

"My father died when I was very young. I had another teacher after I left home." Will could see this line of questions would end up in his time as a Dranger, so he changed the subject. "I know that making yourself look like a boy has kept you off the kidnapping list, but if they think you are a young man, you will be on the kill list."

"I know. My dad talked to me about that too, but I like this look. It's part of me, and I'm comfortable."

"Then I will teach you to fight like a man, so you can be yourself and be safe."

"Thanks. I mean I can shoot a bow. Everyone learns that, but my pull strength is crappy."

"We can improve that, but your structure is not a man's structure. You will need to get closer to your targets without being detected. We will work on that. I will also teach you techniques for close combat moves to use if you're about to be captured." They walked down by the stream, and Will showed her a large clump of dogwood brush. A little further downstream, he found a hemlock tree. "These will make good arrows. This is a good time to prune its branches. The chill of fall has slowed the sap, and it will make the shafts stiffer. It also encourages the tree to grow more shafts next year if we return."

"What do you mean if we return? We may not live in the same place, but we summer in this area. It's what we know." Tommie looked concerned.

"Yes, but the Drangers know this. That is why they found you again."

"We couldn't leave our garden."

"Some choices are very hard, but staying alive is always the best choice."

"We need our garden to survive."

"Then you need to have better camouflage and effective defense strategies." Will could see the wheels of her mind traveling through his words. He believed his intellect was the most important tool to carry him through a problem. He resisted being told what to think and focused Tianna's training on how to think. "I can teach you the problem-solving method I was taught."

"I would like that."

"You can join Soft-Heart as my student. Of course, you need to ask your dad."

"I think he would be happy to have me train with you and Soft-Heart."

"Rule number one, Soft-Heart is not the teacher." Tommie laughed at the humor, but Will held a straight face, and she knew he meant it.

They each had a bundle of branches, so they made their way back to camp. When she had the branches trimmed, Will showed her how to stake them to dry straight. With the ones he had already dried, he showed her how to finalize the straightening process before the fletching feathers and heads were attached. Next, he would go through the salvaged scrap pile at the edge of the camp and choose the best pieces for the heads. She was impressed by his meticulous techniques, so she followed every detail of his instruction, becoming more skilled with each attempt.

Will learned the tribe had wheels sitting at the edge of the camp, and most items, including Relic's desk, transformed into carts. They had a stash cave to hide the gardening and other summer items they would use if they returned here.

It seemed unwise for them to return, but he kept it to himself, remembering the stress it caused Tommie. The road was in rough shape, and their burdens would make their progress slow. This year's Harfest location had been a secret up until the day of departure, and even then, only the council members were told. It was only fourteen miles away, but with the terrain and their loads, it would take at least two days to reach their campsite.

Chapter Twenty-Three

Will was surprised at the tribe's stamina, but their pace was painfully slow. He had imagined them making better time, but they didn't travel like soldiers. They were bogged down by their piles of wanted rather than needed supplies. Soft-Heart's weak and apprehensive attitude was day by day being replaced with determination and cooperation. He helped others without being asked. Maybe he just needed to feel like he belonged. He was no longer shackled or treated like a prisoner. He had been accepted into the tribe. Trusting him would take more time, but each day he demonstrated his loyalty and that he could be a valuable contributor.

When the group stopped near the Harfest celebration, they quickly set up the covered cooking area and the group tent, normally used as the gathering place, for sleeping. With the extra daylight, Will trained his class of two in bow techniques. Tommie knew how to use a bow, but not a gun. The opposite was true of Soft-Heart. Both believed they were accomplished in those skills, but Will found numerous improvements were needed. Denter taught him a lot about shooting the bow, but he had developed a style of his own since living in the woods where the bow was his only means of hunting and defense.

While working with the Fringers, Will was also honing his skills as a teacher. Telling someone what you know does not teach them how it is done. Through trial and error, he developed his method. He used every idea he could think of from modeling, chunking up the steps, assessing along the way, and having the group share their results to analyze their progress. It often took several rounds, but he wouldn't move on to the next lesson until a sufficient level of mastery was achieved, or an acceptable substitute method was devised.

He liked teaching, and he no longer dreaded training the tribe at the winter site. He was excited to start, and now he'd have two assistants. When they arrived at their Harfest camp, he continued working on making the bows. Tommie and Soft-Heart wanted to stay behind and train, so only nine of their people went to the festival. Will asked Tura to trade some of his things to get Soft-Heart a warm blanket and a coat.

He was making him a knife too. Soft-Heart had left his blade with the men to free themselves, and it had never been returned to him. Neither Will nor Soft-Heart felt right asking for it back. Two men had lost their lives that day, and he had been a part of that, whether he was a willing participant or not.

Will made the blade from a broken saw he found in the scrap metal pile. He carved a mountain range into the hardwood handle and polished it into a sheen with a heated, pine-pitch coating, turning it into an amber glaze. When the blade was tightly secured in the handle, Will held it to check its balance.

It was a fine weapon, and he was proud of his craftsmanship. He finished it off with a deer hide sheath and holster for his belt. He thought about making something for Tommie, but she had a bow, a knife, and clothing, and she was still under the care of her father. Soft-Heart had nothing.

When the cold weather moved in, Jellybean told Will that when he gave him his gifts, she would add Cutter's old clothes. Will was relieved that he would have what he needed to stay warm. He was going to need them.

Will found Relic in a corner of the group tent where a small folding table was set up for him. He was poring over Tianna's book and writing numbers on several fingerboards. A fingerboard was a framed white surface that allowed one to write with a stylus or even a finger, and wipe it away by dragging the sliding bar across it. It was a safe, non-electronic way to write something that could not be retrieved later.

"Got it figured out yet?" Will asked since everyone else was outside.

"Well, no. It's not that easy. Let me show you." He put his stylus at the center of the shell. "Shells form in very mathematical patterns. This point is zero." Then he moved to the next level in the swirl. "This point is 1. This is 2 and so on." So far Will was unimpressed, but he listened. "To find the next distance we add the newest number and the sum. Like this: $0 + 1 = 1$, $1 + 1 = 2$, $1 + 2 = 3$, $2 + 3 = 5$, and so on. It's like math magic."

"Seriously, $1 + 1 = 2$ is magic?"

"Ahh, but now it gets interesting. By adding the consecutive numbers in order, you get the perfect distance between each expanding level in the spiral, and the sums get big in a hurry. The thirteenth number is 144, and the next is 233. The Fibonacci pattern and the golden ratio are standard mathematical patterns that naturally occur everywhere in nature.

"It can be used to build sound structures and understand many things including music, art, populations, and even trading patterns. At the High-mind Center, we found it could even predict human behavior surprisingly well. That gets pretty complex, but for this book, I think it is a system of identifying symbols that untangle a message scattered within it. I just have to figure out how to use the sequence and whether it refers to letters, words, numbers, or a combination of them. Do I use the whole book, just one section, or maybe several sections? Without a computer to run all the scenarios, it will take some time."

"Wow, okay. I'm guessing that's why she didn't give the book to me. Tianna gave me the blade because she trusted me, but she gave the Robin-hooders the book because they could find someone to decipher it. It surprises me they did not accomplish that."

"I believe she meant for the book to be returned to you when you were ready. You knew her better than anyone, Will," he emphasized. "She trained you to know this book. You remembered that she focused your attention on the shell, which is probably the Rosetta Stone to decode it. If Denter gave it to you last year, that means the Robinhooders didn't have the knowledge, and they have had this book for years waiting to give it to you. You know the book, and you knew Tianna. You were meant to be involved."

"Huh," Will's sigh revealed his brain was processing. "Well, carry on then." Will walked outside knowing better than to ask what the Rosetta Stone was. He didn't need another history lesson right now. He needed to be out in the fresh crispness of this sunny autumn day.

Tura let Kory go to the gathering today. She'd go tomorrow when the trade fair was held. She was playing a game with her daughter Filly and Jellybean's sister Cammy. Their parents had gone to Harfest, but Jellybean had stayed back, not wanting to lie about Cutter. They sent out the story that Cutter was ill, and she stayed to care for him. They said Leita had no kin at Harfest, and Miles decided to stay with her.

The Fringers were usually honest about their interactions with Drangers, but this was a different situation. That Will took out the whole pack with a bow would have generated a lot of suspicion. Will, Wurden, and Relic agreed no one needed to discover who he was.

The smells of dinner wafted in the air when Will saw the band walking back to camp. Remi, Dixie, and Kory headed the pack, laughing and joking. They were followed by Jedi, Baylee, Zinge, and Dart. Levi and Wurden pulled up the rear, walking some distance behind the rest. Today's purpose was to catch up with everyone and set up the Harfest site. Some trading happened today, but most of it was in the form of information. Wurden pulled Relic and Will out beyond the camp area to talk about the news he heard.

Before he spoke, he pulled out a canning jar with clear liquid inside. He took a swig and passed it to Relic and Will.

"Whoa, that is a *solid* burn," Will choked out. "I haven't had moonshine since my Dranger days," and he took another swig. "Is the news so bad we need numbing, or is this part of Harfest day one?"

Wurden took a shot of the concoction. "Not sure what to make of the news this year. Evidently, Kenner has been busy. He killed all the men in a Fringer tribe, but three got away. He took all the females, old to toddler. Fucking bastard!" Wurden said, taking another tip. "He really has to go."

They all agreed with gestures and single-word grumbles. Wurden went on, "There were also rumors of a whole Dranger pack going missing," he winked at Will. "Mostly I listened and didn't share much. Something is different. We've never had trouble at Harfest, but this year, lots of people believe they will make a raid. Fringers look forward to Harfest all year long. It's more than just a need to trade for supplies to get through the winter.

"We share our stories, trade our wares, celebrate weddings and births, engage in matchmaking, and honor lives lived. And no one wants to be the ones to stay back with the camp. But now there is fear, and there couldn't have been more than thirty or forty people there.

"Several tribes decided to only send one or two people while the rest stayed with their supplies. Many tribes said they were afraid to come, and others are waiting on the outskirts. No tribe can skip it completely because we depend on each other for various supplies. I hope it's better once the trading begins," Wurden looked out into the deep of the forest.

"Before I joined, I heard that one year the fair was canceled because the weather was taking an early turn, but that's the only time it was disrupted. Harfest has always been considered a safe place, but safety is just as much about what is out there as it is about what people believe, and both create danger.

"Dermit knows this, and he's upset that Kenner broke the truce and attacked the Fringers. Denver has encountered some Fringer rebellion already, and the Corporates worry there'll be more. They can't afford the

Dailys knowing the truth about us. But the big news is the CS and Denver Neighwah made contact with the Fringers."

Relic choked on the spirits and gave Wurden a stunned expression. "What? How did that happen? Has that ever happened?"

"Not that I'm aware of. I wasn't told how they contacted us, but I would guess it was leaked in a way the Robinhooders would hear of it. They sent word that Kenner has been sanctioned along with the Corporates in his territory. No one knows what that means or if it's even true, but there's more. They also promised that when we moved to our winter camps, there would be no interference from Drangers or Neighwah.

"They even said we could use the main roads. No one is allowed to mess with us until further notice as long as we stay away from the Dailys and don't start trouble. I don't know whether to believe it's a miracle or a trap. It's unprecedented to communicate with us at all. Their stance has always been we didn't exist, and if we did, we're dangerous and crazy. But offering us a treaty, what does that mean?"

"Wow!" Will was stunned. "We were told the Fringers were never to be engaged with, nor should their existence be acknowledged. The Corporates would periodically and covertly circulate gossip about the Fringers being crazy, violent, kidnappers, and murderers, and they threw in that they were cursed too. That kept the Dailys from contacting them.

"Every decision is weighed against maintaining the status quo. It is the foundation of the Dranger and Neighwah protocols. Dailys are fed and sheltered enough to survive and work for one week at a time, so they don't have the means to change their situation. Uppers are given plenty to live on while threatened with being demoted to Daily status if they don't support the system.

"It is the all-important idea that if everyone stays in their lane, the machine will continue to function. If that changes, everything will disintegrate and people will starve. If the Dailys and Drangers started running for the hills to join happy bands of off-the-grid dwellers, they could not stop the bleed-off of bottom-tier workers.

"Even an attack on the Fringers would create news, and the word would get out that way. That they fear the collective will of the people is without question. That they would reveal that position with a sincere agreement is concerning. There is more to this deal, no doubt." Will let out a long puff of air. "Did you discuss the winter camp?"

"We brought it up, but this new development took over the conversation," Wurden explained. "We all agreed it is a red flag for sure, but what it is a warning of, we don't know. It ratchets our normal level of uncertainty when moving, up about ten notches. What the council decided was to sleep on this mess and talk more tomorrow after we meet with our tribes. We need all our adult members involved in this conversation. It's their right to understand the risks and participate in the final decision. We will meet to hash out all the scenarios and develop viable answers after dinner."

"Dinner!" someone yelled from the camp. They nodded to each other and headed out of the trees without saying a word.

It began raining after the evening meal when Wurden called the adults to the supply shelter. It was rather crowded with supplies they needed to keep dry as well as those they brought to trade. The children sheltered in the group tent, where they would be entertained. Jellybean was eighteen and eligible to attend, but she said she would stay with Tommie and the four young ones.

Wurden, Relic, and Will explained what they discussed, leaving out Will's past. Then they opened the floor for debate.

"Do we know where we're going?" asked Baylee.

Wurden crossed his arms as he spoke. "Well, we have some ideas, but we may need to entertain new ones. There was talk of traveling in bigger groups this year for protection, but the council has not decided anything yet."

"If we travel in groups, it would be easier to find us," Tura added, "and they may be looking to kill off all the men and take the women and girls. Then they'd be done with us."

Will held up his hand. "I don't know what they're up to, but it's unlikely they will completely redirect their soldiers to attack us in the thick of the woods. They want things to return to the way they were even more than we do. That being said, we need to make defensive plans as well as decide where we are going. Something I forgot to mention was I have a Dranger truck gassed up and hidden on 24. It may be useful."

"Well, I'm glad you remembered that." Wurden slanted his mouth looking somewhat annoyed, and Will held out his hands and smiled. "Okay, no harm done, and it does give us something to use if we decide to go on the roads."

Remi responded with a sudden idea. "What if we use the truck as a ruse? We arm it to the teeth and zoom through, flushing out any waiting ambush to come out to chase us. They aren't expecting us to have a truck."

"It could be part of a plan, but their drones could throw spikes in front of us. It could be a suicide run. I do have an idea though," Will continued. "I can't help but think there is another shoe drop coming. There has to be an upside for them, and it will be clear when we hear their final terms. What we need to do is come up with our own terms. It has to hit them in the heart of their deepest fears, but not threaten them so much they decide conflict is inevitable."

The discussion went on for another twenty minutes, but it made little headway toward a decision. The goal of informing the tribe had been accomplished, and that was half the struggle. Will and Relic couldn't sleep, and they left the sleeping tent to talk away from camp.

Will watched the quarter moon glowing through the clouds, and he thought of the Yonali myth. "Relic, tell me about the food shortage problems and how they were solved by the Highminds. It's central to their social structure. There may be something there."

"Mostly we threw out ideas, and some were crazy and some were disgusting. I was transferred to work on a fuel problem and wasn't involved, but I heard they mined some uranium and traded it for more livestock."

"Well, I made all kinds of runs as a Dranger, and I had a lot of maps access in the Neighwah. I could never figure out how we made enough food from those thirty ranches. Some of them are quite small."

Relic considered this and threw out another bit of info for analysis. "When I was moved into fuel research, I heard about a couple of scientists, a husband and wife team as I recall. They were working on a hybrid formula that clones food tenfold with minimal degradation, and the byproduct was a carbon-based fuel source. It could duplicate both flesh foods and plant foods. I heard they both died, and everyone was looking for their two young daughters to see if they had the formula. The parents were suspected of being Highminds, but they weren't registered or in the facility. Maybe they found them and got it."

Will thought about the scarce amount of food they were issued as Dailys, but it could be they had that technology. Maybe they turned some of that food into paste before it spoiled.

"What were the other ideas? We could use them as rumors whether they're true or not." Will was still looking up at the sky as if the answers were held there.

"Yeah, there were two pretty ugly ideas sent from Alli, Allied Labor Legislation Intelligence."

"Allied Labor Legislation Intelligence? Yikes, that sounds like a corrupt Corporate group if I ever heard one. What did they say?" Will brought his focus back down to earth.

"Well," Relic showed discomfort at sharing the next idea, "one idea was to use dead bodies to cultivate the fields."

"What? The disease would be horrific. I was uneasy with the two bodies you buried, but I knew we were leaving soon."

"No, that's not true. The bodies naturally decompose and turn into soil. Using the bodies as fertilizer was unsettling, but our figures said it would take too much time to decay and see the results, and crops can be unreliable."

Will was shocked. "It could kill everyone if we used it to grow food!"

"Not if it was decomposed. It's true, we had diseases running wild when so many bodies were everywhere and left unburied. Carcasses smell and attract vermin and parasites, which can cause health issues, but we don't have that problem anymore."

"Yeah, because we rush them to the refrigeration units and then send them to the crematorium. I know. I was on that run five days a week, driving to the drop-off towns in all three territories to pick up the frozen bodies and take them to the crematorium in CS by the Neighwah Headquarters."

"It's the illnesses that people died of that caused the diseases. Living people are far more dangerous than an easily avoidable body. Your fear is unwarranted. But tell me about these body pick ups. You say they were frozen, like solid? Did you put them in the furnaces yourself?"

"Yeah, human icicles. We pushed them through the slot, and the prisoners unbagged them and burned them. We would pick up the clean bags from the storage room and pack them in the van for the next morning. I never saw the inside of the facility, but the smoke continually rose from there."

Relic was leaning against a tree with his brows furrowed, reviewing Will's information. "So, they were immediately refrigerated, frozen, picked up within a week, and taken to the crematorium in CS?"

"Yeah, if people didn't report a death to the morgue immediately for pick up, they would be punished."

Relic had a grave expression as he mumbled to himself, "Why frozen? Hard to burn a frozen body. Jesus!" he said looking suddenly unwell. "How many bodies a week would you say were picked up on average?"

"Over a hundred, more in the winter. Plus, the military deaths I wasn't part of collecting. Relic, what's wrong?"

Relic was deathly pale and holding onto the tree. Will began to worry about him. "The other idea," he said with alarm in his voice, "was to process human bodies into a powder for consumption. The average weekly quota required to supplement the current food supply was one hundred and twenty."

Will froze. His breaths became wild pants, and every muscle in his body became rigid and angry. He clenched his fists and screamed, "FUCK!" followed by shrieks of terror.

Wurden heard the obscene screech and came running while signaling everyone else to stay in the tent. He found Relic sitting down and leaning against a tree. His head was in his hands, and Will was on his knees weeping.

"What the hell is going on?"

"I did that. I picked them up and delivered ... it—them. I even ate it myself." His stomach was roiling.

Relic spoke in a creepy, calm voice. "I think we found our blackmail material. In truth, it may be too threatening for them to let us live. We have to devise a way to convince them we have people in various locations who know their secret, and we can release it whether we're alive or not."

Wurden picked Will up off the ground. He was a sickly grey, and the emotional pain on his face was palpable. Wurden was holding him up as he turned to Relic. "What the hell are you talking about, Relic?"

Chapter Twenty-Four

When Relic was done, Wurden stretched out his arms and cradled his tipped head. He let out a sound of despair in a long, deep breath. Turning away, he paced the area back and forth in a futile effort to walk off the revulsion churning in his gut. He decided to focus on their next move.

"Shit," he finally said, shaking his head. "It makes so much sense. Why didn't I see it?"

"I too believed the disease theory they peddled, and I was in the thick of it," Will confessed. "I was part of the collection, and I even distributed the powder." He had his hands on either side of his head as if he could draw out the vile knowledge causing him to lose his mind.

"Here's the real kicker," Relic replied. "If we spread this rumor, it will probably cause an uprising in the Daily communities. They would be further subjugated and under even more dire circumstances. Their children would be rounded up and used as leverage, or they would refuse to give up their dead and stage a massive hunger strike and starve. It's too volatile. We can't let it out, but neither can they."

Will was shocked at what he was suggesting. "So, we just let Dailys eat each other's dead bodies without telling them. They dutifully turn over their loved ones' bodies, thinking they are saying goodbye. But oh no," Will threw up his hands, "they come back in the form of dinner." Will picked up a rock and hurled it into the darkness. "What the fuck is happening?"

Wurden bent down on his haunches where Will sat on the ground. "We aren't ready for a revolution, Will. What we need to do now is use this to find a safe place to be for the winter. We aren't ready to start a war that will wipe us and thousands of Dailys out, and further tighten the Corporates' grip of oppression. Without the facade of benevolent order, they would have no reason to hide their vicious nature.

"The choice is clear. We can save their sentiment or their lives. Step back and approach this with logical compassion, not emotional impulsivity. When we have a plan, the passion we feel about this betrayal will give us the drive to carry it out."

Will was stunned at Wurden's suggestion. It smacked of the Corporate order bullshit. "My family ate their neighbors for dinner, and you say I should think logically! Is that really what you're asking?"

"Yes, for now, it is."

A part of him knew he was right, but it was so wrong it was too much to ask. Will began to wonder if Wurden had the stomach for war when the time came. He pounded off, crashing through the dark forest in the opposite direction of the camp like an enraged grizzly. They let him go. It was an impossible dilemma and the cruelest of truths to work out.

Wurden left for trade day earlier than normal to attend the morning council meeting. Hours later, the rest of the adults, including Jellybean, went to Harfest, leaving Soft-Heart and Tommie to watch the children. Will hadn't come back to camp that night. He climbed into a tree above the council meeting to listen while the leaders discussed the new plan.

The council opened the meeting before most Fringers were even awake. Wurden told them his tribe had dirt on the Corporates, but it was too volatile to disclose. Without knowing why their enemies would acquiesce, he convinced them to hash out the demands.

When it was time to speak, all the adults were called together. Will couldn't see the people, and they couldn't see him either, but he could hear every word. Grady, the oldest and longest-standing council member, stood before the puzzled gathering.

"As you may have noticed, this is an unusual year. Our peace with the territories has been tested. Several of our tribes have endured attacks, and our women and girls have been abducted by Drangers sent from Pueblo. For as long as I can remember, we have been left to our way of life without much interference.

"But we're not the only ones who have taken offense at Kenner's assaults. Recently, we were contacted by the Tri-Territory Alliance telling us they do not sanction these actions. They want to reestablish the truce that existed between us. But we want more than a truce. We want retribution." Uneasy conversation and angry shouts of agreement showed the diverse opinions of the crowd.

"What would keep them from coming after us and getting rid of us completely?" yelled a woman from the crowd.

"We don't have weapons like they do. They could burn us out quick as moss in a fire," another called out.

"Well, the truth is we have some leverage now. I can't tell you what it is. I won't even hint at it, but letting them know we discovered this will put them in a tight spot. It could destroy their status quo and cause a lot of chaos if we were to spread it around. We are going to bargain with it to be allowed to settle on the west side of the divide, far from the Denver Territory." A loud raucous erupted in the group before him.

"We don't know that side. Why don't we just let the news out and let it give them some grief for a change?"

"Yes, they have caused us much pain. You buried your son, and they took your wife and your little girl. I haven't forgotten that. Many of us have lost more than we should have to bear. But we can't win a war against them. Please, just hear me out.

"For one, it's safer on that side. We got the news this spring that the I-70 tunnel had a radioactive waste spill, so it's closed and blocked off with hundreds of shipping containers. There isn't much up there, and they won't waste resources to rebuild roads and manage the heavy snow removal required. They abandoned several towns there, and there are also quite a few ghost towns, so we wouldn't have to live in tents and freeze all winter.

"Before we accept their truce, they need to meet our demands. They are as follows:

-Return the females taken this year.

-Give us safe passage across the divide.

-Allow us to settle in the abandoned towns of our choosing without interference or hostile actions.

-Provide us with the following supplies: five hybrid trucks, one with a plow, two with winches, six open trailers with tarps and straps, ten; ten-gallon cans of fuel, three chainsaws, and two tow chains. And for our lead and sweep teams, three ATVs with winches, six helmets, four satellite radios, tire goo for flats, and ten five-gallon cans of extra fuel.

-The main group will be allowed to travel through first safely and without incident.

-Each vehicle will be refueled at each town as needed

-All groups will arrive safely and without incident.

-Send out our coded message to Robinhooders confirming our safe passage.

-Leave our towns alone and maintain the peace between us.

"Wow, what the hell do you have on them?" a man in the front asked.

"Enough, Mace, we have enough," Grady answered.

"Why don't we ask for weapons?" asked a young man not more than eighteen.

"We discussed that, but in good faith, we wanted to assure them that we aren't looking to start a war. We just want what they want, or at least what they say they want, which is for things to return to a state of no engagement."

"What about the tribes that aren't here, Grady?" another face in the crowd shouted out.

"We are locating them, and if you know where some are hiding, please get word to them. If they want to travel with us, we need to know soon. We could have almost four hundred people if everyone goes. We probably won't all settle in the same town. That will be up to each tribe once we all get past the last checkpoint. I hope everyone does go because it won't be safe here after we leave. They could try to join the remote Fringers in areas where life is isolated and difficult, but they don't like outsiders, and they can be hostile. Any questions?"

"When would we leave?" Someone from the crowd yelled out.

"We have to see how they react to our demands first, but as soon as I know, you'll know. It would be prudent to trade well and prepare for this journey by prioritizing your belongings. Space will be limited. Now, let's get back to Harfest. I declare the trade fair open."

There was a lot of commotion, and Will quickly and quietly slipped out of the tree and headed back to camp. Soft-Heart asked where he had been, but Will dismissed his inquiries and tended the fire. His mood was sour and brooding.

"Hey, Ninja," Soft-Heart said quietly with an element of uncertainty. "I'm guessing that's your Dranger name. I've seen your brand." Will gave him a look that had him backtracking his conversation. "I can see you're upset. Unless there is something I can do, I'll leave you alone," and Soft-Heart turned to go.

"This mood has nothing to do with you, Hunter." It was the first time Will had said his real name. "I'm satisfied with your progress, so I will not call you Soft-Heart anymore." Will had been thinking about the evil deeds he had been tricked into, and he didn't feel he had the right to stand in judgment of this man any longer. "Let's move on to things we can work on. I want you to practice your strength training this morning. After lunch, we'll shoot the bows. Let Tommie know."

"Got it."

Hunter would have liked to ask Will about his sullen demeanor, but he worried it would reverse his decision. He had only started training a week ago. Ten days ago, he was a shackled prisoner, and now he was ... an unshackled warrior in training. That was something. That was progress.

Hunter's father was a mine worker and rarely came home. Will was the closest thing to a positive role model he had ever had, and he would do anything to gain this man's trust. He knew the answer lay in showing his determination and honest effort, but mostly it would take time.

It was just before dinner when everyone but Remi and Dixie came home. There were only two weddings taking place out of the five that were scheduled. It was a great time to meet other single people and celebrate with family and friends, but Jellybean and Leita were not up to the jubilation. It was not only the secrets of their losses. The interaction with the Corporates weighed heavy on their minds, and they worried about retaliation.

Tura gave Will the items he sent her to find, and he set them and the clothing Jellybean gave him on Hunter's cot and went to find him.

"You shot well today. I can see marked improvements with every lesson."

"Thanks. That means a lot coming from you."

"Come to the tent. I have some things you will be needing," Will said and turned in the direction of the group shelter. Hunter assumed it was tools to complete tasks or a new weapon he needed to learn. But when he threw the tent flap aside, he saw his bed was full of clothing. "These things are for you. Since you will travel with us this winter, I don't want you to freeze to death."

Hunter looked at the pile of goods on his patchwork bedroll. First, he unfurled the blanket at the top of his bed. It felt heavy and warm and was expertly made. The dark red bands were striped with honey-gold lines within, and on either side were orange and black stripes. Hunter rubbed his hand over it, wondering if it was wool.

"Is this wool?" he asked.

"Yes, I was told we have access to the goods Drangers are given by the Uppers to trade for the unsanctioned, recreational concoctions they want."

"Huh, I guess that makes sense." Hunter set the blanket down and picked up the deerskin coat. It was lashed tightly together with leather cording. The inside hide had been scrubbed into a soft suede while the outside had been rubbed with animal oils to make it shed water. Rabbit fur lined the hood and around the neck. It sported two side pockets and two on the chest. He tried it on, and it was big but not too big.

"Wow, I don't know what to say. Where did you get this stuff?"

"I had some items I knew I had to leave behind, and Tura traded them at the fair for me. The knife I made myself."

"Knife?"

Will pointed to the coat he was still wearing. The stunned apprentice stuck his hands in the side pockets and pulled out the smooth, weighted item. It wasn't just a knife; it was a beautifully crafted weapon. He pulled it out of its sheath. It gleamed and felt good in his hand. It was undoubtedly the nicest thing he had ever owned.

"Again, wow! Thank you! This knife is amazing." Hunter moved it around, impressed with its weight and balance. Wow, who knew you were a badass *and* a craftsman."

"Don't go trying to make a move on me. It'll go badly for you." Will gave him a crooked smile.

"Of that I am sure."

As Will walked out, Hunter was sitting on his blanket and going over the garments sent by Jellybean. He hung his coat on the pole hook and proceeded to secure his knife onto his belt. Will went to sit by the fire, and it wasn't long before Hunter went to join him.

"I'm living my best life," Hunter said as he sat down, "and I have you to thank. You're rough on me, and I get that, but you're harder on yourself. I know you don't know me well yet, but I hope someday I gain your trust.

Whether you believe it or not, I'm all in. If you ask me to fight, I'll fight. I'd fight to the death if you asked me. I respect the hell out of you, and someday, I will earn yours."

"I believe you mean what you say, I do. But it takes time to see all the sides of a person. I know you had weak training from a weak leader, but it took courage to follow your convictions and help your captives escape. But to do so, you betrayed your pack brothers. Not saying I disagree with your choice.

"I too have made hard choices and been trapped into horrible deeds. I'm just saying, be careful where you place your loyalty, and don't give it too quickly. People have many sides to them. They change from second to second with each new role and relationship. Every person is capable of great kindness and horrific evil. It just takes the right situation." Will was drowning in his melancholy. Hunter wondered what had changed in the past twenty-four hours to cause it.

"Do you think, knowing those things about me, you can ever trust me, respect me?"

"I understand the choices you made. What you did not do is plan that choice out. If I hadn't been thrown on your path, it would have gone badly. You are only alive because I used you. You are impulsive. You pledged loyalty to me, but I didn't give you a choice. Not really, and I apologize.

"If you knew all the choices I have made, you might decide I am unworthy of your loyalty. You know very little about me. You see my skill and strength and that I used them to help the vulnerable. But you do not know me. Loyalty can be pledged to a leader you don't know or trust, but respect for them takes time. I have mighty demons and powerful enemies. As hard as I try to fight them, they multiply despite my efforts and sometimes because of them. If you knew who I was inside, you would think differently and follow someone else."

"I know who you are," Hunter said, leaning low on his knees to look at Will's down-turned face. "On the outside, you are a shrewd and formidable warrior, and on the inside, you are a fierce protector. The very nature of your business is messy, but your purpose is crystal clear. I don't know the details of your end goal, but even I can see you are laser-focused on it." Hunter stood up, signaling his departure. "I see exactly who you are, and I choose to follow you." Will was focused heavily on the orange flames curling around the blackened logs. He nodded his head slightly, and Hunter knew it was to acknowledge his commitment.

Wurden, Grady, and another man Will didn't know left early the next morning to meet with the three Neighwah soldiers on Highway 24. Will hid to discourage any trouble. From his perch, he saw two Neighwah soldiers waiting. They had secured the perimeter with at least two men in the weeds. When the three Fringers approached, the five men faced each other and gave the expected cold greetings.

"Who is in charge?" asked the Neighwah.

"That would be me," answered Grady.

"You called this meeting, so what are you after?"

Grady spoke for the group. "I need you to take me to see the head Corporate of CS. He is going to want to see me immediately, so don't delay. What I carry is for his ears only. Any deviation from that will have you dead by his hand. My friends will expect me back here at 2:00 p.m. tomorrow." Will had to admit the guy had guts to demand an audience with the top elite and turn himself over to the Neighwah.

"What is this?" the head soldier asked, not believing what he was hearing.

"I warn you, if I am not delivered directly to your top guy, the consequences will be devastating."

"Whatever, it's your funeral." They handcuffed Grady and hauled him into the truck.

Will had his doubts the egotistical soldier would follow Grady's commands, but Will tried to remain confident in the plan. The team went back to camp, but Will stayed. After he was sure no soldiers were prowling around, he went back to camp. Spending just enough time to gather food and water, he went back to watch for soldiers and wait for Grady's return.

His muscles were stiff from a cold and uncomfortable evening, and his belly was growling. The dried meat and bread he brought had been eaten long ago, and he had just emptied his canteen. Based on the sun, he presumed it was between 12:30 and 1:00 in the afternoon. He let his thoughts wander to his comfortable days as a Neighwah soldier.

He thought about the fancy watch he had left behind in his dorm room. It would have been handy about now. He remembered his cushy life, real food, and nice clothes. He remembered Dean and Molly. Especially Molly. How he missed them. How he wished his time and thoughts were spent on her instead of his enemies, destinies, and secrets. But then the great betrayal came back to him.

The very price of his comfort was more despicable than he could bear. The guilt rolled over him like a powerful spring tempest. His anger growled and roared, threatening unspeakable violence. So many happy moments all shadowed by shame, and he was prohibited from doing anything to change it.

If only he could find out about his family and his friends Dean, Nash, Calen, and Molly. Did Dean survive? Did any of them? Were his family and friends questioned, harassed, or worse? Why did he let people get close to him? He was a death trap, a ticking bomb, a curse. He lived in a horrific nightmare overflowing with if-only wishes.

He was snapped out of his vile thoughts by a line of five trucks barreling down the road, each followed by a trailer. They came early to avoid the greeting party at 2:00. Will repositioned himself. He saw heaps of equipment and three ATVs loaded on the trailers. Suddenly, women and children hopped out of the last truck bed. *Holy shit!* Will gawked at the scene. *They caved!*

Will counted twelve females. All of them were quite young, and all of them were crying. Will realized that none of the adult women accompanied them. He expected some kind of compromise, but he was hoping it would be on items, not people. No doubt, they were leveraging the women as hostages to ensure silence. It would be an excruciating blow to their families.

Remi and Wurden came down the trail just as the Neighwah drove away. They marveled at the supplies, and Wurden checked the gas, tires, fluids, and other under-the-hood systems. He deduced they weren't the best trucks, but they should easily make the five-hour journey as long as the roads weren't too bad. Will made a note to search the Corporate gifts for tracking devices before they headed down the road. He fully expected that would be the case, and since the Fringers' safety was tied to their own, it wouldn't be a deal breaker in his mind.

He knew from his road repair runs that they only maintained the primary highways. Using the main roads had not been in the agreement, but it would benefit all concerned if the Fringers got safely away while the Corporates watched them leave.

He hoped there weren't any rogue soldiers with vengeful trouble on their minds because that could topple the whole territory into chaos. He would have loved being a fly on the wall of that briefing. It was unprecedented, and no explanation would be offered to the curious, battle-ready soldiers. Their frustration made him smile, but their questionable self-control made him worry.

Grady and Remi left to lead the girls down the trail to be reunited with their families. When they were all gone, Will hopped down and went over to Wurden, standing guard over their haul. He expressed how sorry he was the women had not been included. Wurden said Grady had talked with the families, saying getting back their kin was the one demand he didn't expect them to honor. But he agreed the news would be rough, and each tribe leader would have to handle it their own way.

"What happened to the women who stayed?" Will asked.

"They were removed from the brothel, but they were sent to be Dailys in CS and Denver. It was their insurance plan."

"Won't they tell people they were Fringers and how Fringers live?"

"Nooo," Wurden said with certainty. "They would be called witches or liars."

"How do we know they were removed from the brothel?" Will questioned.

"Not sure, Grady didn't get that far, but if they weren't, the Robinhooders will tell us."

"Hey, I'm gonna grab a bite and send some guys from our tribe to relieve you."

"Thanks. When they arrive, I'm going to get the truck I hid up the road."

"Oh, yeah," Wurden added, "Grady said he asked for five and admitted we had one. That ensures the orders will allow all six trucks to pass.

When Will got back, he got the full story about the women from Relic. They were given new names, and their life stories were rewritten. They were told that the safety of their families and tribes relied on their silence. Grady would get the Robinhooders to verify they were resettled and treated fairly as Daily standards go. But he didn't think they would be able to retrieve them without breaking the contract.

"Grady wasn't taken seriously at first, and they refused to take him to the top guy. He convinced them what he had was not for their eyes, and they finally got him in front of the right person. Then poof, everything quickly fell into place," Relic concluded.

"Wow," Will sighed, "it's hard to believe. I mean, I know how the Neighwah works. They don't bargain."

"It was unprecedented. It feels strange to me too. But Grady believes his power of persuasion nailed it." Relic rolled his eyes. "He did have some great speech lines. 'War is ugly. Let's end it.' was my favorite." Relic laughed.

"So original," Will said sarcastically. "His success couldn't have anything to do with the power to topple their control over the Dailys. I told him to say something like, 'This is the only way to protect your status quo'. Those are the kinds of buzzwords that get their attention."

Will paused for a moment, lost in his analysis. "This whole deal feels too easy. Do you think they'll let us go? Or, more importantly, do you think they found Cali Bantu? They wouldn't need to honor the deal if they did."

"Hmm," Relic thought, "I don't see how. We have most of the clues. Besides, we would have detected some movement, some kind of action. It's a terrifying thought, though."

The word was given that the first group would leave tomorrow shortly after breakfast. That meant they'd be loading the trailers most of the night. Will and Hunter remained hidden from the other tribes' members, so they packed the items in the carts while others walked them down to the trucks. Will, Hunter, Kory, and Remi gave a quick lesson on how to drive the trucks to seven men and women.

They taught several others to ride ATVs. It would be ideal for each vehicle to have two people who could drive. Then, drivers could be traded around as required. Between the tribes' ATVs and the ones they got from the Corporates, they had eight four-wheelers. Five would travel in front equipped with weapons, but also chainsaws and the equipment needed to clear the road of obstacles. Three would be the sweep.

By midnight, all the camps except for the group tents were packed in the trailers. Will showed Wurden where the trackers had been placed, but he suggested they remain there until they passed the last Neighwah checkpoint. Will had little doubt that part of the trackers' purpose was to ensure the caravan was unimpeded by soldiers or highway robbers. It was in the Corporates' interest that this trek went through without issues.

Will went to get a couple of hours of sleep while the trailers were being loaded and secured. Tomorrow evening, they would be in their new home.

Not a place to set up a frigid campsite, a real town with buildings and fireplaces.

Before he drifted off, he thought back to his childhood, when he would listen to Omar tell tales of his travels. There was a town he said he wished he could live in. It was up north, on the other side of the divide, in a protected valley. McCoy had been renovated with large multi-room condos and lodges during the pre-hit days. Many prepper features were incorporated to support a cooperative community.

It was a well-kept secret from the panicking fray, and he convinced several of the tribes to give it a chance. While studying the map to find a new home, Will saw the label in a very small font, McCoy. That's where the tribe, his tribe, was headed.

Chapter Twenty-Five

The trailers were loaded, tied down, and hitched up to the trucks. Seven tribes of two hundred and eight Fringers decided to travel in the caravan. Others chose to travel the trails on their own and meet them in the area. Some set off to unknown destinations, not trusting the Corporate deal. Though not all would settle in McCoy, all the Harfest tribes were heading north.

It was an emotional day. They were leaving their precious Pike Forest grounds to live where winters were colder, but they were skilled at surviving the cold. What they were leaving behind was the familiar world where their skills worked. The world where they knew the best fishing holes and hunting grounds. Where they knew the patterns of the seasons, and it allowed them to garden successfully. Where all their memories lived and loved ones were buried. This northern area may be safer from the Corporates, but it wasn't home.

Nomad Fringers were small bands of friendly wanders who hiked to the remote corners searching for tradeables and plentiful hunting grounds. Their most valuable commodity was information. According to them, the area they were settling was sparsely inhabited. After the tunnel accident, most Fringer townships folded due to the high traffic to secure it and the fear of radiation leaks.

Many stood hugging and sharing the loss of their world while the youngest children were piled into the big cab trucks. It would be a long day, and they needed to be kept warm during the cold ride. Many would take their turns riding the twelve bicycles with solar assist while the rest rode in the truck beds and trailers bundled to the hilt.

The six trucks and large trailers were filled to the brim with people and supplies, but it was a fraction of the Fringers' belongings. Most individual tents were discarded in favor of a few large canvass shelters. Travelers huddled under blankets to keep warm and hide whatever weapons they had for protection.

The plan was for the caravan to check in every thirty minutes and give a report on their location. It was expected that the transmission would be monitored, but Relic developed several strategies to protect their communication. Relic also took charge of the book and the blade, and he didn't tell Will where they were hidden. It gave Will some trepidation, but he believed Relic had devised a safe apparatus for smuggling the treasures.

The Neighwah had provided them with an up-to-date road map highlighting the best and worst roads heading north. Normally, believing them would be foolish, but under the threat of their secret being revealed, they assumed they wouldn't lead them onto a non-passable road. Even without the blackmail material, it was in the Corporates' best interests to have them move further north into a region far away from the Dailys.

Based on the map's information, the area around Leadville was decidedly the toughest section of the journey. Due to the weather and road issues, much of that section was labeled poor or hazardous. After that, they would be traveling on roads without information about their condition. Again, if one believed the Corporate reports, the highway on the west side of the tunnel had not been maintained for several years.

A massive radioactive waste spill inside it required the owner to barricade both sides of the tunnel. The only other route, Loveland Pass Road, was marginally maintained, and most of the year, weather issues made it difficult, if not impossible, even for the Neighwah to use.

The handful of the territory's residents living on that side of the tunnel were relocated. Many Corporate Uppers were relieved the only reliable entry into Denver from the West was eliminated. However, the leaders were disappointed when their dreams of expanding the territory had to be abandoned. It would be impossible to bore another tunnel, so the Fringers did have security there.

It was the sole reason the tunnel was sold to the Corporate owner, who promised to repair it. Instead, he was ruined and is now missing. That kind of mistake was not tolerated.

Both Relic and Will believed the Corporate strategy had a long-game agenda. It wasn't comforting, but it would give them time to get settled and evaluate their own long-term goals. One of those plans included raising and training an army. With the north effectively cut off by the poisoned tunnel, there would be many recruitable people. Grady had a vision of an army for defense, but that differed greatly from Will's vision.

Four riders on two ATVs, Hunter among them, had already started up the road and would be joined by three more ATVs with six riders from other Fringer tribes. Their job was to evaluate and clear the road for the caravan. It was expected they would run into snow, so they had a small snowplow on one of the four-wheelers as well as a large plow on the front truck.

Three more ATVs with five riders would be the sweeps at the end to help anyone who fell behind and make sure they didn't encounter trouble. Corporates weren't the only dangerous people on the road. Some Fringer tribes were quite unscrupulous, and ostracized Fringers were worse.

Will drank the hot coffee substitute as he watched the menagerie from his perch. The snowplow truck made its way down the bumpy road, followed by the truck and trailer caravan. It was six a.m. which was over an hour later than Will wanted to leave. He knew the reality of traveling on old roads. He hoped they could make it to McCoy before the darkness settled in completely. It was a long way to travel in one day, and road troubles were a certainty. Spending the night on the way was not something he wanted to risk with such a vulnerable flock.

He was deep in thought, trying to prepare for every possible threat. But the result was an overwhelming weight on his heart. Once again, he had set a plan in motion that put innocents in danger. He shook off the dread and got back to focusing on the desired result.

As the travelers set off on their adventure, they were awash with a mixture of sadness and excitement, but bubbling up through those feelings was pure fear.

When the last trailer was far enough down the road, that Will could no longer see it, he rode back to the other two ATVs. The three riders were standing by their vehicles. The only person in the group he knew was Steve, and that introduction was only an hour old. He had not met people outside of his tribe because he had not gone to Harfest, and no one visited their camp. But he was in charge of this end, and he'd have to make that clear to them.

They had their helmets under their arms and their backs to Will as he approached, but they turned as he pulled up. Will stood to climb off and froze. His eyes were playing tricks on him, so he removed his helmet. The man in front of him also froze in his tracks.

"You fucker," Rival yelled. "I thought you were dead."

"You were the one leaking all over the place. I thought *you* were dead," Will answered as he hopped off his four-wheeler.

"Well, thanks for checkin'!"

"Sorry, asshole, I was busy getting drugged, kidnapped, and almost blown up."

Their comrades were ready to pounce on them, unsure where this greeting was heading, but the shock and distance between the two combatants instantly morphed into a fierce embrace.

Rival gave his explanation without disclosing their true names. "I woke up in this Fringer camp to someone telling me you were dead, so I had to be relocated."

They repeated their embrace with hard slaps, emotional yells, and expletives.

Steve stepped toward Will and Rival. "Well, I guess you already know Rival, but Indy and Ricco meet Ninge." Rival understood why Will had to change his name, but Ninge! Seriously?

They shook hands and exchanged the appropriate greetings. Indy had kept her helmet on and only flipped her visor. She was the only female on ATV duty, and Will had little doubt she was Rival's recruit and backseat partner. Rival hadn't changed much, but Will had. The two walked away from the team for a much-needed conversation.

"Ninge?" Rival said sarcastically, "Really? For what? Ninja?"

"Yeah, I had to make a hasty choice! Why didn't you change your name? Aren't they looking for you?" Will asked.

"It was kinda too late. I was hit with shrapnel, and it knocked me out. When I regained consciousness, the Fringers taking care of me were already calling me Rival."

Will grabbed Rival's hand in a firm shake and leaned in for one more hug. "I missed you, man. The RH staged my death and spread the word around. I'm sure it destroyed Taylor, Nash, and Calen." Will paused before continuing. "My mentor and pack leader, whom I respected big time, gave his life for me. I lived alone without any contact for a year and a half. I went full wooly mountain man for over a year."

"Opposed to what I'm lookin' at now?" Rival reached over and grabbed the collar of his deer hide coat. "Geez, remember how stylin' we used to be? We look like shit now. Why couldn't the Robinhooders let me get my cool duds before whisking me off to Fringer land?"

Will laughed. "My mind has been plagued with thoughts of my family, you, and Molly. Have you heard anything about Molly?"

"No, sorry. I mean, my last day was the same as yours. Last I heard, Lewis was still sniffin' around Molly though. He's the marrying kind, did it once before. Maybe they're hitched and raising brats."

"I guess I should hope that's true. Mostly, I hope she wasn't targeted for questioning."

"Who are you? Why are you so valuable to them?"

Will tipped his head and looked sideways. "I'll tell you someday, but for now, you don't want to know."

Remi called, "I hate to break up this bromance moment, but we have to talk about our plan." Will and Rival walked back.

"Okay," Remi began, "Ninge is in charge, but I have the final route sanctioned by the Corporates, so listen up." He pointed to the map he propped on his seat as he walked them through the highlighted path and the warning about certain sections. "We will be going through several towns, that we have been promised safe passage. We don't know if these intersections are marked by signs or soldiers pointing the way.

"We are here on 24, at Lake George. We follow 24 to where it takes a sharp turn north of a ghost town called Buena Vista. We continue on 24 into Leadville. We can't take 24 beyond Leadville because the suspension bridge collapsed years ago. So, we'll take the detour on 91.

"This part of the journey is full of winding and potholed roads. We've been told most of it has been repaired and passable for vehicles, but there is a large section in the middle where a slide took out some trees and part of the road. The work crew in front will need some help, so when we get to that section we will hop in front and assist them.

"As high as it is, we can expect some mean weather, so watch for rocks, unstable roadbeds, mudslides, and anything else that could go wrong. Just before 91 dead ends onto I-70, we'll hit a deserted town called Brecken-ridge. That's where the first group will grab their gear and get off, with our assistance, while the caravan takes off.

"We go west on I-70 until we hit 131. Two tribes will take a couple of trucks and continue to go west where we turn north on 131. Twelve or so miles down the road we'll reach Route 301, and a mile down that road is McCoy. That's our final destination. We did not disclose it to the

Corporates, but they may figure it out if they drone us. It's supposed to be abandoned, but no one we know has been there since the tunnel accident, so we don't have confirmation on its status other than it wasn't hit in the meteorite storm."

Will took over to clarify their roles in the mission and the acceptable terms of engagement. "When we're riding through the uncivilized areas, we will use a line formation with me in the front followed by Steve and Ricco then Rival and Indy. Every time we approach a town, we will use a well-spaced wedge formation, and when we leave, we'll use a vee formation with plenty of distance between us. Those at the edge of the vee, surveil the woods for soldiers, devices, or any other threats.

"Each time we get through one area, our order and formation will change back to a line. Watch where I move to, and you will know where you should go." Will used a stick in the dirt to teach them the various formations and their places in them.

The radio sounded off with Hunter's voice. "Come in Tail Team, this is Lead Team."

"Tail Team here, give us your location and situation."

"When we left Hartsel about twenty minutes ago, sentries were posted along the street, but not another person was along the road to see us, and the Neighwah just watched us go by. We've been running about twenty-five to thirty MPH. How's your end?"

The Tail Team answered as they rode down the rough but cleared road. Thirty minutes later, the next check-in came over the radio with Hunter giving the report.

"Everyone is fine here. We're on 24 still. The road through our old woods was pretty rough. A trailer got stuck where the road had been reduced to a dirt road. We're finishing up road work. We had to clear several trees and some brush here and there. The road was pretty overgrown, like most Fringer territory, but we never needed it to be this wide because it wasn't for vehicles. The roads ahead are marked in good condition, so we should make better time."

"Do you need assistance?" asked Steve, the designated communicator. Will and Rival could not let their voices be heard in case a voice ID tag was scanning for them.

"No, plenty of hands available."

"Rodger that, talk in thirty."

They called again when they were at 285 Interchange and reported the roads were in much better shape. The caravan got back on 24 going north and was four miles north of Buena Vista when they made their next call.

Grady reported snow was beginning to fall, and they were taking a needed break. Some of the travelers were ill from the rough ride and needed to get out for a minute, while others needed a bathroom stop.

The weary group took a needed twenty-minute break, but the weather and the time urged them onward to reach Leadville. It was the last section of road the Neighwah would be guarding, and from there the Fringers were on their own to find their settlements. With the bridge beyond the town uncrossable, they would need to take the more treacherous 91 route. Will told Grady to give Wurden a message.

"Check your rigs after you are well past Leadville. And remember, keep the pace up. We're on a schedule." It was more than a routine check-in message. It was the signal of where to stop and remove the trackers. It would be instantly realized by the soldiers, and it was likely they would discover their winter settlement soon enough, but there was no need to make it easy for them.

When Will's team reached Leadville about fifteen minutes after the caravan, slushy snow was starting to pile up leaving telltale white fluffy ruts down the road. The threat of slippage caused them to slow their pace. The huge, soft flakes floated down as gently as a peaceful dream, contrasting its foreboding reality, and it was quickly piling up the further they progressed northward on the winding mountain road.

The Lead Team had reached the unrepaired section of 91 and started working on the mud and trees blocking their way. It was minor as mudslides go, but they had a schedule, and they called the caravan to send help. It didn't take long for the ATVs on sweep duty to catch up with the train of trucks and trailers. They were slipping on the snow, and one trailer came so close to sliding off the road that two passengers fell out and tumbled down the embankment. They were lucky that only minor injuries were incurred.

Will unhitched the trailer on the snowplow rig at a pullout spot and sent it ahead to help clear the road. Indy got the travelers out and pushed them on a jog up the road to get them warmed up. Will and Rival connected their ATVs and pulled the mostly empty trailer, yanking it out of the ditch. When the road ahead and the trailers were set, another hour and a half had passed.

It was an arduous twenty-five miles to Breckenridge and another seventy-five to their final destination. With the sun beginning its indifferent descent, Will guessed they had no more than four more hours of daylight with the heavy tree cover. They were seriously behind schedule. Many of these drivers were new to the task. It was hard enough to pull a trailer and manage the slippery snow, but adding icy dark roads may prove to be too precarious for the student drivers.

They would be able to keep moving as long as the snowplow driver could clear the roads without getting stuck. But this section of the road had no guide stakes, causing the edges to disappear into the white surroundings, and going off the pavement was likely. That wasn't the only issue. The cold would be unbearable to those in the back, and they were already showing signs of fatigue.

Will looked up at the misty glow of the sinking sun. Later they would only have a quarter moon, which did not give much light even if the snowy clouds were to take pity on them and let it shine fully. He set his mind on attacking the issues one at a time, and he hoped he would not have to add any souls to their litany of loss.

The trailers were reconfigured to accommodate the snowplow trailer's occupants into the other ones. Will had the strongest and biggest ATV, so he would pull it allowing the plow to clear the road better and quicker. Slipping and spinning in the heavy, wet accumulation took a lot of man-handling for the already worn-out rider, and the trailer only added to the ache and strain.

As they closed in on Breckenridge, the falling snow and its accumulation waned, making the roads easier to manage, but they were behind schedule and even good roads wouldn't make up the time.

The expected two hours allotted for 91 turned into three and a half. Along with unhooking and reconnecting trailers, winching stuck vehicles, and monitoring shivering travelers, it was a miracle all were well when they reached Breckenridge.

Passing through the town, they saw a few curious residents, but no Neighwah soldiers. It was a small but friendly group. When the Fringer tribe wishing to join them explained their intentions, the community seemed agreeable. However, endless questions were asked about how they acquired their vehicles. The risky answer was replaced with the decided story of a trade for the Fringers being banished from the Southlands.

The daylight was quickly failing, and they were still well over two hours from their destination. I-70 had much less snow than the road they were just on, so the trailer was reattached to the snowplow. The Tail Team let the caravan travel on while they waited behind to maintain the sweep.

Will wasn't surprised to hear that the smallest ATV on the Lead Team was overheating. It wasn't meant to pull two riders on such a long haul. It was decided one of the riders would wait with a radio on I-70 at the road's edge five or so miles outside of the 91 Interchange.

Wurden hopped out of the plow truck when the group met the ATV rider. With the two positioned on either side of the road, they quickly examined the caravan as it passed to spot issues, saving them the time to make another stop. Wurden joined the crowd in the last trailer and waved at the rider who was to wait for the Tail Team and hop on the back of Will's ride.

When they hit I-70 it had been almost eleven hours since they left the Harfest area. The sun's light was low on the horizon, teasing the voyagers with its control over time and perhaps their fate. They still had two to three hours to go, and it was already five o'clock. Driving in the dark was no longer a threat. It was a certainty. But the I-70 road was in very good shape, so they had that in their favor. Hopefully, it would be enough.

When they were several miles down I-70, the overcast glow of daylight was hanging low. The night was tightening its grip and robbing their visibility. They stopped when Steve got the call from the rider left by the Lead Team. The voice on the other end said he could see them, so they slowly drove until they came upon a bundled figure with a helmet on. He waved them down and was about to hop on the back of Will's ride, but Will stopped him.

"Wait, who are you?" Will demanded. The twilight was dim, but Will shone his bright lights at the stranger. The Neighwah and possibly other foes might know where they were. He needed to see this rider and get confirmation that he was the one left on the road. He cursed himself for not arranging a code word or something to verify this person's identity.

"Back at cha," came a muffled voice.

"Take your helmet off," Will pointed at the stranger.

The man removed his gear, and Will gasped while removing his helmet immediately.

"Holy shit!" was the response of the man before him.

It was instantly followed by Will holding up his hand and saying, "Brother."

"Brother," Nash said, understanding the message to keep info safe. "I was told you died," and he hugged his dear friend.

"Seems to be a lot of that going around," Rival said.

"I'd love to catch up," Will answered, "but let's move on before this storm decides to get going again." It seemed overly coincidental, but it made sense when he thought of the vehicle training both Rival and Nash had.

Will saw the tracks of the second group that turned off toward their destination around Vail, and he quickly glanced at them to ensure they were alone. They made good time, arriving at the 131 turnoff in an hour and twenty minutes. They paused before heading north toward their destination.

While Steve and Ricco filled the tanks, Will, Nash, and Rival closely verified that only two sets of truck tracks with the following trailers had continued west toward their destinations as planned. Indy decided it was a good time to take a bathroom break.

"So far, the Corporates have kept their side of the bargain perfectly," Will said while they all took a much-needed pause. They said goodbye to Steve and Ricco, who were settling with the tribes down the road. Indy returned, and they headed down the last segment of their journey.

The four riders reached County Road 4 off 131. The snowplows had done a good job of clearing the worn-down road, but the snow had turned to icy cold rain. Neither the loud motors, abused bodies, nor the biting cold could block out the questions they had bouncing around in their heads. But Will and his friends' conversations would have to wait. They were dangerous and needed a convenient time in a private place. It was unclear when that would occur, but it would be in this new and unknown town they must learn to call home.

Will saw the glow of a township on the turnoff to McCoy, and the team picked up their pace. He envisioned the tiny town defending itself against the invading army of weary travelers. When they pulled up, he saw a warehouse building with all three trucks and trailers parked in front. A sea of people could be seen through the open bay doors, and several individuals were happily ushering everyone inside, saying a meeting was about to begin.

Will, Nash, Rival, and Indy secured their rides and removed their helmets. Indy shook out her long dark hair, and Will realized it was the first time he had looked at her without a helmet. She was very pretty and gave Rival a sexy sideways glance. Of course, he'd have a beautiful female partner. Rival just smiled at Will while shrugging his shoulders.

"Everyone, I need your attention," Grady said, taking the lead. "I have been talking with the townsfolk who live here. Let me introduce their mayor, Jessica."

The woman standing next to Grady took a slight bow and addressed the crowd. "If you come in peace and want to work, we are happy to welcome you. When the tunnel accident happened last year, many pulled up stakes and left. Since then, we have been in desperate need of more hands to keep up with everything. Thank you," she said and gave the small stage back to Grady.

"We have much to talk about and decide, but tonight we just need food and rest. They have a town meeting hall down the street. It's big and maintained and warmer than this warehouse, and tonight it's where we'll sleep. So, grab your overnight bags. We'll sort out our supplies and find you homes tomorrow. But tonight," Grady turned toward the thirty or forty townspeople standing together, "dinner is on us."

"Thank you," said Jessica, and then she whispered something to Grady. It made him smile, and he made a gesture that she take over. "We also have a large kitchen in the town hall for gatherings, and we appreciate your generous offer of supplying the food. But we are familiar with the kitchen, so we'll head up the cooking crews."

"We are delighted to work with our new friends," said Grady. A cheer went up from the crowd, and joy radiated from every face.

Will and his team stood quietly in the back. He thought it odd that these townspeople weren't more guarded and suspicious. The Robinhooders must have let them know they were coming, and it made sense that RH would do that.

Will had been waiting to talk with Nash. And now that the town meeting was over, people were exiting through the bay doors with their overnight totes. Will took this opportunity to grab Nash and pull him to the side.

"How did you get here? Where are Taylor, Pierce, and Calen?"

"I have answers I want too, Will, but yours first. Your family, our family, they are here, and we go by our real names. They don't know you're alive. But Calen and his family..." Nash bowed his head and shook it from side to side.

"Tell me!" Will had a fierceness that might threaten most people, but Nash knew him too well, and he pushed back.

"Get a grip, Will. This won't be easy to hear." Will stuffed his mood down to listen to his friend. "Seems all along, Calen's dad was a Neighwah informant, a plant. I mean from way back before you crossed the border." Will was flabbergasted in disbelief. Jonah had been so good to him, but he stayed quiet as Nash continued.

"He was sent to keep track of you because of your dad or your mom. I don't know why. Evidently, Calen wasn't even their son. They took him from another family as a toddler. They were a make-believe family working for the Neighwah. I heard they were promised Upper status, but I doubt they knew it would take so long.

"Calen had no idea, and when he found out, they told him he had to betray you. He said there was something they wanted him to find, a book or something. He gave me a coded signal that he was going to find you, and I said you were Neighwah. If they wanted something, they already had you.

"I guess he headed to GZ, probably to find the book and hide it, but they followed him there. They tore GZ apart. The next thing I knew, he was dead. They said it was from a rebel's gun, but I heard he escaped, and the Neighwah shot him like a rabid dog as he tried to get away. I watched his fake parents cry their fake tears, and I thought I would lose it."

Will covered his mouth and let a whimper slip, but he let Nash continue. "That's when the Robinhooders took our family. Grabbed us in the dead of night and dropped us in a Fringer camp. I thought you were dead, man. That's what the Robinhooders told us," Nash's voice began to crack. "I thought both my blood brothers were gone, and I'd be alone forever." Nash started to weep, and Will took him in his arms.

"This is so fucked up, Nash." Will was trying not to cry as emotions flooded him. "I'm so sorry about Calen. I know how it feels. I know how it feels to find out you're not who you thought you were. To have your life assigned a purpose without your permission. I know. God, Calen. He was so ... kind. This is all my fault."

"Will, stop. If your purpose has anything to do with taking on the Corporate bastards, Calen would have wanted in. Damn, *I* want in. I will go to the bowels of hell with you. Do you know why?" Nash asked, and Will shook his head.

"Because, Will, if you believe in it; I believe in it, and you don't need to explain it. You are the most honorable and brave man I know. I can't explain how ecstatic I am to see you, my best friend, my brother. Please let me join you. I know you're cooking something up. I can tell. I want to be part of something bigger than surviving. I want to be part of something ... with kick-ass honor."

"I'm so glad to see you, Brother," Will said. The short message communicated the years of understanding between them, and no more words were needed. The two hugged and slapped each other's backs, splattering mud and snow behind them. Will asked, "Could you take me to see Taylor?"

"Yeah, come on."

Chapter Twenty-Six

Will entered the large sprawling building and searched through the sea of sore and shivering travelers bearing their luggage. When he found his family, he silently walked up behind them while they listened to the person giving the evening's directions. Peirce was holding hands with a woman and standing next to his dad. Taylor was holding the hands of his stepson, and Nash's mom, Francine, was holding her toddler. The instructions were short, to the point, and quickly done, causing the crowd to move about. Before he lost them in the mass of wanderers, he tapped Taylor on the shoulder.

"I'm home," he said softly.

They turned, and there was no hesitation. The three men hugged. "I knew you were alive," Taylor spoke with emotion. "There was no scenario I could believe in with you gone."

"Good to see you, little bro," Peirce said, smiling through his watering eyes. The woman standing next to Peirce held his hand and had a protruding belly. "This is my wife, Susan. Susan, this is ..."

"Ninge," Will answered quickly. He was glad that they all knew to play along. The familiar hope that he could have his name back fluttered through his brain but quickly dissipated into the place impossible wishes go.

"We're expecting a little one in three months," Pierce added, though the coming addition was already obvious.

They talked briefly, but the rest of the catch-up conversation would have to wait until everyone was settled in for the evening. This group was bone cold and beyond weary. The hardwood floor of the large open room offered plenty of space for stretching out on blankets. The area was warmed by two wood furnaces cranking out the heat they desperately needed.

Will could see this town building was once a school. The cafeteria was the large kitchen area the mayor, Jessica, had referred to, and the gathering house was the gymnasium. Hunter, Remi, and Jedi stood guard over the supplies in the warehouse building where Rival, Nash, and Will came to join them.

"Okay, Will, let me get this straight. Your best friend in the Neighwah was Rival? I thought you wanted to kick his ass," Nash laughed.

"Oh, trust me, it happened several times," Will quipped.

"Yeah, and then he woke up," Rival slapped Nash's back.

"So, you're Ninja?" Nash laughed, looking at Will. "How did you get that name?

"I'm not loud, like you," Will smiled. It was good to joke around with people who knew him so well, even if it wasn't completely.

"So, how many names have you had, Will?"

"Too many. But seriously, you need to stop calling me that."

Rival and Nash were getting along so well that it made Will think of Calen. They must have been looking for Tianna's book, and they thought Will had left it with him when he went to join the Drangers. Will wasn't sure how the RH got it, but it was on that horrible day so many years ago. Though Calen had been dead for over a year, this grief was new to him. Will wondered when his losses would ease up. It was as if he woke up every day to a mythical harpy eternally gnawing away his gut.

The men shared their stories in between wandering through the trailers and checking the accesses. Just then, someone banged on the door. It was a boy, and he had three dogs that wiggled their way past him and into the warehouse.

"What's up, kid?" Will asked the boy who looked no more than twelve.

"They said they can't be in the sleeping room. They told me to put them in here." The sleepy kid turned around and left.

"Whose dogs are these? Are they strays from the town?" Will asked.

Nash explained, "When I was checking for issues on the Fringer parade, someone came and got me. We walked to the end of the caravan, where I saw three dogs tied up. Everyone felt bad for them and couldn't bear to leave them to die."

"Are you shittin' me?" Will yelled. "You're lucky it wasn't a trap."

"Well, actually it was, but there were so many of us, the scavengers must have run away," Nash added.

"Whoa! So reckless. I can't believe you didn't protest."

"Oh, I did. I even volunteered to put them down humanely, but everyone was pleading with Grady to save them, and Grady okayed it," Nash answered, throwing out his hands.

"This is bad. This is really bad. If we don't get some serious training and discipline going, we're all doomed." While Will was talking, he was rubbing the dogs' heads. "Well, if we have to take care of them, I say we get to name them."

"Good point. This one is Fletcher," Rival said, playing with the dark tawny pup. "I had a book about a dog named Fletcher who looked just like this."

"This black and white one is a female, and I'm calling her," Nash paused for a minute. "Tessa, her name is Tessa, after my grandma."

Will looked at the male dog at his feet, shyly wagging its tail. The dogs looked so different they must be from different litters, probably the runts. He looked calmer, and maybe older, than the other two, but not by much. He had soulful eyes with a touch of mischief.

"Give me a minute. I'll think of something." The burnt orange colored dog peered up at him. Will thought of Leita and her beautiful hair. It was the color of polished copper and a roaring fire. "Copper," Will said. "He's Copper."

They played with the dogs while patrolling the area. When it was Will's turn to crash, he realized how exhausted he felt. His muscles screamed from the abuse of the long, cold ride. Every part of him ached from manhandling the ATV all day. He took out the liniment Tura gave him and rubbed it into his sore body. It took a couple of minutes, but soon the warming lotion sent him into a deep, hard slumber.

The next morning after breakfast, Jessica and Grady presented the housing plan. There were over forty condominiums with five apartments each, and numerous homes dotted the streets and hillsides. Most were in decent shape and ready to move into. Figuring the tribes would want to live near each other, they assigned areas to each. It would be their job to sort where their people settled, but there were plenty of homes to go around. Rival, Will, Nash, Hunter, Jedi, and Remi found a six-bedroom cabin half a mile away from the town center and claimed it without asking. They gathered their things into a truck and drove to settle into their bachelor pad.

The massive log cabin had a welcoming wrap-around porch. On one side of the wide entrance door hung a sturdy wood swing tucked beneath two front windows, and a large picture window adorned the other. The front door led to a spacious great room with a huge stone fireplace and a built-in nook for firewood.

The furniture included two couches, two lounge chairs, and side tables between them. Matching their environment, they were made from thick logs, but unlike the walls, these were richly stained and polished smooth with lacquer and many years of wear. They were missing the soft cushions to make them feel inviting, but trading could solve that.

The kitchen had a long, smooth, light-grey concrete counter with black flecks. An old wood stove sat on the outside wall. It had a stovetop and four lift-out lids on the edges, a warming section in the center, an oven, and burn boxes on both sides of it. Will couldn't wait to try out some new recipes on it.

There was indoor water, but it came in the form of a hand pump at the sink. Hunter cranked it a couple of times and water began to pour out. It wasn't clean or coming in a steady stream, but who knows how long it had been left idle. Regular use would get it working perfectly.

At the end of the long hall was a moderately sized room with a small wood stove and a multitude of racks for drying clothes. A gorgeous view could be seen out the full-length window, and parked in front of it was a sizable soaker tub. Also downstairs were a bathroom and two bedrooms. Will and Rival claimed those quickly, saying they were the oldest and boldest. But in all honesty, no one was fighting for the coldest rooms during winter.

The upstairs had less room because of the slant of the roof, but there were four bedrooms and two bathrooms, which included composting toilets, and a hand pump sitting over big basins for washing up. Without a water heater, showers were unrealistic.

The pups, Fletcher and Tessa, were already slated to live in two other homes, but Copper wouldn't leave Will's side, so he came home with them. Will went to his room. The large bed made of knotty pine comically dwarfed his bed sack, leaving a border of unclaimed space. A desk sat in front of a large picture window that desperately needed curtains.

Will noticed an odd wooden board nailed haphazardly on the wall at the end of the bed and in between two windows. He walked outside to see if a huge hole was the reason for the covering, but it was a stone chimney. Perfect. He knew a lot about repairing those. He'd get right on it.

He opened the closet and found that it was full of treasures. First, he took out the three large pillows. The cloth covering them was dingy and dusty, but he ripped them open and used the stuffing for his bed sack and pillow. Next, he found a pair of snowshoes and poles and a wooden sled with metal rails.

Another thing he found in the closet was a nicely framed painting of a strong male African lion. He was sitting and staring out across a grassy field at a large grazing animal. A slight breeze flowed through his impressive mane, and his muscular body radiated power and dominance. Will saw a nail jutting out at the top of a discolored square on the wall, so he returned the art to its rightful place. *This is my lion's* den, Will thought to himself. *Now it's home.*

When he turned back toward his bed, Copper had stretched out across the center, signaling he was home too.

Many Fringers had mixed feelings about settling into the permanent accommodations of McCoy. They had lived in tents or abandoned buildings, but they were always close enough or the walls thin enough to hear calls of distress. It was the first time most of them had lived in a house. The individual dwellings were the best most had ever experienced. Everyone agreed the efficiency of the town was impressive, but being so detectable in a permanent place seemed precarious.

The town was under constant guard, but most knew they couldn't fend off attackers. They had their blackmail weapon, but there was little doubt the Corporates were already working out a response to discredit or dismiss that accusation. The winter was pretty much guaranteed to be trouble-free, but after that, it was a gamble.

The town of McCoy had been transformed to accommodate residents after the meteorites left the country in turmoil. The self-sufficiency and sustainability were well-thought-out and impressive. They had established a simple system of government that held general elections for a few top positions every three years, and town meetings were once or twice a month.

After several tragedies and bouts of emigration, they had dwindled their number of one hundred and eleven down to eighteen. But now, overnight, they had grown into a thriving community of one hundred and forty-seven, and three more on the way. With their combined supplies and accomplished hunters, the town was well set for the winter months.

Before long, they were enjoying the permanence and the comfort four walls provided as well as the freedom of privacy.

The maintenance of many places and things had been neglected. Repairs and improvements on all the inhabited homes consumed most of the initial workforce, but the homes were inhabitable within two months.

It took time to finish the repairs and improvements on the other buildings, but a modest medical facility and indoor trading area were established. The chicken coop was tripled, and they planned to multiply the flock when the new grain supply was harvested. Everyone was responsible for chopping wood for their heating and cooking, but they had to add to the town's supply as a kind of tax.

The town generated electricity from a waterwheel at the river, and five windmills set on a nearby hill. Though solar panels were set atop every building not all were still working. Relic promised to try to find the supplies needed to repair them, but some required mining and refining processes that were distant plans. Every home had lights, a refrigerator, and a communication device that was networked within the town. The rest of the power went to the machines to repair and create needed items.

Will was excited to hear they had a reloading room in the maintenance building. He had never reloaded bullets himself, but he wanted to learn more about it. The town used to have an extensive supply of guns, but many of those went with people leaving the colony. Since then, the reloading room and the guns had been locked up, but Will hoped he would be allowed to at least take inventory.

The winter was long, and each day was filled with hard labor. There had been no time for defense training, and Will often registered his opinion on the dangers of disregarding it. Finally, the spring sun began to push back the snow, and Will planned to get his volunteers into a training regime, but then the garden project took off.

The new garden was to cover twenty-five acres, with a lot of room between each row. Will shared the technique Tianna had taught him, and the town decided to incorporate it in a section of the garden to test its outcome. When the garden was well on its way, the town council voted to focus attention on the roofs before winter returned.

After that, he thought, another project would be deemed more important. Will's concern for their security was reaching a boiling point. Rather than his usual brief suggestion, Will planned to give a well-thought-out speech to get his military defense force established in the town charter.

"Good evening, I know many of you have heard my suggestion for preparing ourselves against attacks. It's a mistake to think we can live here forever without the Corporates interfering. Our free society is their worst nightmare. Don't kid yourselves. At this very moment, they're devising ways to end it. Everyone here knows we have a secret agreement with them, and you believe it would cross the line to train for our defense. That may very well be true, but they are only going to leave us alone until they find a way to take us over.

"We are fortunate this tunnel is impassable. It cuts us off and makes it difficult for them to reach us and their outskirt towns. But you can bet they will eventually improve Highway 24 to gain access to Fairplay, Leadville, and Breckenridge. And they might even develop the Loveland Pass Road.

"Last week, we found two drones. They were within miles of our town. We don't know why they fell out of the sky. They had no signs of being shot down, and we assumed they malfunctioned, but you can bet there are more out there in working order. It's also likely they will come looking for them. Maybe we could turn them over, and they would believe we are upholding our part of the bargain, but it is more likely they will accuse us of knocking them down. Some of you know how the Corporates work, but you still believe they will honor an agreement that is not in their interest.

"We have to ask ourselves, do we trust them to leave us be, or do we prepare to defend ourselves? Both of those scenarios have serious risks. I have found Corporates to be predictable in their actions and reactions.

They may see our training as an act of aggression, and in response, they will assess our threat level.

"In my experience, as long as we don't spread our philosophy or solicit people from their towns, our threat level will be deemed low and not worthy of engagement. However, if they see us as complacent and weak, they may decide to deal with us swiftly and covertly. In other words, we could be victims of one of their tragic accidents or well-planned plagues.

"Here is the readiness schedule I propose. All able-bodied men and women will train a minimum of two hours twice a week. We will establish a reserve unit that will train for three hours three times a week, and we will have an elite unit that trains for five hours five times a week. The elite unit will start with fifteen qualifying volunteers. The reserve unit will begin with twenty to thirty volunteers. Also, at the school, we will train all able-bodied students in the art of self-defense.

"No matter what the scenario, trust me, they will come. It's a matter of when, not if. Freedom has never come easy. It has always been traded in the blood of good men and women. I am willing to fight and spill my blood for what we've achieved. If I am alone in this belief, you can ask me to leave, and I will.

The silent and attentive room burst into numerous pockets of vivacious conversation. Jessica quieted the room. "We need to hear the town's opinions, so we can assess your plan together. I will split the room into fourths." She explained the divisions and continued. "I will give each section ten minutes to address the town. This is not the time to say yes or no. It is the time to present ideas and ask questions. Section C in the back, if you have a question or a statement, please stand and you will be called on, and Ninja will answer your questions."

Five people stood. Jessica called on the first one. "Does your plan include drills for taking cover?"

"Yes, that will be included in the training."

"Do people have to qualify to be on the reserve team?"

"No, you just have to put in your hours."

"How do you know so much about the Neighwah and the Corporates?"

Will had anticipated this question, but he wasn't sure the answer would be accepted. "We've heard the rumors, and we've studied their responses."

"Are you talking about the Robinhooders?"

Jessica interrupted before Will could answer. "I highly suggest we not affiliate with, or talk about that group if they even exist. I hope that is the last time we hear mention of that group, especially in a public setting."

The man who asked the question was visibly annoyed and had more to say, but he held his tongue.

"Group D in the back, it's your turn."

The meeting continued with each group until the proposal was called to a vote. The first vote approved the training and its schedule. The second vote was on where the training would take place. There were three choices. One was in the gym full time, so it wasn't seen, but that meant the students lost their gym and long-range weapons training was compromised. The next was outside full-time unless the weather was too bad. The third was to find a different place away from town. The final decision was the second choice, but finding a new place was given a timeline of two months.

It was mid-summer, and the weather was still mild. It was Will's job to find the training site. It would have to include a building for inclement weather and overnight stays. He was one of the main hunters for the town, and he went out several times a week. But in all his excursions, he had never found such a place. He would have to extend his search, but not too far. The place had to be close enough that the people could travel back and forth from town.

In his mind, he went through scenarios of the groups taking turns living offsite for training. Making trips every day would get unwanted attention. It gave him an idea of how big his search should be. Will packed up for his solitary trek the next morning and left his roommates in charge of getting the schedule and lessons started as well as leading them.

Leita sat diligently teasing out tangles with her hair glowing vibrantly in the firelight. She often looked his way with flirtatious smiles and enticing stares. She grew more beautiful to him with each encounter, but he knew better than to let her be involved with him. Belonging to the same tribe was enough trouble, but personal connections could bring her unspeakable suffering. She had also recently lost her husband and miscarried her child. He walked away from the fire to shake off his loneliness and reclaim his solitude.

Under the light of a full moon, he headed to his favorite spot by the river. The summer sun was setting, and the air began to chill. He listened to the Colorado River tripping over rocks and swirling in eddies. The wilderness brought him freedom, and it was the one place where he could claim freedom and embrace his independence.

A twig snapped behind him, and he immediately took a defensive position. It was Leita.

"Did you follow me, or did you need time alone?" Will asked. "I could find another spot."

"I came here to think, and take a break, but please don't leave. I am not opposed to some company," she said as she wrapped her generous shawl around her slender frame." I liked your speech, and I agree with your plan. It's smart."

"Thanks," he answered. He was in a crouched position and focused on the calming flow of the river. "I am not used to addressing a crowd."

"Well, I have to admit, you spoke more words tonight than all the ones before combined, but you did well. Even though many people don't want military exercises held here, they understand the need for them," she said and she sat down beside him.

"I hope so." She was sitting so close, he could smell the herbal lotion she often wore. His body was beginning to flood with desires, all of them inappropriate. Needing a distraction, he picked up a flat rock and walked to the shore. He flung it across the river and counted eight skips.

"Have I offended you in some way?"

Stunned by the statement and her interpretation, Will turned quickly. "No, why do you say that?"

"You are a puzzle to me," she said. "You look at me with wanting eyes, yet you shun my company. Just now, I sat down, and you got up and walked away." Will looked out over the shimmering river while she continued. "If I bother you, say so. I just want to know where I stand."

"You have been through a lot. I just meant to show respect for you and your late husband."

"My only love was a Dranger who brought me here to be safe and free. I found out I was pregnant after he was killed. Miles stepped up to be my mate and father to my child. We never were in love, and we never made love, but he was a good man, and I respected him. Love may have grown if we had been given more time. I miss him terribly, but not like that."

"And then you lost your child. That is a sad tale. I am sorry it happened."

"Me too. So can you sit back down now?"

"You tempt me," he said, looking at her before he turned back toward the river, "but I am not an easy or safe man to know. I have many enemies. People close to me become targets. Too many have died because of me. I am not looking to add a woman to that list."

"I am not looking for a public camp date or a future husband, and when I do, it will probably be someone more settled. You are like a wild stallion, strong and dangerous. Although that intrigues me, I have no intention of beating myself up trying to tame you. I like my independence too, but I miss the closeness a man can provide, and I am very attracted to you. You invade my dreams. Perhaps if no one knew we spent time together, there would be no danger."

The same fire in her eyes was blazing in his own. She was beautiful, tall, toned, and outspoken. He was resisting, but it was increasingly difficult. He sat back down beside her. Without word or warning, she kissed him softly, letting the touch grow more passionate when he did not pull away. Will's head was spinning. This was more temptation than he could refuse.

His body was responding and drowning out the warnings in his head, and they soon faded into a whiny whisper. It had been so long since he held a woman in his arms, and primal desires surged through him. He traced his hand gently along her shoulders and up to the ribbon that tied her hair back. Softly, he tugged at the ribbon imprisoning the fiery ringlets. The black silky string was still tangled in his hand as he lost his fingers in her untamed curls.

She moved her hands under his shirt and along the ridges of his abdomen. He was all male and muscle. She caressed his smooth skin rippled with strength and predatory power. Making her way upward, she found her quarry. She grasped his nipples between thumb and finger, tenderly at first and slowly increased the pressure until a soft moan breached his lips.

He mimicked her movements, caressing her toned, flat stomach and up to her perfect breasts. All the while their lips joined to fuel their rising passion.

Will moved his kisses to follow her cheekbone. "I don't want to spoil the moment, but ..." his speech was a soft sigh.

It was so different from his normal deep tone, and it sent Letia higher. "Don't worry. I am healthy and will not conceive tonight. I planned a rendezvous, not a bonding."

"Bold, clever, and gorgeous, my kind of woman." Will moaned. "I'm obsessed with your hair. It's all wild with fiery energy."

"It's like that everywhere."

"Oh, damn," Will smiled. "We have to get to that."

Clothing began finding its way onto branches and boulders until the moon gleamed over every inch of their flesh. The chill of the deep night couldn't cool the fever of their embrace, but when she shivered, mostly with excitement, he grabbed her ample shawl and draped it over them. They had both deprived themselves for so long that their excitement rose quickly. By the time he entered her willing body, they were both decadently in touch with their needs.

Unlike Molly, this was pleasure for pleasure's sake. No emotional promises or expectations for tomorrow or fears of its cost. It heightened his selfish desires, and the more he indulged his hunger, the more she responded in kind. When she was on the verge of her climax, he slowed the pace. Breathing deeply, he looked at her, and she lifted her heavy eyelids and smiled with parted lips.

He settled a deep, hungry kiss on her slightly opened mouth, which quickly compelled him to resume his fevered pace. It rocketed them in a united burst of ecstasy. The waves of pleasure ebbed into the warm afterglow of fulfillment.

For some time, they lay there side by side and fully embraced as if the ride had not yet come to a complete stop. Will broke the bond and rolled onto his back, looking up into the indifferent universe. He felt boundless and devoid of earthly burdens, and he bathed in his insignificance. It was so clear at that moment.

All things had a purpose, a fate. Though the sinking moon and the babbling river followed nature's path, they had a destiny too. Tonight it was to provide a melody and a mood for their love-making under the starry heavens. They lay in contented silence until they left the river, following different paths.

Chapter Twenty-Seven

Will slept under the spell of a rare, solid sleep. Without nightmares and worries stirring in his mind, he felt refreshed and ready for his journey. He would be traveling to areas he'd never been to find a place for a training camp. It was dangerous, exciting, and his kind of outing.

It had to be far enough to disassociate itself from the town, but close enough to reach in a short day's drive or a hard couple-day hike. He doubted he would find a place suitable before the coming winter, but he knew he could find a place to build. He expected to construct barracks of some kind as well as a training course. Though it would eat up a lot of time and resources, he didn't want to wait. Call it intuition or premonition, he felt something was changing, and the Corporates were coming.

Before winter, the facility would require bedding, a kitchen, and access to water. He needed open ground for target practice, and so much more to truly get a force ready to face other highly trained soldiers. The list looked like a Herculean task, but as Relic would often say, destinies are like that.

He was deep in his head when Taylor approached him. "So, what are your plans for searching? Did you file anything with the council?"

"No, they would have found something to stick their controlling fingers in. But I'll tell you my direction, for no other reason than to know where to send a search party," Will smiled.

"I highly doubt there is anything in those woods you can't survive, but it's a good idea."

"I planned to follow the Colorado River east, which would address three issues. It's near water; it would be, more or less, out of the treacherous mountains in winter. Plus, there is an old road for trips back and forth. We could repair it and have easy access."

"Well, old roads can be repaired, but that makes others know they're used. But we'll deal with that another day. I like it. It's well thought out. Good hunting, Will." Taylor shook his hand firmly and pulled him in for an embrace.

Will had looked forward to this adventure since it had been okayed by the town. Remi, Hunter, and Nash asked to go with him, but he declined their offers. He was a loner by nature, and he needed time and seclusion in his world of woods. He missed his easy days at his hunting cabin, where he enjoyed walking slowly and listening to the sounds of the forest. It was a language he understood. He felt the spirit of the mountain landscape before him. It was wild, free, alert, and dangerous, like him.

Being on foot, Will expected to be gone for at least a week. He used his map book to follow the Colorado River, but on the second day, he turned off and headed south down the Blue River. He wanted to check out Green Mountain Lake. He expected to run into a Fringer village at Heeney, and he was surprised to find it so deserted. It became obvious as he walked past the recently scorched buildings that something deliberate had happened here.

Not one structure was large enough or undamaged enough to claim. It looked like the people or the town was taken out. It would be important to find out why. He found no bodies, so he assumed someone needed to make sure the town was not inhabitable, interesting.

He took an early morning dip in the lake and remembered the swims he would take with Rival. This would be a great place to settle the camp. It was far enough away but not too far, and it had water. It seemed perfect, but nagging at his head were three critical questions. Who or what destroyed Heeney, why did they need to, and will they return?

It was high noon on his fourth day, and he was enjoying the journey. In pure Will fashion, he analyzed the issues as he walked. He decided that if he had to build a facility, he would make constructing it part of the training. It wasn't the perfect scenario, but if he worked the recruits hard enough, the construction would be finished sooner while building their strength and endurance. It was almost nightfall when he made it to the narrow end of the Lake and settled down near Black Creek.

He was scouting the next morning and thinking a thousand thoughts, as he often did, when a thud on the ground came from behind the brush up ahead. He crouched down and silently approached the area. Just then, a large, reined head rose from the brush followed by a whinny. It was a horse! A domesticated horse with tackle and a saddle which meant someone was near. Will remained hidden.

"Ugh," came a deep groan from behind the tall grasses. Will crawled closer. It was the rider. He was hurt and lying on the ground. Will could not see anyone else, but that didn't mean he was alone.

Will edged through the grass to where the man lay with blood-soaked clothes and a smell signaling he had a gut wound. It was clear he was not going to make it.

"What happened to you? Can I help?" Will asked more than a means of reconnaissance than any belief he could help.

"Are you Dranger? Show me your brand, or I'll shoot." He weakly held up the gun for credibility, but his hand was shaking from the effort.

Will stood up and bared his scar for the man to see. He worried he might shoot him because he was from a different Dranger Territory, but the man's hand with the gun fell to his side. "Did they send you already? It was yesterday morning, I think, when we engaged them. Our mission failed. The intel was wrong. You have to give my report for me. I'm not gonna make it." The man was struggling greatly to give his report, but he kept going.

"We followed them here as ordered. We were supposed to ambush and capture them when they met the other rebels, but it went wrong. They must be protecting those buildings. We weren't told about the buildings. There was a lot of gunfire. I ran off to try to report back because I was already been hit. I was going for help. They don't know where we are. Please don't let them think we went Fringer and deserted."

Due to their northern position, he must be a Denver Dranger. He knew that Prefect Gunner headed their packs. He decided to use what he remembered from the Drangers he met on the body runs to glean information before the man passed out.

"I'm one of Prefect Ender's lone lion scouts, but I work for Prefect Gunner too. I know nothing of your run because I left over a week ago for solitary recon duty. Tell me about your mission so I can give your report." Will hoped that both of the prefects were still in charge and the man bought the lion story.

"Smart of our prefects to have scouts out here during this mission. We heard chatter that a rebel group we'd been watching was going to meet out in the middle of nowhere. When we got the run details, we were curious why they would travel so far for a meeting."

The man was struggling to speak and breathing erratically, and he was extremely pale and clammy. His body was experiencing the final stages of shock. "It was just a meeting place. That's what we were told. We were to gain access to the building for cover, so we could capture and interrogate the rebels. But they had so many people in full gear and armed to the teeth. The building, it's hard to see," he strained through the pain and Will grabbed his hand to steady him.

"It's camo'ed up good, a damn fortress. How could we have known? These rebels," he groaned a pitiful sound, "better armed." He yelled and tried to roll onto his side in great agony. "Their soldiers ... more trained," his words were breaking up, but he pushed on." You have to warn ... You gotta..." He wailed in pain.

"Are there still people in the building? Where is its location? Who should I report this to?"

He was barely conscious now, and his voice was reduced to a mumbled whisper. "Go north, follow creek, to lake. In the woods, hundred yards up there. Don't know if they're still there. Been here since last night, waiting for death," he yelled in pain from the effort spent on the conversation. His next words came in broken phrases.

"This badge lets you in. Rifle pack, all dead." His last words came in a cry, and his eyes squeezed tight with agony. He began convulsing, and Will held his hand. He helped his brother Dranger die as his breaths became ragged then they ceased completely, and his body slumped.

Will was disturbed to learn there had been such an important mission, and he was, by his proximity, in the thick of it. It was also within fifty miles of the McCoy homestead. They may know of it, but it sounds more like they stumbled upon it. He assumed that destroying the town by Green Lake was used to ensure the privacy of this 'fortress' the man spoke of. *If it wasn't the Corporates, who was stationed there?*

He buried the Dranger in a shallow grave and spoke over the mound. "I ask that your people thank you, honor, and remember you." He took the horse by the reins and secured his gear on the back of the saddle.

Since living in McCoy, he had taken full advantage of the library. He read a fictional story about a cowboy who trained people to ride horses. The book gave great detail about the techniques and the philosophy of control. Will was fascinated. He hoped the author had done her research because he was going to put those lessons into practice. Having confidence that he was in charge was the most important trait for controlling a horse, and he had that in spades.

He put his left foot in the stirrup and threw his right leg over, settling himself in the saddle. The first thing he noticed was how high his position was, but he reeled back his unease of being thrown and landing from such a height. Holding the reins up, he gently kicked the animal in the sides, and it moved forward. *So* far, *so* good, he thought. He pulled out his compass and steered the horse northeast back to the creek.

When the horse came upon a log in its path, it started nervously prancing. Will figured he was getting ready to step over when suddenly the horse backed up and leaped over the log with more height than required. It sent Will bouncing out of the saddle, landing him on the horse's back end. He held on tightly to the reins and grabbed the saddle horn.

"Whoa," Will commanded firmly, and the horse stopped and started munching on a bush with new buds. Will resettled himself and laughed. "Okay, Horse, let's make a little bet. You think you can make a fool out of me, but I bet I can make a friend out of you.

"If I win, I'll feed you grains and find a place to keep you warm and safe in the winter. If you win, I'll feed you to the wild things. What do you say?" The horse nickered and shook his head as Will pulled him away from the tasty bush. "Okay, Little Bet, let's go." Will clicked his cheeks and gave a firm kick to his sides. Little Bet moved onward.

Will was about to give up on this mysterious compound. He surmised from his map book and the directions he was given, that the Dranger was referring to Black Creek Reservoir. He had found the lake, but he saw no structures. He decided to travel up the ridge before he gave up on the Dranger's directions. The man had been delirious with fever and pain, but he gave a solid report, and someone shot him, so there had to be something here.

The ground leveled off, but the forest was thick, making it hard to see through it. Too thick in fact, and it caused Will to look closer. The slight visual abnormalities had him on full alert because those kinds of defects suggested camouflage, just as the Dranger said. He took Little Bet back down the hillside fifty yards or so and secured him to a bush. Grabbing his binoculars, he climbed back up and into a tall tree to get a better look.

There it was. It was huge, and he was impressed with its camouflage technology. Four large, single-story, rectangle buildings were set in a weave pattern. The word Alpha was lettered vertically, like the spine of a book, on the building closest to him. The camouflage on the roof and the pavement was technologically advanced, like the type the Neighwah used in high-level security outposts.

A gravel road led to the camo-pavement surrounding it. This place screamed more resources than any rebel forces he knew of. If it was a Neighwah outpost, why would Prefect Gunner be attacking it? Could it be another territory infiltrating Denver's borders? With this kind of technology, he was probably being watched, but he saw no movement. *What the fuck is going on here? Who built this place and why?*

This structure was well-funded on the exterior, and he could only imagine who and what was locked inside. Whoever they were, they had defensive capabilities to take out a whole pack of Drangers and not be on high alert now. That meant he should be.

The side he was looking at had the scars of intense artillery fire, with dried blood on the walls and the pavement. This place was throwing off countless warning signs, and it was in McCoy's backyard. He needed to head home immediately and bring some soldiers, and he needed Relic.

He estimated the distance using the existing roads was around a sixty-mile trek. On horseback, it would take three days to get home. It would take him a week to return, but he couldn't risk getting closer without a team.

He pushed himself and Little Bet the first two days, but took his time the next two. He arrived late in the evening on the fourth day and secured Little Bet outside of town. Though exhausted and sore from the ride, he called Rival, Nash, Hunter, and Relic to a private spot. He told his friends he needed their help to assess a building he found, and they needed to leave at dawn. Beyond that, he didn't elaborate.

He neglected to tell them he had chosen them because they were soldiers, and a grave and deadly battle had just been waged there. Nor did he tell Relic that the technology of this place was like nothing he had ever seen.

He had no intention of informing anyone about anything yet. Political interference and a town panic were the last things needed before he even knew what they were dealing with.

He explained to the people of the town that an old dying wanderer had told him of a place that might work for them. It wasn't a complete lie, but he left out the meat of the story, including the horse and the man had the Dranger brand. Before they set out to leave, he told Wurden they were checking out some possible prospects. He told him who was coming with him because he wanted their opinions.

Tommie overheard the discussion and begged Will to let her go with them. Will knew this mission was anything but routine, and she needed more training before she went into possible battle situations.

"Tommie, we only get two ATVs, so some of us have to double-time it. We have little space for supplies as it is. We will have to jog a good portion of the way. But I do have a favor to ask you. Will you take care of Copper for me? Copper trusts you, and you're the only one who disciplines him. Remi and Jedi will have him climbing on the furniture before I get back."

He wished there was time to see Leita, but the questions and possibilities swirling around this fortress demanded answers. He was in a hurry and had much to do before they left.

They packed a week's worth of gear and headed out under a vibrant orange sky. Rival, Nash, Hunter, and Relic met Will, and they headed out on two four-wheelers. Three on an over-packed ATV was precarious, but when Will stopped and introduced them to Little Bet, they began to ask questions. But there was no time to chat. Will wanted to be back at the site as quickly as possible.

Because Little Bet was tired from his first jaunt, they stopped just past the ghost town of Yarmony. It was near the Colorado River, and they ate the dinner that had been packed for them. Will gave Little Bet a good rubdown with a curry comb along with some oats he found in the barn. His horse needed a day of rest. But it wasn't going to come.

The mystery and threat of this place were stalking his thoughts like a predator. Once again, his good intentions had stirred up deadly trouble for the people near him. He knew all the platitudes of people making their own choices, but time and time again he was the deadly factor.

They sat by a small fire, and Will told them the whole story. He talked about Little Bet, the Dranger, and what he found. They were still for a moment waiting for the punchline, but Will stared at the fire with hypnotic intensity.

"Sooo ... umm," Rival spoke first, "I guess it's a good thing we brought a couple of guns and bows and arrows to fight this high-tech unit of lethal warriors. Maybe we could collect some rocks too. Do we have a plan, or are we hoping for mercy?"

Will stirred the fire with a stick and looked up at his friends. "I just need, we just need, to know what is in our backyard here. Be they friend or foe, this is too much neighbor for our small town of farmers. The plan is to get as much information as we can. And we may get the chance to use this." Will held out the access badge. "It opens the door, at least that's what he said."

The fire was dying, and the darkness was taking over. Hunter rubbed the brand that ran across his knuckles and recalled the pledge he had made. He had meant what he said, and this was his opportunity to prove it.

He held his fist upward and declared, "I fight with the Ninja."

Immediately, Nash and Rival followed the gesture.

The next morning, they were all excited to get going. They still had at least two more days of travel to the site at a pace accommodating Little Bet.

"Tell me again why we had to bring the horse," Nash complained.

"I can't leave a horse that belongs to a Dranger pack in our town when all its best warriors are away."

Relic had been quieter than usual, and Will knew he was thinking about his role in this military mission. But he found his voice when they stopped for lunch.

"Exactly what is it you expect me to do when we get there? It seems likely we will be shot at or captured, probably both. As you say, I suck at those."

Will smiled. "Relic, I don't think the inhabitants are aggressive. I wandered all over those woods, and with the technology they appeared to have, I'm sure they saw me. But they did not act. They are hiding inside, which means they prefer peace, or it's empty. And if it's empty, I'm taking it."

"Well, whoever resides inside has proven they have a mighty sting. They left no survivors the last time someone came to visit. And if it is empty, it sounds like it would be hard to hold."

"One day at a time, Relic."

When they rejoined the Colorado River, they encountered numerous blowdowns across the road. When Will traveled on foot, it was easy to climb over them, but the ATVs could not find a suitable detour. Will kept moving on Little Bet while the rest of the crew dealt with the roadblock. They met up in Kremmling and set up camp. Little conversation was exchanged due to the heavy work they had done that day, and sleep came quick and heavy.

Around 2:00 p.m., on the third day, they arrived at the burnt-out town of Heeney. Relic said he saw numerous boxes that might house cameras. It would be a strategic place to watch for approaching intruders. They were not the camera boxes Will knew from the Neighwah, but this group was most certainly not affiliated with them.

They passed through the town and stopped for a late lunch, but they didn't set up camp because they planned to move into their observation site that evening. The moon was beginning to wane, but it was still reflecting a strong gibbous glow into the night. Once they passed Green Mountain Reservoir, they would turn on Black Creek Road and find a suitable place to set up camp.

Though the day was particularly long, their rest was restless due to the edginess of the area, but soon they fell into a cautious sleep while Little Bet and Will took the first watch.

Today was the day they would see the compound, and excitement ran high. But it was also the day they may feel the full power of this fortress, so apprehension ran just as high. They left Little Bet on the ridge like before and crept up to a good vantage point.

Upon seeing the facility, they became invigorated, and their curiosity compelled them closer. They had been watching the quiet buildings for hours now. They had even stood up enough to evoke some kind of response, but nothing stirred. The hesitation was unsettling to the tenacious troop, and Will wondered how long this standstill would last. The group inside could wait indefinitely, but his team's supplies were limited. He needed a new plan, and his team needed to help decide it.

"It was clear the Drangers breached the compound," Will said, "but the sole survivor didn't give me enough intel about the security before he died. There was a fierce battle, and everyone in his pack died. You can see the bullet holes in the building wall and the blood on the walkway. There could be hundreds of soldiers in there."

"I say we throw a rock at this wasp nest and see what comes out," Rival suggested.

"That sounds very risky," Relic quickly piped in. "Why don't we just knock on the door?" The four men stared at him with incredulity. "Well, that looks like a hard no."

Will was tired of simply observing this incredible find. "So," he stated, "we've been squirreling around here and nothing has stirred. This place is a formidable stronghold. They aren't defenseless. How much time do you think they would let us spend snooping around before they reacted? I mean, think about it. I've returned after a week of being away. If they valued their privacy, I never would have made it home."

"Even though we're just farming townsfolk, they don't know that. They know we are interested enough to bring more people to their hideaway. How much time are we going to spend waiting to get some answers?" Rival was smiling at the possibility of some action. Being a Fringer had more to do with hiding than fighting, but he was no Fringer. He missed fun, women and easy living, but mostly he missed the thrill of battle. He enjoyed hunting, but harvesting prey was not the same as facing an enemy.

"I agree with him," Hunter pointed at Rival. "Let's poke this nest."

"It could go really bad, but we can't sit here forever," Nash added.

"Okay, let's send the horse out there in full view and see what happens," Will decided.

Will led Little Bet to the edge of the clearing and slapped him onward. The gelding meandered until he found a clump of fresh grass to graze on. Will had a visual on two buildings, and the cameras on one building tracked the horse's movements, but there was still no response. He motioned for the others to come down to his location. The evening was creeping in, and with no outdoor lights, they needed to attempt breaching the structure.

"How is it possible that this place is abandoned?" asked Relic.

"Shit, if it is, it won't be for long. I just wonder who will return, or who else will want it, and whether we can hold it. But hell, it's worth a try." Rival's excitement was pounding like a war drum through Nash and Hunter while Relic was backing away.

"Relic, you come with me. You have the best chance of getting through the technology. Rival, Hunter, and Nash cover us."

"That building is riddled with bullet holes, and my warrior skills are untested," Relic said with obvious trepidation.

Rival smiled at Relic. "Well, here's your chance," he said with a slight chuckle.

"You'll be fine. Stay behind me," Will said as he crept the rest of the way down the embankment. Rival pushed Relic after him. To Will and his soldiers, the persistent stillness of the stronghold was more unnerving than any confrontation. They crossed the open ground to a side entrance. There was a padlock on the door, and Will was about to slam it with his hatchet, but Relic stopped him. He opened a leather case with numerous metal tools. He removed a long pick and began fiddling with the padlock. Even now, no one came to stop them, and the lock clunked open. Will slid the badge through the slot, and the door clicked.

Rival, Nash, and Hunter came down, and they all went inside, piercing the darkness with their battery lights. They were in a hallway with several doors. The one directly in front of them opened easily with the same card. It was a medical facility, and though it was mostly empty, some equipment remained.

The next door wouldn't open, so they left Relic and Hunter to work on it and went down the other side of the hall. Down the hall was an empty room and another full of boxes. They'd have to check them out later.

Relic smiled when he felt the subtle tick of tumblers aligning. He yelled for his friends and opened the door. It had several offices, barracks-style sleeping quarters, and personal sleeping quarters for a commander. Hunter was still speechless when Nash, Rival, and Will stepped into what looked like a command room. Relic had settled himself in, and he was already in his element tapping on the blinking computers.

"This place is a fucking goldmine!" Hunter yelled. "And we haven't even seen the rest."

"These people left in a hurry," Will said, "but it was recently. There's no way they won't come back. Let's check out the rest of this place. Hunter, stay with Relic." Hunter collapsed in one of the chairs and spun it around. He would follow Will's orders, but he would rather go exploring.

Rival and Will shined their flashlights into a hallway leading to a large open space with chain-link barriers. A mess hall to his right had folded picnic tables and a fenced-in area directly in front of it. Suddenly, a buzzing sound came from the ceiling, and the overhead lights came on one by one, making a thunking sound as each set lit. *Nice* work, *Relic* Will said to himself. This place was huge, and there were four more buildings this size.

Now he could see the full kitchen and the fenced-in area for physical activities. It even had basketball hoops. The next room smelled and looked like a barnyard. Woodchips covered the floor of a large but short stall on one end with a water trough and hose. Will told Nash and Rival to get Little Bet and settle him in with some feed.

What was the purpose of this place? It seemed too cushy for soldiers. Who built it, and why did they leave?

Rival walked up and pointed to the shipping container structures beyond the fence. "The three trailers over there each have restrooms, showers, and laundry areas. There are tables and tubs for children. The water and electricity for them are still turned on. Why would anyone leave? Is it cursed or something?"

"This place just gets stranger and stranger," Will said.

Relic came out, followed by Hunter, who was looking around all wonder-eyed. "I believe this place was a sanctuary for families. I only hacked into the first level, but I found an inventory list to support that. Each building held forty to fifty people and support staff."

"Well, they had more than enough space for that many. Okay, let's get settled for the night. I want a list of what appliances and utilities are working as well as any supplies you find. Hunter, check out the boxes in the storage room. Relic, you can keep working on the computer. Rival, check in the offices for supplies. Nash, check out the storage in the kitchen and see if you can get the kitchen appliances going.

"I'm pretty sure I speak for the group when I say we're hungry. I'm going to investigate the infirmary." Will suddenly worried this place might be under quarantine, and they had been exposed. Will shared his quarantine theory with Relic, and he said he would look for signs of that.

Walking from the mess hall, Rival approached Will. "Hey, I want in on the whole brotherhood thing. Nash and Hunter became blood brothers, and Hunter took some oath that no one else did. Dude, did I miss a memo or what?"

Will thought for a moment. He would not be able to slash his fist for every recruit he gathered, but an oath was a good idea. He decided to bring Rival in himself, and they went to the infirmary.

Nash used the state-of-the-art appliances to cook their supplies along with some canned goods Hunter found in the storage room. After dinner, they each enjoyed a long, hot shower. Will found a forgotten basketball, and he and Rival showed Nash and Hunter how to play. Will settled in the commander's office and Nash in the barracks while Rival and Hunter took the first watch.

The next morning came, and there was still no sign of the previous owners. Relic told Will that the last time the infirmary was used was during the battle just over a week ago, and there was no mention of diseases.

Relic said he could get them into the other buildings with the use of the card fabricator he located. He worked for hours getting clearance to the other buildings, but he couldn't open the computer rooms yet. He and Will understood the security for entering the buildings, but both were curious why there was just as much security to keep people inside.

Will and Relic walked outside to the center of the complex to get to the other buildings. The ground was covered in camo paint with a strange sheen to it. Relic said it was brilliantly designed. It deflected camera images as well as heat sensors, and it mimicked foliage. He may have been apprehensive before, but now he was enjoying the bliss of exploration.

One by one they did a quick check of the three other buildings labeled Beta, Delta, and Gama. They all had similar arrangements, but it was apparent the Alpha building was the primary.

Chapter Twenty-Eight

Will let his mind wander while he groomed Little Bet. Horses made a lot of sense for this terrain, and he could see boarding several here. The current animal areas were meant for smaller livestock, and some were set up as gardens. He would have to add a bigger enclosure for horses. He had so many visions of running this incredible complex.

There was no question he had to claim it. The question was how to recruit enough people to hold it. He planned to round up Fringers as quickly and quietly as possible from all over the area. He'd start with the ones who traveled with them and settled in other towns.

He had to go back and face the council. He needed to convince them they were on a time crunch to have the training facility up and running. Just like a mean-looking summer thunderstorm brewing on the horizon, their enemies would soon come looking for their soldiers. It didn't matter whether they stayed here or hid at McCoy, their quiet lives had come to an end when Kenner broke the Tri-Territory Treaty. Will was done with waiting and slow-walking plans. They needed to act fast.

Nash, Hunter, Rival, and Relic would stay, and Will would return to McCoy. Relic found a program for outer defense measures, and he was sure they could hold it until he returned. Will was packing the ATV when Relic came running out.

"Ninge," he called and motioned him over. Will wished he could be called Will, but it was wise to keep the habit, so slip-ups did not occur. He hid behind false names to protect others, but it was hiding just the same, and every time someone called him Ninge, he bristled. Will walked over to Relic letting Rival finish securing the few items they needed for the ride. "I found something."

"What?"

"I have been deciphering Tianna's book. There are things added at the end that are not in her handwriting. It is in an old signaling system called Morris code consisting of dots and dashes sent by long and short flashes or beeps. It was invented for mariners to communicate across the water and ..."

"Get to the point Relic."

"Written in that code is 'safeband'. I thought it meant a secure way to communicate. But then I found a file on this computer called SaFeBand. The letters SFB are capitalized which is not shown in Morris Code. I haven't been able to open it, yet," his eyes gleamed, "but it is called SaFeBand. Have you ever heard of SaFeBand before?"

Will shook his head. Will had noticed the marks at the end of the book, but he assumed they were added by Tianna. He wondered how Relic could tell from dots and dashes that it wasn't written by her.

"Well, I guess that settles it. If we can't claim this place we have to destroy it."

"We can't do that, Will! We need the answers in that file. I don't know if we could find it again."

"Trust me, Relic, this place is too good to let go, especially if it leads to Cali Bantu. I'll fight like hell to keep it. That also means it's too good to let the Corporates have it. We will decide that shit when we face it, but if it truly is part of our destiny, then we will make it happen."

He turned to see Rival walking the ATV to him.

"It's all charged up and ready. We are very low on fuel, so you'll have to go slow and use the solar option. Relic looked excited," Rival said. "Did he find something on the computer?"

"It's unclear what he found. His head is buzzing with input, and when he gets that way, we have to wait for him to sort it out before it makes sense. What he needs is sleep, but I doubt he'll take it willingly."

Will was deep in thought about what to tell the council. He trusted Wurden, but Will worried he would want to walk away from such a risk to avoid trouble. He knew that's what Grady and Jessica would want. They would throw a fit that he found something that required protection. He had to convince Wurden to support him.

Before he left, Rival turned to his friend. "Will, spill it. I can hear the wheels in your head churning."

"I'm just not sure how I should present this to the council. They see the world differently than we do. Their answer is to hide from danger, but we know one can only hide for so long. This conflict is inevitable, and we must prepare before it attacks. I worry they will see this facility as a threat, and they may wish to run from it. That can never happen. I just don't think they're willing to sacrifice what it will take to keep it."

"So the bottom line is not do we keep secrets; it's which ones? What is the likelihood that anyone but soldiers would visit?"

"Hard to say, but eventually they would know, and they would feel betrayed."

"This sounds like a Taylor question. Do you trust him with this kind of information? It seems like you do from my observation of your numerous side talks."

"Maybe so," Will smiled. Not much gets by Rival. He wanted desperately to tell him everything, but he couldn't yet. It wasn't about trust; it was about protecting Rival from knowing too much and protecting the information from too many.

Relic knew a lot about Will. Wurden and Rival knew much, and Taylor knew some. He found it tiresome remembering who knew what. He vowed to dispatch this destiny endeavor with all its arduous secrets as soon as he could.

He arrived just as dinner was being set up. The familiar way Will asked Taylor to walk with him told Taylor it was about something troubling and highly secretive.

"Here's a scenario: what if we found something we can't let go of but the council will be afraid to keep? What should I tell them?"

"How dangerous is it potentially?"

"More dangerous by far to let it go than to keep it, but there is no safe choice. I fear tucking our tails and running would be the council's choice, but that wouldn't work for long."

"Sounds like you located a weapon."

"The whole place is a weapon."

"Oh, well, can you tell me about it?"

"Yeah, I think I should. I need help delivering the intel in a way politics can't deny the necessity of claiming it and defending it. You're so much better at that than me."

They put the details into three categories. What all should know, what some should know, and what the team kept to themselves for a while. All should know they found a safe place to train, and the schedule they already agreed upon should begin with the elite group leaving tomorrow.

The council should know where it is, that it is abandoned, it is camouflaged, and it could be a shelter for the town if trouble came to McCoy. He would also let them know there were utilities available, but not a computer room with access to surveillance, weapons, and potentially top-secret information.

In other words, he wouldn't disclose how valuable it might be to the Corporates, but he would tell them how perfect it was for their needs. He would say that based on the observations of his team, it was abandoned and is not part of the Neighwah.

The things he didn't say were the things he couldn't quantify safely. He met a dying Dranger who had been sent there on a run. He wouldn't share why he knew how Drangers and Neighwah operated. Even though it would help his cause, he would leave out it was unlikely the Corporates would send Drangers to a place like this if they knew more about it. They would have sent the Neighwah, and now that the pack was missing in action, that was bound to happen sooner than later.

Will was gambling with other people's lives again, but it was a forced ante. He didn't know who it had belonged to, but as far as he was concerned, it was theirs for as long as they could hold on to it. That the Neighwah might come, or worse, be on their way, was unknown. Whether they held it or left it, their town and probably several others stood the chance of being eliminated, so running wouldn't work. However, with the weapons inside, they had an obligation to defend it, and if all went wrong, they had a duty to destroy it.

Will gave his report and recommendations to Grady and Jessica, with Rival and Taylor present. He said they had much to do before the hard winter months set in. It was more of a metaphor than a lie.

Will was surprised when Jessica said she was happy they found a spot a solid distance from town, making deniability more plausible. She was naïve about the enemy they faced, but it was a win for the people, and he would take it.

Their questions proved they had no clue what he had found, or that he had held back information. They assumed it was a worn-out warehouse of some kind that no one was around to care about. This lie wouldn't last long, but hopefully, winter would provide them with time to recruit enough soldiers to have the compound up and running.

Will found Leita gathering herbs and vegetables for the soldier group that was being sent off the next day. She smiled and went back to her task while he went to grab a couple of sacks of grain for his horse. The barn had been restored enough to shut out the weather and the predators for the goats, pigs, and chickens. Wood chips lined the stalls, and clean water sloshed in the troughs. These were very efficient people. They saw what needed to be done and did it without complaint.

He heard her soft footsteps on the earthen floor and felt her hands run up his back. He spun around and looked out the open door. They were alone. They climbed into the hay-filled loft, and he saw the blanket and moon wine already set up. *Very efficient and very* lovely, he thought. He had until morning to thoroughly enjoy her company.

The elite team, including Nash, Rival, and Hunter, was four members short of the fifteen Will had hoped for, but by morning two more joined, including Tommie. Taylor accompanied them, but he was not joining the army. The supplies were packed into a truck and onto the three four-wheelers. Some complained about losing them, but their extra fuel was almost gone anyway. This would allow them to move a lot of food and supplies to their new military base. They packed many fresh vegetables and the supplies to can them, as well as seeds for the garden areas.

The trip over the ridge and down the river was all on old but now passable roads. Taylor, Jedi, and Remi rode the heavily and precariously packed four-wheelers cautiously. Will drove the truck with the other recruits, more supplies, and Copper.

They arrived the next day after clearing a minor amount of debris from the road, so the truck could pass. Everyone standing before the complex had the same expression—stunned. Their reaction only increased when they went inside, where their excitement and awe quickly turned to fear. Will sat them at the picnic benches in the cafeteria for their first briefing.

Remi was the first to speak. "There is no way the people who built this are gone for good. If, or should I say when, they want this back, the resources they must have would crush us."

Tommie jumped in, "What about our families? They're defenseless!"

"Okay, first, this place is top-secret. I need to remind you that you will be severely punished if you disclose it. Understood?" They all nodded. "I don't believe the Corporates know of this place, or they wouldn't have left it unguarded. But we have evidence ..."

Tommie cut Will off again and asked, "What about the Neighwah drones? They'll just shoot us down!"

Will continued, "We have evidence that the people who built this place are peaceful and believe in a government by the people. This place was built to house families, and they gave lessons on democracy and job training. If we're right, and if they come back, we should do everything in our power to join them.

"As far as the safety of our towns and this place, the camouflage technology here is like nothing I've ever seen. We are virtually undetectable from the air. We have surveillance capabilities too, and the cameras here are amazing. We also have seven working drones, and we have more that we are getting up and running. Relic discovered booster stations in a ten-mile area around here. They supply a secure line between the drones we found and the command center. We can communicate with and watch McCoy from here. We will be setting up a line so we can warn them, and with the reserve soldiers there, they will have defensive capabilities until we arrive.

"They can just access the space satellites and see everything we see and more," added Remi.

"Relic says something has happened to the satellites required for long-range drone communications. It's why we found some that malfunctioned. Without instructions, they either returned to their launch site, landed, or crashed."

"I for one, want to hear Ninge. Let him talk," said Taylor.

"Thank you, I do want to hear your input, but there are some things I need to explain. There was a battle here, and during or shortly after it, this place was abandoned. We know all the Drangers sent to check this place out died. There is no evidence the Corporates knew these buildings were here. They sent a Dranger pack to follow and apprehend the rebels when they met with their contacts. The Drangers were never able to report back, so the Corporates have no idea where to look for them.

"The Corporates are bound to conduct a search for the missing pack. The last thing we want them to do is find and occupy this facility. The residents may also come back someday. You can bet both will be considerably armed the next time they come. But the reality is we would probably get swept up in that battle whether we are here or in our villages. We are better armed and more prepared with this place than we are hiding.

"The good news is, we have evidence that the owners of this facility are also rebels, meaning they are against the Corporates. They may even be freedom fighters like us. If we could meet, I believe they'd let us join them.

"But now, we need to get set up, so we are up and running to work on our number one objective—being ready to defend our people."

They nodded their heads, and Will asked for questions, but they were all speechless. Will delegated a long list of tasks, ordering Rival, Nash, and Hunter to oversee them. Tommie and Remi trailed after the three men discussing the list, while Taylor followed Will.

Will took Taylor on a quick tour. Taylor followed Will to the outer edge of the main area to check on the accommodations for his horse. Little Bet was munching a mixture of grains and grasses in his corral. He snickered when Will passed by and patted his neck.

He noticed the fence had been raised to make it suitable for a horse, and the corral was quite large, too large for one horse. He imagined several more stalls being added if they could get more horses. Kenner had quite a few on a ranch outside of town. Will smiled as he imagined stealing them away.

The next door led to the utility room, and Taylor marveled at the shiny new, state-of-the-art technology. They passed by a door with an access keypad, which Taylor surmised must be the control room, but Will said they would go there at the end of the tour. Taylor followed Will through the main area to reach the medical facility.

The infirmary held a reception area and an office with partitions to separate two desks and a records area. The exam room had four sections divided by curtains. Next to it was a storage room with an empty, locking glass cabinet for medicines.

Down the hall were two rooms, each with two hospital beds, and another that looked like an operating room with overhead lights and various strange outlets. The equipment that remained had been cleaned, and a written inventory of supplies lay on the treatment bed ready for inspection.

Taylor was overwhelmed by the valuable equipment left behind. He was confident and concerned that someone would be returning to claim such a prize. It was clear the previous tenants had removed most of the items and relocated. But it was unlikely they planned to abandon these resources unless serious trouble was headed this way. Something was off, but he decided to wait until the tour was over to discuss it.

A separate office was next to the infirmary, followed by another storage room with boxes and other random items. The main area had four curtain tents set up, but the vast size of the available space suggested it could hold many more. The nearby mess hall was clean and already in use.

Will had described to Taylor that they had found the place in the kind of disarray that suggested those who had stayed here left in a hurry. But it looked quite orderly now, and both were impressed at the progress the small team had made in such a short time. Taylor could see they respected Will and were proud to be part of this new organization.

Nash let them into the command center. He told Will that Relic passed out in the barracks five or six hours ago, and Will said to let him sleep.

Will looked over at Taylor. "So, what do you think of this place?"

"It's way more than I expected. I doubt it was left for you to just move in for free. You do need an army just to keep it, and it better be one hell of an army because if this is what they left, I can only imagine what they have. Are the other buildings the same?"

"Very similar, but this one seems to be the primary. It's a masterpiece of technology. Relic said he hadn't seen anything like this outside of the

Highmind camp. If he can figure out the weaponry, I think we can hold it," Will interjected.

"I think you were right. This whole compound is a weapon," Taylor said as he stared in awe at the numerous camera feeds displayed on screens that covered two walls. Not all were working yet, but if anyone could access them, it would be Relic.

"Yeah, but the weird thing is there are accommodations that suggest children lived here."

"So, you think it was a sanctuary, not a military base," Taylor said.

"Actually," said Relic, who was walking in behind them, "I think it was both." Hearing the discussion through the open door, he got up and resumed his seat at the computer station. "I think they called this place the Hold. I found numerous entries referring to this compound as the Hold, with each building being given a Latin letter designation. I also found a file called "New Haven". It was buried deep, like it was top-secret. Maybe it was a forgotten file that wasn't fully erased. It's encrypted, so it may take me some time to open it. This is an isolated server, so if it's not on this hard drive, I can't hack my way into a network to it."

"Maybe New Haven is what they decided to rename this place. I mean, who wants their hometown name to be the Hold? It sounds like a prison." Will thought some more and offered, "Or maybe it was where they were going. But why move? According to a video file we found, they had one encounter, which they won, leaving no survivors, and no reason to believe they were discovered."

"One did escape," Relic added, "and the people here had no way of knowing he didn't survive or send word. There is an abundance of mysteries surrounding this place. How did they finance it and build it without being detected?

"This place is quite new, so why build this at all if they had another place to go? How is it they have these kinds of resources? Was it because they had children and civilians here and they didn't want to risk putting them in harm's way? When did they discover they had another place else to go? Or did they build two?

"Did they join this New Haven or conquer it? I need to investigate this New Haven file because it is the key to understanding who we are dealing with." Someone called Relic on the com-line. He left the command room, leaving Will, Taylor, and Nash to worry it out.

"Everything he just said about this place is screaming, threat," Will had to admit it, but he still was compelled to invent reasons these residents left, the kind that justified his army should stay. "Maybe after they left, they all died somewhere. As sad as that would be, it would answer why they haven't returned. No matter what, look around. This place is amazing, and for now, it's undiscovered, undisturbed, and ours, and I just can't let it go."

"Well, it's only been two weeks since the 'Holders' left, if that Dranger is correct about the battle. And it isn't empty," Nash added. "We're here, and even though there's something strange about it, maybe throwing you advantages like this is how destiny works. I say hang on to it as long as we can."

"Holders, I like that." Will smiled, and then he sighed, "You're right about one thing. We can't let it go, but defending this place demands an army. I'd like to have around three hundred soldiers, but I'd settle for one hundred before winter hits."

"Well," Nash interjected, "right now, we have fifty-two, and though most of them are part-time, it's a good start. We'll keep hitting the towns we know of, but I'm going to send out the drones to find more Fringers in this area. I think there are a lot more groups out there. I believe we can make your goal, but we need to plan that kind of first contact."

Taylor had been quietly listening to their discussion, and before Will could answer, he spoke up. "Yes, I agree. That calls for finesse and a deal or trade. How about I help you work on that?"

"I'd appreciate that," Will replied. "Nash, you and Taylor will work on that and let me know what you decide."

Will saw Hunter walking into the command room with an excited look that suggested he had new information.

Hunter blurted out his news in a fast stream of sentences. "We found fuel tanks buried underground, and they're full! They are fed by a small pipeline, from where we don't know. It isn't enough to keep all these buildings going all winter, so maybe they have more than one pipeline or an alternate energy source. But we can fill up the ATVs and the trucks and charge them too. That means we can cover a lot of ground in a short amount of time.

"We also found two utility task vehicles. One is big, and it can carry twenty passengers and a driver easily, and thirty-something if we go for some standing and the seats squeezed full. It's not running, and it needs work, but one of the other buildings has a maintenance shop. The other one is smaller and also has a few problems.

"This place is incredible! As much as they took, they left a lot too. For some unknown reason, they left here in a hell-fire hurry."

"Yeah, I get that." Will added, "How did the first drone run go? Were you able to fly them? How long before we can search for Fringer tribes?"

"Yeah, hey, those are so fun. It was cool. We could see from really high and far away."

"Hunter!" Will asserted, "calm down."

"Yeah, I know, but we got two of the drones flying. Relic taught me how to use the controls. It took me a bit to master flying one. Then I taught Nash. He learns quick, and after spending an hour or two, he got really good at it. We can send those two up whenever you want."

"Okay, keep me informed. And dude, breathe. You're throwing off sparks. I need to call everyone together, so..."

"Allow me," Relic said as he came back in and sat in front of a computer with a microphone. "Attention, there is a mandatory meeting in the mess hall now." Relic smiled and held out his hands with obvious pride and joy. He loved his new toys, which made Will chuckle.

"Relic, you're a genius," Taylor complimented.

"I know," he replied.

Will sat on a table with his feet on the bench and faced the eleven elite members in front of him. He gave a brief overview of the benefits and risks involved in securing this stronghold.

"Our first order of business is understanding our vision, so we're united. Then, we will pledge our loyalty to it. You will not be swearing an oath to me. You will swear an oath to our overall vision, our code of conduct, which is to protect our people and secure freedom for our realm. As your current commander, you are swearing to follow my orders. Are you ready to swear?"

Shouts of yes rang out from the tiny army. "Pull out your knives and come to the kitchen," he said as he walked that way and they followed. "Heat your knife, make a fist, and cut across your fist with the hot knife. Make sure your knife is hot enough. It's the burn that will leave the scar as well as sterilize and seal the wound. Don't get carried away. I don't want to see any fingers dropping on the floor."

"And no yelling or whiney sounds of pain allowed," added Nash, remembering that day in GZ so long ago when he, Will, and Calen became brothers. Nash, Rival, and Hunter motioned everyone over to the massive gas stove. Will let his top soldiers initiate this new group of soldiers. And this group would initiate the next, and so on. No one would have more than two marks except Will.

"Repeat after me," Will stated. "With this oath, I pledge my allegiance to the Guard. I will be loyal to its goals and fight bravely with honor to restore liberty and better the lives of all." Will realized the magnitude of the moment. If there was ever a time to believe in his destiny and bear its burdens, this was it. They now were united in a cause, and they swore to it in blood. To fight with honor and allegiance to better the fate of all. This was more than an oath taken by individuals; it was their creed and the sum of all worthwhile endeavors.

"Remi," yelled Jedi, "I know you got moonshine. Time for a shot."

Jedi began searching the kitchen cupboards for cups, and Remi jogged to his tent. Jedi was handing out cups when Remi returned, holding aloft a large mason jar full of clear liquid to shouts of celebration. After a boisterous couple of toasts and twenty or so few minutes of festivities, they got back to discussing the lengthy list of tasks before them.

"Our first mission is to get more towns to join our alliance and recruit more soldiers to defend it. What I need is good ideas about approaching skittish Fringers."

"Well, some of the tribes that split off will remember us, but we have to find them. No matter what, we should come with goods to trade," suggested Taylor.

"Offer to let a representative come here to see what we have," said Relic. Everyone stared at him in disbelief. "Listen," he added, "we would blindfold their representative on the way and leave one of our guys at their township. We could clear out one of the other buildings and use it to show recruits. If we're going to ask for their trust on one hand, we can't mistrust them on the other." Will smiled, remembering when he had said that to him.

"I like all these ideas," agreed Will," but I will add one more. We need to pledge that we will protect each other and the townspeople if this situation goes south. An individual can join the Elite team, but if the town wants to join the alliance and be entitled to our protection, they need a percentage of their people to be reservists."

"Hey, what is it we have on the Corporates that made them cower? Could we use that?" Tommie asked.

"Well, that will be a card we play someday, but we need to be a lot stronger because once that's out, they'll have nothing to lose." Will looked at Relic, and he was nodding his head.

"Damn, that must be some mean secret," replied Jedi. "Are you sure we shouldn't know it?"

"Trust me, you don't want to know it," sighed Relic.

Remi, Rival, and Jedi visited the first tribe while Will hid in the trees. They were very wary, but they got a volunteer to travel to the base while Rival stayed with them. They removed his blindfold inside the Gama building. Nash thought they had left it too sparsely furnished to entice the potential recruit, but he was thoroughly impressed.

They got one elite and five reservists from that tribe to join their alliance. It didn't take long before the council members of the tribes knew about them before they showed up. It increased the membership of already allied tribes, and others began requesting membership.

Chapter Twenty-Nine

B y mid-September, Will had a total force of one hundred and fifty-four soldiers. Seventy-three were elites and eighty-one were reservists, and more were joining. He also set up his top trainers to go to the allied tribes and train the rest of the people in defensive moves and evacuation plans. Will was encouraged by their bravery. They knew they could be up against a formidable force, but most agreed things were changing, and preparing for it was the only way to survive.

Fall was driving back the summer, and the harder the weather was, the less likely the Corporates were to strike, and the better trained their forces became. The army was taking shape. What surprised Will the most was the weapons and ammo the tribes added to the cause.

Relic ran anxiously up to Will. "Will, I've picked up some chatter from the Corporate grapevine. They are deliberating a plan to send several Dranger squadrons on a reconnaissance/takeover mission at the Poison Tunnel."

"You mean the Eisenhower-Johnson Tunnel, where that nuclear waste accident occurred?" Will asked.

"Yeah, that's the one. It's over fifty miles from here, so we should be okay. Since the Kessler Effect, surveillance has required close proximity."

According to an RH report, a group fighting the advancement of technology had successfully taken control of hundreds of satellites. They systematically used the weaponry aboard to obliterate certain strategic systems in orbit. That in turn initiated the Kessler Effect of billions of shrapnel trajectories continuously devolving the orbiting traffic into a dense and useless debris field. It disabled the fleet orbiting the Earth and effectively cut off communication and imagery for surveillance. It would also be some time before any repairs to the net could be addressed.

"Why attack a toxic site?" Will was getting tired of confusing clues popping up.

"They must believe there is something there worth acquiring," answered Relic.

"Interesting. Theories that the radioactive accident was a ruse had been circulating in the Neighwah since I was there. They were dismissed because there was evidence of a nuclear catastrophe. Radioactive signatures were detectable by radiation-sensitive satellites before the Kessler Effect took them out. It proved there was a radioactive issue. Since that kind of energy doesn't dissipate for decades or centuries, it would still be hot.

"Except for the crews sealing it up, there hasn't been a peep in almost two years. It shut down the east-to-west access within the territory as well as access to the Fringer tribes. Something on that front has changed if they're doing recon on it. They must think there's something or someone in there. They aren't sure, or they'd send a more serious military force than a couple of Dranger packs. Hmmm," Will paused. "See what you can dig up Relic, but do it very carefully. We don't want them noticing us."

Will lay awake in his bedroom in the command center. The bed was quite comfortable, but sleep evaded him. His head was buzzing in full analysis mode ticking off questions and possible answers. What if the accident was a deception? Maybe something is stored there. That would be a lot of storage room. Maybe it was Cali Bantu."

Suddenly he sat up. He remembered the Neighwah officers laughing that one of the troublemaking Corporate business owners had lost every-thing. He spent years depleting his father's vast legacy and becoming a hoarder of ridiculous volumes of worthless items. He hunted down failing companies and purchased their surplus overstock inventory of products, many unsaleable in this post-apocalyptic world.

He purchased the huge tunnel, which was smart because the tolls could have brought in a lot of credits, but the disaster closed it indefinitely. Most thought the Corporates sabotaged him because they didn't want him controlling or providing access to the neighboring territories or the wilder Dailys on that side of the mountain range.

Will remembered when he did body runs in Denver, seeing the file of shipping containers one after the other being rolled down the road toward the spill. The ambitious Corporate was forced to entomb the toxic waste, taking every resource he had left. No one knew what happened to him after what was left of his company was taken over.

Will accessed every memory he could about the tunnel. *What was his name? Ralden, Belgel, no Vogel!* Never once was there any evidence of substantial weaponry being stolen or purchased, and a manmade tunnel didn't fit the description in the song. It seemed untenable to use this place to house a massive armory in Denver's backyard.

Suddenly, he had a new thought. This guy would have had a lot of resources. He owned an enormous shipping and supply company. *Maybe this Hold was his creation. Maybe this place wasn't renamed New Haven. Maybe this Hold was a stopping-off place before they moved to New Haven.*

Even the name supports that theory. Maybe with this guy's funding, they created a town in the tunnel. It would explain the supply gathering. It had over three miles of space and would be a perfect hideaway, a true sanctuary from the tyranny of the territories. Whether it was a town or Cali Bantu, they had to check it out.

Did they know they were under investigation and may be attacked? Did they need help? Were they a free society or just another oppressive regime? He needed answers about the previous residents here and the possible residents there. With the resources they appeared to possess, these were exactly the kind of allies they needed.

Having arrived at some answers to his questions allowed him to drift off to sleep until his routine five a.m. stirrings. He took a quick shower in his private bathroom and walked by the computer room to the mess hall area. He found Taylor worshipping a steaming mug of the coffee substitute they had recently discovered in storage. It seemed they were the only ones awake except Rival, who was on guard watching the cameras in the control room. It gave him the perfect opportunity to run his ideas by Taylor.

"Well thought out," Taylor responded after a moment of consideration. "Do we have a timeline on when they plan to make their move on the tunnel?"

"From what we gathered, the Drangers had not yet been hired. As of this morning, it was still in the planning stage, but both Denver and Colorado Springs are involved. Here's what I know about Dranger runs. After they're hired, they will request supplies and transport. Then they have to travel around the divide to get to the west side."

"Why aren't they making their stand on the east closest to where they are located?"

"Relic and I believe they will attack both sides, but first, they will build up a large force on the west side so whatever resources are in there can't escape out to the wilderness. Denver can easily replenish soldiers as well as capture escapees and their assets from the east, so their initial focus would be to beef up the west entrance. They want to salvage everything they can. Prisoners are particularly valuable because of the intel they possess."

"So how much time do we have to seek out these assumed residents? And how will we vet them? I mean, why don't they just wipe us out assuming we are enemies? We have very little reliable information. They could be allies with the Corporates, and this is just in-fighting. We're flying blind here, Will." Taylor didn't see a viable plan yet.

"Well, from the records we have found, we know quite a bit of information about the routines of the people who lived here. We know this was not an oppressive place. They provided security, educational programs, medical care, healthy food, hell, they even had a counselor. There were families with children and, evidently, they celebrated a wedding. The people came from various statuses, but everyone was treated the same.

"That just doesn't sound like the Corporate way. They think and behave like us. They even hide like us. I don't know what deal the benefactor of this place made with the citizens, but as far as we can tell, the benefits were shared equally among them. We need to join a group like that. Our only hope is that they need us." Will couldn't let go of this place, and now the idea of gaining powerful allies was locked in his sights.

"Okay, first things first. How do we contact them? Before the attack or when it starts?" Taylor asked. "I think we need to make both plans and present them to the Allied Council. Then we have to call up all of our forces." Taylor was trying to reign Will in, but he had watched him grow from a child to a man and the one trait that never wavered was his stubbornness.

Taylor continued his persuasive attempts for Will to release his jaws that were locked onto the Hold and now unknown allies. It required a comprehensive think-through. "They are going to balk about the poison tunnel. It is a very prevalent story. Rumors abound about the dead plant zone and the bodies found near there with terrible burns."

"Yeah, I thought about that," Will answered thoughtfully. "I find it very convenient that they scoured the area to scrub the affected debris but left dead bodies about. Only one team will go near the tunnel for now, and they will be volunteers. I plan on being one of them."

Over the next few days, several teams were established to perform specific tasks. The Reconnaissance Team was assigned to get as close to the tunnel as possible and make contact if allowed. The Supply Team gathered, constructed, and secured supplies and weapons. The Communication Team maintained the lines of communication among their existing Fringer allies and continued to seek out new tribes to join the alliance. The last was the Training Team which oversaw the combat instruction of all soldiers. All the teams had the part-time goal of manufacturing weapons and ammo.

The initial Recon team consisted of four people, Will, Rival, and two seasoned recruits. They drove the repaired smaller utility vehicle up Black Creek Road, down Highway 9, and east on I-70. Though the four-lane road showed the result of the harsh winters, they had few issues navigating the potholes. They traveled by nightfall until they approached the last five miles before the tunnel. The utility vehicle was hidden off the road, and they camped out.

That next morning, they set out on foot. The elevation of over eleven thousand feet had them moving at a slower pace than normal. They were careful to stay well hidden, but a mile and a half away from the tunnel they heard drones overhead. Not long after that, they were assaulted by an ear-piercing sound that had them running for at least a mile back down to their vehicle. The sound grew fainter the further from the tunnel they went.

Rival was the first to talk. He spoke in broken words, panting in between them due to his winded state from the high elevation. "Well, if that... doesn't prove someone... is there and watching... I don't know what does," he was bent over, supporting his hands on his knees. All of them were struggling to breathe, and they took a few minutes.

"If they were with the Corporates ... they'd... just shoot us," Will added, having his own breathing issues. Will took out a small device Relic sent called a bronchodilator inhaler. They each took a couple of hits. It helped, but they moved down to a lower elevation just the same. Will decided that making contact was going to require more thought.

The other teams were much more successful in their goals. The Supply team tripled their ammo and made fifty more bows. Relic and Nash found a substantial stash of guns, ammo, and reloading equipment in an under-ground storage room at Delta Hold. The troops looked more like soldiers thanks to the Training Team, and the Locate Team got two more tribes to join the alliance, acquiring five full-time soldiers and twelve part-time. Through their networking with the other tribes, they had increased access to spy intel.

They now had information coming from various status levels in all three territories. They were receiving a steady flow of RH intel from the east side of the mountain range. At some point, they were going to be noticed. They desperately needed to find a powerful ally, and the tunnel people were their only prospects.

It was a year ago that they moved into the town of McCoy. They began the militia to defend their families and homes, but no one counted on the discovery of the compound. It injected their little unit with the momentum to quickly morph into a well-armed and highly organized coalition. It was a constant topic of the town meetings. Some opposed its existence and wanted to abandon the compound, while others wanted to expand it further, but everyone agreed that the soldiers were needed, and it was time to officially name them.

They decided to make the name the soldiers already used official. The Guard was formally recognized and established, and Will was its unopposed commander. An artist among them created an emblem of a forward-facing lion's head, with a predatory stare. The words Loyalty, Honor, Liberty, and Bravery formed an arch around the lion icon with Guard written below it. Several seamstresses were employed to embroider the decals using the three-foot-pump sewing machines found in one of the small shops in town.

It was the last days of September, and at the Hold the occasional sunny day was being replaced by cold winds and threatening skies. Any day now, the scenery could change from frigid rains to a blinding world of frosty white. Though winters were harsh, many Fringer settlements wished for their return. It was an effective deterrent for the Corporates and Drangers, who could reach them easily during the warmer months. Only a few of the southern roads would be maintained after the snow began piling up, safely isolating them.

While working on a strategy to connect with the tunnel, they received concerning intel from their contacts in Central City. A large group of Drangers and Neighwah were set to investigate the tunnel before winter set in. Several squads of heavily armed Drangers and Neighwah were scheduled to flank the tunnel on both sides. The troops coming to the west side were slated to move out within a few days. Will called his top-ranking officers to an emergency meeting.

As he read the intel report, he addressed his top officers. "The threat to the tunnel is credible and imminent. We must find a way to warn the tunnel inhabitants without suffering their attacks. I am riding to McCoy this morning for an emergency meeting with the council. I'll be back by dinner."

Will stood before the Allied Council to get approval of the manpower and resources to assist the possible allies. The resulting word fight was intense. The council members seemed split down the middle.

"It is clear many here support your request for troops, Ninge, but I doubt the majority of our peaceful town would vote for war. The council needs to meet in the conference room. We will return with our decision in thirty minutes or less. Feel free to grab some lunch while you wait." Jessica folded her overconfident hands and looked at him with the resolve of her already-formed decision.

As they left the room, Will knew that there wasn't time for a meaningful meeting and the explanation and debate that would be required to follow. He also knew she had already made her decision, and she would bully the other members to acquiesce. He was deep in thought as he went to the kitchen and hardly responded to the greetings from friends who saw he was in town. He grabbed a pre-made sandwich and quickly headed back to the town hall, so they couldn't try to put him off for having left. He got there just as they were filing back in.

"Before we continue," Jessica said, taking the lead as usual. "I have, we have, a few questions. Including the elite team and the reserve unit, how many soldiers are in the Guard?" Grady and Jessica had been running the town since they arrived last fall. Jessica was unhappy that their "just hide" protection strategy was slipping away. Grady was the head Fringer, and a bit more moderate than Jessica, but they did not vote pro-military in any scenario. Will saw himself as a realist, but he could understand why people thought he was a war hawk.

"There are two hundred and forty-eight people in the Guard," Will responded. "Thirty-three are elite soldiers with twenty in supervisory roles in various positions, ninety-one active duty personnel, and one hundred and twenty-four reservists. Though all soldiers are combat-trained, not all have combat posts. We have medics, food service, weapons construction, maintenance, and research."

"Okay, Ninge," said Jessica. She didn't trust Will or his fake name, and she seemed to add a bit too much inflection when she spoke it. Before she could continue, Will spoke.

"I have a point of order," Will announced with confidence. "From now on, I wish to be addressed by my true name, William." There was a murmur in the crowd, but it died down suddenly when the room was called to order.

"Any reason you chose this moment for your reveal?" asked Grady with honest curiosity.

"It is time for reality. If I expect us to stop hiding, I should also be forthcoming."

"Can we know what you have been hiding from?" Jessica asked. Will looked back at Wurden, one of the few people who knew his secrets. Wurden was shaking his head no.

"We all escaped the Corporates here, and many of us discarded our birth names. Those stories are for another day."

"I agree, for now," said Grady. "We have something more pressing."

Jessica continued, "So, you have one hundred and twenty-four full-time soldiers. How many ear protectors do you have to combat the newly reported sound assault drones we learned about?"

Will knew she thought he was caught off guard, but they had already prepared for it. In the compound, they had located seventy adult sets and twenty child-size sets. They were in the process of altering the child-sized sets to fit adults. "Seventy-nine on hand and eleven more in assembly," he answered with confidence.

She paused for a moment and seemed taken aback by his response. "I see. We agree to allow you to take a fourth of your full-time people to the tunnel, IF, they volunteer."

"According to my math, you are only approving a total of thirty-one soldiers to fight the battle of our lives. You will be sending us to a massacre!" Will said with a sweeping arm gesture.

"That is why we are only allowing volunteers!" Jessica slammed him back.

"I want to go on record that I vehemently disagree with this decree."

"I'm afraid that's the council's final decision, William," Grady said with a calm conviction. "By the way, I think William fits you better than Ninja. Thank you for sharing that."

Grady always tried to mend fences and keep the peace, but Will was not grasping this olive branch. His men and women and probably the whole alliance had been put in grave danger. Will gathered his notebook and headed for the door with a mean stride. This town would eventually fight, but he was worried if they waited, they'd be caught on their heels. He knew with every cell in his body their only chance of survival was to be in front of it.

The aggressive ATV ride back to the compound gave Will the time and venue to release some anger, but not enough to quell his frustration. Rival met him before he got to the garage, and he could see the fire in his eyes.

"So, how did the meeting go?" Rival asked with hesitation, knowing Will's verbal sparks would be flying. Will described the gist of the meeting, interjecting numerous expletives and sarcasm. Though the language was inflammatory, it was the substance that had Rival equally enraged. He knew the meeting with the council had not gone well, but this was a catastrophe.

"Thirty troops! We'll be slaughtered," Rival began his seething rant when Will finished his report.

"Thirty-one," Will corrected him with animated sarcasm. "Well, there is one sliver of good news. You won't have to call me Ninge anymore."

"No shit, you dropped it? Or did you add another name to your collection?"

"Nope, it's been dropped. Not sure how long it will take for someone to figure it out, but my guess is it will be awhile. Rival, call a meeting at the afternoon shift change with everyone. I need to get these plans going. Our window is closing."

Rival walked away wondering if Will would ever divulge what his name meant to the Corporates. The repeated suggestion that he wouldn't want to know had suddenly changed into what he needed to know. Shift change was in an hour, so he announced the mandatory meeting early. After Will filled Relic in on the meeting results, Relic told him he would stay and man the cameras while he addressed the troops.

There were two shifts per day. Soldiers worked four twelve-hour days followed by three days off. Flexibility was built into the schedule, allowing the soldiers to address their personal responsibilities as well as ensure every minute of the day was covered. Soldiers could hitch a ride on the supply runs and most opted for eight days on to get six days off.

Hunter found two folded-up structures that hitched behind a vehicle. To his surprise, they opened up into lodging facilities. Each base had a kitchen and restroom, and bedrooms could be added as required. The units could be easily assembled at their destinations. They were hauled to two different places, providing an offsite lookout and shelter for those traveling back and forth.

Will stood before the troops in the Alpha building. The Alpha yard had been emptied of everything that couldn't be easily moved aside to accommodate a gathering of the growing organization. The Guard men and women, stood at attention in straight rows. They had come a long way from the green recruits that had arrived over the last couple of months.

"At ease, Guards. I have several announcements. On the mission we're calling Avalanche Strike, we have been permitted to approach and assist the tunnel." Cheers rang out, and Will put his hands up to quiet the outburst. "But," he paused, not wanting to deliver the next part, "we will only be allowed to send thirty-one soldiers. Since I will be one of them, I'm looking for thirty volunteers."

Gasps and expletives rumbled through the large group. "I want to be one of them!" a soldier yelled above the fray. Many more volunteers joined him.

"If you want to volunteer, put your name tag in this bucket, and I'll choose thirty from the volunteers."

Though the crowd was still grumbling, the bucket was passed down the rows. One by one, the soldiers ripped their Velcro name tags off the Guard patch sewn on their camouflaged shirts. There weren't resources available for uniforms, so they modified their shirts and trousers to look reasonably similar.

As big as the bucket was, it could barely hold the volume of name tags, and Will was touched when it made its way back to him. They were brave, ready, and willing to serve.

"Thank you. I couldn't be more proud of your dedication to our cause. All volunteers are to meet back here in one hour, and I will read off the list."

He dismissed them, and they scattered in every direction, leaving the huge main room of the Alpha building empty. "Well, at least they believe in our future," he said to Rival. His voice echoed slightly, reminding him of his lonely job of choosing who would serve and very possibly die.

"They believe in you," Rival responded without hesitation.

He met with his top officers. Without going through the bucketful of names, they constructed a list of forty of the best soldiers to fill the positions. With the fullness of the bucket, he could be assured that out of the forty listed, all thirty positions would be filled. He called the troops back. As he called out the names one by one, they came up to the front line. When he finished, he looked out at the remaining soldiers.

"The rest of you, I thank you for your dedication, but you are dismissed." A hand shot up in the crowd. "Yes?" Will couldn't imagine what the man would add.

"Sir, I've thought long and hard about this, and I'd like to resign from the Guard."

Will was shocked. This man was not known for being a poor sport or a sore loser. "Look, I know how hard you have trained, and everyone here deserves a spot, but I can't go against the council. Trust me, I still need you. Please don't make a rash decision like this."

No mandate kept soldiers from quitting like the Drangers and the Neighwah armies, and Will suddenly realized the value of that condition to hard service. Though he had revisited that issue several times, he erred on the side of incentivizing the much-needed recruits who may still be conflicted. But now, he wondered if that had been a mistake on his part.

"Yes, sir, I understand, but I'm sure. However, I would like to check out a gun and a bow to go hunting. Maybe you know someplace my time would be well spent."

Will tried not to smile. Dozens more hands went up with the same request. They had found a loophole, and no doubt they discussed it during the lapsed time. These patriots of the Guard found a way to serve, and now he had an army. He couldn't be prouder to be a part of this unit.

No law prevented civilians from "hunting" where they pleased or defending themselves if threatened. Those were their rights as Fringer citizens. Weapons were available for soldiers and trained civilians, who didn't own one, to check out as needed.

Rival spoke up. "And if you want to rejoin after you come back from 'hunting', you will be reinstated at your current rank."

Will glared at him for taking charge and authorizing such an action without his consent. He made a mental note to reteach that. The chain of command is critical in executing dangerous missions, and it crumbles when subordinates take liberties beyond their rank.

It reminded him of the advice Relic gave him. It was a quote by Alexander the Great. "I am not afraid of an army of lions led by a sheep; I am afraid of an army of sheep led by a lion." That being said, if Rival had brought it up as a request, he would have praised him for the idea. He would honor the suggestion, but Rival would have to be taken down a notch.

Nash yelled out, "We follow the lion! We follow William of the Guard!" The shouts and stomps were deafening, and the room vibrated with rowdy pride. Will was overcome with humility and dire responsibility.

Forty Guards needed to stay behind to monitor the movements around the Hold and to defend it if necessary. The reserves were activated and stationed on the roads leading to the nearby allied towns should any enemy soldiers come their way.

Those wanting to "resign" had their paperwork ready and signed but not dated. Relic would stamp the final discharge papers as the troops moved out giving Will plausible deniability if the council tried to blame him. That meant the team briefings and drills had many more attendees than the handful authorized.

The intel also gave a detailed report of the number of troops the Corporates were sending and where. The tunnel was a mystery to both the Corporates and the Guard, but the Corporates were following their time-honored agenda. Catch the rebels unprepared, capture the resources, and question the prisoners. The Guard was trying to navigate a meet and greet in a war zone. *What could go wrong*, Will said to himself cynically.

Chapter Thirty

The Guard's plan was to entrench their teams ahead of the enemy on both sides of the tunnel and engage them from behind, pushing and trapping them toward the tunnel barriers. True, it wouldn't allow them into the battle until it was thick in its business, but it would systematically diminish the enemy's expected reinforcements. It additionally made retreating an option if it was decided.

The intel reported the Corporate army planned to drive to Silverthorne and march their soldiers in four troops to the west barrier. The information for the east side was less reliable because it was designed to be responsive, but two troops were expected to be on the march.

The good news was none of the chatter had the Guard on their radar. The enemy expected to surprise their target, and they expected their only conflict would come from the tunnel ahead not behind. This was the Guard's best advantage, however, their disadvantages were alarming. Not only did both of the armies ahead possess better weapons and more experienced soldiers, but the Guard wasn't expected by anyone making it highly probable they would confront two armies at once.

Sleep was scheduled, but it didn't come easy for soldiers primed for battle. They were tightly coiled into striking mode waiting for their journey and the call to fight. The fear of the realities and imagined battle horrors cause a natural inclination to flee, but not one soldier gave in to its siren song.

The next morning, Will and Rival traded salutes with the Eastside Team before they began their final briefing for the Avalanche Strike mission. They would be the first to leave. A team was sent to clear and secure Highway 9 to Silverthorne. On the edge of that town was the drop-off sight, position 0, and that was where their secure path ended. The Eastside team would cross I-70 to Highway 6, Loveland Pass Road. It was the old road from before the tunnel was bored. It looped back to I-70 and was the only current option, but its condition was unknown, and it came out extremely close to the east tunnel entrance.

It was unlikely they would run into Corporate soldiers because it was too visible for a large group to use with any advantage. Will expected the enemy troops heading to the east side would come from Denver and Colorado Springs would supply soldiers to the west.

Though the enemy had no reason to use Loveland Pass, the Guard's Eastside Teams did. The Guard teams who traveled on it would have to evade the tunnel drone scouts and whatever other defenses were positioned there. Then they would find a secure place to hide until Rival gave the order to engage. The official number was to be twelve, but twenty-four more "non" soldiers sat in the briefing and would make the trek to the east entrance.

"Eastside Teams you're heading out soon after this briefing. You'll ride in the troop vehicles and be dropped off near Silverthorne. We can take all of you, but it's standing room only. In Silverthorne and Dillon, Rival will lead the recon crew. It may take a little time to make sure the area is clear, but it's worth the effort. We don't know if they belong to the tunnel or the enemy, so disable everything you find.

"We gave you all four electric ATVs for a quiet approach. They are stashed here," Will pointed to a spot on the map just past Dillon. "If it's clear, leave position 1 and cross I-70 to the Pass, and secure your rides at position 2. Sound detectors are most likely what they will use on this road since cameras take too much bandwidth and require a good signal.

But sound detectors are very effective at detecting manmade sounds, so no chatter.

You may be tempted by the many side roads where surveillance is less likely, but land mines are probable. Before you enter Keystone, Rival will lead the recon team again to check for surveillance.

"Then drive like hell to get your gear and team members to position 3 at Faerie Spring. Even riding three at a time, it's not enough to transport all of you, so some of you will have to walk until the first group can come back for you. Use the heat-reflective, camo blankets for cover and stay there until dusk.

"Your next trek will be dangerous. The road condition is unknown, it will be dark, and you can be assured surveillance will get heavier the closer you get to the tunnel. At position 4 on this side," he pointed, "of the second switchback, hide your vehicles, remove the batteries, and cover your rides." Will turned the next part of the instructions over to Rival.

Rival stepped onto the small platform and turned to the screen to address his team. "When you get to the top of the ridge, you need to locate chair lift number three. The moon will be full enough for you to see the lift." He switched the screen image to a picture of the aging lift with a faded number 3. "Evaluate its condition as you were trained to do." He proceeded to review the zipline lessons from last week using the familiar pictures and diagrams.

"Attach your zipline trolleys and make your way down slowly. Secure your trolley to the return line for the next rider and hide here at position 5. If the line isn't in good enough shape, you'll have to hike down. The air is thin up there, so drink water and pay attention to your breathing and each other. When everyone is down, Rival's team will go to position 6 across the road. This is where the watching and waiting starts. You will find this part of your mission intensely stressful. Stay focused. "

Will stepped back up on the platform. "Unless you are discovered, don't jump into the fight until the order is given by Rival. We believe the Tunnel people will be able to take care of themselves, but we will be assisting from the sidelines. The tunnel drones carry sound devices, oxygen limiters, and guns. All of which are very unpleasant. Have your ear protectors and inhalers handy in case you need them. The Corporate army will have drones too, but they tend to be outfitted with guns exclusively.

"We will have three teams on the ridge tops, two on the west and one on the east. It's where the drone operators will pilot from and the medics will wait till they're needed. Our drones are the green ones. You can shoot down all the others unless instructed differently. Both the east and west side teams will have drone support on the hill. Your leaders and seconds will be able to hear the chatter, so watch their lead.

"When we get into the fray, our strategy is to trap the enemy between us and the tunnel. Many of the soldiers will have bulletproof armor, but their hands and feet are unprotected to give them more mobility. Those are their weaknesses, but their weapons are fierce. Remember, we aren't there to win the war for the tunnel or be lambs to slaughter. Our goal is to assist them where we can, to make them our allies."

"The reality is we don't know the nuances of this battle, and I have no intention of getting caught between two warring factions. But the fact is, we will be in a three-way war. Like the Westside teams, you wait for the enemy to pass and then engage them, but you only have two teams, so stay behind the enemy at all times.

You will probably take fire from both sides. It is also true that the Drangers and the Neighwah out-gun us, and we believe the tunnel is equally armed. They have sophisticated armor, shields, radio helmets, mean drones, and experience. Fire from safe cover and don't enter the battlefield unless Rival gives the call.

"Because our mission is to let the tunnel know we are friendlies, everyone will wear these around their heads." Will held up a green strip of cloth. "And if you have a helmet, it will be painted with a green stripe. It is our hope the tunnel soldiers will recognize we are fighting with them."

He looked out over the silent gathering. They were intently waiting for his next words. Their loyalty amazed and frightened him at the same time. He faltered, but just for a second. "We may not want to accept this, but I may call for a retreat if they both turn on us, and it stops being in our best interests. If that happens, follow your team leader."

While the Eastside Team loaded gear and supplies, the Westside Teams filed into the yard for their briefing. Their instructions were very similar, minus the zipline trip. When the gear was loaded and the second briefing was done, the entire Guard army stationed at the Hold filed in, lined up, and stood at attention.

Will stood before all the active-duty members. He studied the dedicated men and women before him. He could see they were loyal and prepared to let the battlefield deliver whatever fate decided for them. But he didn't want to bring home a pile of dead bodies to mourn and honor. He wanted victory. He thought of all the books he had read at the academy and the ones assigned to him by Relic. He had studied them dutifully, but being exposed to wisdom and having it were not synonymous. Understanding and believing it took time. But he remembered being inspired by the St. Crispian's Day speech from Shakespeare's King Henry the Fifth.

Henry's troops were outnumbered and out-weaponed, but they were loyal and willing to die for their king and country. But Henry didn't want them to die for him; he wanted them to fight and win for their country and their king. That's what gives a soldier honor. His troops went into full victory mode after their king motivated them with a passionate rallying cry of determination, tribute, and his belief in them.

After he concluded the business of introductory necessities, Will took a long cleansing breath. "I know we face great odds, but we have a weapon they'll never have. We have something worth fighting for, our freedom. Of our own free will, we took a blood oath. And though we come from many tribes, by this day's end, we will forever be brothers and sisters, related by battle and blood.

"Our stories will be passed down through generations. Our descendants will speak of Avalanche Strike with admiration and of the fortunate few who fought here. They will recall annually the Guards branded and bonded with warriors' teeth who soared on liberty's wings to victory. Those who hear the tales and dreams of this day's glory will lament they were not here. We who fight together will be immortalized, and every year from here on, cups will be tipped in gratitude in remembrance of our victory. And we *will* win, because we *can* win, but mostly because we *must* win."

The troops raised their arms with oath scared fists held high and roared with fervor and might. A chant rose above the individualized shouts, "LION, LION, LION!"

Will humbly held his hand on his heart and tipped his head, and then he stepped off the platform. Relic had been standing with the support team in the back and approached Will as he left the stage. He had to yell to be heard above the still-energized crowd.

"That sounded like a bad version of Henry the Fifth," he smiled. "Well done." Will grinned. "Here is the list of our alliance statement and supply requests that we discussed," Relic said as he handed Will the paper.

"Let's hope we get to use it," Will said as he tucked it in his shirt pocket.

The three small Eastside teams left immediately after the morning briefing. At noon, the Westside teams began traveling to their drop-off spot just above Silverthorne. Unlike the Eastside Teams, it would take both utility vehicles and two trucks to bring all sixty-five soldiers and their gear to the drop-off site. From there, they would travel on foot, keeping to the woods to reach their observation positions.

Relic, Taylor, and Pierce manned the command at the compound in the computer room of the Alpha building. Relic was monitoring the large area screens for any drone activity in their area. He had finally accessed the hard-wired cameras from Heeney, Ute Pass Road on Highway 9, and some on I-70. Besides watching for troops moving toward the Hold, it allowed him to extend their communications to the Westside Team by flying them back and forth to relay information. They would report the changes and movements of the enemy on I-70, and if needed, they could have the drones join the fight. The Eastside teams, however, were on their own due to the distance and terrain.

On the days before deployment, the road crew had made a thorough check from the Hold to the drop-off position 0, an abandoned neighborhood in Silverthorne, east of the Triplet Ponds. The rest of the team hunkered down in the trees and waited for Rival's signal as they made their way to position 1 near I-70. Upon receiving the signal, the team packed the gear to position 1 and waited to advance to position 2. It took fifteen minutes to get the okay signal to go but only five to efficiently pack the gear across the Interstate to position 2. Then they secured all but their light packs on the four-wheelers.

All in all, they disabled three cameras and four sound detectors. Seven soldiers rode the four laden ATVs on the quick ride to Keystone, disabling any devices they saw on their way to position 3 at Faerie Spring. The rest of the team would hike stealthily through the trees to meet at position 3. Their radios would allow them to communicate any issues. At position 3, they recharged the ATVs while the sun was high.

Everyone was rested by the time the sun set hard over the mountainous range. The next group began the journey up to position 4 while eight riders headed up on the ATVs. When they all arrived, they would tackle the zipline and secure themselves on either side of the tunnel entrance.

It was silent and serene as they journeyed on the beautiful trek up Loveland Pass. The dim glow of the waning moon helped them make their way up the winding and steep road. Lonely patches of recently fallen snow demonstrated the short window for using this thoroughfare as access across the divide. They were one storm away from being trapped.

After several trips, they all were at position 4, with vehicles secured, and batteries removed. They downed a quick meal before they went to locate the chairlift. They placed the batteries and the chargers on top of a struggling outbuilding, so they would be ready for their retreat.

Rival hoped their evacuation wouldn't require great haste because not everyone would fit on the available vehicles. He knew the plan to shelter his team members, but that contingency was fraught with unknowable danger. The good news was, so far the tunnel had not reacted to their approach. He assumed the camo and infrared blocking blankets had kept their movements covert.

Rival chose a volunteer to climb up to the lift station and assess the line of stability. Using her binoculars and low light from a drone, she traced the line for defects and ensured all the chairs were detached. She looked down from the lift wheel and gave the thumbs up.

The trolleys had been specially designed to run on the ski lift cables, but they only had three. When the first zipliner slid down, he pulled two lines with him to be used for retrieval. So as one flew down, the empty trolley would be hauled back on the looped retrieval cord. Three times a drone from another faction came near their vicinity, causing them to hunker down under the blankets.

It took over an hour to get everyone down the ridge. Cautiously, they made their way to position 5 on the southern side of the road and settled themselves on the ridge overlooking I-70. The first team crossed the road to the northern side and situated themselves at position 6. The drone and medic team set up high on the south ridge. They took turns sleeping and watching for the enemy troops to approach the tunnel barrier.

The Eastside Teams were set and ready at their positions. He knew it could be a day or two before the fray began. He had been in many battles, and he looked at the faces of his inexperienced recruits. It didn't help that they were on their own, cut off from the other teams. The untried soldiers were fidgeting and losing cohesiveness.

Rival knew it was the waiting that ate away at one's resolve. He needed to keep their minds focused and in lockstep with his. He had them glass and creep in methodical search patterns as well as practice hand signals between the two teams on either side of the road to occupy their minds, maintain contact, and allow him to redirect any negative thoughts.

The Westside Teams had arrived at Silverthorne late that afternoon. The course of action was similar to the Eastside Team's strategy, but their teams would take positions along I-70. Position 7 was around five miles from Dillon at Hamilton Gulch. This was Will's team, and they would act as first contact. Remi's team would be the second sentry at position 8, just over six miles from position 1. Tommie had position 9 and Jedi would be the closest to the tunnel at position 10, seven miles from position 1. The teams would be in a zig-zag pattern on the road's edge. Position 11 indicated one was within the barrier or inside the tunnel and was not a mandatory objective.

The hike down I-70 involved maneuvering in the trees and on steep hillsides to avoid detection from the tunnel and any surveillance devices planted by the Corporates. Both Will and Relic gambled the Neighwah would not risk the element of surprise to plant new equipment. They would use the existing ones, which Rival had intimate knowledge of from his work at HQ.

When they reached position 1, Will quietly and in code gave his final instructions to the Westside Teams.

"Our mission is to demonstrate our allegiance and make contact with the tunnel. Our tasks are to observe from a secure location and defend the tunnel when necessary and if possible. We do not want the Corporates to know the Guard exists, or that we assisted the tunnel. We don't need them coming back here to hunt us. My team will secure position 7 and watch the road for Teams as they make their way to positions 8, 9, and 10. Drone and med teams find suitable positions, one on each side of the ridge."

Will left with his group while the rest stood by waiting out the twenty-minute intervals between each team's advance. It was almost four hours before all the Westside teams had reached their positions without incident. Will hoped the same was true of the Eastside Teams.

The slow wait was stressful, and on day three, even Will began hoping the enemy would show soon. At most, they had three more days of supplies, and leaving would be hard without accomplishing anything. He began devising a way to contact the tunnel without provoking its defenses.

It was mid-afternoon on the fourth day when the waiting came to an end. Relic reported the enemy moving at a ruck march pace and was last seen around Dillon moving up I-70. Will knew the ruck march pace of a soldier was a fifteen-minute mile carrying full gear. That meant the first group could reach his team in ninety minutes and the tunnel in two hours. Will intended to slow down that pace.

He sent a scout to get a visual around the bend and send a signal when he had eyes on them. They were marching down the middle of the road. No attempt was made to hide their approach, suggesting they didn't believe the tunnel posed a credible threat, and this was just a recon mission. They sent the four troops in waves with the most experience at the back because the Drangers at the front were expendable. They had a sizable group of soldiers, and it would be a credible poke at the nest to see how many wasps, if any, it held.

As if the fates didn't believe the war was enough drama, the barometer, which had been stable and high, was starting to fall at a quick and steady pace. It signaled a massive storm front was marching their way, and it could reach them by mid-morning. If it hit too hard, it would be challenging to transport all their troops back home, especially the Eastside Teams.

Will dismissed the report for the time being. He couldn't worry about the weather right now. He was focused on the details regarding the locations of the four enemy packs down the road plodding ever closer.

Up on the ridges at both ends of the tunnel, two on the west and one on the east, were three groups of drone operators and medics. The strategy of the staggered teams was to take on the last troop as they passed. Will's team was the best-trained and armed group. The same was true of the last enemy troop, so they would take them out and systematically move up to assist the other teams.

Relic reported to Will that the first group was closing in on their position, so Will contacted the other teams. They sat patiently watching the first three packs trudge by. The first two consisted of frontline Drangers. They had shields that offered some cover but were made of crappy metal. Their guns were old and inferior, and they didn't carry either item in a ready position.

Will contacted Jedi, whose team was the closest to the west entrance. Jedi reported the soldiers were lying on top of the razor-wired barrier with rifles ready. That confirmed the tunnel was inhabited, and they were prepared to defend themselves.

Will told him that the poorly armed and barely protected Drangers were on their way. Jedi's team should stay where they were unless detected and help the tunnel armies by adding their firepower to the fray from the treed ridges as needed.

The tunnel people wouldn't worry where gunfire aimed at their adversaries came from, and would probably assume it was their tunnel comrades. The enemy, hiding beneath their worthless shields, would believe it came from the soldiers on the rim, at least initially. Will knew at some point, they would viciously pursue those shooting them from the side.

Two more enemy troops of fifteen or so men filed by. Relic radioed Will that the last foreseeable group was approaching his position. Will signaled his team to get ready. They had been briefed that this team would be mostly Neighwah soldiers and would be the most heavily armed and protected by state-of-the-art gear. But Will explained the soft spots in their armor, and they practiced aiming at them in their training.

It was finally time to end the waiting and begin the hunt. The last three men in the Neighwah unit were lured out of the ranks to check out a flash Will's team created. Two enemy soldiers went in to check it out, and the team ambushed them quietly. One enemy was shot with an arrow while the other soldier was delivered a quick twist of the neck from behind.

The third soldier, who was waiting for the now-dead men, radioed that he was going to check on his buddy. The troop was quite far down the road now, but the Guard could see them well enough to know they had stopped. Will executed a third unarmored man swiftly with a swishing arrow through the heart. Within a couple of minutes, the halted troop locked their shields to form a tiny fortress.

It was then that the drones began to fly and the bullets to attack. Two black and four green drones engaged in a dogfight. The bangs and pops among the sound of an angry swarm could be heard above while arrows found their way through the shield gaps. The enemy drone operators were caught unaware. Based on their tactics of focusing only on the hillside and not above, assuming they alone would command the skies.

The arrogant enemy birds fluttered down to their owners, but two more black drones came whining back from the troops up ahead. At that point, the green drones had already fled the scene.

At the same time, Will's team pulled back up the hill and hunkered down behind the boulders they previously located for this purpose. They had taken out three of the fifteen most formidable foes and two drones. They confiscated their guns and shields, and the enemy on the road was wasting their ammo shooting blindly at the hill. Will knew they couldn't win this skirmish unless they charged up the hill, which would make them particularly vulnerable.

Will discovered that one of his crew had a bullet wound. It was a deep grazing slice to his shoulder where his vest failed to cover him. He was quickly treated and told that he could hang back a bit, but his response was an adamant shake of his head. Guard blood had been spilled in battle.

The reality of war and the heartbreak of it was dripping down their comrade's arm. But they did not lament; they rallied. It triggered them, coalescing them into warriors fueled with pure resolve.

Their opponents begin to move down the road with their shields in formation. Will's team followed them like silent shadows through the woods. When they focused more on running than protecting themselves, Will's team sent a cloud of arrows, nailing their feet and ankles.

That decommissioned three more, down to ten. The wounded adversaries were left by their comrades to the rebel woodland band. They moaned and pleaded on the edge of the road with their weapons and shields, and Will sent two of his soldiers to dispatch them. The two Guards carried the shields they had collected in front of them.

As luck would have it, their opponents believed their comrades had returned for them. They let their protection down just long enough to be dispensed. The Guards gathered as many good arrows as they could, as well as the shields, weapons, and ammo of the enemy. Then they hurried to catch their team.

The remaining Neighwah soldiers had been running and crouching each time the gunfire erupted from the ridge. At two miles down the road, Will let loose another round of fire, and two more soldiers dropped from bullets penetrating their weakened shields. The enemy made their way down the road and around the next curve using a painful crouching advance. Will waited in patient silence as they clamored up the opposite hillside with their eyes focused on the direction of his assaults. Will's team lie low and quiet, knowing the enemy just entered Remi's location.

It was about five minutes later that the first screams were heard. Remi's team split up to draw their prey close to their noose and drop traps and yanked the triggers to activate them. Three more were killed by traps and two were slain. Down to five. They started running between the two Guard teams, and that was a big mistake. All five enemy soldiers surrendered. They were not killed. They were tied to trees. Will had plans for these men.

Will and Remi's teams came upon Tommie's team struggling with Drangers and Neighwah mixed. Some of the Drangers in the last group had better armor under their clothing, and it took more firepower than anticipated to penetrate it. But like the last unit, they had been caught unaware, and over half died before they could get into formation. Numerous men lay motionless on the broken road, and several more were moaning. Only two bodies were covered. They were Guards, the first two Will knew of who died in this battle.

A group of seven Dranger soldiers came back to help the Neighwah troop, but all that was left were three bodies stripped of shields and weapons. Four of them died, and the other three were captured, hidden, and tied up. Half of the enemy troops had stopped and lay in wait for their unknown foe following them. Will's three teams pushed them steadily onward toward the tunnel, but the cost was three more Guards.

"Commander," came a call from Jedi. "They're here and climbing the wall faster than the tunnel army can stop them. We can't leave cover because the tunnel army is firing at us. We are taking it from two sides."

"Injured?" Will asked.

"Yeah, two, but they'll make it if we can get them back."

"Pull back. We're coming."

There was a long pause, but the reply finally came, "Yes sir."

By the time Will, Remi, and Tommie's teams arrived at the tunnel entrance, Jedi's team was silent on the ridge, but they rejoined the battle when they saw their reinforcements had arrived. With the confiscated shields and Neighwah rifles, the Guard was holding their own, but the tunnel barrier was being breached.

A brave Guard soldier charged from the edge to protect a comrade, thinking the Neighwah shield would protect him. He discovered tragically some enemy soldiers shot bullets with drill tips. It bore through his armor, flesh, and bone until it buried itself in a rock on the hillside before it stilled.

He died before his Guardmates could get to him. The drill guns were easily identifiable with their large barrels, and the enemies carrying them immediately became prime targets. Though only a few carried those weapons, they were given solid cover by the other soldiers.

Will was fighting a soldier on the edge of the woods. He was giving an assist to a tunnel soldier who had run out of ammo and was being attacked. Will felt the jab of a knife in his arm from a clumsy ambush attempt. Then he felt the soldier being pulled off his back. He turned around to see a tunnel soldier had given him an assist. As he looked around, it appeared the tunnel company had realized the Guard was fighting with them.

The two armies began to fight as one. Nash grabbed a Dranger off of a tunnel troop, turned him around and the tunnel troop ran him through with the bayonet on the end of her rifle. Nash gave a nod, and she gave a casual salute back. Tommie was dragging a Guard under her command to the edge of the battle scene.

"Hang on Dayven. I got you." She was holding him, and he was gurgling blood and bubbles from his chest, nose, and mouth, Jedi ran to her.

"Tell ... tell, ..." Another volume of blood retched out of his mouth from the chest wound, ebbing the life from his body. Tommie was losing it watching him die before her.

Jedi appeared behind her and filled in the dying man's words to save him the effort. "We'll tell your family you love them and how honorably you fought. But try to stay with us. You can tell them yourself." But before Jedi finished his sentence, the soldier's eyes glazed over, his face went limp, and his head slumped forward.

His still, breathless form lay limp in Tommie's arms, and she pulled him closer, rocking him as she wept. Jedi knew it was her first real loss as a leader in a battle. He'd been there, and he wished he could help her through it, but this wasn't the time, and it definitely wasn't the place. Jedi pulled her away, leaving their honored friend heaped in the dirt.

"Come on, girl. It's not over yet," Jedi said sternly.

She watched the body of Dayven get further away as she was dragged to the cover of the trees. She tried to remember what she knew of him, but it wasn't much. He was twenty, lived with his mother, and was engaged to be married. *Oh, God*, she realized, *as his leader it was her job to tell them that they lost their son and fiancé.* When she started to weep again, Jedi shook her gently.

"Get a hold, girl. We have people to save and others to send off. War is ugly business. We've all been where you are, but you have to push all that down until the fight is over. Time to be a soldier and do your job, Tommie." Jedi had a hold of her shoulders, and he was looking her straight in the eyes, She was so young, like so many soldiers before her. "You are strong enough to finish this. Let's go"

She felt dizzy as she stood up but shook it off. Trying to focus, she followed Jedi back into the fight. She didn't look down at Dayven's body as she ran past him to duck behind a fellow soldier's stolen shield. She aimed her bow and let go of the thin spear. She watched her pain travel with it as it crumpled her target to the ground.

Chapter Thirty-One

The battle ended soon after that. All the Guard troops were wandering around in front of the barrier sorting out the wounded and dead, be they friend or foe. Will walked the outer area and checked on each of his wounded soldiers and then his fallen comrades. He was checking off their names to make sure none were missing. He discovered nine Guards were injured, but they were expected to recover. He was upset to learn they had lost seven good people. Though it was less than expected, it was too many. Too many families to inform, too many tears to shed, and too many good people with unfinished lives.

In the background, the Guards were rounding up the prisoners, many of whom were pleading for mercy. They had their own miseries to mend. He couldn't hate them. He had been one of them once. His mind was on how Rival's team was doing, and if everyone had made it through.

Will shouted to his army, "Guards, unless you are involved with serious medical duties, stand before the barrier wall with your hands raised." Will had a white cloth in his raised hands, standing with all able Guards behind him. Will was yelling and hoping they could hear him. "I need to speak with someone in charge."

Soon a drone flew over the wall and lowered a communication device to him. It was a lot like the ones he had used in the Neighwah, but he held his suspicions down.

"I am William of the Guard, and I am a friend of the sanctuary tunnel." Will waited for a response that seemed to take forever, and he began assessing the communication device.

"How did you find out about us?" came a voice on the other end.

"I've been running the Guard underground, and I learned about the attack on your offsite facility. The Neighwah know you are here. I don't know where they got their intel, but you are on the grid, and they are interested in taking you down. This was just a recon mission," said Will.

"I don't know if what you say is true, but we do seem to be in your debt. Is this army all of you? Are there more of your underground Guard?" the voice answered.

"I too, am hesitant to give away information, but if you refer to the Guards on the east side, those are ours. We sent reinforcements when we heard about a small faction going up there."

Again, there was a long pause on the other end. *He's testing* me, Will thought. It was exactly what he would do. Militarily, this man had the advantage, but the tunnel was only safe when it was hidden. Now that it was discovered, their strategy needed to change. That gave Will an advantage too, and he intended to claim it.

Finally, the voice returned. "Are any of your soldiers wounded? Do you need medical supplies?"

"Yes, that would be appreciated," William replied.

"Give a list to my medic, and we'll send them over the wall." A geared-up tunnel medic climbed down a rope ladder thrown over the wall, and Will sent him to their head medic to relay the supplies they required. He followed the Guard medic and took notes on each soldier's injuries and needs, then climbed back up the wall and disappeared.

Will was getting tired of this detached conversation. He was just about to say as much when the voice asked, "William, leader of the Guard, what do you want?"

"I want to be allies, to join forces. I believe your people are honorable, but we are strangers. How do we make a pact with this thick wall between us?"

The silence on the other end was getting annoying. He stood holding the phone, feeling like that kid so many years ago when he was standing before his supervisor saying he wanted to quit. Like then and like now, he knew the move was considered too gutsy, and it just wasn't done. Maybe he had crossed a line, and he pondered having his Guard take cover. But he had come too far, so he stood his ground.

The rope ladder was lowered again, and a tunnel soldier waved at Will to climb up. He was being invited in. It could be a trap, and he'd seen his share of those, but he had always come through. He ordered Jedi and Remi to get everyone home if this went south.

He walked up to the twenty-plus foot wall and grabbed the rope, trying not to wince as he climbed. The exertion caused his wound to bleed through his ripped sleeve bandage and seep down his arm.

They pushed aside the razor wire and ushered him to a metal ladder on the other side. Before he went down, he took in the view of the inner area before him. He was impressed at its size. He figured it must be almost three acres of space. Soldiers were loading the bodies of the deceased enemies onto a cart. The medical staff was triaging the ambulatory wounded sitting on small trailers with benches on either side.

There were no wounded combatants begging for help or mercy like there were on the perimeter. All the enemy soldiers in this enclosure area were dead. Will wondered if they had been killed where they lay, or perhaps they had been taken inside to a medic station. Taking them into their secret tunnel seemed unwise, so it was more likely any survivors were executed.

Will looked over at the massive entrance wall with two monstrous gates and several doors set within them. Through one of them came a self-assured man striding purposefully across the huge yard. Will knew instantly it was the man he was to meet. He climbed down the ladder. He made his advance with all the confidence he could muster as a lone soldier surrounded and confined by an unknown army.

The man was tall, but not as tall as himself. He had a confident gait, and he had removed his helmet. No other tunnel person had done that, and it was reassuring to see a human face among them. His uniform was the same high-tech gear as the others, but it appeared untouched by battle. *He didn't need* it, Will said to himself. *He had commanded this battle from a desk.*

Will looked down at the leather armor he had tanned and lashed himself. It was made of thick elk hides on the chest and back, and sandwiched between the outer layer and the inner layer was a metal plate. It wasn't completely bulletproof, but it would slow one down. His rifle was slung across his right shoulder, and his bow was on his left. He saw the battle blood he wore, and though he was thankful little of it was his own, he knew he must look like a barbarian.

He could feel the dried blood splattered on his face and made an attempt at civility for this critical meeting. He ripped off the other sleeve of his undershirt and grabbed his water bottle to dampen it, but only a dribble came out. He chuckled to himself. *I guess I'll go for barbarian negotiator today.* He spat on the rag and wiped his face.

As the man approached, Will looked down at the man's bare hands, and then at his own covered in the blood of war. Finally, the gap between them closed, and the two men extended their hands. *Well, at least he isn't a germaphobe* Will reasoned. With a firm grip and a confident stare, they exchanged the traditional greeting.

Several soldiers carried a small foldout table and two chairs. The man told one of the soldiers to bring some water and gestured for Will to sit. Will could see he had trained his force well, and the soldier's demeanor showed more than discipline. It demonstrated respect. With what Will knew so far, he knew he would either end up hating this guy or respecting the hell out of him.

"Welcome to New Haven, William of the Guard. I'm Gray, the Senior Security Officer of the Defenders." Just then, someone came with two tumblers and a pitcher of water. Gray poured the water into his glass, drank it down, and then offered some to Will. It was a time-honored symbol of good faith to prove the consumable was free from additives.

"Yes, thank you," Will answered, partly because he really was thirsty but mostly because it showed good faith on his part. "It is good to put a name to the mysterious community and a face to a voice," Will suddenly realized. This was the one part of the plan he had not worked out well. He had no idea how to start this conversation. But he did have a pressing question that required an answer. "Gray of the Defenders," Gray smiled at the reference. "I do not have contact with my Eastside Teams. I do not know how their mission went."

Gray clicked on his communication with a somber nod of understanding. "Gabe, come in."

"Yeah," came the voice on speaker mode. It was one more sign of transparency between them. This commander was earning his respect, or setting him up neatly.

"Give me a rundown on the condition of the Greenbanders."

"Greenbanders?" Will mouthed. Will had forgotten about the green headbands all Guards wore. He'd have to thank Remi for the suggestion.

The voice responded. "We know of twenty-eight Greenbanders who came to the east entrance. The med team is treating nine of them with non-life-threatening injuries. One man, however, is seriously injured, and Maya's team is treating him. And, sir, three died. I hope it wasn't us."

Gray had left the device on speaker, and he looked at Will knowing he had heard the message. "Alright, Gabe, thanks. Get me the names of all of those soldiers."

"Will do, sir."

Yeah, sorry we didn't know what to call you, but it was easy to see you all had green bands on," Gray said.

The two discussed the battle and the intel safe to share. Will shared the story of his discovery of the compound, which they called the Hold, and that he had more soldiers secured there. Tidbits of information were shared, but neither disclosed their military capabilities nor other strategic intel. Nor did they engage in diplomatic small talk. In that they were like-minded.

"So, not to be repetitive, but exactly what do you want from us?" Gray asked.

"Our mission is to make a pact between us for mutual defense and trade. I think we need each other, and neither of us would benefit from an armed quarrel between our clans." Will watched for Gray to react, but he was maintaining a straight poker face. Will was gaining respect for this commander.

"However, since you asked," responded Will, " I have a list here of some of our needs." Will fished around and pulled out the list tinged with blood and sweat. "I believe we can better serve each other if we have an understanding about the compound you call the Hold. I also have requests for some supplies we believe you possess."

Will read off the list which included: the Guard retaining residency at the Hold, fencing to repair damaged sections, access to the cameras and other defensive applications, establishing secure communications for continued dialog, a power source for winter, medical supplies, and other less critical items.

"Though none of these supplies are demands, all of these items will be used for our mutual benefit. But we are well settled in the Hold and willing to fight to maintain control of it."

There was a silence when Will finished. He already recognized Gray's signature move and almost smiled. With the obvious break in their conversation, a medic approached the two men sitting in the middle of the yard. "Sir, may I clean your wound?" Will bristled, and Gray saw his hesitation, understanding it was a low priority for him.

"Look, William, it's just smart not to get an infection," Gray offered. Will held his gaze for a moment and then nodded, but he refused the pain-relieving injection. He'd take the sting of cleaning and stitching the wound to avoid being drugged. They were building trust between them as men and as communities, but it was too new and unearned.

Gray seemed to understand, and he used this time to distract him from his pain. He explained he had no power to grant his requests on his own, but would present them to the council immediately. A soldier came with a paper and handed it to Gray.

"I have the names of your casualties. Kade, Wayne, and Julie. I'm sorry, William. It's never easy to receive a list of the dead and recall the faces who followed you into battle."

"Kade never should have come," Will sighed. "Though he was young, he was fighting the cell sickness. He wanted to be remembered for helping his people before the disease took him. Julie was his wife. He begged her not to come, but they had a bond ...," Will's voice trailed off as he winced. Gray didn't know if it was from the needle piercing his inflamed wound or the news he had just received. "I'm sure," Will continued, "they fought side by side and caught the same round of fire."

"Yeah, cancer is a bitch," Gray let a moment pass. "But I can think of worse things than a noble death in the arms of someone I love."

Will acknowledged the truth of his words with a nod. "There was one soldier who was seriously wounded. Was that name given?"

"Oddly, no," Will could see Gray's mind was evaluating the omission. "I will get that info for you, but I'm sure medical assistance was provided. They would do everything but bring him or her inside. That would have to go through the town legislators." Gray rolled his eyes slightly. Will gave a look signaling Gray he had also dealt with legislative quagmires.

Gray's com-box buzzed. This time he had the setting on private, and Will could not hear the conversation. "It appears I have my own wounded to address, and I must go. It's been a pleasure, William," Gray said and held out his hand.

"It has been my pleasure as well, Gray," Will said, reaching out his hand to conclude what he hoped was the first of many meetings. "And Gray, call me Will."

Gray smiled. "Okay, Will, I'll present this to our town and get back to you." And with that, Gray gave a casual gesture and turned toward the door, dodging a line of defenders carrying tents, bedding, and food for the Guard.

Will was informed that the Eastside Team was also getting similar supplies. Will thought back to the approaching storm. He had messaged Relic that all was well, and the battle was over. He said he was working on contacting the tunnel, and he'd get back to him.

He needed to start transporting soldiers back to the Hold, but it was getting dark and the roads could have straggling enemies. For now, they were safer where they were.

Will sent a small squad to retrieve the tied-up prisoners, which had totaled eleven. He hoped the abused, oppressed, and unappreciated men would be willing to join his army after some months of retraining under house arrest. They would have no access to the outside or knowledge of where they were. It might help if they were enticed by the possibility of rescuing their family members. If they still did not want to join after that, they would be driven so far into wild Fringer territory that they would never find their way home.

The Defenders and Guard proceeded to work side by side, treating the wounded, setting up tents, and serving meals to the soldiers, but neither spoke much to the other. No one knew where the line of silence was. They had fought together, but were they allies, or were they circumstantially and temporarily on the same side?

When all the Defenders left, campfires sprung up, and Will called his team leaders to debrief him. Outside, rowdy talks of battle stories and tears for lost comrades rumbled through the camp. Many took advantage of the wash stations, but some, like Tommie, couldn't wash away the day's hardships just yet. She clung to the last remnants of her friend's lifeblood as if it kept him connected to the living.

By morning, the tent walls were snapping in the wind. The storm was beginning to flex its muscles, and Gray contacted Will. "We need to get you back to the Hold as soon as possible. We have two large transport vehicles we can loan you until the storm breaks, and you can return them. I have a feeling we will be meeting again. You said you had ATVs stashed on Loveland Pass. We know where each other lives, so I'll hold those for you until we can trade. Oh, and William, I hope you don't mind. I contacted the Hold and spoke to a man named Relic and gave him an update."

"Thank you, so I guess one of our requests has already been installed. I will contact you when we arrive. I'll have the Eastside Team disclose where they stashed the batteries they removed."

Gray responded. "We are transporting your troops in covered buses through the tunnel. The pass is already too dicey. Oh, and Will, the name of your critical soldier is Hunter."

Will's heart sank. Hunter was loyal to a fault. He felt guilty for taking him prisoner and making him into one of his soldiers. He never really had a choice. Will's destiny burdens returned, and he felt the weight of all the death and pain inflicted upon those who followed him. They had accomplished their goal so far, but like all battles, the cost was great.

As his army worked with the Defenders to take down the camp, Will waited by the barrier for the Eastside Team to return. He wanted to check on Hunter and begin whatever treatment they could administer immediately. The outer door that connected the yard to the road had been opened.

The three covered vehicles were followed by two large rigs piled with the soldiers' gear atop three long boxes. Rival hopped out of the bus first and went directly to Will's side.

"Hunter isn't with us, but don't react, and don't say anything to anyone," Rival spoke softly. "I'll explain later away from listening ears."

Will nodded at Rival, trying to act nonchalantly. Rival went to assist in the activity, but after a long ten minutes, Will pulled him away. He led him down the road spanning the front of the tunnel. When they were far enough away, he spun Rival toward him.

"Tell me now!"

"He's hurt badly, Will. He took some shrapnel in the neck and one in the leg. He was struggling to breathe from the one in his neck, and he lost a lot of blood from the one in his leg. He was unconscious when the lady doc came out. I don't know how this place can fix him, but she said she'd try. She said she could get in trouble for bringing him inside the town, so we need to keep quiet until she finishes operating on him."

Will bristled at the thought of someone cutting on Hunter. He could only hope it was done humanely, and she knew what she was doing. Yet, from the sounds of Hunter's injuries, it was his only chance, so, for now, he would follow Rival's lead.

Will walked back to connect with the Eastside Team and assess the wounded. It seemed none of them were in immediate peril as long as they got them back to the compound. He spoke to the Eastside Team and ordered them to not talk about the battle until they debriefed him first. Will had a million thoughts in his head, and there were many tasks and meetings in his immediate future. However, the first order of business was to get his soldiers home. After the storm, he would contact those family members who had lost a loved one. It was one of the worst and most important jobs a commander had.

Will wanted to check on Hunter as well as talk with his soldiers before they left, but they had to move. He wasn't going to be allowed inside the tunnel town, and Hunter could not be moved. He had to trust this New Haven doctor to care for him.

Each trailer could fit sixty people, but they had a lot of supplies packed in with them, so they still had to push the bench limits. They had the trailers loaded quickly, and soon they were rolling down the road.

Just outside of Dillon, where they hid a truck, a pack of Drangers blocked the highway. They had tried to start the truck, but they soon discovered the battery had been removed. The Drangers waited to ambush them and retrieve the part. The Guards were refreshed and ready, while their foe was exhausted and freezing.

The Guard quickly overtook them and shot at the ten or so more running to their inevitable death from bullets or hypothermia. The battery was restored, and some supplies were quickly loaded in the truck bed. This allowed six soldiers to ride in the truck while the additional prisoners were piled into the transports. Two were considerably wounded, and their survival was uncertain.

They were met on Highway 9 with the snowplow clearing their way. Again, Gray established that he was true to his word. *Promising, very promising,* Will thought. Relic said the tunnel told him they would give you guys what you needed to get home, but the road might need to be cleared.

The heroes were greeted with cheers and shots of moonshine when they arrived at the compound. Hot spaghetti and mountain salad were heaped onto plates. The two more seriously wounded Guards along with the two wounded and shackled Drangers were checked into the infirmary where the compound's healer addressed their wounds.

Will grabbed Rival to the side for a talk. Although he trusted him, he had once again gone over his head. They had won the battle, and it looked like they would have their allies. He should be celebrating with his soldiers, but things were still unsettled. He had left a man behind, and ten men and women lay in a cold truck outside waiting for their final goodbyes.

"Rival, what happened?" Will's temper was flaring.

"Calm down. It was out of my hands."

"I am as calm as I'm going to get until you tell me everything that happened."

"Just before the enemy retreated, Hunter was hit in the leg. He was bleeding badly and couldn't get to cover before one of those things they call sticky bombs exploded, sending sharp shit in every direction. That's when it hit his neck. When the medics came out, they looked at him and talked to someone referred to as Dr. Maya. She told them to pack his wounds and bring him inside the yard where she could evaluate him."

"So you let them just take him?"

"Hell no! I said wherever they took him, I was going too. So, they let us through the wall. She meets us, and she's all garbed up for germ protection and shit. She tells me, 'I can save him, but he needs to stay here for a while. I'm not supposed to do this without the town's permission, but I won't let him die if I can help him. You can't tell anyone. I need time to operate on him. I will let my superiors know when he's in recovery. I promise you, they won't hurt him, but please keep this quiet. Can you do that?' And what could I say except, yeah, go save him."

Will thought about it and calmed down. "You did the only thing you could. I get it, but we have now deceived the people we are trying to align ourselves with. I can't say I would have done anything differently, but it does complicate things."

Will waited until the next morning to try out the secure com-line with New Haven. He also knew he didn't have enough information on the town to report back to the council, and he hoped Gray could give him something to calm their concerns.

"Gray, Will here. I feel the need to tell you something… problematic. You have one of my men in your hospital. I didn't know until my lieutenant gave me details of what had happened last night. I'm not excusing his complicity, but he says your Dr. gave him an impossible choice and swore him to secrecy. Hunter, my seriously wounded man, was graciously given a spot in your hospital, and although I appreciate it, you can understand my concern."

"Well," came Gray's reply, "that sounds like something Maya would do. I hope you don't think this jeopardizes our alliance proposal because it doesn't."

"I am glad for that, but I also want to learn how my man is doing."

"I am calling her as we speak. She's very dedicated, and he's lucky to have her as his physician, as is my brother, but she can go rogue when she believes she's right."

Will sighed, "I have a couple of those too."

"Just a minute, Will, she's calling in." Will heard short, mumbled responses, and then Gray returned to their conversation. "Okay, your guy's surgery was successful, and he's been stabilized in the Intensive Care Unit. She says that the next twenty-four hours will give a better prognosis. She also said he needs to stay there for at least a week to recover. I'm glad Maya helped him. We both lost people. I am sorry for yours."

"As I am for yours." So much suffering Will grieved. He hoped it ended with the promise of a better future for all people, but war seemed to be the eternal curse of mankind and the solemn price of destiny.

"Thank you. And your brother, if I may ask?"

"He's better, but his recovery will take time. I guess we both have a couple of prayers to send up."

"You practice religion in New Haven?"

"The freedom to practice religion is honored here."

"That's exactly what we believe in too, freedom. Do you have a moment? We have waited so long to meet you, I want to know more."

"Will, I would love to learn more about your people and you about ours, but I've got a hornet's nest stirred up here right now. The people of New Haven are shocked they were discovered. Frankly, it's their naiveness that shocks me. They've filled the streets, wearing down my exhausted Defenders."

Streets! Will suddenly grasped how big this town must be. He knew it extended over a mile, but he imagined one long hallway.

"Plus," Gray purged on, "my younger brother was wounded and he's on the edge. My sister-in-law is in labor, and the legislators are taking advantage of the chaos by grabbing political points. And that's before I tell them Maya took one of your men inside the tunnel without permission."

"Wow, yeah, you've got a full bucket of...,"

"Shit, you can say it." Will heard Gray exhale his tension with a long breath. It felt comfortable talking with this man, maybe too comfortable. Will reeled back the slack in his demeanor and returned to his protective mode.

"I sympathize. Seems no matter the size or the intentions of a government, politicians find a way to over-complicate things," Will sympathized.

"True that," was the frustrated response.

"Gray, would you get word to Hunter? Tell him we're ... praying for him. And don't be too hard on this Dr. Maya. Thank her personally for me. Hunter is kind of like my little brother."

"You got it. The meeting with the board will happen tonight, so I'll call back soon, Will. I'll let you know if there are any changes with Hunter."

"Roger that, Gray, thanks."

Will pushed the button that ended the call, but the conversation had just begun.

Reclamation

Will over thought his attire for the meeting of his career. He didn't want to appear overly militant or inappropriately casual. He wanted to show respect and strength. He landed on black jeans and a collarless white button-up shirt. Leita said he looked more delicious than scary. He laughed and told her he'd remember that.

Looking out of the large utility vehicle, his post-battle penitent mood returned. It was why he liked to drive rather than ride. He set his mind on imagining what a tunnel town would look like. He wondered if it would be dark and dank because underground places were like that. He thought about Hunter, one of his soldiers, who was too badly injured to return to the fort. He was being cared for at their hospital, where he was reported to be in good health and ready to go home. *How could he heal in a place like that?*

Still staring through the window and lost in his thoughts, he didn't notice they arrived until the vehicle pulled up to the entrance at the barrier. He briefly opened his window to take a deep breath of clean air. The driver went through several layers of security before being allowed into a small underground corridor. They traveled down the dimly lit passageway, and again they had to pass through more layers of security. Will was impressed.

But when the driver pulled into the town, Will was astonished. It was bright and beautiful, and when he propped open his window, the air smelled fresh, and the oxygen level seemed higher than the air outside. *Interesting.* They drove past windowed enclosures where people tended livestock. Then the corridor opened up to a bustling little city. It took him a minute to notice that every structure utilized shipping containers for its construction, but the final product was stunning.

The homes and offices featured colorful and creative designs with windows, porches, and balconies, and they were decorated with attractive foliage and other décor. The ceiling did not fool one into thinking it was the sky, but it provided a cheerful ambiance. People were bustling about, working and strolling together. It was like a scene from a forgotten time.

They were met by the Defender, Gabe. Will remembered his name as the one who reported the status of his troops at the east entrance. Gabe explained that they would eat lunch and then see Hunter before attending the meeting at Town Hall.

The organizers decided to allow the visitors to walk through the town and understand its scope. It was a notable show of trust. They walked the streets, passing municipal buildings regularly interrupted by blocks of housing, while attracting the stares of the citizens, unaccustomed to outsiders. Arriving at the dining area, they were inundated by school children weaving past them, stealing glances, and giggling as they were herded to the park next door.

The dining area was nicely decorated with slate flooring and separated from the street by a faux weathered fence laced with green ivy. Scattered within the dining space were dozens of tables, charmingly accented with jars of wildflowers that looked stunningly realistic. A lattice wall woven with delicate vines gave privacy to the tables where they were seated.

The server arrived with water, and the day's lunch choices flashed on the electronic unit she set before them. The main course options included chicken, sausage, or a peanut butter and jam sandwich. The sides were raw carrots and reconstituted pears. Before Will could ask, Gabe assured them that Corporate additives were not used at New Haven. Gabe said something about hating it as a Daily, but he didn't give any hint that he knew how nefarious it really was.

Will, Taylor, and Relic asked as many questions as the time for lunch would allow before they were back walking down the street. As they passed the Rapid Aid Center, which seemed small for a hospital, Will wondered where Hunter was being kept. His concerns were soon answered when they turned down a side street corridor, and he saw a mint green and blue building that extended beyond his view. It was labeled the Asilo Hospital of Goodwill.

When they were completely out of the corridor, Will was stunned by its impressive size. While most of the structures were two shipping containers wide and two high, this one had multiple sections on either side that were three wide and higher than the neighboring roofs. Though it encroached on the street, it didn't block the traffic in any significant way. In between the two sections was an alcove where an emergency cart was parked at one end, leaving the front double doors easily accessible. Two potted plants flanked a bed of pink flowers, dividing the alcove and the street.

Inside the lobby, Gabe talked to the receptionist, who buzzed them through the door to where the admitted patients were housed. They took a short walk to the elevator and rode it to the second floor. Down another hallway, they were led into a room where Hunter was being fussed over by two nurses.

"Slacker," Will said, crossing the room in two large strides. "All this pampering and flirting is going to ruin you. I might have to go back to calling you Softheart." Will smiled and joked, but he could see Hunter's bandaged neck, and his leg was heavily wrapped up from ankle to mid-thigh. Concerned about his wounds, Will shook his hand gently. The nurses left, and the four talked about the battle, the comrades they lost, and the town of New Haven.

"They have treated me well, sir. Yesterday, they took me out in a wheelchair, and I saw just how incredible this place is. I was taken to a place they call the Rec Room, with all kinds of games. Then we went to a charming diner for lunch. I even heard they have a bar! This place is beyond belief!"

Hunter exclaimed enthusiastically. He was in good spirits, which relieved Will considerably.

Acknowledgments

I am thankful to be in a nation where I can express myself freely. It is not this way for everyone. I write dystopian fiction as a tribute and a warning that liberty is a fleeting concept, not a permanent structure, and it is our duty to protect it.

I cannot express enough gratitude for all the support I received from my beloved family, friends, and business partners.

In loving memory, I thank my parents, Harold and Carolyn, for providing me with a loving home to grow and learn in.

I thank my husband, Bryan, for standing by me and encouraging me. I thank him for being my business manager, which is a frustrating job, while still being my biggest fan.

I thank my family and friends for all their support, suggestions, reviews, and help.

I thank Kennedy for bravely taking on my digital media world and expanding my brand. Thank you to RG Graph X Design for his work on this amazing cover.

Most importantly, I thank God for his guidance, forgiveness, love, and compassion. And for surrounding me with so many good people. Amen

Conversation with the Author

What inspires me to write? Everything inspires me. It's exhausting. As a child, my dad called me his "what-if girl" because I envisioned endless scenarios for everything in my life. I used to call it my crazy side, but I quickly discovered that my introspective creativity allowed me to develop valuable connections and intriguing possibilities.

Why do I write science fiction dystopian novels? I love the paradoxical nature and intense drama in dystopian fiction. When married with science fiction, it presents a possible future where the hard-won advancements of society have been destroyed or confiscated by the few for power and control over the many. Paralyzed with fear, the masses wait for a hero, one who possesses the duality of a selfless compassionate moral code while harboring a ferocious warrior side. It feels purposeful to share the foreshadowing scenarios of this genre which go beyond recreational reading.

How do I develop characters? I use the traits I see in real people be they admirable, tragic, or despicable. I love hero quest stories that test everyday people in extraordinary circumstances. They are compelled to defend the vulnerable, but in doing so, they must cross the ethical boundaries that make them worthy. The characters I create are like children to me. I watch them grow and evolve, and I grieve every time I cause them pain and misery or make them stray to advance my plot line.

roxannewarauthor.com

9 798988 001027